UNDER MY SKIN

Also by Lisa Unger

LISA UNGER

UNDER MY SKIN

PARK
ROW
BOOKS

PARK
ROW
BOOKS

Recycling programs
for this product may
not exist in your area.

ISBN-13: 978-0-7783-6978-3
ISBN-13: 978-0-7783-0840-9 (Library Exclusive Edition)

Under My Skin

ParkRowBooks.com
BookClubbish.com

Printed in U.S.A.

To Connie, Donna and Pat,
Faithful readers who have become friends.
Your support means more than you know.

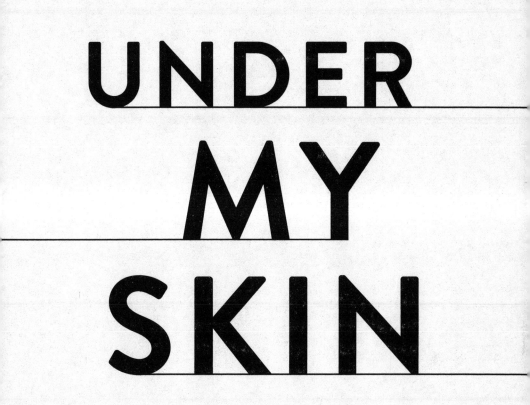

UNDER
MY
SKIN

PROLOGUE

I like him. I do.

But.

There's always a *but*, isn't there?

He's talking and I should be listening. I'm not. Does he see it, that I'm scattered, distracted? Doubtful. He doesn't seem especially observant, has that way about him that people do now. As if they are putting on a show of themselves, as if the moment is being *watched* rather than *lived*. He glances about as he talks. Up at the television screens over the bar, all on mute, all tuned in to different sporting events. Down at the phone that sits dark beside him. Back to me, off again to the rowdy table across from us—a postwork gathering I'm guessing from the rumpled suits and tired eyes.

I soak in the details of him: his shock of ink black hair, thick—any girl would kill for it; dark stubble on his jaw, just enough—sexy, not unkempt, style, not neglect; his gym-toned body. Beneath the folds of his lavender oxford, the dip of cut abs, the round of a well-worked shoulder.

If I had a camera in my hand—not a smartphone but a real camera—say a mirrorless Hasselblad X1D, ergonomic, light—

old-school style with high-tech innards—I'd watch him through the lens and try to find the moment when he revealed himself, when the muscles in his face relaxed and the mask dropped, even for just a millisecond. Then I'd see him. The man he *really* is when he steps off the stage he imagines himself on.

I already knew he was handsome, stylish, in shape, before we agreed to meet. His profile told me as much. He works in finance. (Of course he does.) His favorite book is the Steve Jobs autobiography. (What else?) But what's under his skin, that carefully manicured outer layer? Beneath the mask he puts on in the morning—what's there? The camera always sees it.

He runs his fingertips along the varnished edge of the table between us, then steeples them. I read somewhere that this is the gesture of someone very sure of himself and his opinions. It tracks. He *seems* very sure of himself, as people who know very little often are.

He laughs, faux self-deprecating, at something he's just said about himself. His words still hang in the air, something about his being a workaholic. What a relief that it's just drinks, not dinner. No point in wasting time, if *it's* not there, he wrote. Who could disagree? So adult. So reasonable.

I never thought it would be. It can't be. Because *it* has nothing to do with the way he looks. *It* isn't about his eyes, black, heavily lashed and half-lidded. Or the bow of his mouth, full, kissable. (Though I might kiss him anyway. Maybe more. Depends.) Attraction, desire is nothing to do with the physical; it's chemical, a head trip. And my head—well, let's just say it's not on straight.

A woman laughs too loud—a cackle really, harsh and jarring. It startles me, sends a pulse of adrenaline through me. I scan the crowd. I really shouldn't be here.

"Time for another?" he asks. His teeth. They're *so* white. Perfectly aligned. Nothing in nature is so flawless. Braces. Whitening.

The rim of the glass is ice-cold beneath my fingertip. The

drink went down fast, too fast. I promised myself I wouldn't drink, not with everything that's been going on. It's been a long day, a long week. A long *year*. The weight of it all is tugging at me, pulling me under.

I take too long to answer and he frowns, just slightly, looks at his phone. I should just leave. This is crazy.

"Sure," I say instead. "One more."

He smiles again, thinks it's a good sign.

Really, I just want to go home, pull up my hair, put on my sweats, get into bed. Even that's not an option. Once we walk out of here, it's back to the jigsaw puzzle of my life.

"Grey Goose and soda," he tells the waitress when he's flagged her down. He remembers what I'm drinking. A small thing, but so few people pay attention to the details these days. "And Blanton's on the rocks."

Straight bourbon, very manly.

"Am I talking too much?" he says. He looks sweetly sheepish. Is it put on? "I've heard that before. My last girlfriend, Kim— she said I ramble when I get nervous."

It's the second time he's mentioned her, his "last girlfriend, Kim." Why, I wonder? Carrying a torch? Or just trying to market himself as someone who's been in a relationship? Also, "last girlfriend." It begs the question: How many others? Maybe I'm reading too much into it. I do that.

"Not at all."

I am a seeker. I want to explore the world. Don't you? I love to learn, to cook, to travel. I get lost in a good book.

That's what his profile said. In his picture, he smiled, nearly laughing, hair wind-tossed. It was a good photo, could have come from a magazine—which is always suspicious. Photographers know all the tricks to capturing beauty, the right angles, the proper lighting, the magic of filters. The truth is that most people aren't *that hot* in person. Even beautiful people, real ones, are flawed in some way—not airbrushed, or prettily windblown, eyes glittering. Lines around the eyes and mouth, an almost imperceptibly crooked nose, a faint scar—chicken pox or a childhood fall from a bike. People, real people, have a little stain from lunch on their tie, maybe something hanging from their nose or in their teeth, patches of dry skin, shoes that need replacing. These imperfections make us who we are, tell the truth of our lives.

But to his credit, he is close to as good-looking as his profile picture. But something's off. What is it?

There's nothing special about *my* profile picture, nothing misleading, just a photo snapped by my friend Layla, who set the whole thing up. Of course, she's a talented photographer, my oldest friend and knows how to shoot me. No filter, though, no Photoshop tricks. What you see is what you get. Sort of.

"What about you?" he says.

The waitress delivers the drinks to our high-top. Her ears are lined with silver hoops; another in her lip. She is fleshy but pretty with startling green eyes that give her an otherworldly look. I bet she reads a lot of teen fantasy novels. *Twilight. Harry Potter. Hunger Games.*

"Thank you, *darlin',*" he says to her. He drops the *g* and inflects the word with a twang, though I know he was born and raised in New Jersey. She beams at him, flushes a little. He's a charmer in a sea of snakes.

I notice that he has a way of looking at women, a warm gaze, a wide smile. It seems like a choice. A technique. He knows that women like to be gazed upon, attended to with male eyes. It makes them feel pretty, special in a world where we too rarely feel like either of those things. She smiles at him, does this quick bat of her eyelashes. She likes him. I can tell; she glances at him from time to time as she shuttles back and forth along the bar, between the other high-tops she's also serving. Even if I walk out of here, I'm sure someone will go home with him.

Good-looking, charming guys emanating the scent of money rarely go lonely.

"What do you want to know?" I ask when he turns back to me.

He takes a sip of his bourbon, gazes over his glass, mischievous. "In your profile, you said you were a runner."

Did Layla put that in my profile? Layla—this dating thing? All her idea. *Time to get back out there, girlfriend.* I honestly don't remember what we put in the profile.

"I *run*," I say. The truth is that I *used* to run. "I don't know if I'd call myself a runner."

"What's the difference?"

"I run—for exercise, because I like it, because it calms me. But it doesn't define me. I don't have a group, or register for races, travel to do marathons or whatever."

Am *I* rambling?

Finally, "I run. I am not a runner. Anyway, I'm more indoors lately, at the gym."

He nods slowly, a pantomime of the careful listener, looks down at his glass.

I almost tell him about Jack then; it's always right on the tip of my tongue.

My husband was killed last year, I want to say. *He was attacked while he was running in Riverside Park at 5:00 a.m. Whoever it was— they beat him to death. His murder is still unsolved. I should have been with him. Maybe if I had been… Anyway. I don't find running as enjoyable as I used to.*

But then he's talking about how he started running in high school, ran in college, still runs, travels for marathons, is thinking about a triathlon in New Mexico next year, but his work in finance—the hours are so crazy.

Kim's right, I think. He talks too much. And not just when he's nervous. Because he's not nervous, not at all.

It's his nails. They're perfect. They are, in fact, professionally manicured. Expertly shaped and buffed squares at the ends of thick fingers. He steeples them again on the table between us. That's the *but*. Vanity. He's vain, spends a lot of time on himself. The gym, his clothes, his skin, hair, nails. Which is fine for tonight. But in the long game, when it's time to stop worrying about yourself and start thinking about someone else, he's not going to be able to do it. The lens would have seen it right away.

Should I mention my nervous breakdown, the one I had after Jack died, how days of my life just—*disappeared*? Probably not, right?

The space grows more crowded, louder. It's one of those Upper East Side sports bars with big screens mounted at every angle, games from all over the country, all over the world playing. It's filling up with the after-work crowd, men who are really still babies with their first jobs, fresh out of school, girls—tight-bodied, hair dyed, waxed and threaded, tits high—who have no idea what the next ten years will hold, how many disappointments small and large.

It's Thursday, tomorrow the end of the workweek, so the energy is high, exuberant voices booming. Our waitress drifts back and forth, deftly balancing trays of clinking highballs, frothy pilsners of beer, shot glasses of amber liquid. Shots? Really? Do people still do that?

There's a buzz of anxiety in the back of my head as I scan the crowd, turn to look through the big windows to the street. *Someone's been following me*, I almost say, but don't. *I've been suffering from some sleep disturbances, some unsettling dreams that might be memories, and to be truthful my life is a bit of a mess.* But I don't say those things. He's still talking, this time about work, a boss he doesn't like.

It's closing in, all the laughter, cheering, bodies starting to press, ties loosening, hair coming down. I let him pick the meeting place. I'd have chosen a quiet spot downtown—in the West

Village or Tribeca, someplace soothing and serene, dark, where you speak in low tones, lean in, get to know someone.

Note to self: don't let them choose—even though the choice speaks volumes. In fact, this dating thing, maybe it's not for me at all.

"I've got an early day tomorrow," I say, in the next lull between things he's saying about himself. He's been practically yelling, to be heard above the din. I *should* get out of here. Huge mistake.

I see it then. A flinty look of angry disappointment. It's gone in a millisecond, replaced by a practiced smile.

"Oh," he says. He looks at his watch—a Fitbit, wouldn't you know it. "Yeah, me, too."

"This has been great," I say. He picks up the check, which the bartender must have laid in front of him at some point.

I take my wallet out.

"Let's split it," I say. I prefer to pay or split in these circumstances; I like the feel of equal ground beneath my feet.

"No," he says. His tone has gone a little flat. "I've got it."

It's not just the nails. There's a sniff of arrogance, something cold beneath the flirting. I can see the glint of it, now that he knows he's not going to get what he came for. Or maybe it's not any of those things. Maybe there's nothing wrong with him at all. Very likely it's that something is wrong with me.

Or most likely of all, it's just that he's not Jack.

Until you let your husband go, no one else will measure up. That's what my shrink said.

I'm trying. I'm dating.

Setting them up to knock them down isn't dating.

Is that what I'm doing? Just killing time with men who can't help but to ultimately reveal themselves as *not-Jack*. They won't be as funny as he was, or know just where to rub my shoulders. They won't run out at any hour for anything I need, without being asked. *I'll go grab it for you.* They won't have his laugh, or that serious set to his face when he's concentrating. They won't bite on the inside of their cheeks when annoyed. They won't feel like him, or smell like him. Not-Jack.

Until one day, says Dr. Nash, *there's someone else who you love for all new reasons. You'll build a new life.* I don't bother telling her that it's not going to happen. In fact, there are a lot of things I don't bother telling Dr. Nash.

On the street, though I reach out for his hand, he tries for a kiss. I let his lips touch mine, but then I pull back a little, something repelling me. He jerks back, too. It's awkward. No heat. Nothing. I shouldn't be disappointed, should have *long ago* lost the capacity for disappointment. I suspected (knew) that *it* wouldn't be there. But I thought maybe if there was heat, some physical spark, I wouldn't need the sleeping pills tonight. Maybe we'd go back to his place and I'd have a reprieve from putting back the pieces of my fractured life.

Now I must decide where I will go tonight—back to an apartment I was supposed to share with my husband but where I now live alone and no longer feel safe, back to Layla's penthouse, maybe to a hotel.

A police car whips up Lexington. *Whoop. Whoop.*

"Maybe we could run this weekend?" He's still working it, though I can't imagine why. "Ever try the trails up in Van Cortlandt Park? Short but pretty—you feel miles away from the city."

"Nice," I say.

Unless there's someone lurking in the shadows, and no one can hear you call for help.

"Should I text you?"

He'll never text me, of course.

"That sounds great."

Even if he does text me, I won't answer him. Or I'll put him off until he gets the hint. It's easy like that, this dating thing in the age of technology. You can dangle someone off the edge of your life until they just float away, confused. Ghosting, I think the millennials call it.

"Can I see you home?" he asks.

"No," I say. "I'm fine. Thanks."

I feel wobbly, suddenly. It's after nine, and those two vodka sodas are sloshing around in an empty stomach, not to mention the other chemicals floating in my bloodstream. I haven't eaten anything since—when?

"You okay?" he asks. His concern seems exaggerated, his tone almost mocking. There are other people on the street, a couple laughing, intimate, close, a kid with his headphones on, a homeless guy sitting on the stoop.

"I'm fine," I say again, feeling defensive. I didn't have *that* much to drink.

But then he has his arm looped through mine, too tight, and I find myself tipping into him. I try to pull away from him. But he doesn't allow it. He's strong and I can't free my arm.

"Hey," I say.

"Hey," he says, a nasty little mimic. "You're okay."

Of course I'm okay, I want to snap. But the words won't come. There's just this bone-crushing fatigue, this wobbly, foggy, vague feeling. Something's not right. The world starts to brown around the edges. Oh, no. Not now.

"She's okay," he says, laughing. His voice sounds distant and strange. "Just one too many I guess."

Who's he talking to?

"Let go of me," I manage, my voice an angry hiss.

He laughs; it's echoing and strange. "Take it easy, sweetie."

He's moving me too fast up the street, his grip too tight. I stumble and he roughly keeps me from falling.

"What the hell are you doing?" I ask.

Fear claws at the back of my throat. I can't wait to get away from this guy. He pulls me onto a side street; there's no one around.

"Hey." A voice behind us. He spins, taking me with him. There's someone standing there. He looks distantly familiar as the world tips. Somewhere inside me there's a jangle of alarm. He has a dark hood on, his face not visible.

It's him.

He's big, bigger than—what's his name? Reg, or something. Rex? The big man blocks our path up the sidewalk.

"Hey, seriously, dude," says Rick. Yes, Rick, that was it. "Step aside. I've got this."

But the world is fading fast, going soft and blurry, tilting. There's a flash, quick-fire movement. Then a girlish scream, a river of blood. Black red on lavender.

Then arms on me.

Falling.

Nothing.

PART ONE
Hypnagogia

Between the dreams of night and day there is not so great a difference.
—Carl Jung, *Psychology of the Unconscious*

1

"I think someone's following me."

I almost kept this to myself, but toward the end of our session it just tumbles out.

Dr. Nash wrinkles her brow with concern. "Oh?"

Her office is a cozy living room, all big furniture and fluffy throw pillows. There are shelves and shelves of books and pictures, and trinkets, small art objects from her travels. It's exactly the kind of office you'd want your shrink to have. Warm, enveloping. I sink deeper into my usual corner on her plush couch, leaning heavily on the overstuffed armrest. I resist the urge to curl up in a ball and cover myself with the cashmere blanket that's tossed artfully over the back. A grouping of those faux candles flicker on the coffee table; she made me some tea when I arrived. It sits in front of me, untouched.

"The other night when I left the gym, there was someone standing across the street. I think I saw him again this morning on a park bench near my office."

Even thinking about it, there's a flutter of unease.

The doctor shifts in her leather Eames chair; it's too well

made to creak beneath her weight. She's a wisp of a woman. The leather just whispers against the fabric of her pants. Afternoon light washes in, touching her hair and the side of her face. There are these longish pauses in our conversation where she chooses her words, letting mine ring back to me. She takes one now, considering me.

"Are you certain it was the same man?" she asks finally.

A cool October breeze wafts in the open window, street noise carrying up from nine floors below. A horn, the rumble of a manhole cover wobbling beneath the weight of passing vehicles, the yipping of some small dog. I imagine a Yorkie in a little sweater, straining against a slender leash.

"No," I admit.

"But certain enough that you're uneasy about it."

I'm already sorry I brought it up. I *did* see someone, a man in a black hoodie, sneakers, faded jeans. He stood in a dark doorway across the street when I left the gym last Tuesday. Then on Thursday as I headed to my office clutching my daily quadruple espresso, I saw him again. I felt his eyes on me, the details of his face hidden in the dark shadow of that hood.

I dismissed it. There are lots of staring men clad in jeans and hoodies in this city. Any girl will tell you, there are always eyes on you, unsolicited comments, unwanted noises, unwelcome approaches. But then maybe I saw him once more over the weekend, when I was coming home from the farmers' market. Still, it's hard to be certain.

"Well," I backpedal. "Maybe it wasn't the same man."

I shouldn't have said anything. I don't want her to think I'm backsliding. Stumbling toward another *breakdown*. When something like that happens to you, there's this energy to the people who care about you, like they're always waiting for signs that it's going to happen again. I get it; they don't want to miss the tells a second time and run the risk of losing you again, maybe for good. Even I'm wary. I feel a little sick about that black spot in my memory where I took a vacation from reality, how fuzzy are the days surrounding Jack's murder.

So. I try not to think about it. It's one of the things from which I am trying to *move on*. That's what you're supposed to do, you know, when the worst thing happens and you're still standing. Everyone's very clear about it: you're supposed to move on.

"It's probably nothing," I say, stealing a surreptitious glance at my watch. My smartphone, my tether as Jack liked to call it, is off and tucked into my bag, as per Dr. Nash's office rules. *Here we free ourselves of distractions and try to be present in a world that conspires against it*, she has said more than once.

Dr. Nash watches me, prettily brushing away an errant strand of her lovely gray-blond bob. Behind her there's a picture of her family—her chiseled-jaw, graying husband, her grown children both with her same delicate features, intelligent eyes. They all stand together on a terrace overlooking a beach sunset, smiling, faces pressed together. *We're perfect*, it seems to say. *Wealthy and gorgeous, without a single stain of darkness on our lives*. I look away.

"I noticed you're not wearing your rings," she says.

I look down at my left hand. The finger is slightly indented from my wedding and engagement rings, but bare.

"When did you make that decision?"

My hands swelled the other night, and I took the rings off and put them in the dish beside my bed. I haven't put them back on. I tell her as much. Jack has been dead almost a year. I'm not married anymore. Time to stop wearing the jewelry, right? Even though the sight of my bare hand puts a painful squeeze on my heart, it's time.

"Was it before or after that you started seeing the hooded figure?"

Dr. Nash is the master of the pointed question.

"I see where you're going with this."

"I'm just asking."

I smile a little. "You're never *just asking*, Dr. Nash."

We like each other. Sometimes, lately, our sessions devolve into chats—which she says is a sign I need her less. A good thing, according to her. Progress on the road to healing, the new normal as she likes to call it.

"How are you sleeping?" she asks, letting her other question rest.

I have the nearly empty pill bottle in my purse. Last time I asked for more, she wrote me a scrip but lowered the dosage. *I'd like you to try to get off these.* Honestly, it hasn't been going well. My dreams are too vivid. I'm less rested, so edgier, jumpier during the day.

"I was going to ask for my refill."

"How's that lower dosage?"

I shrug, trying for nonchalance. I don't want to appear fragile, not to her, not to anyone. Even though I am, terribly. "I'm dreaming more. Maybe I feel a little less rested."

"You're not taking more of them, though, are you?"

I am. I'm also doing other things I shouldn't be doing. Like taking them with alcohol, for one.

"No," I lie.

She nods carefully, watching me in her shrink way. "You've been taking them for eleven months. I'd like to go down to the minimum dosage with an eye toward your being off them altogether. Want to give it a try?"

I hesitate. That chemical slumber is the best place in my life right now. I don't say that, though. It sounds too grim. Instead I find myself agreeing.

"Great," she says. "If it's an issue, we'll go back up to the dosage you're on now. And those dreams? Go back to the dream journal you were keeping when Jack first died. It's an important part of our lives, our dream world. As we've discussed, we can learn a lot about ourselves there. Do you still keep it by your bed?"

"Yes."

She hands me the white slip of paper.

"Well," she says. I stare at the crisp sheet, her doctor's scrawl. "I think our time is up for today."

I'm always a little startled by the end of a session, the abrupt reminder that no matter how intimate, how I strip myself bare in these sessions, ours is a professional relationship. If I stopped paying, these chats with Dr. Nash would come to an unceremonious end.

"And, Poppy? If you see him again, call me."

A siren from the street below drifts up, a distant and ghostly wail. This sound, so frequent in the cacophony of city noise, always makes me think of Jack. About an hour after he left that morning, emergency vehicles howled up the avenue beneath our window. There should have been some premonition, some dark dawning, but there wasn't.

A lingering head cold had kept me in bed instead of going with him as I normally would have.

You could have died that morning, too, Layla says when we go over and over it.

Or maybe it wouldn't have happened at all. Maybe we would have run in a different direction. Or maybe we could have fought off the attacker together.

Or maybe, or maybe, or maybe—on and on. Infinite possibilities, myriad ways Jack might still be with me. He overslept; a light caused him to cross another street; I was there and twisted my ankle, causing us to return home. I turn to those scenarios in blank moments, in dreams, when I should be paying attention in meetings. So many other paths he could have taken and didn't.

"I'm not imagining him." It seems to come out of nowhere.

Dr. Nash cocks her head at me. "I didn't say you were."

I bend down and grab my bag, come to standing as she does.

"And lock your doors. Be mindful," she adds.

"You sound like my mother."

She chuckles. "We can talk about that next session."

"Very funny."

★ ★ ★

I walk toward the subway, needing to get back downtown for a two o'clock meeting. I'm probably going to be late—again. The city is such a mess, a constant crush of traffic and delayed trains. I think about a cab or an Uber, but sometimes that's even worse, snaking through jammed streets, trapped in a box, trying to decide if it would be faster to just get out and walk. The whole city seems to conspire against promptness.

I text my assistant, Ben. Running late, I tap in quickly and descend beneath the street. It's Monday midday, so it's not as crowded as it could be. Though the day is mild, the platform is hot as an oven and smells like piss. My stress level starts to tick up.

Jack wanted us to leave Manhattan; he'd grown to hate it. *Everything that was cool about it is gone. It's just an island for the rich.* He dreamed of a historic property upstate, something with a lot of land, trees, trails to wander. Something we could renovate and make ours. He longed to disconnect from the rush of wanting, grasping, striving, at least on the weekends. He wanted time back behind the camera. He didn't get any of those things.

We *were* packing when he died, boxing up the one-bedroom Upper West Side apartment we'd shared for five years. But instead of moving out of the city, we were moving to The Tate, a luxury high-rise in Chelsea—a gleaming tower of apartments with floor-to-ceiling windows, offering stunning vistas, high ceilings, wood floors, chic open-plan kitchens, pool and gym, a 24/7 building staff. It was me. I was the one who wanted it; he acquiesced.

He loved our dark, cozy place on Ninety-Seventh—with views of the other building across the street, with radiators that clanked, and mice in our ridiculously dated kitchen, and the old doorman Richie, who'd worked there forever and was sometimes asleep when we walked in. He loved our crazy, colorful cast of neighbors—Merlinda, the psychic who read clients in her apartment; Chuck—or Chica—accountant by day, drag queen by night, who had the most beautiful singing voice I'd ever heard; Bruce, Linda and Chloe, public school teachers and their adorable, gifted daughter, our next-door neighbors who never failed to invite us for Sunday dinner.

Now I live in a starkly beautiful space that looks out onto lower Manhattan—alone. I don't even know who lives in the apartment next to me. The hallways are gray tunnels, lined with doors that seem to rarely open. In my apartment, the furniture is placed appropriately—bed in the bedroom, couch in the living area—but most of the boxes are still unpacked. To say I miss my husband, our wacky neighbors, that dark old apartment, our life—well, why? There are no words to adequately describe that slick-walled gully of despair. Suffice it to say that I can't seem to fully move into my new life without Jack.

I'm sorry, I tell him. *I wish I had listened to you.*

Dr. Nash says it's okay to talk to him, if I understand he's not talking back.

Time drags and I'm ever more fidgety, annoyed. More people file down the stairs. The platform grows dense with bodies, the air thickening with impatience. Still the train doesn't come. I lean over the edge of the platform to see if I can spot the glow of an oncoming headlamp. No.

I glance at the clock. There is officially no way to be on time now. A bead of perspiration trails down my spine. A glance at my phone reveals that there's no signal.

When the train finally screeches into the station, it's already packed. I wait by the door, letting the flow of people exit. There's no guarantee that the next train will be any less crowded, and that waiting meeting looms. I shoulder myself on, shimmying toward the door that connects one car to the other; find a space with a little breathing room. The cars fill.

Stand clear of the closing doors.

The doors close, open again, then finally shut for good. The train lurches forward, stops, jostling everyone, then onward again. I close my eyes, try to breathe. The crowded space is closing in already. I am not great in tight spaces, which is an uncomfortable condition for a city dweller. It's worse since Jack died; the fingers of panic tugging at me more than they used to. I lean my head against the scratched, foggy glass. *Breathe. Just breathe. Imagine you're on a trail in the woods, plenty of space, the tall green trees giving oxygen and shade. There's a bird singing, the sound of the wind in the leaves.* It's the meditation Dr. Nash gave me for dealing with anxiety in crowds or anywhere. Occasionally, it works.

But when I open my eyes again, he's there. That hooded man, pressed in among the crowd in the other car, a statue amidst the clutter of shuffling, jostling passengers. His eyes are hidden by the shadow of the hood, but I can feel them. Is it the same man? My heart stutters, a suck of fear at the base of my throat.

Reality cracks, a fissure splits in my awareness. For a moment, quick and sharp, I'm back in my own bedroom. The space beside me on the king mattress is cold when it should be warm. The covers are tossed. Jack left for his run without me, letting me sleep.

"Jack?"

Then I'm back, the train still rattling, rumbling. I'm stunned, a little breathless; what was that? A kind of vivid remembering, a daydream? Okay. It's not the *first* time it has happened; but it is the most vivid. The woman next to me gives me a sideways glance, shifts away.

Pull it together, Poppy. The stranger—he's still there. Is he watching me?

Or is he just another blank commuter, lost in thought about home or work or whatever it is we ponder when we're zoning out, traveling between the places in our lives. Maybe he's not seeing me at all. For a moment, I just stare.

Then, unthinking, I push through the doors, stepping out onto the shaking metal platforms between the cars. This is a major subway no-no, I think as I balance and grope my way through the squeal of metal racing past concrete, metal on metal singing, sparking, then through the other door into the relative quiet of the next car.

He moves away, shoving his way through the throng. I follow.

"What the fuck?"

"Watch it."

"Come on."

Annoyed passengers shoot dirty looks, shift reluctantly out of my way as I push after him, the black of his hood cutting like a fin through the sea of others.

As we pull into the next station, he disappears through the door at the far end of the car. Trying to follow him, I find myself caught in the flow of people exiting, and get pushed out of the train onto the platform. I finally break free from the crowd, jog up the platform searching for the hooded figure among tall and short, young and old, backpacks, briefcases, suits, light jackets, baseball caps. Where is he?

I want to see his face, *need* to see it, even though I can't say why. Distantly, I'm aware that this is not wise behavior. Not street-smart.

Don't chase trouble, my mother always says. *It will find you soon enough.*

Then the doors close and I'm too late to get back on. Shit. My phone chimes, finding a rare spot of service underground.

A text from Ben: ETA? They're going to wait a bit, then reschedule. Assume you're stuck on the train.

It isn't until the train pulls away that I see the stranger again, on board, standing in the door window. He's still watching, or so it seems, his face obscured in the darkness of the hood. I walk, keeping pace with the slow-moving train for a minute, lift my phone and quickly take a couple of pictures. I can almost see his face. Then he's gone.

2

I arrive at the office frazzled, sweaty, full of nerves, late for the meeting. In the bathroom, running my wrists under cold water, pulling shaking fingers through my dark hair, I stare at my reflection in the mirror.

Pull. Yourself. Together.

My face is sickly gray under the ugly fluorescents, as I dab some makeup on the eternal dark circles under my eyes, refresh lipstick and blush. A little better, but the girl in the mirror is still a tired, wrung-out version of the person she used to be.

Rustling through my bag, I find the bottle of pills Layla gave me. It's blank, the little amber vial, no label. *For nerves,* she said. I hesitate only a second before popping one in my mouth and swallowing it with water from the faucet, then try to take some centering breaths. Dr. Nash is not aware of my unauthorized pill-taking, one of multiple things I keep from her. I know. What's the point of keeping things from the person who is supposed to be helping you?

As I walk past Ben's desk, he rises and hands me a stack of messages.

"They're waiting," he says, dropping into step beside me. "You're fine."

"Great." My smile feels as stiff and fake as it is. "The subway is a mess."

"Everything okay?"

He inspects me through thick, dark-rimmed glasses, tugs at his hipster beard. He's a stellar assistant; I keep trying to promote him but he doesn't want to go. My clients love him—he's on top of all their contracts, tracks down their payments, helps with grant and residency applications. Over the past year, he's been more agent to them than I have. He could probably just take over and I could slip away. It's tempting, that idea of slipping away, disappearing—another life, another self.

"Yeah," I say unconvincingly. Ben watches after me with a frown as I push into the conference room.

"His work," Maura is saying. "It's stunning."

"Whose work?" I ask, taking my seat at the head of the conference table. "Sorry I'm late."

All eyes turn to me. When Jack was alive, I could come and go unnoticed. He ran the meetings and I was the number two—critical to the running of the office, but not the magnetic, energetic head of the meeting table. He brought a light and enthusiasm for the craft, for the business into every gathering. I am not the captain he was, I know, but I'm doing my best. They watch me now—respectful, kind, hopeful.

Jack picked out everything in this room, from the long sleek conference table to the white leather swivel chairs, the enormous flat screen on the wall. His photo from an Inca Trail trek, featured in *Travel + Leisure*, is blown up onto an enormous canvas. He took it from his campsite above the cloud line—orange tents blossom in white mist, as clouds fall away into a landscape of jade and royal blue, the dip of the valley dark and the sky bright.

"Alvaro's," Maura says. "He took that Nat Geo job to photograph the okapi living in the Ituri Rainforest, just got back yesterday."

The photos come up on the screen—lush, jewel greens and deep black, a red mud road twists and disappears into a thick of forest; a girl, her eyes dark and staring, stands on a riverbank in a grass skirt, her expression innocently teasing. A blue-and-white truck travels precariously over a swaying wooden slat bridge.

Maura runs a manicured hand over her black hair, pulled tight into a ponytail at the base of her neck. She's young, but her almond-shaped eyes reveal an old soul. Olive-skinned, almost birdlike in her delicacy, she's a firebrand agent, fiercely protective of her clients. She worries over them like a mother hen.

"The colors, the movement, the energy," I say. "They're wonderful."

The trunk of a tree, hollowed out and haunted, twisting, branches reaching up into deep green black. The shots of the okapi, an animal that is partially striped like a zebra, but related more closely to a giraffe, are stunning—a mother nursing her young, a young male hiding in tall grass, a small herd underneath a wide full moon.

"They are," Maura agrees. Her smile is wide and proud. "He's—*amazing.*"

I wonder, not for the first time, if something is going on between Maura and Alvaro. It's not a good idea for an agent to fall in love with a photographer she represents. In fact, it's not a good idea for anyone to fall in love with a photographer. The unfiltered world never quite measures up to whatever he sees through that lens. Alvaro Solare, Jack's best friend and the firm's first client, is the typical roving photographer, always in pursuit of the next perfect shot. Which means the rest of the world can go to hell. There are a string of heartbroken women in his wake. I'd prefer Maura not become one of them. But it's not really my business.

The rest of my agents run down the status of their clients' assignments. Our firm, Lang and Lang, mine and Jack's, represents photographers. We are a boutique agency, small but successful, with some of the top names in fashion, feature and news photography on our roster.

What started as a small enterprise in our apartment, has grown into an agency with a suite of offices in the Flatiron Building. Jack, affable and mellow, was a natural mediator. When Alvaro was in a dispute with the *New York Times* travel section, Jack stepped in and resolved it over drinks with the photo editor, an old friend of his. Alvaro paid Jack 15 percent out of appreciation. One thing led to another, and after a year Jack was turning down photo assignments, and representing more of his friends, including me.

So, after years of hustling as travel photographers, scraping together a living, we traded in our life of adventure for a firm dedicated to protecting the rights of people who make a living with a camera in their hands. Alvaro thought it was a mistake, that we were wasting our talent and our lives. And he never lost an opportunity to tell us so. But we thought it was time to settle down, start a family. Except it didn't work out that way.

I half listen as the other agents run down problems and successes. I comment, make suggestions, offer to make a call to a contact of mine at *Departures*. But mostly, I am still on that train, chasing after the man in the hood.

I wonder if anyone notices that I am a ghost in my life.

It's another half hour before I am back in my office, scrolling through the blurry, useless photos I took on my smartphone. The light was poor, too much motion. That dark form is just a smudge, a black space between the grainy commuters all around him. I use my thumb and forefinger to enlarge the image on the screen, but it looks ever more amorphous as a low-quality image will.

I start to doubt myself, my grip on reality. What did I see really, after all? Just a man with a hood, who might or might not have been looking in my direction.

I don't even notice Ben until he's sitting across the desk from me. There's a look I don't like on his face, worry, something else.

"What?"

He leans back and crosses his legs. "When were you going to tell me?"

"Tell you?"

"That you're dating again."

I shake my head, not wanting to get into it. "I'm not."

"So, who's Rick, then?" He slides a message across my desk. There's another one from him in the stack I've just barely started to sort through. I'm old-school; I still like paper messages to toss when calls are returned, write notes on, keep as reminders.

"He's no one," I say.

I wouldn't say I'm exactly dating. There's a snow globe on my desk, a little farmhouse surrounded by trees. Jack gave it to me one Christmas. *This is what our house will look like, out in the country. Quiet. Away from all the chatter.* I tip it and watch the snow swirl around the black branches.

"I saw your profile online," says Ben. He peers over his glasses, a gesture he thinks makes him look wise, worldly. It really doesn't. He's far too young to be either of those things.

Putting the snow globe down, I lean back in my chair and frown at him.

"What are *you* doing on an online dating site, a young hottie like you? They must drop like flies."

He shoots me a faux-smarmy eyebrow raise. "That's what we do. The millennials? It's how we *roll.* Tinder, OKCupid, Match.com. Love is just a swipe away." He makes a wave motion with his hand.

"So, it's not just for old people, then?" I sift through the tiny white sheets of paper. "The divorced, the forever single—the widowed."

Widowed. I hate that word; it evokes black veils and wails of grief. It defines me by the loss of my husband, as though I'm less now that he's gone. Of course—I am. I regret saying it as soon as it's out of my mouth. The word hangs in the air between us. When I look up from my messages, Ben has me pinned in a thoughtful gaze. Another youngster with an old soul; it seems we have a type in our small firm.

"If you must know, it wasn't my idea."

"Let me guess." He shifts forward, puts his elbows on his knees.

"Layla came over. Wine was consumed. The next thing I know, I'm back in the dating scene."

I don't think you can *clinically* call what I'm doing dating. In the olden days, we used to refer to it as sleeping around. A relationship? A boyfriend? No. I don't want those things. Not yet. Maybe not ever. But, wow, does it ever feel good to be touched again. I don't share this with Ben, who is studiously massaging that hipster beard he's so proud of. I wish he'd cut it off. It's borderline offensive, though I can't say why precisely.

"It's a good thing," he says finally, rising. "And Rick sounds like kind of a nice guy. He's hot, too. Looks like he could have money."

"You checked him *out?*" I say, mock mortified.

"Uh," he says, widening his eyes. *"Yeah."*

I smile at my young friend, my assistant who has outgrown his position but still likes it. If he has a girlfriend, or a boyfriend—or whatever—he never says so. I open my email; an impossible number of messages await.

"Two calls in a day," says Ben, moving toward the door. "I like his confidence. A man who knows what he wants."

"Confidence or arrogance?" I ask. "Desperation?"

"Let's call it—" Beard rubbing, word searching. "Assertiveness."

"Send him an email, will you? Tell him drinks on Thursday?" I ask.

"From you or from me?"

"Would it be weird if it was from you?"

"Seriously weird," he says, then rethinks. "Well—more like pretentious. Have your people call my people? Do you want to be *that person*?"

"Fine—from me."

Ben frequently sends emails at my direction from my account. Never anything big, just setting meeting times, quick one-line answers to various questions.

"Where?"

I shrug. "I don't care. He can choose."

Ben hesitates in the door a minute, his lanky form in my peripheral vision. Then he leaves me and I am alone with that image staring back at me from my smartphone. I close the photo app and put the device down, shut my eyes and draw in a few deep breaths. That's the other thing you're supposed to do when you're trying to move on, to smooth out the edges of the panic, sadness, anger or whatever overtakes you—focus on the breath. Breathe, they tell you.

Whatever that pill was, it has smoothed out the edges some, for sure. I'm lighter, less shaky.

But—honestly—I'm scared; fear tickles at the back of my throat. There's a white noise of anxiety in the back of my head. It's not just the man in the shadows, on the train. He *is* scary, sure. If there *really is* someone following me, then yes, it's weird and frightening. What's scarier, though, given my history, is if there *isn't*.

I finish out the day, and work late, pushing everything else away. There are contracts to review, emails to answer, a dispute between a fashion photographer and a model she supposedly came on to, then ejected from a shoot when he refused her, another dispute between a feature photographer who'd submitted photos to a travel magazine, filed for payment via their

Kafkaesque system, and ninety days later still hadn't been paid. Work is easy, a cocoon that keeps the chaos of life away.

When I look up from my desk again it's after seven and all the other offices are dark. The refrigerator in our break room hums, a familiar and weirdly comforting sound. Half of the hallway lights are off, leaving the space dim and shadowy. I know Ben was the last to leave and he locked me in on the way out, reminding me to set the alarm when I finally took off for the night.

As I'm packing my bag, a phone starts ringing in one of the offices. It bounces to the main line, and I reach over to pick it up. There's no number on the caller ID, but I see that it came from Maura's extension. Maybe it's Alvaro; he used to call late for Jack. We've drifted since Jack's death, not that he and I were ever really friends. In fact, despite his extraordinary talent, and his close friendship to Jack, I've always considered him a giant asshole. I really hope, for Maura's sake, that she hasn't fallen for him.

"Lang and Lang."

There's just a crackling on the line.

"Hello?" A strange sense of urgency pulls me forward in my seat.

There's a voice but so much interference that I can barely make it out. I hang on awhile longer, listening. A strain of music. The blast of a horn. That voice, it's throaty and deep, talking quickly, unintelligible through the static. Is it familiar?

Poppy. I think he says my name. Something about it sets my nerve endings tingling.

"Yes, this is Poppy. Sorry—I can't hear you."

I press my ear to the phone, cover the other to hear better. But the connection finally just goes dead, and a hard dip of disappointment settles into my stomach. I wait, thinking the phone will ring again. But it doesn't.

With a niggling sense of unease, I move away from the phone. That voice. My name on the line. Or was it?

I pack up my bag and loop the office, making sure lights are down and doors are locked. It's a small space; there are only five of us. Walls are made from glass, so there are few places in the office that can't be seen from wherever you stand. Still, I feel uncomfortable, like I'm being watched. I lock the door behind me, head down in the elevator.

"Working late," says Sam, the night security guard at the desk. He has a worn paperback novel in his hands. He and Jack used to talk about books, sharing a love of science and history. I glance at the title: *The Future of the Mind* by Michio Kaku.

"Light reading?"

"The brain," he says, tapping his capped skull. He has dark circles under his eyes, a strange depth to his gaze. An insomniac who works nights, a veteran who did two tours in Iraq. "It's the ultimate mystery. We know less about it than we do about space."

Jack would know what to say; he'd probably have read whatever Sam was reading. They'd chat for ten minutes while I kept busy answering emails on my smartphone. But I just nod, aware of the sad way he looks at me. Most people look at me like this now, at least sometimes. The widow.

"Take care of yourself," he says as I head toward the door. There is a gravity to his words, but when I turn back, he's already gone back to his reading.

On the street, shadows fill doorways and pool around parked cars. But no hooded man, just a young couple walking, hands linked, leaning into each other, an old woman with a shopping cart, a lanky kid walking and texting. A yellow cab swiftly pulls to the curb. Safe inside, I turn to look behind me once more.

Maybe, maybe something moves in the shadows across the street. But it's hard to be sure.

3

Instead of going home, I head to Layla's, dropping her a text so that she knows to expect me. Not even five seconds pass before her reply. She's always half expecting me for dinner these days— which makes me feel some combination of grateful and guilty.

We're having meatloaf. Gma's recipe.

Whose grandma she is talking about, I'm not sure. Mine, hers or Mac's? There certainly wasn't any famous meatloaf recipe in my family. Layla's brood wasn't exactly the gather-around-the-Sunday-table type, and most of them are long gone. Mac comes from a long line of glittering one percenters; meatloaf is not on the menu. Maybe she was just being ironic.

Yay! I type. Uh—whose gma?

When the phone pings again, the text is not from Layla.

Hope you're well, it reads. I'd love to see you again. No pressure. Just drinks?

The name on the phone gives me pause. Of all my recent assignations, he stays with me. I try not to think about the night

we shared, but it comes back in gauzy scenes. His touch—
gentle but urgent; his laugh—easy, deep. Sandy curls, like Jack's.
Something else just beneath the surface—what was it? There's
a little catch of excitement in my breath, but I quickly quash it.
No. I'm not ready for anything more than we shared. I've told
him as much. I briefly consider responding. It would be another
easy night, an escape hatch from my life.

Layla's text distracts me: I was just being ironic. I got the recipe from the internet—like everything else.

I hesitate another moment, remembering the feel of him, then
delete his message without response.

Cold. I know.

Layla's Central Park West address is gray and regal with a private motor court, multiple sparkling, marble lobbies manned by
a small army of smartly uniformed doormen. It's a fairy tale, a
castle for the ultrawealthy. The towering lobby ceiling dwarfs
me as I enter. The scent of fresh-cut flowers and the glitter of
the chandelier above create a ballroom effect. Story-tall abstract
oils, white leather sectionals, a twisting metal sculpture—there
are museum lobbies with less grandeur.

Real people don't live in buildings like this, Jack would say. He'd
seen too much of the world in his lens—people living in poverty, children starving, cities ruined by war, nature decimated
by corporate greed. Obscene wealth offended him. Me—not
so much. I drift through worlds, as comfortable in a hostel as I
am at the Ritz. Living in opulence or squalor, under the skin
people are just the same. Everyone suffers. Everyone struggles.
It just looks different from the outside.

My heels click on the marble, the staccato bouncing off the
walls. Allegedly, Sting lives here. Robert DeNiro lives here.
(Though I've never seen either of them.) Those mysterious Russian billionaires you always hear about live here. My dear friends

Layla and Mac Van Santen live here with their teenagers, Izzy and Slade.

I still don't *completely* understand what Mac does. Finance, of course. Hedge fund manager—but what does that really *mean*? I also don't get how in the last ten years, he got so crazy-beyond-ridiculously rich. Something to do with "shorts" and the mortgage bond crisis of 2007. Suddenly there was a move from the perfectly spectacular Tribeca loft to the Central Park West penthouse. The monthlong summer trips overseas. The family driver, Carmelo. The private plane at an airport in Long Island.

Layla and I share a laugh over this now and then—mirthlessly—how much things have changed since we were kids together. How her mother worked two jobs. How my parents bought her prom dress when her family couldn't afford it, how *her* parents fought in the kitchen over stacks of bills they couldn't pay. How my dad and I would drive to her place and pick her up when she couldn't stand the yelling and worse. Her parents are both dead now, having led, short, unhappy, unhealthy lives. But Layla still bears the scars they left on her, literally and figuratively.

The doorman, unsmiling but deferential, knows me and waves me through without bothering to call up.

"Have a good evening, Ms. Lang."

The floral scent from the lobby follows me into the mirrored elevator. I drift up to the twenty-eighth floor as though on a cloud, silken and silent, emerging in the private foyer.

Pushing through the door into Layla's penthouse apartment, I'm greeted by the sound of Izzy practicing her violin in the room down the hall. Whatever piece she's struggling through is unrecognizable. The sheer size of their space, the thick walls, keep the sound from being unbearable as surely my early instrumental attempts were to my parents—the clarinet, later the flute. I remember their strained encouragement, their palpable relief, when I discovered that my passion was the totally silent artistic endeavor of photography.

Let's just say that Izzy is no musical prodigy, either; I wonder when or if she'll be told. She practices with gusto, though, attacking the same few musical phrases over and over. If it's a matter of sheer will alone, she might improve. She's a high achiever like her father, focused, unrelenting, a star student.

Slade, her younger brother, is at the kitchen island FaceTiming with a friend on his iPad while they play some weird world-building game on a laptop. Two screens are apparently required for this interaction. I plant a kiss on his head, am rewarded with a high five, and his megawatt smile. Slade's more like Layla—or like Layla used to be. Easy, laid-back, distractible and artistic.

Layla's at the stove; the table set with fresh flowers, cloth napkins, gleaming platinum silverware. There are only four places, which I take to mean that Mac is not going to be home for dinner. The usual state of affairs.

"Please put that away and tell your sister it's time to eat," Layla says to Slade as she comes over to give me a hug.

"Izzy!" Slade bellows, startling us both into laughter. "Dinner!"

"*I* could have done that," says Layla, swatting him on the shoulder. "Tell Brock you have to go. Goodbye, Brock."

"Goodbye, Mrs. Van Santen," comes the disembodied voice from the iPad.

"Did you finish your homework?" she asks Slade when he's closed his laptop.

He looks at her with Mac's hazel eyes, an uncertain frown furrowing his brow. He's a heartthrob, all big eyes and pouty lips, thick mop of white-blond curls. Fourteen years old and already towering over Layla and me.

"No more gaming until it's done," says Layla. "Now go *get* your sister. Clearly, she can't *hear* us."

More screeching from behind Izzy's closed door as if to punctuate the point. Slade moves in that direction as slowly as a sloth, knocks, then disappears into Izzy's room.

"That violin teacher keeps telling me that she has promise," Layla says, moving back over to the stove. "Am I crazy? She sounds truly *awful*, right?"

"I heard that," yells Izzy, emerging. No one ever *says* anything in the Van Santen house. "I *am* awful! Obviously. This was your idea, Mom!"

Layla rolls her eyes as Izzy tackles me from behind, kissing me on the cheek. Her hair is spun gold; she smells of lilacs. She's lean and fit, but no skinny waif. I've seen her and her field hockey–playing girlfriends put away their body weight in pizza.

"Save me from all of this, Aunt Poppy," she says. "Can I come live with you?"

"I know, darling," I say, holding on to her tight. She used to sit in my lap, kick her chubby legs and laugh as I changed her diapers, and squeeze her tiny hand in mine as we crossed the street. Is there anyone dearer than the children of people you love, especially when you don't have your own?

"How *do* you bear up under these conditions? It's miserable."

"Mom, please," says Izzy. She walks over to her mother, picks a carrot out of the salad and starts to munch. "I'm just *not musical*."

"It's good for you, sweetie," says Layla easily. She pushes a strand of stray hair from Izzy's eyes. "To do something you're not *great* at immediately. To work for something."

"That's—*ridiculous*."

The teenager, so like her mother, blond with startling jewel-green eyes, casts me a pleading look. "Isn't that *ridiculous*?"

Savory aromas waft from the oven and range top, making my stomach rumble. I used to cook, too. Jack and I both loved being in the kitchen. Lately, when I'm not here, I survive on a diet of salad bar offerings and maybe Chinese takeout when I'm feeling ambitious. I help Izzy get the water.

At the table, I let the chaos wash over me—Izzy going on about some mean-girl drama, Slade begging to add a robotics club to his already packed schedule. All the heaviness, the strangeness of my day lifts for a moment.

But my inner life is a roller coaster. I think: this is the life Jack and I could have had; maybe not the insane wealth—but the chattering kids and the food on the stove and the homework. The happy mess of it all; it could have been ours. And then the ugly rise of anger; we were robbed of this. I stare at the water in my glass. Followed then by the stomach-dropping plummet of despair: What is there when I leave here? A dark apartment, void of him and the life we were building.

Layla's hand on mine. The kids are looking at me.

"Poppy?" she says softly. "Where did you go?"

"Nowhere," I say. "Sorry."

A ringing device causes Layla to rise from the table. I hear the electronic swoop as she answers.

"Wait, don't tell me," she says. "You're going to be late. I shouldn't wait up."

Her tone is light, but there's an edge to it, too.

"There's just a lot going on right now." Mac on speaker apparently. No—FaceTime. She comes to the table with her iPad, sits back down beside me. Even on the screen I can see the circles under his eyes. He rubs at his bald head, his tie loose and the top button on his shirt open. "You know that, honey."

Layla softens, smiles at the screen. "I know. We just miss you."

"Hi, Mac," I say.

"Hi, Dad," the kids chorus.

"Hey, guys."

"Poppy's my husband now," says Layla. She tosses me a smile. "She's in your place."

"I hope you two will be very happy together," says Mac with a light laugh. "Poppy, good luck."

I blow him a kiss.

"Izzy, sweetie, how did you do on your calculus test?" he asks.

Layla passes her the iPad.

"I'm confident," she says, covering her mouth, still chewing. These kids, all confidence, no worries. When did that happen? What happened to teen angst? I used to lie in bed at night worrying—about grades, about friend drama, about *everything*.

"Did you check your work?" he asks.

More chewing. "Uh-huh," she says. "I got this, Dad."

Izzy hands the iPad to Slade. "Dad, this is the last week to sign up for robotics."

"What did your mother say?"

"She said not unless my grades come up." Slade casts a sad-eyed look at his mom, which she ignores.

"Then that's the decision."

Is it fatigue that makes his voice sound that way, flat, distant? Or the crush of it all—work and family, marriage, pretty from the outside, exhausting from the inside.

Slade, still undeterred, launches in about how by the time he can prove he'll get his grades up, it will be too late. They go back and forth for a few minutes.

"FaceTime parenting," whispers Layla. I don't like her flat tone, either, or the kind of sad distance I see on her face; it's new. "It's all the rage."

"You okay?"

She puts on a smile, but looks down at her plate. "Yeah," she says, false bright. "Yeah, of course. Just—tired."

I catch Izzy watching us with a worried frown.

"Dad says what if I sign up for robotics and quit if my grades don't come up?" Slade cuts in.

Layla looks to the screen, annoyed. But the iPad is dark; Mac is gone.

"Your father and I will discuss it later and give you a decision tomorrow."

"Robotics is the future, Mom."

Layla puts down her fork and locks Slade in a stare. "Ask me again and the answer is no."

Everyone knows that tone; Slade falls silent and looks at his plate. The mom tone—which means you've reached the limit of her patience and you're about to lose big. I take a bite of meatloaf. Wherever she got the recipe, it's great. I've cleared my whole plate. I didn't realize how hungry I was. Layla's barely touched hers. Which I guess is why she's a size zero.

"Okay," he says, drawing out the word into sad defeat.

Izzy gets up, scraping the chair loudly, clearing her plate. "I promised to call Abbey."

Somehow the mood has changed, the happy chatter died down, a stillness settling.

Layla and I settle into the white expanse of her living room— everything low and soft, the gas fireplace lit, photography books laid out on the reclaimed wood coffee table, a bottle of pinot opened between us. I want to tell her about the hooded man, but I don't. She'll panic, launch into fix-it mode, and I don't need that right now.

We've been friends since eighth grade. But *friend* is such a tepid word, isn't it? A throwaway word that can mean any level of acquaintance. What do you call someone who's shared your whole life, who seems to know you better than you know your-self, accepts all your many flaws and weaknesses as just flubs in the fabric of who you are? The person you can call at any hour. The one who could show up at your house in the middle of the night with a body in the trunk of her car, and you'd help her bury it. Or vice versa. That's Layla.

"Mac's working late," I say, tossing it out there.

She lifts her eyebrows. "That's Mac. It's what he does. He works."

She seems to wear the opulence around us, slipping into it easily like a silk robe. The expensive fabrics on her body drape; her pedicured toes are pretty, white-pink squares. Her skin prac-tically glows from regular treatments. It would be easy to think she came from wealth, that this was all she knew. But I remember how she grew up. The fingerprint bruises on the inside of her arm from one of her father's "bad nights." How my mother used to pack extra food in my lunch box in case Layla came to school without and with no money to buy anything. We don't talk about it much anymore, the abuse, the neglect. Ancient history, Layla says.

"It's easier I think," she says, looking down into her glass. "For him. To be at work than here with us. It's messy at home, you know. Lots of noise, emotions, ups and downs—family, life. Numbers sit in tidy columns. You add them up and it all makes sense."

When Jack and I first started the agency, Mac helped figure out the finances.

One night, he came to our apartment after work, and sat at our kitchen table covered with a swath of spreadsheets and documents. Layla and I grew bored, drifted away from the table. But the boys stayed up late talking about pension plans and salaries, quarterly taxes, insurance costs.

Layla and I opened a bottle of wine, lay on the couch listening to their voices, low and serious.

"Are you sure this is what you guys want?" she asked that night.

"The agency?"

"Yeah," she said. "Won't you miss it? The assignments, the travel, you know—the excitement of it?"

There was something odd in her tone. "Do *you* miss it?" I asked.

She shrugged. "The kids keep me busy," she says. "But, yeah, sometimes."

I was surprised by this; it never occurred to me that Layla was less than happy.

Her Facebook posts and Instagram feeds were a cheerful tumble of beautiful pictures of the kids, family trips, idyllic

Sunday breakfasts, strolls in the park. Layla and Mac in love, wealthy, with two gorgeous, gifted children. *Fakebook*, Jack liked to call it. *A bulletin board of our pretty moments, all the rest of it hidden.*

"I guess we all make our choices," she said, flat and final. "I mean, we're blessed. I'm—grateful."

"Mac loves the kids," she says now. "He's always there for them. He's never missed a performance or a party—they call, he answers."

"He loves *you*."

That much I know. Though Mac can be stiff and isn't exactly a sparkling conversationalist, sometimes even a little blank, his face lights up when Layla talks. He watches her with love in his eyes. Personally, I think he's on the spectrum, a genius with numbers but maybe struggling elsewhere. Not an unusual combination. But since Jack's death, Mac has spent many an evening at the office with me, educating me on everything Jack used to handle. He's patient, gentle, explaining and re-explaining as often as necessary without a trace of annoyance. He's been there for me, just like Layla. These people—they're my family.

Layla rubs at the back of her shoulder, seems about to say something but then it dies on her lips, replaced by a wan smile.

"I know," she says. "Of course he does. Seventeen years."

She takes a sip from her wineglass, the lights behind her twinkling in a sea of dark. In daylight, the room looks out onto Central Park—an expanse of green, or autumn colors, or white. "It's okay. We can't change each other. Most of us who stay married know that."

Jack and I had just passed our eighth-year wedding anniversary before he died, so I don't comment. But I don't remember ever wanting to change him.

"I'm sorry," she says, sitting forward and looking stricken. "The stupid things I say sometimes."

I lift a hand. "Don't walk on eggshells. Don't do that."

"So what's going on with you, then?" she asks. "Something—so don't lie."

"Nothing," I lie. She doesn't buy it, doesn't push, but keeps her gaze on me.

"I saw Dr. Nash today," I say, just to put something out there. "She wants me to get off the sleeping pills."

"Why?" says Layla, pouring us each another glass of wine. I don't stop her, though I've had enough, and the pills earlier. This is our second bottle. "Fuck that. Take what you need to sleep. This year's been hard enough. You tell her—"

I tune her out. She's always had a mouth on her, always the fighter, the one standing up, speaking out. For some reason I flash on her arguing with one of her high school boyfriends. We were in the parking lot after a football game. She hit him on the head with her purse. *You fucker!* she'd screamed, as we all watched. I dragged her off; she kept yelling. The look on his face, like he'd never experienced anger before. Maybe he hadn't. Layla wept in my car afterward. What had she been so mad about that night? I don't even remember—or who the boy was, or who else was there. Just the bright spotlights from the field, some girls giggling, the smell of cut grass and Layla's voice slicing the night.

"Poppy," she says.

"What?"

I'm getting the mom look, the one she gives her kids when they're not listening.

"I asked if she took you off the pills."

"She lowered the dosage."

"And."

"My dreams." My dream images of Jack from last night mingle with the shadow on the subway, the odd daydream I experienced on the train. "They're more vivid. I don't feel as rested."

"Tell her to put the dose back up," she says sharply. "You need your rest, Poppy."

"I *want* to get off them." The words sound weak even to my own ears. Do I really? "I don't want to take pills to sleep for the rest of my life."

"Why not? Better living through chemistry. Lots of people are medicated all their lives." She lifts her glass like she's proving a point.

I don't know if she's kidding or not. What's certain is that I'm duller, mentally heavier. I haven't had a camera in my hand since Jack died, haven't taken one serious photograph. The truth is I don't even feel the urge. Is it the grief? The drugs? Some combination of those things. I put the glass down on the table, where it glitters accusingly. How many have I had? Is it weird that I don't even know?

She drops it. We chat awhile longer, just gossip about the firm, how I think Maura and Alvaro might be involved. I think I see something cross Layla's face at the mention of Alvaro's name, but then it's gone. She tells me that she's started shooting again. Layla has an eye for faces. They blossom before her lens, reveal all their secrets. Her favorite subjects in recent years, naturally, have been her children. She still maintains her website, has an Instagram feed with a decent following. She has real talent, more than I ever had.

"Don't worry," she says. "Not more beautiful shots of my gorgeous children. After Slade and Izzy go to school, I head out the way I used to. Just looking for it, you know, that perfect moment."

"Show me," I say, curious.

"I will." She looks away. It's not like her to be shy. "I'm *rusty*. I've spent so many years on the kids—maybe I've lost my eye. What small amount of talent I had, maybe it just withered up and died."

"I doubt that," I answer. "Be patient. Maybe you just have a new way of seeing things now."

She shifts on the couch, folds her legs under her. Something about the way she's sitting seems uncomfortable, as if she might be in pain. Too much kickboxing. She rubs at her shoulder again. "Life does that I guess."

She looks at me too long, too sadly. I look away.

"I should get home." This happens. I'm okay where I am and then suddenly I just need to be alone, like I can't hold the pieces of myself together anymore.

"Stay here," she offers. But I've spent too many nights in their guest room. Tonight, I need to think. Layla's life is a cocoon. When I'm here, everything else disappears—the real world seems fuzzy and insubstantial.

I get up, and grab my stuff, get moving before she can talk me into it. She watches me a beat, seems like she wants to say something. But then she rises, too, and doesn't stop me.

"Wait a second," she says, then rushes off down the hallway. She's back in a moment, as I'm pulling on my coat.

"Take these," she says, pressing a bottle of pills in my hand. "They're mine. I think that's the dosage you were on originally."

I look at the bottle. "Don't you need them?"

"I can get more."

"How?" I ask. "Dr. Nash watches me like a junkie."

Layla smiles. "I have my ways."

I shouldn't take them. I should hand them back to her and ask her what the hell she's talking about. Where is she getting all these pills? And why? But I don't. I just gratefully shove them in my pocket, promising myself that I won't take them. Unless. Unless I absolutely need to.

"Sure you don't want to talk about it?" she asks. "Whatever is going on? I'm here when you're not okay. Always. Don't forget that."

It's tempting, to come back inside and tell Layla, let her take over in that way she always has. *This is what we need to do...*

"I'm okay," I say instead.

4

The Lincoln Town Car waits for me in the motor court. When he spies me, Layla's towering, refrigerator-sized driver, Carmelo, climbs out quickly and rushes to reach the door before I do, smiles victoriously as he swings it open. He has long blond hair pulled back into a tight ponytail, faded denim eyes and a jaw like the side of a mountain.

"I got there first, Miss Poppy," he says.

"This time," I concede, slipping into the buttery leather interior, and he closes the door.

It's a thing we have; how I find it ridiculous to wait by the door while he comes around to open it. And he considers door-opening a critical feature of his job, and a terrible dereliction of duty if I open it and get in before he sees me. He's the rare person who cares about the minute details of his profession. I shouldn't mess with him. But he's sweet and funny and we enjoy our little game.

"Home?" he asks.

"Home," I say, even though I don't have a home. I have a place where I live, but not a home.

The city rushes past—lights and people, limos, beaters, taxis, bicyclists. I am light, the wine, the pills—I let my head rest against the seat, which seems to embrace me. The hooded man is a distant memory. The car is quiet, except for low jazz coming from the radio; I let my eyes close. Sometimes Carmelo and I chat about his aging mother, his young son, Leo. But he rarely speaks unless I talk to him first, unless he has a question. It's another standard of his job, to disappear, to be only what you need him to be. When I open my eyes, I catch his in the rearview mirror, watching.

"Long day?" he asks.

"Yes," I admit. "You?"

"The usual," he says with a shrug. He takes the kids to school, Mac to work, shuttles Layla through her busy day, waits for Mac in the evenings, takes clients (and friends) around; his day ends when Mac's does, often not until after midnight or later. Carmelo was always the driver for boys' night out, when Jack, Alvaro and Mac got together. Shuttling them from bar to bar, maybe to some private card game at Mac's club, who knows where else.

What could Carmelo tell us about our husbands? Layla mused.

Are you kidding? I'd quip. *He'd never tell us anything.*

"The city, though, lately. What a mess."

"Ever think about getting out?"

"Nah," he says. "Born and raised, you know."

He pulls to the curb and I just stare for a second, my heart pulsing.

"Carmelo."

He turns to look at me questioningly, then out at the street. His eyes widen as it dawns.

"Oh, no," he says, then covers his mouth in a girlish gesture of embarrassment. "Miss Poppy. I'm so sorry."

He's taken me to my old apartment building, the one on the Upper West Side where I lived with Jack, not far from Layla's. A couple I don't recognize climbs the stairs, laughing, carrying sacks of groceries. She's petite and wearing jeans, a light black jacket. He's taller, broad, with an inky mop of hair—young, stylish. It could be us. It *was* us.

"It's okay," I say, biting back a brutal rush of grief, of anger— not at him, at *everything*.

He pulls away from the curb quickly, cutting off another car and earning the angry bleat of a horn.

"I don't know what I was thinking," he says, voice heavy with apology. "I'm *so* sorry."

"It's okay," I say again, trying to keep my voice steady. "Easy mistake."

I look back at my old street, but then he turns the corner and heads downtown. It's gone. I want to go back; I want to get as far away as possible. I wish that he would drive and drive and that we'd never reach our destination; that I'd just drift in the space between Layla's life and what's left of mine forever.

Back at my place, I open another bottle of wine, pour myself a glass and look around the space. The pain from the sucker punch of seeing my old block has subsided some. And I experience a brief flicker where I feel distantly inspired to decorate, to settle in, as Dr. Nash keeps encouraging. At least unpack the boxes that are still stacked everywhere.

But that moment of inspiration passes as quickly as it came and I find myself reclining instead on the couch. I turn on the television, close my eyes and listen to the local news—an armed robbery in the Bronx, the Second Avenue subway near completion, a missing child found. The measured, practiced voice of the newscaster soothes; my awareness drifts.

"Jack?"

The bed beside me is cold, the covers tossed back. The clock on the dresser reads 3:32 a.m. I push myself up, sleep clinging, lulling me back.

"Jack."

I pad across the hardwood floor. I find him in the living room, laptop open.

"What are you doing?" I ask, sitting beside him on the couch.

He drops an arm around me, pulls me in. I love the smell of him, the mingle of soap and—what? Just him, just his skin. No cologne. He'd wear the same three shirts and pairs of jeans all week if I didn't buy his clothes. He doesn't always shave, wears his hear longish, a sandy-blond tangle of curls. Has a pair of black-framed glasses instead of bothering with contact lenses.

"Just catching up on email."

His email is open, but so is the web browser, the window hidden.

"What is it?" I tease. "Porn?"

"Yeah," he says. "I'm out here watching porn while my beautiful wife sleeps in the next room."

I nudge in closer, wrap my arms around him.

"Porn's easier, though, right?" I offer reasonably. "Isn't that what they say? Porn's never tired, doesn't say no. You don't have to satisfy porn."

"Stop," he says. I reach for the computer and open the web browser before he can stop me. The face of a beautiful dark-eyed woman stares back at me. But it isn't porn; just a news article he's been reading. A photojournalist was beaten to death in her East Village apartment, a suspected robbery gone wrong, all her equipment stolen.

"Who is she?" I ask.

He shakes his head, a beat passing before he answers. "Just someone I used to know."

I scan the article. "She was murdered?"

He stays silent.

I feel a rush of urgency. "Jack, tell me who this is and why you're reading about it in the middle of the night."

He doesn't answer, just stares straight ahead.

"Jack," I say again. "Who is she?"

★ ★ ★

I wake up with a jolt on the stiff fabric of my couch, disoriented, reaching for him. The dream lingers, clings to my cells. *Who is she?* My own voice sounds back to me. I'm tangled in that strange weaving of the real, the remembered and the imagined. Jack's scent, the feel of his arm, stays even as the shapes and shadows of the apartment he's never seen assert themselves into my consciousness.

I reach for the dream—the woman's face on the screen, the news article. *Someone I used to know.* But it's jumbled, makes no sense. A dream? A memory? Some weird hybrid?

The couch beneath me is hard, not soft and saggy like the one in our old place. This one I bought online because I thought it looked sleek and stylish; when it arrived, it was as stiff and gray as a concrete slab. I didn't have the energy to return it.

The television is on, the sound down so low it's barely audible. Radar images of tomorrow's weather swirl red and orange, a storm brewing, unseasonable heat.

Slowly, Jack, the dream begin to fade. I reach for him, but he's sand through my fingers.

This is not new. Since his death, I vividly, urgently dream of my husband—embraces, lovemaking, his return from this place or that, maybe the store, or a business trip. The joy of his homecoming lifts my heart. These moments—though they are twisted and strange, places altered, patchworks of things that happened and didn't—are so desperately real that I often awake thinking that my real life, the one in which Jack has been taken from me, is the nightmare.

And then, when I wake, there's the hard, cold slap of reality: he's gone. And that loss sinks in anew. Every single time. How I dread that crush when he's taken from me again, when the heaviness of grief and loss settles on me once more, fresh and raw, its terrible weight pushing all the air from my chest.

I wipe away tears I didn't even know I was crying. And I

reach for the remote and let our stored pictures come up on the screen. Photos from our travels scroll—a canopy walk in Costa Rica, lava tubing in Iceland, a selfie that we took while kissing on the Cliffs of Moher. The images transfix, the girl I was, the man he was. Both of us gone. Many nights after work, this is what I do. Lie here and watch our hundreds of photos scroll silent across the screen.

It's going to get better, Dr. Nash has told me. *With time, the weight of this will lessen.*

It isn't, I want to say but don't. *How can it?*

Outside my towering windows, the city glimmers.

I pull myself up, dig the new lower dosage prescription out of my bag, pour a big glass of water. Just about to drink the medication down, I pause. It sits in the palm of my hand, blue and seductive.

What if I just stopped taking them? What would happen? I should do some research. Jack wouldn't approve of the amount of medication I've been taking, I know that. He wouldn't even take Tylenol for a headache.

Or…

I remember the higher dosage Layla handed me; I grab them from the pocket of my coat, hearing her voice, always so certain: *take what you need to sleep.* I think about the other pills I took today. How many? What were they? How much wine did I drink?

To be truthful here, there's not much of an internal battle. I *need* the utter blankness of dreamless sleep, the dream life Dr. Nash so values be damned. I need a break from grief, from my thoughts—from *myself.* I shake out one of the higher dosage pills. Then another. I drink them down. Just for tonight.

With images twirling around my sleepy brain, I enter the bedroom. On the bedside, the black dream journal rests by my bed. I haven't written in it in a while, but Dr. Nash's advice from today is still fresh in my mind. *We can learn a lot about our-*

selves there. I flip it open, and scrawl down what I remember, but it's faded to nearly nothing. I scribble: a dark-eyed girl on the screen. Who is she?

The pen feels so heavy in my hand.

There is no furniture in the bedroom except a low white platform bed, covered by the cloud of a down comforter, big soft pillows. I close my eyes, let the journal and pen drop to my side—pushing away thoughts of Jack, and the stranger shadowing my life, Layla, Dr. Nash. I wait for that blissful chemical slumber.

5

The surface beneath me is cold and hard, my head a siren of pain. Nausea claws at my stomach and the back of my throat. My shoulder aches, twisted under me. A sharply unpleasant odor invades. I don't want to open my eyes; I squeeze them shut instead.

Where am I? I should know this.

I open them just a sliver, peering through the fog of my lashes. Silver and white, a filthy tile floor, feet walking by, high heels, sneakers, flats. Scuffling, voices. Music throbbing outside, someone laughing too loud—drunk or high.

You must be kidding me! a voice shrieks.

I push myself up. I'm in a bathroom stall, curled around a toilet bowl. That odor—it's urine. I'm on the floor in a bathroom, in a nightclub by the sound of it. My heart starts to race, my breath ragged. I look down at myself. I am wearing a dress I don't recognize; tight and red, strappy high heels.

Okay, okay, okay, I tell myself. Just think. Just think. What's the last thing you remember?

Jack's funeral beneath a cruelly pretty sky, leaning heavily on Mac, his strong arm around my waist practically the only thing holding me up. Layla holding my other hand. Mac's whisper in my ear: *It's okay, Poppy. We're going to get through this. All of us together. Hold on. Be strong. He'd want that.* Our old apartment filled with friends, damp eyes, whispering voices; Jack's mother, her face ashen with a tray of sandwiches wobbling in her hand; Layla taking it from her, laying it down on the table. My mother chatting with Alvaro, flirting as if this wasn't her son-in-law's funeral. I can hear her throaty laugh, inappropriate enough to draw eyes. Me wishing for the millionth time that my father was still alive. Daddy, please. I need you. How silly. A grown woman still calling for her father. Those are the last things I can remember. Where am I now? How did I get here?

I pull myself unsteadily to standing, the walls spinning. Someone pounds on the stall door.

"One minute," I say, voice croaky and strange. I don't even sound like myself.

Whoever it is finds another stall, slams the door. The door outside swings open, voices and music pour in, filling the whole room. Then it goes quiet again.

There's a bag lying beside me, a glittery black evening purse. Even though I don't recognize it, I grab for it and open it. My cell phone, dead. Five hundred dollars in cash. A thick compact, which I pry open with shaking hands.

The woman in the mirror is a mess, long black hair wild, mascara running down her face in sad clown tears, pale, blue eyes wide with fright. I sit on the seat and use some toilet paper and my own spit to clean my face. I do a passable job, running my fingers through my hair, using the makeup in my bag to fix myself up. In the small shaking mirror, I'm almost normal again. Except for the fact that I have no idea where I am, or how I got here.

Okay. Deal with that later. Breathe. Breathe. Breathe. I just need to get myself home. I can figure everything out once I'm safe. I'll call Layla then. We'll figure it out. She'll know what to do.

I wobble through the stall door, tilting in heels too high. Two women—one black, one white—applying makeup at the mirror glance at me, then at each other. They both start to laugh.

"You okay, honey?" one of them asks, not really caring. She smears a garish red to her lips.

"You need to Uber your ass home, girl," says the other, frowning in disapproval. Her hair is dyed platinum blond, her lips dazzling berry. I feel a lash of anger, but a wash of shame keeps me from answering back.

Their laughter follows me out the door, until it's drowned out by the heavy techno beat. Bodies throb on the dance floor as I push my way through the crowd, wondering where the exit is. Instead, I find myself at the bar, taking a seat. I'll rest here a minute, my legs so unsteady, head spinning.

The bartender comes over and leans in to me. She brings me a glass of ice water. Embossed in ornate script on the glass, a word in red: Morpheus.

"Your boyfriend's been waiting for you all this time," she says as I take a long swallow. "If you thought you lost him, you didn't."

I glance in the direction that her eyes drift—they are violet, eerie and strange. Color contacts. On her arms, tattoos—a dragon, a tower, a woman dancing. I stare, fixated by the lines and colors. I can't focus on anything for very long.

"He sees you."

Who is he? Long sandy hair, pulled back, a thick jaw and strange eyes that seem to defy colors—amber, green or steely blue. He gets up and comes over, leans in behind me.

"I thought you left." His voice in my ear sends a shiver down my spine.

He spins me around, tugs me into him. The heat between us; it's electric. He snakes one arm around my back, the other around my neck and leans in, as if we are not in a crowded club, but alone. His draw is magnetic, irresistible. And then we *are* alone, the world dropping away, music fading, as he kisses me long and deep. I am on fire with desire, a deep ache inside me. It's embarrassing how badly I want him.

Jack. Jack.

But it's not Jack.

"Who is Jack?" he wants to know. "Doesn't matter. I'll be Jack, whoever he is. I'll be anyone you want me to be."

Then, as if by magic, we are in his car—or at least he's driving. I have no idea whose car it is. But it's a nice one, leather, glowing blue lights, soft music playing on Bose speakers. Everything smells clean, new. The city skyline is in the rearview mirror, streamers of white and red lights around us.

"Where are we going?" I ask, barely even recognizing my own voice.

"Don't you remember?" he asks gently.

"No," I say with a rising panic. "I'm sorry. I don't remember at all."

He looks at me with a strange smile and just keeps driving.

6

I'm sorry. I don't remember at all.

The words burrow into my sleep, taking on urgency, growing louder, until the sound of my own frightened shout wakes me.

I bolt upright, breath labored, T-shirt soaked through with sweat. I'm in my own bed, the covers tossed to the floor. A weak Tuesday morning sun bleeds in through the blinds, shining on my clothes from last night in a messy tumble on the floor.

The details of the dream are already slippery. What kind of car? What club? It's *important* to remember; I *must* dig into that place.

Coffee brews in the timed pot that's set for six, its aroma wafting through the apartment. The city is awake with horns and distant sirens and the hum of traffic. Slowly, breath easing, these mundane details of wakefulness start to wipe away my urgency. The dream, the panic to remember, recede, slinking away with each passing second like a serpent into the tall grass of my wakefulness.

Sleep is the place where your mind organizes, where your subconscious resolves and expresses itself. In times of great stress, dreams can become like a whole other life, Dr. Nash said. A terrifying, disjointed life that I can't understand.

I reach for my dream journal and start writing, trying to capture what I remember:

Morpheus, a nightclub?

Black-and-white-tile floors, kissing a faceless man?

He takes me somewhere in his car, a BMW maybe. Afraid. But relieved, too? Who was he? Where was he taking me? Why did I go with him?

Red dress?

Powerful desire. Jack. I thought he was Jack, but he wasn't.

The impressions are disjointed, nonsense really in daylight. As I scribble, the sunlight brightens and begins to fill the room through the tall windows. Too bright. I must be late for work.

Finished writing, I flip back through to the earlier pages, looking to see if there's any other dream like this one. Reading what I wrote late last night, before I took the pills, it's the scrawl of a crazy person, loopy, jagged:

Jack, computer, looking at porn? Who is she?

Another sentence that I don't even remember writing: *Was he hiding something from me?*

I stare at the black ink bleeding into the eggshell page. There's a little stutter of fear, as if I discovered a stranger had been writing in my dream journal. But no, the handwriting is unmistakably mine.

I start flipping back through earlier entries. One page is filled with a twisting black spiral. It begins at a single point in the middle of the paper, spins wider and wider until it fills the whole sheet. It's inked in manically, scribbled at so hard that it leaks through to the page beneath. There's a tiny black figure that seems to be falling and falling deep into the abyss.

No one tells you about the rage, I'd written. *I could fall into my anger and disappear forever. How could he do this to me? How could he leave me like this? Who did this to him? To us? Why can't they find my husband's killer?*

Again, that feeling—a stranger writing in my dream journal. But no.

That rage, what a sucking black hole it is, devouring the universe. I remember that there was a terrible, brilliantly real dream about finding the man who took Jack from me. I chased him through the streets, finally gaining on him and taking him down in a lunge. I beat him endlessly, violently, with all my strength. It was so vivid I felt his bones crush beneath my knuckles, tasted his splattering blood on my mouth. It went on and on, my satisfaction only deepening. I confessed this tearfully to Dr. Nash.

Anger, in doses, can be healthy, Poppy, she said. *It's healthy to direct your rage toward your husband's murderer, to not hold it in. Rage suppressed becomes despair, depression.*

How can it be healthy to dream of killing someone, to imagine it so clearly? To—enjoy *it?*

There's darkness in all of us, she said serenely. *It's part of life.*

I shut the dream journal hard; I don't want to go back to that place. That rage inside me; it's frightening. I don't want to know who I dreamed about last night, where I was. Maybe it's better to let these things fade. After all, if you're supposed to remember your dreams, if they mean something—why do they race away? Why do they never make any real sense?

The hot shower washes what's left of it all away. I can barely cling to even one detail. But there's a song moving through my head, something twangy and hypnotic.

I've seen that face before.

Images resurface unbidden as I head to the office—I flash on the man at the bar, the blue lights of the car interior. It's an annoying, unsettling intrusion, these dreams so vivid, so disturbing. And I'm not rested at all; I'm as jumpy and nauseated as if I'd pulled an all-nighter.

I ask myself a question I might be asking too often: How many pills did I take last night? And: How much wine did I have?

Not enough, apparently. Not enough to achieve blankness.

Nervously aware of my surroundings, I scan my environment for the hooded man. Though the day is bright, I see shadows all around me, keep glancing around like a paranoiac. There's a group of construction workers, all denim-clad, with hoodies pulled over their hard hats. One of them stares, makes a vulgar kissing noise with his mouth. I stride past him, don't look back.

Finally, in the office, at my desk, I feel the wash of relief. It's early still, at least an hour before anyone else comes in. I pick up the phone.

"Hey, there," answers Layla. "You didn't call me back last night."

Her voice. It's a lifeline. She's so solid. So real.

"Did you call?" I ask, confused.

"Yeah," she says. "Just wanted to check on you. I didn't like how you looked when you left."

Scrolling through the messages on my phone, I see her call and a text, left after eleven.

"Oh—sorry." How did I miss that?

"Seriously. What's going on?"

Layla is the first one to start worrying about me. She was the first to think that maybe something wasn't right a day or two before my "nervous breakdown" or "psychotic break" or whatever we're calling it these days. Dr. Nash just refers to it as my "break." *Think of it as a little vacation your psyche takes when it has too much to handle. It's like a brownout, an overloading of circuits. Grief is a neurological event.* And Layla was the one to bring me home.

I tell her about the dream, anyway the snippets I can almost remember.

She's quiet for a moment too long. I think I've lost her.

"Layla?"

"Poppy," she says. "Maybe you should call Detective Grayson."

I'm surprised that she would bring up the detective who has been in charge of Jack's murder investigation. A murder investigation that has petered to almost nothing. It's been almost a year since Jack was killed and every lead has gone cold. There are no suspects. No new information. But Grayson is still on the job, checking in regularly, always returning my calls to query about progress. I used to crave justice for Jack, for everything we lost. It used to gnaw at me, keep me up nights. But, with Dr. Nash's help, I've let that idea go somewhat. What justice is there for this? No matter what price paid, the clock will not turn back. So this question sits like an undigested stone in my gut. Who killed Jack?

"Why? What does Grayson have to do with this?"

Another moment where she draws in and releases a sharp breath. I can hear the street noise so she's probably leaning out the bathroom window with her cigarette so that the kids don't smell it when they get home from school. She's supposed to have quit; obviously, the nicotine gum isn't cutting it. I'm not going to hassle her about it. Who am I to get on her case, pill popper that I've become?

"I was just thinking," she says finally, carefully. "The days you can't remember. Maybe what you dreamed last night. I mean, maybe that wasn't a dream at all. Maybe it was a memory."

Her words strike an odd chord, cause an unpleasant tingle on my skin. "Why would you say that?"

"Honey," she says. A sharp exhale. "When I found you, you were wearing a red dress."

Ben comes in singing. He has his headphones on, clearly doesn't see me. He's belting out Katy Perry, singing about how this is the part of him you'll never ever take away from him. He reaches into my office to flip on the lights I've neglected to turn on and his eyes fall on me. He blushes and gives me a wide smile, takes a bow. I'd laugh if my body didn't feel like one big nerve ending, sizzling with tension.

"Maybe—you're *remembering* things," says Layla when I stay silent.

"Dr. Nash said I probably wouldn't, that likely those days are gone forever."

It was two days after the funeral that I disappeared. Four days after that I woke up in a hospital, remembering nothing. Even the days before Jack's murder and through the funeral are foggy and disjointed. Part of me thinks that it might be a blessing to forget the worst days of your life; I'm not sure I want them back. Dr. Nash has suggested as much, that my memories haven't come back because I don't want them.

I remember the day he was killed in ugly, jagged fragments, sitting in the police station, reeling at Detective Grayson's million, gently asked questions. Was he having trouble at work? Did he have any enemies? Were there money troubles? Affairs? Were either of you unfaithful? Hours and hours of questions that I struggled to answer, grief-stricken and stunned, trapped in a tilting unreality. There were these long stretchy moments where I pleaded with the Universe to *just let me wake up.* This had to be a nightmare. Grayson's grim face, the gray walls, the flickering fluorescent lights, all the stuff of horror movies and crime shows. This wasn't my life. It couldn't be. Where was Jack? Why couldn't he make it all go away?

Finally, my mother showed up with our family attorney and they took me home. I remember stumbling into my apartment—*our* apartment, falling into the bed we shared. I could still smell him on the sheets. I remember wailing with grief, facedown in my mattress.

Take this, honey. My mom forced me to sitting, handed me one of her Valium tablets and a glass of water. I didn't even hesitate before drinking it down. After a while, the blissful black curtain of sleep fell.

For a while, I know Detective Grayson suspected me. After all, I would inherit everything—the life insurance payout, the business, all our assets—when Jack died. But I think at some point he realized that for me it was all ash without my husband. Then he became my ally. *If you remember anything, no matter how small, call me.*

The case, it bothered him. Always. Still. Stranger crime is an anomaly. A beating death of a jogger—it grabbed headlines. The city parks are Manhattan's backyard; people wanted answers and so did he. Jack was a big, strong guy, fast and streetsmart. He'd traveled the world as a photojournalist, dived the Great Barrier Reef to find great whites, trekked the Inca Trail, embedded with soldiers in Afghanistan, attempted to summit Everest. It never, ever felt right that he'd die, a random victim, during his morning run. He had a phone and five dollars on him. A year later, his case is still unsolved.

"But maybe Dr. Nash is wrong?" suggests Layla. "Maybe it means something."

Now it's my turn to go silent.

"Let's do it tonight," Layla continues. "Work out, eat, talk it all through. In the meantime, call Dr. Nash and Detective Grayson."

Layla, queen of plans, of to-do lists, of "pro" and "con" columns, of ideas to turn wrong things right. She corrals chaos into order, and heaven help the person who tries to stop her.

"Okay." I release a breath I didn't realize I was holding. "That's a plan."

I flash on that moment at the bar, that man, again. Who was he? Someone real? Someone I know?

"You're okay, right?" asks Layla. "You're like—*solid*?"

"Yeah," I lie (again). "I'm okay."

Detective Grayson agrees to meet me in Washington Square Park for lunch. So around noon I head out. The coolish autumn morning has burned off into a balmy afternoon as I grab a cab to avoid even worrying about the hooded man.

The normalcy of the morning—emails and the ringing phone, conversations about understandable things like contracts and wire transfers—has washed over the chaos of yesterday and last night, my dreams where they belong, the grainy, disjointed images faded into the forgotten fog of sleep. I don't have the urge to look over my shoulder every moment as I make my way under the triumphal Washington Square Arch and into the park. My chest loosens and breath comes easier. Grief and trauma, I remind myself, are not linear experiences. There are good days and bad ones, hard dips into despair, moments of light and hope. My new mantra: I'm okay. I'm okay.

Grayson sits on a shady bench near a hot dog vendor, by the old men playing chess. He already has a foot-long drowning in relish, onions, mustard, ketchup and who knows what else. It seems to defy gravity as he lifts it to his mouth. A can of Pepsi sits unapologetically beside him. No one else I know would even dream of drinking a soda, in public no less. It's one of the things I like about him, his eating habits. It reminds me of Jack. Jack and I would be walking home from a client dinner that had consisted of tiny salads and ahi poke with some slim, fit photographer who turned in early so he could make a 6:00 a.m. yoga class, and Jack would make us stop at Two Guys Pizza, where he'd scarf down two slices.

God, when did people stop eating? he'd complain.

I grab a similarly gooey dog, and take my place beside Grayson. He grunts a greeting, his mouth full. He's sporting his usual just-rolled-out-of-bed look, dark hair a mop, shadow of stubble. He's wearing a suit but it needs a trip to the dry cleaners, his tie loose, a shirt that has seen better days. Still, there's something virile about him, maybe it's the shoulder holster visible when he raises his arm, the detective's shield clipped to his belt.

The leaves above us are bold in orange, red, gold, but they've started to fall, turn brown. I dread the approaching winter, the holidays where I imagine I'll drift between Layla's place and my mother's, a ghost—people giving me tragic looks and whispering sympathetically behind my back.

Jack and I used to have our whole ritual. We'd put the tree up by ourselves the weekend after Thanksgiving, have a big party for all our friends. On Christmas Eve, we'd go to my mother's house, where she would show off whatever new man she was dating, drink too much, then try to pick a fight with me—honestly because I think it's the only way she knows how to connect. We'd spend Christmas Day at our place with Jack's mother, Sarah. We'd plan the meal for months, then hang around in our pajamas all day—cooking, watching movies, playing Scrabble. It was my favorite day of the year.

Last year, just months after losing him, I couldn't even get out of bed. The holidays passed in a grief-stricken blur with the phone ringing and ringing. Layla, Mac, my mother coming by to try to coax me out of bed.

It was Mac who finally got me up, convinced me to come to join them for Christmas dinner. "We're your family," he said, pulling open the blinds. "You belong with us. I know it hurts but there's no way out of this but through. Show the kids that you're not going to let this crush you. Show them that they're not going to lose you, too."

Guilt. It works every time. He offered his hand, which I took and let him pull me from bed and push me toward the bathroom. As I ran the shower, I heard him call Layla, his voice heavy with relief. "I got our girl. She's coming."

It seems like yesterday and a hundred years ago.

"Funny you called," says Grayson now. He's prone to manspreading so I leave a lot of space between us.

"Oh?" I take a big messy bite of the hot dog, and try not to spill anything on my shirt. Yellow mustard and white silk are not friends. Actually, white silk is no one's friend. Wearing it is like a dare to the universe: go ahead, bring it on—coffee, ketchup, ink—I can take you.

"I've got something maybe." He does this thing, a kind of bobblehead nod. "Maybe. Might be nothing."

There's a file under his Pepsi can.

"They brought some punk in this weekend for armed robbery," he says when I stay silent. I wait while he devours that dog in three big bites. It's impressive. He wipes his mouth with gusto, maybe building suspense.

"Perp was caught in the act, more or less. A couple of uniforms brought him down as he exited the bodega in the East Village. I think he got like two hundred bucks if that. Anyway, he tells the arresting officers that he knows something about a murder in Riverside Park last year, so they call me in."

My whole body goes stiff; my appetite withers. Putting the hot dog in its paper tub beside me, I try not to think about that dark day, not let the barrage of images come sweeping in. But it's a flood, the uniformed officers in my lobby, the cold marble as I sank to the floor, the gray interrogation room. Weird details like a ringing phone that no one picked up, the scent of burned popcorn somewhere in the station.

"I'm sorry," he says. He rubs at the stubble on his jaw. "I knew this was going to be hard."

He's watching me with a kind of curious squint. It's warm, but it's knowing. Dark brown eyes, soft at the edges, heavily lashed like a girl's. He's taking it all in, filing it away—the moments, the details, the gestures, things said and unsaid. There's something sad in that gaze, and something steely. I wonder if I could get it. If I had a camera in my hand, could I capture everything his eyes say. Sometimes there's not enough light; sometimes there's too much. Some people you just can't get. They won't let you.

"I'm okay," I lie (again). It's the easiest lie to tell because it's the one people want to hear the most. That you can take care of yourself, that they don't have to worry. Because in a very real sense, they *can't* help. Most of the time, we're on our own.

He tosses the tub, the napkins, into the nearby trash can and lifts the file. It looks small in his thick hands. He picks at the edge with his thumbnail, opens it.

"Anyway, this mope says he knows a guy who claims to be a killer for hire. For a thousand bucks, he'll kill anyone with his bare hands."

The words sound so odd, so ridiculous. I nearly laugh, like people laugh at funerals, the tension too much.

"My guy, the armed robber, let's call him Johnny for the sake of clarity, was on a bit of a bender, so his memory—it's cloudy. *Johnny* says he met this killer for hire at a bar, and the guy got to bragging. I brought a healthy skepticism to the situation, naturally. But I gotta admit some of the details fit. Like, he knew Jack only had five bucks on him, that the assailant smashed Jack's phone to a pulp. Little things that weren't out there in the news."

"So," I say, feeling shaky and strange. Those few bites of hot dog are not agreeing with me. "You got a name? He's in the system? Saw if the DNA matched?"

Detective Grayson shakes his head, leans forward.

"No name. Johnny didn't know the guy's name, street-smart enough not to ask. But he gave the sketch artist a description. It matches accounts of a man witnesses saw fleeing the park the morning Jack was killed."

I appreciate how he often uses Jack's name, doesn't call him "your husband" or "the victim." I feel like he knew Jack, that they might have been friends. The detective is exactly the kind of guy that Jack liked—smart, no bullshit, down-to-earth.

Grayson hands me the file and I open it. The black-and-white pencil drawing stares back at me, full of menace. Head shaved, wide deep-set eyes, thick nose, heavy brow. There's something about it, something my brain reaches for, but then it slips away. It's like when I try to force myself to remember those missing days. There's *truly nothing* there, just a painful, sucking dark.

"Anything?"

I shake my head. "Nothing. I don't know him."

"Johnny says he was a big guy, maybe 6 feet, well over 200 pounds. Ripped, thick neck, big hands."

There's that familiar tightness in my chest, that feeling that my airways have shrunk when I think about him out there. I imagine Jack lying on the path. I see wet leaves and blood, the curl of his hand on the pavement. *I'm sorry. I should have been with you.*

"He'd have to be big, right?" My voice catches. "To overpower Jack."

Detective Grayson puts a hand on my forearm, easy, stabilizing.

"It's something," he says softly. "The first something in a while."

"A killer for hire." The words don't feel right in my mouth. "A thousand dollars. To kill someone."

"The random mugging," he says. "It never sat right."

"But who would *hire* someone to kill Jack?"

He takes a swig of his Pepsi. "You tell me."

"No one," I say. It sticks in my throat and I cough a little. "Everyone loved Jack."

Grayson pulls himself out of his constant slouch, twists a little like he's trying to work out a kink. I notice he's saved a bit of his hot dog bun, has it clutched in his hand. He tosses it, and a kit of pigeons clamor, their pink-green-gray feathers glinting in the sun.

"I'm going to go over all my files again tonight," he says. "See if this new information sheds light on anything old. We'll find this guy. And when we do, maybe he can answer that question."

We'll find this guy. "*How* are you going to find him?"

"I went to the place where Johnny says they met," says Grayson. "They've got the sketch up behind the bar. Patrol in that area is on the lookout."

It seems impossible that you could find someone that way, just hoping they come back to a place they've been. And anyway, there's that part of me that thinks: What does it matter if we catch him? Jack is not coming back. Not even if the guy, whoever he is, gets caught and goes to the electric chair. What does it fix? Nothing changes.

I imagine a trial that drags on, a conviction, or not. Years and years of appeals, tied up in more rage, misery, grief. Jack wouldn't like it. *Let it go*, he'd surely say. *Everyone dies, somehow, someday. Don't let this eat whatever's left of your life.*

"*You* called *me*, though," says Grayson. He takes the file that sits open in my lap and closes it, tucks it under his leg. I'm glad that face is gone. "So...what's up?"

I almost tell him about my dream, the one in the nightclub, that maybe—maybe—could be a memory. It's why I called him, because of Layla's suggestion that it might be a memory. But he's so pragmatic and the images seem so strange and nonsensical now, especially in light of what he's told me. And I don't want to recount the part where I kiss some strange man. Even in a dream, it's shameful, sordid, isn't it? There's shame, too, about those missing days. I imagined myself stronger than that, not the person who shatters in the face of tragedy.

But I am that person; I did shatter.

Instead, I just tell him about the hooded man, how I think I'm being followed.

He digs his hands into the pockets of his pants, listens as I tell him about the encounter on the train.

"Big guy?" he says, looking down to open the file again. "Six feet, heavy?"

"I think so." Bigger than Grayson, taller, broader.

"You're sure?" He pauses and looks up at the sky, which is a bright blue through the red, gold, orange, of the leaves above, the gray of the buildings. "Of what you saw."

He knows my history.

"Not completely," I admit. "No."

"You couldn't see his face?"

"The hood."

"Yeah," he says, drawing out the word. He dips his head from side to side, runs a hand through his hair, considering. "But his face was *completely* obscured by the hood? That doesn't seem right. You can usually see *something*."

I shake my head, pushing into my memory. "No."

Then I remember the pictures on my phone, scroll through the shots and show him the clearest one, which isn't clear at all. He takes the device and squints at it.

"Hard to see his face, you're right. Email it to me," he says. "I'll have our guys work their magic. Maybe we'll get something."

He hands the phone back to me. I quickly forward the image to his email address. We sit a moment, both of us lost in thought.

"So, look," he says, dropping a hand on my arm. "The next time you see him, call me right away. Linger if you can safely. I'll get there fast or send someone."

"Okay," I agree.

We talk awhile longer. He promises that he's following up this lead with everything he has. He must have other cases, other priorities, but when I'm with him he always makes me feel like Jack is the most important thing on his mind. He's convinced his superiors not to close the case, won't turn it over to cold cases, even though he's hinted that there's pressure on him to do that. It's been nearly a year.

"This new information," he says. "I have a feeling about it."

I do, too. Why does that make me feel worse instead of better?

"I'm not letting this go," he says. "I promise you that."

Though I'm not really dressed for it in heels and a pencil skirt, I walk up Fifth Avenue. My head is vibrating, thoughts spinning—Detective Grayson, and killers for hire, how maybe for a thousand dollars someone ended my husband's life. A thousand dollars. And if that's true, is the man who killed Jack the same hooded man following me? I swallow hard, there's a bulb of fear and anger stuck in my throat.

I let the current of the city take me. Its energy pumps and

moves; it doesn't stop for any reason, ever, not even the death of the most important person in your life. It just keeps pulsing, pushing, a flow that you have no choice but to follow.

At the light, I dig into my bag and find that amber vial Layla gave me—not the sleeping pills, but the pills she said were for nerves. I dry swallow a white one. No idea what it is. I really don't care as long as it quiets the siren of anxiety in my head.

Then I put my headphones in, and listen to my go-to, a David Bowie playlist. I keep walking, heading toward the office. I'm just getting into it, feeling lighter, less mired down, when the music stops and the phone starts ringing. Dr. Nash returning my call.

"Poppy?" she says when I answer. "Everything okay?"

Still marching up the street, I tell her everything—the dreams, Layla's ideas, Detective Grayson's revelations. I always think it looks crazy, when someone has her headphones in, gesticulating, walking, talking to someone whom no one else can hear. The modern age has turned us all into ranting schizophrenics.

"That's a lot," Dr. Nash says when I'm done. "Why don't you come in on Thursday? We can talk it through."

I almost tell her. That I've been mucking with my dosage, taking mystery pills, drinking, that last night I took Layla's stronger sleeping meds, two of them. That I just took something else without even knowing what it is. But what does that make me? I stay quiet.

"Okay," I agree. "Why am I dreaming more?"

It feels disingenuous to ask this question when I know she only has part of the information she needs to answer it. Still I'm hoping for an answer that makes me feel better.

"You're probably not dreaming *more*?" It sounds like a question. "Perhaps you're just *remembering* more, which—could be a good thing."

How? I wonder. How can it be a good thing to lose Jack again night after night? I know her answer about dreams being the gateway to our subconscious, how it's a place where we work out the things our conscious mind presses away. That pain is a doorway we must pass through to get to the other side of grief and loss. She's saying something to that effect as I flash on the filthy bathroom floor, the heat of that stranger's kiss.

"I'd like you to stay on this lower dosage," she says.

Here again I almost spill it, then don't. I silently vow to give Layla back her pills, stay on the dosage Dr. Nash prescribed. I'll tough out any hard nights ahead. Because I want to get off the pills, too. I don't want her to know how badly I need them, how painful is the night. Daytime is easy; I can busy-addict myself into constant motion. It's when dusk falls, and energy lags, that the demons start whispering in my ears. When the sun goes down, darkness creeps in, coloring my world gray.

"If you dream vividly again, don't forget that journal," Dr. Nash is saying. "Write everything down for our session. Poppy, I really *do* want us to think of this as good news."

"Good news," I repeat, not feeling it.

"If your memories of that lost time are coming back, it means that you're stronger. And if Detective Grayson has a lead, you may be closer to closure on what happened to Jack. I know you don't think it matters, but it could be *so healing* to finally understand."

That sketched face swims before me, just a drawing of someone who may or may not be real. Was that the last face Jack saw? The thought gnaws at my stomach, cinches my shoulders tight. *Why wasn't I with him?*

I want to argue with her. How would it be healing to think someone hired a man to kill Jack? Who would do that? Why? A thought, something dark, tugs at me, something from one of my dreams last night. When I chase after it, it disappears.

"Maybe," I say instead.

"I'll see you Thursday," she says. "But call me if you need me. Day or night. You know that."

Then, just as I end the call and stop to put my phone in my bag—there he is, following a half a block behind me. A hulking man in a black hoodie, head bent. He stops suddenly when I turn to him, disappears into a doorway.

I quickly dial Detective Grayson, but he doesn't pick up. Most people would be running away. But instead, I start moving back downtown in his direction.

"He's here," I tell Grayson's voice mail. "Following me up Fifth Avenue. I'm at Fifth and Eighteenth, moving south, back downtown. He ducked into a doorway and I'm following."

Which is *crazy*. Maybe even—dare I say it—suicidal. But I keep walking, hugging closer to the buildings, waiting for him to pop back out of the shadows. It's broad daylight, the avenue as ever a rush of professionals, artists, students, tourists, shoppers flitting between Sephora and Armani Exchange, H&M, Victoria's Secret; traffic a stuttering wave of sound and motion. But it's all distant white noise as I move toward where I'm *sure* I saw him disappear. I press myself against the building and then spring into the doorway that's set back from the building wall.

There's no one there. How can that be?

I reach and pull on the handle of the large black metal double door between Aldo and Zara. But it's locked tight. Suddenly seized by anger, I find myself pounding on it.

"I saw you," I yell. "I know you're *following* me."

The door stays locked, and no one comes. I get a few sideways glances, but what's one more shouting crazy person on a city street?

I pound on the door again, the metal cool, the sound reverberating.

What is it? A delivery entrance? I stand back to look at it; it's the armored entry to a keep, a demon hiding inside. Pure rage rises, a tidal wave. I don't even try to hold it back, let it wash over me, take me away. I get to pounding again. Not just knocking, but channeling all my anger, all my frustration into that metal, barely even noticing that I'm hurting myself, that the door doesn't budge, that no one comes.

And that's how Detective Grayson finds me, violently banging on the door, yelling.

"Hey, hey," he says, coming up from behind. I feel his hands on my shoulders, turn and shake him off hard. He steps back, hands up.

"Take it easy, Poppy."

He's illegally parked his unmarked Dodge Charger right beside us, traffic flowing around it, honking and annoyed at yet one more pointless obstacle to traffic flow.

"He disappeared through here," I tell him. I'm breathless, sweating from the heat, the effort, the fear. I don't like the way he's looking at me, brow creased with concern.

"Okay," he says putting strong hands on my shoulders. "Take a breath."

I do that, feel some calm returning now that he's here.

The door swings open then, and an impossibly young, svelte woman in a black shift dress and thigh-high boots stands before us. She looks back and forth between us, blankly annoyed.

Grayson flashes his shield.

"We're pursuing a suspect," he says. His tone is comfortingly official, validating. There *was* someone there. There *was*. "Did someone come in through this entrance in the last ten minutes?"

She shakes her head and her long black hair shimmers.

"No," she says. "I'm the manager here and this is the service entrance. There's a *bell*?" She points to it meaningfully. "You ring and someone comes to open it. But there haven't been any deliveries this afternoon."

"I saw someone come in here," I say, more sharply than I mean to. She blinks glittery eyelids to express her displeasure. Her eyebrows are shaped into high arches; a hoop sparkles in her nose.

"No," she says as though she's never been more certain of anything in her life. "Not this door."

"Mind if we have a look around?" asks Grayson easily. She regards him uncertainly, then steps aside. We both walk into the storage area—boxes, racks crushed with clothes, standing steam irons, gift-wrapping station, no menacing strange men in hoods. Adrenaline, the power of rage, abandons me, leaving me feeling foolish, hot with shame, shaky now. Did I really see him come in here?

Grayson's standing by the door. "Where does this go?"

"Back to the shop," she says. "There's a fire exit through the break room on the other side of the store, but an alarm sounds if you push through it."

"There's no other exit from this storeroom?"

"Well, just out back, to the alley behind the buildings, where we dump the trash."

Grayson follows her and I trail behind. The dim alley reeks of rotting garbage; fire escapes track up the surrounding buildings giving way to a stingy square of sky up above.

"The street gate is locked," she says. "Only the super has the key. Want me to get him?"

Detective Grayson looks at me and I shake my head.

"I'm sorry." My voice is a rasp. "I was sure I saw him come in here."

There's that look again from the detective. I know it well—worried confusion. *What's wrong with Poppy?*

On the street: "Are you okay?" He rests a steadying hand again on my shoulder. "You seem—"

"What?" I ask. "Crazy, unstable, a wreck?"

"Let's go with—unsettled."

His comforting grin settles me a bit. For a second, I flash on my father, how good he was at talking me through spirals of emotion, bouts of worry. *Oh, you're too sensitive,* my mother would sniff. *You better get a thicker skin.* But not my dad; he always knew what to say. *Okay, just breathe. Let's break this down. What's really going on?*

"Let me give you a lift home," says Detective Grayson when I don't say anything else. I can't prove what I saw, so there's no point in trying.

We climb into the Charger, plain and white on the outside but high-tech within, a buzzing radio, mounted laptop, all manner of blinking lights on panels. The button for the siren is a tantalizing shiny red, and I fight the urge to press it.

"Maybe he ducked into a different doorway," he offers as we snake up Fifth.

"Maybe."

I'd have sworn it was *that* doorway. But obviously not, and that's the hard part. Because what we see, what we think we see, what we remember, isn't always reliable. In fact, it rarely is. Like for months after Jack died, he was everywhere. I'd see a tall man with a lion's mane of hair and my heart would lurch with joy and hope, crashing into despair milliseconds later. Or I'd imagine him so vividly walking into the room that I almost saw him. Or like those lost days of my "break." I lived those days, went places, saw people, did things, but the more I press in, trying to remember, the deeper and darker that space becomes.

The eye, the memory—they're the trickiest liars. Only the camera lens captures the truth, and just for a moment. Because that's what the truth is: a ghost. Here and gone. As Grayson drives, I scroll through the pictures on my phone again and find that grainy image of my shadow stalker.

Who are you?

Who was I during those lost days?

Layla spent two days looking for me, visiting all the places we frequented together with a picture of me until finally I came stumbling into her lobby, apparently wearing the red dress from my dream. Did I know that detail? Had she told me at one point what I was wearing, what I looked like, and I just filed it away? Or was my dream, as she suggested, an actual memory?

"I'm going to hang around awhile," Detective Grayson says

as he pulls in front of my building. "Out here, in my car. I have some calls to make, emails to answer. I can do it here for a while, just, you know—in case. Why don't you get some rest?"

Part of me wants to tell him that I'm grateful. Thankful that he hasn't given up, doesn't urge me to let it go and move on, that he still cares about what happened to Jack, what happens to me. But a bigger part of me is not grateful. How urgently I wish we'd never met, that I had no reason to know Detective Grayson. I leave the car without a word.

I tap over the limestone floors of my lobby, breezing past the day doorman, who is on the phone but offers a friendly wave. In the elevator I text Ben and tell him to cancel my appointments and calls for the afternoon, that I've come down with a stomach thing. It's not ideal, but I'm addled and shaky, in no condition to talk to clients or anyone else. Inside the apartment, I close and lock the door.

Leaning against it, I slide down and sit on the floor, the long hallway that leads to the rest of the apartment dark, lined with photographs—his, mine, us together. The only thing I've managed to do since moving here is hang those photographs. Sitting on the hardwood, I think tears will come, but they don't.

Instead I notice that one of the photographs lies on the floor, surrounded by broken glass.

I haul myself up and walk over to it, the apartment unnaturally quiet. The thick-paned windows on the twentieth floor keep most city noise at bay. The glass crackles beneath my feet as I retrieve the picture. Me and Jack, on our honeymoon in Paris. *What a cliché!* he'd complained. He'd wanted to go Thailand, lie around on some isolated beach, sleep in a thatch hut. But a Paris honeymoon was my only girlhood fantasy and he complied, because he always did. He always wanted me to have the things that I wanted. I can't even tell where we were, a selfie so close that everything behind disappeared, our faces so goofy with love that it's almost embarrassing to see.

I hold the shattered frame. The picture hanger is still on the wall. And the photo seems too far from its original space to just have fallen somehow.

My breath comes heavy. I should move back slowly toward the door and run downstairs to Detective Grayson. Instead, I turn and walk toward the living room.

It takes me a moment to notice it, but when I do my stomach bottoms out. Sitting on the low coffee table between the couches is an orchid in a pot. A fat, snow-white bloom drips heavily from a bowed stalk. There's a single white card tucked into the thick green leaves at its base, a note in black scrawl.

I remember you.

Don't you remember me?

7

"Let's go over this again," says Grayson.

He sits on the couch across from me, leaning forward, his dark gaze pinning me to my seat. I know that look; he's been watching me like that for a year. As though he might still suspect something dark just beneath the surface of what he sees.

Layla's already here, ministering. She's gotten me a blanket, which I'm not using, brewed coffee that I'm not drinking. Now she's hovering, sitting on the couch beside me, leaning in so close that her thigh is fused with mine. Her foot is tapping in that way it does when she's nervous or annoyed. She's staring at that white blossom as it quivers in front of us, at Grayson, around the apartment, with a kind of narrow-eyed suspicion.

"You entered your apartment—" he leads.

This is another thing he does, asks me to repeat what I told him, once, twice, three times. Looking for the inconsistencies of lies, I suppose.

"And I saw the picture fallen on the floor at the end of the hallway."

"Why didn't you leave the apartment right away?"

"I didn't think," I say. "I walked down the hallway and picked it up. Then I saw the orchid and called you."

"Weren't you afraid that there might have been someone in your place?"

"No," I say. "I mean—it didn't occur."

He's frowning at me, like this doesn't make sense. "But you suspect someone's following you."

"That's right," I say, feeling foolish. "I don't know. I just didn't think there was anyone here."

I'm so tired. Whatever I took on the street, I can feel it warm and tingling in my bloodstream. I wish I hadn't taken it. I want to be more alert for this, more plugged in. But my awareness is swimmy and strange.

"Ms. Van Santen here has a key to the apartment. And there's another key with the building staff. They have permission to enter your apartment to make deliveries."

I nod, a faint ringing in my ears, a wobbly quality to the space around me.

I see Jack walking around the unfurnished space, standing in front of the floor-to-ceiling windows looking out onto the expansive view. It was late afternoon when we first came to see it, the sun low in the sky.

If you like it, I like it.

I want you to like it, too.

He walked over to the open-plan kitchen, touched the marble countertop.

What's not to like?

But?

He stared at the refrigerator, ran a finger down its gleaming metal surface.

It just feels a little—too cool. Like a museum.

We'll make it ours.

I wrapped him up, my arms tight around his waist. He looked down at me with that smile, indulgent and half-amused. At any contact, there was heat. His lips on mine, then his arm around the small of my back.

What do you think? The Realtor had returned, catching us making out like teenagers. *Oh, I'm sorry!*

Jack looked up at her, unflappable. *We'll take it.*

"Poppy." Grayson's voice brings me back. His frown has deepened.

"I'm sorry. What?"

Two uniformed officers dust for prints; they are comically mismatched. He is a towering thick-shouldered black man; she's a petite strawberry blonde, a full head shorter. They move quietly, with purpose, from the doorknob, to the plant, the note, the photograph frame, leaving bursts of black residue behind on the too-white walls. Does that come out? The apartment, which I've just barely settled into, feels tainted.

"So, *anyone* who works in the building has access to your apartment? The doorman, the maintenance staff—" He lets the sentence trail.

The staff, with permission, delivers packages, dry cleaning, laundry directly to the apartment; the cleaning service comes in on Wednesdays. I never thought of it as strangers coming into my apartment, though of course that's precisely what it is. Under Detective Grayson's disapproving frown, it seems like a terrible failure to safeguard myself, the apartment.

"Yes. I guess that's right."

"There's no sign of forced entry at the door. Of course, no chance that anyone comes in through the windows." He walks over to the window—which only opens a sliver to let air in. He pushes back the gauzy drapes and peers out at the view. "So how many people would you say are on staff here?"

I try to picture the various doormen, the cleaning staff, the superintendent, the maintenance guys. Had any of them seemed odd, menacing? Had I seen anyone lurking where he didn't belong, feel eyes lingering too long? No.

But the fact is that I'm a specter in my life now—floating, going through the motions, white-knuckling my way through days that seem to have no meaning. There it is. The thing I haven't even said to Dr. Nash—I'm not sure what the point is without Jack. I'm not sure I even want to be here.

"Maybe twenty?" It's just a guess, though. I have no idea how many people work here.

"Does this mean anything to you?" Detective Grayson points at the flower, the note.

Dangling and snow-white, it hangs between us, the heavy blossom bending the stem.

"It reminds me of your favorite flower. The ghost orchid," says Layla.

"But that's not a ghost orchid. It's a phalaenopsis, a moth orchid, found in any corner deli or supermarket. It's as common as a carnation."

"Close enough," says Layla with a shrug. "Whoever left this *knows that* about you."

"Maybe," I say.

The ghost orchid blooms only once a year, between June and August, and is found in the swampy forests of southwestern Florida, Cuba and the Bahamas. Rare and elusive, it perches on scarious bracts, appearing to float in midair, hence its name. It can only be pollinated by the giant sphinx moth, the single insect with a long enough proboscis to access the flower's extremely long nectar spur. Jack and I spent two months in Florida, wading through the Fakahatchee Strand with a Seminole guide to get pictures for a *Smithsonian Magazine* feature.

We spent our days in waders, sweltering in the thick humidity, savaged by mosquitoes and no-see-ums, on the perpetual lookout for water moccasins and alligators. And then, at the beginning of our final week, we finally found the blossom. It hung in the murky light, roots clinging to the cypress tree, a shimmering apparition, bright white, with delicate, dancing tendrils, curling, disappearing into the shadows all around. The pulsing throb of cicada song, the squawking call of a great blue heron, the rippling of water, the perpetual scent of damp rot that's somehow the cleanest thing you've ever smelled, and among all the wild, this perfect creation of nature. We were hours, taking shots, waiting for changes in light, switching lenses, filters. It passed in a heartbeat and then the light disappeared and we had to leave.

After that, all other flowers wilted in comparison to its delicate, spectral beauty, its rarity. Who knew that? Jack, of course. Layla. Maybe a few of our friends, a client or two. The ghost orchid cannot be had, though. You won't find it at any florist. It's a protected flower. It can only be observed in its natural environment.

"Poppy?"

Layla has her hand on my shoulder, is staring at me, brow wrinkled with worry.

"What?"

"Where did you go?"

To Florida, with Jack, a hundred years ago. I would give anything to go back.

"Sorry." My tone is as flat and numb as I feel. Layla's scowl deepens.

She rises and I catch Grayson staring at her, though he looks away quickly.

Wow, he *is* human. For some reason, I don't think of him as a person, exactly. He's a reaction formation, someone who appeared in my life on the very worst day. If Jack hadn't died, he wouldn't even exist. Observing him watch Layla elevates him somehow. He's a man, probably younger than he looks. That gray in his dark hair premature, I think. Beneath the rumples of his ill-fitting blue suit, there's a man with a life. Divorced. He may have mentioned a son, a teenager.

"You're not staying here," Layla announces. She casts a quick dismissive look at Grayson. "Pack a bag."

"Poppy," she says when I don't answer. It's precisely the tone she uses when one of the kids isn't moving fast enough for her.

"*Okay*." And I sound a little too much like a sullen teenager.

"I have to agree," Grayson says, watching me again. "You shouldn't stay here until you've had the locks changed. Even then maybe—until we have a handle on what's happening here."

When I still don't move, Layla heads to the bedroom, issuing a sigh. I hear her taking my overnight bag down from the closet, opening drawers. My limbs are filled with sand.

"You're telling me everything, right?" Grayson asks. He sits in the chair across from me and leans forward on his thighs.

"Of course," I snap, annoyed. "I'm being followed. Someone broke into this apartment. My husband is dead. What *more* do you think I have to tell?"

He leans back, lifts his palms in surrender. "I'm on your side, remember."

That orchid dangles between us. "Sorry."

"I get it."

I can't bring myself to look at him again, just stare out the window at the Freedom Tower glinting in the distance, the sun drifting down toward the Henry Hudson. September 11. I thought the world had ended that day. Who could have known that it would begin and end again?

"You just seem *off*," he says, still frowning. "Out of it."

"I haven't been sleeping." And I'm popping pills left and right, Detective. Not even sure what they are, actually. Also, I often take them with alcohol. Do you think that's a problem?

"I'm going to check with the super, see who was on duty today," Grayson says when I don't say anything else. "I strongly suggest that you rescind your permission to let building staff enter this apartment."

"Okay," I concede.

Then he gets up and leaves the room, striding down the hall, door shutting behind him. The uniformed officers are gone, as well. When did they leave? It's just me and Layla.

"When were you going to tell me about all of this?" She stands in the doorway.

"Maybe never," I admit. "I was kind of hoping I was just imagining the whole thing."

"*Hoping* for that?" She cocks her head, squinting at me.

"I don't know." We both wait for me to make any sense at all. "I don't know what's worse."

Layla has my overnight bag over her shoulder, her hand on her hip. The blond highlights in her hair pick up the afternoon light. She's dressed in her workout gear—yoga, kickboxing, Pilates; she's in killer shape. She's shaking her head slightly, her lips just parted. She's considering.

"I don't know, either," she says finally. "Let's go home."

I look around the apartment, most of the life I shared with Jack still in boxes. His clothes, his books, his old yearbooks, his shoes, portfolios of his photographs, our pots and pans, Christmas ornaments, collected items, his black-framed glasses, his wedding ring, which I placed in the box it came in, his lucky sweatshirt, his wallet, the bear he slept with as a baby, a picture album from his childhood. God. It's all still in there, all the little fragments of his life and ours, the items collected so meaningless now that they've gone a year inside a box without seeing the light of day. Layla's right. This place isn't home.

"When it's done, *whatever* this is," Layla says, "I'm going to help you get settled in here. Or wherever you want. Do you want to stay here?"

"Do you want to stay here? Sleep in?" Jack whispers.

"No," I tell him. "I'm coming."

"Sure? You were up a lot, coughing."

"It'll be good for me."

We don't turn on the lights, just feel about for leggings, sweatshirts, socks, beat-up runners that we've left in hopeful piles by the door. If you turn the lights on, the magic of a predawn run leaks away. Once the lights come on, the morning has begun and that secret hour between sleep and the rest of the day is lost.

Richie, our doorman, is sleeping as we slip outside, snoring, head tilted, a paperback spine up in front of him. The morning is perfect. I already feel the fog of my cold lifting, sinuses clearing in the morning air.

We cross at the light and jog onto the path. We don't talk much in the morning; sometimes I even wear headphones. We don't always keep the same pace. Jack's faster in a sprint, but can't match me for distance. We let each other be. He looks back at me, and I wave him on. He moves off into the dark. I know I'll catch him by the underpass. He burns out after a point, slows down. There are lots of people around— joggers, walkers, bikers zipping past. I have never, even for a moment, felt unsafe on the streets of New York City. Of course, it's not safe. But really, what is? Bad things happen everywhere.

I slow, a cough coming up. I walk in a circle until it passes, but I feel light-headed and weak. This cold; it has got its hooks in. Jack loops back for me.

"You okay?"

"Yeah," I say. "I think I'll head back after all. I'm not up for it."

"I'll go with you."

"No," I say, waving him off. "Go ahead."

He needs it. He's like a Labrador; he needs lots of exercise or he gets antsy, has trouble sleeping, is prone to worrying.

But he loops his arm through mine. We go home.

Jack never intersects with the man who killed him. We make breakfast, head into the office together. Our life continues, good days, bad days, fights and lovemaking, successes and failures.

It's a thing I do, run a scenario where he doesn't leave that morning, or where I go with him. Or he turns an ankle and comes back. Or we oversleep. Anything but him getting up, not waking me, and leaving in the dark by himself.

"Well, no matter," Layla says now, tugging me off the couch. "You don't have to decide anything today."

8

Don't you remember me?

The words dig deep into my pill-induced nap in Layla's guest room. Sleep is an abyss, and I swim up through its murky layers, emerging to the caterwauling of Izzy's violin practice down the hall. The clock on the bedside glows, a neon-green accusation. 5:00 p.m. Something has slipped away from me: another day when I could have been closer to that "new normal" Dr. Nash keeps promising. Like a mountain in the distance, it just seems ever farther.

I sit still for a moment, trying to make sense of it—the disjointed images of my dreams last night, this morning, my lunch with Grayson, the hooded man, my pounding on that Fifth Avenue door, the orchid in my apartment, the note, the shattered wedding photo. There's too little difference between the things I've dreamed and what's really happened, waking memory bleeding into dream. How do all the pieces fit together? Or do they? Am I so addled that I'll never be whole again?

My phone lies slim and dark next to the clock. I reach for it, dial Ben.

"Hey." He answers on the first ring. "You okay?"

"Yeah." The word pitches, unconvincing and wobbly.

"Layla told me what happened," he says, his voice lowered.

I really wish she hadn't done that.

"I let the security guys in the building know about it," he goes on when I don't say anything. "So, they're aware. Layla says you're going to hire someone, you know, for protection?"

I don't remember saying that. But it sounds like an idea Layla would have and put into action without consulting me. Her philosophy: if there's a problem, throw money at it. On the off chance that the world doesn't bend to your will, start beating it with your fists. If this is something she's decided is a good idea, she may have already made calls.

"Tell me about the day," I say instead of getting into it.

Contracts signed, assignments late, a payment dispute. I let his words wash over me, offer comments, suggestions. I know what to do. He has questions. I have answers. Work is easy, even the problems and negotiations. At the office, everything makes sense. I guess I can relate to Mac on this point, my workaholic friend. Life, on the other hand, is a messy, unmanageable tangle, the Gordian knot I can't seem to untie without Jack. Ben and I chat for a while. I am grateful that he's there, that he's been there for me this long, ugly year, picking up my considerable slack.

"Why don't you take the rest of the week off?" he suggests. "I can handle things."

"No."

Somehow, planning to not go in to the office is like giving in. The agency has been my lifeline, pulling me out of bed and back into the world. I am the steward now of what Jack and I built together; it means something. "I'll be there tomorrow."

I can hear him clicking on the keyboard, checking the calendar.

"Oh," he says with a click of his tongue. "What about your date on Thursday?"

I'd forgotten all about him—runner Rick, Rick who works in finance, volunteers for Big Brothers. These dates I've been going on, they've been good—easy, no strings so far. Just a little too much to drink, a stumble back to some strange apartment, disappearing into someone else's body, life, bed where I can close my eyes and pretend I'm with Jack. For a few seconds here and there, it even works. Then I leave before the sun comes up.

"Cancel it," I say, even though a part of me doesn't want to, even with everything going on. Or maybe because of it. I have come to look forward to those little escape hatches, where I can slip off my skin as Poppy, the widow, and be someone new, someone not dogged by grief, popping pills to get through the day. I think again about the text I received in the cab yesterday, the warmth I felt, the excitement. I tamp it down hard. Get a grip.

"Okay," Ben says. "Probably a good idea."

"Messages?"

"Alvaro came by your office when he was here to pick up Maura. He wanted to see you. Asked if you'd give him a call when you have a chance."

"Did he say what he wanted?"

"No," said Ben. "He was typically reticent and brooding. What's with that guy, anyway? I always wondered how he and Jack could be friends. They couldn't be more different. He's just so—dark."

"I know what you mean."

The truth is, I actively avoid Alvaro. And since Jack's death, he seems to be avoiding me. People drift apart when someone dies; grief can be a schism, one that keeps widening. When I look at him, I see Jack. It hurts. And maybe we never liked each other much anyway; there wasn't much reason to hold on, Jack the only thing that ever linked us. I wonder what he wants, make a mental note to call him.

Mercifully, Izzy has stopped playing the violin by the time

Ben and I end the call. A pleasant silence has settled, though I
hear the television in the kitchen, Slade's voice intermittently. I
lie a minute absorbing the peace of the room—charcoal, dove
gray and cream, every surface plush. There's an oil painting of
a cherry blossom tree, trunk bent, wind taking the pink petals away. How many nights have I spent here since Jack died?
Too many. I force myself up, the room tilting, my head aching.

Even though my life is built on quicksand and there's a persistent roar in my ear, I manage to help Layla with dinner, proof-
read Izzy's essay and stare confused as Slade tries to explain how
his video game works. The activity of the evening is a river that
carries me away from anything that might be going on in my
head. Layla and I, in a tacit understanding, don't discuss anything
that's happening in front of the kids. That's the beauty and tor-
ture of children; they don't allow you to spend too much time
reflecting on your own inner life. It's all about them.

But once the apartment is quiet again—Izzy chattering on the
phone with her friend, Slade finally settled in with his homework and Layla taking a shower—it all crowds back, questions
churning. Having convinced Layla to let me clean the dinner
dishes, I get to washing, pour all my nervous energy into scrub-
bing and wiping, loading the dishwasher, wiping the countertop until it gleams. Did I really see someone on the street? Who
brought that flower into my apartment? *Was* it meant to evoke
the ghost orchid? Does anyone know me *that* well now that Jack
is gone? I dial Grayson, but he doesn't answer. What did he find
when he talked to the building staff? Why hasn't he called?

I'm just finishing up, deep in thought, when Mac comes in.
He holds two bouquets of tulips—one pink, one white.

"I heard you had a rough day," he says. He hands me the
white bouquet. "For you."

Knowing I was here, he'd never bring flowers for Layla and
not for me. That's Mac.

I take them from him and draw in their scent, instantly cheered. "Thank you. That was sweet."

"You deserve a little sweetness," he says. He looks like he's had a rough day, too, fatigue sitting on his shoulders, around his eyes. They both look so tired.

I find two crystal vases in the cabinet by the range, then clip the bottom of the stems and arrange the white flowers. I leave the pink, knowing he'll want to hand them to Layla.

He shifts off his bespoke suit jacket and sits at the kitchen bar. He fills a room, dominating not with size—he's tall but slim—but with a kind of intense aura. Whatever it is, it doesn't photograph. In images he's slouched usually, towering over Layla, the features of his face disappearing into shadows. He recently shaved his head, tired, Layla said, of trying to pretend he wasn't losing his hair. He's grown a goatee as a kind of hair counterbalance. Tonight, he looks a bit like a washed-out Russian mobster—embattled, his face set in its natural scowl.

"I did have a rough day," I admit. "Are you hungry? Layla left you a plate."

"I ate." He rubs at his eyes. "Thanks."

He looks toward the freezer, then casts a glance back down the hall from which Layla might emerge. He offers me a quick, mischievous lift of his thick eyebrows. I don't need a translator. Layla doesn't like him to drink on the weeknights. But I grab the bottle of Reyka from the freezer, and pour the Icelandic vodka into a lowball over ice. Mac and I are old drinking buddies, tossing them back long after Jack and Layla had begged off. I'm having enough problems without adding hard liquor to the mix. Still, I join him, pouring myself a generous serving. The heat of it, that blessed tingle.

"Okay," he says, taking a swallow. "Tell me everything."

I run it all down for him, starting from my first sighting of the hooded man, through the afternoon, my conversation with Grayson, the break-in, the orchid. He watches me, as if he's taking in the elements of what I'm saying and what he's seeing and entering them into a challenging equation that he's trying to solve. He sits quiet a moment, looks down at his glass. Then:

"Can I see the photo? The one on your phone?"

I pull the phone from my pocket and find the image, hold it out to him. He takes it, puts his glasses back on, uses his thumb and forefinger to enlarge the image.

"There *is* someone there," he says, handing it back. "He does seem—menacing. But it's just a guy in the crowd. You couldn't see his face. How do you know he was following *you*?"

I look at the image again, a pit forming in my stomach.

I'm not crazy. I may have lost it after Jack died, but I *do* have at least a tenuous grip on reality. There *was* someone on that train. He *was* staring at me. There was a man on the street today, a stranger in my apartment. Who is it? What does he want? But I stay quiet. The more you must assert your own reality to people, the crazier you seem.

"So what about Grayson's lead? A killer for hire?" He inflects the last sentence with disbelief.

"That's what he said."

"That just sounds crazy to me." He pours himself another finger of vodka, his glass quickly drained. "There was no one better. No one more upright and good. Who would want to hurt Jack?"

"That's what Grayson asked me," I say. "I don't have an answer. No one. Everyone loved him."

Another pour, both our glasses this time. We both sit with our thoughts.

"Sometimes—often," he starts, then stops.

"What?"

"Occam's razor, you know it? A theory in problem-solving which states that the simplest explanation is the best explanation."

"Meaning?"

He takes a sip and rubs at his temple. When he looks at me again, his eyes are so sad.

"The thing none of us wants to accept, that Jack was in the wrong place at the wrong time, the victim of a random street crime. One that might go unsolved."

It is hard to accept, the randomness of that, the pointlessness. I find myself shaking my head. It doesn't feel right. It might be the simplest explanation but it never seemed like the right one, not even to Grayson.

Mac drops a hand on mine. Our eyes meet and he offers that smile, kind, bolstering.

"But listen, there's a company we use at our firm, a private security group," he says. "I gave them a call today."

I blow out a breath. This has Layla written all over it.

"You shouldn't have done that." There's a thrum of anxiety in the back of my brain.

He lifts his palms in supplication. "Hear me out. It's been nearly a year. The police don't have anything solid, and now maybe there's someone following you, this odd lead. On the off chance that it wasn't random, maybe, I've just been thinking—"

"Thinking—"

"You hear about it you know, a person appears to be one thing, then you start digging through the layers, into the past, and he's someone else completely. I mean, maybe there was something going on with Jack—something we didn't know about. Something even *you* didn't know about."

The words hang between us. He reaches over and touches one of the pink tulip petals.

"We think we know each other, right?" Something dark crosses his face; it passes like cloud, dissipates quickly. "But do we really? Do we ever really know what goes on deep inside?"

The words slice, a razor blade to my tissue-thin psyche. What is he saying?

"I knew my husband, Mac." My voice shakes a little. "So did you."

He looks down into his glass, nearly empty again.

"What—you think we're going to find out there was another family? Or he was into something illegal?" I say with a laugh. "No."

He shrugs. "Maybe we only knew a piece of him. Maybe that's all we ever know of each other."

Layla sweeps in as I'm about to protest, a vision in dusk-gray silk pajamas edged with lace. She moves in next to Mac, kisses him on the cheek, casting a meaningful glance down at his glass. He stands and wraps her up, kisses her. I look away, busy myself with filling the second vase with water. He hands her the flowers and she peers at them lovingly.

"What a lovely husband," she says. "Thank you, darling."

Is there something stiff about it? She notices me watching them, shakes her head slightly and moves away from him. What's going on with them? Something. But maybe it's just me.

"Mac and I have been talking. We think you should hire someone." Layla pulls up the chair beside her husband. She hands me the flowers and I put them in the vase. "Someone to watch out for you. Someone to figure out who's doing this. Someone to deepen the investigation into Jack's murder."

Mac offers his glass to Layla, who after a stern look takes the last swallow. It's a beautiful vodka, glacier cold and slick in the throat.

"Poppy and I were just talking about it," he says. The dark tone of our conversation is gone; he's all business now. I let it go, eager to move on from whatever it was Mac was suggesting. "Our clients often need a security team when they travel overseas. They have a division of private investigators, as well. Very effective."

I imagine myself being flanked by a couple of beefy men in

black as I walk up the street. Some gumshoe in a wrinkled rain-coat investigating my "case."

"That might be overkill."

"How is it overkill, Poppy? Someone's *stalking* you. Whoever it is *broke* into your apartment," says Layla. "Jack was murdered, his case still unsolved. Now this new suspect? A killer for hire?"

I start to offer some further protest.

"Poppy," she says. "You're not safe. I mean, you can see that, right?"

"It's done," says Mac. "Look, if there's one thing I know, Jack would want us to take care of you, keep you safe. Tom Jager from Black Dog Security and Crisis Management will contact you tomorrow. You'll like him—he's the kind of guy who just gets things done. The two of you will come up with a plan together, and this will get handled."

Honestly, it's like standing in front of a freight train. Layla's always been so sure of herself. And since she and Mac got crazy rich, there's no stopping them. They'll help you whether you want it or not. It's annoying but kind of sweet, too. How can you be mad at people who want so badly to protect you, even as they're trampling your boundaries?

"At least they can keep you safe until we know for sure what's going on," says Mac.

Layla seems satisfied. "And you'll stay here until it is."

Checked off, managed, sorted.

She's as bossy as your mother, Jack always used to say. *Kinder, more well-intentioned, but still domineering as hell.*

It used to bother me that Jack never quite got Layla—and that she never quite got him. She grew up in chaos with a vio-lent, alcoholic father, a mother who couldn't stand up to him until the day he died, a brother who is currently in prison. She seeks control now over the lives of people she loves. It's text-book: the adult child of an alcoholic. Jack on the other hand couldn't stand to be controlled, railed against authority of any kind. He was a wanderer, a nomad with a camera in his hand. Free range. There was never the same ease between them that there is with Mac and me.

"Okay." I don't remember being such a wuss. I'm just so damn tired.

Layla comes over to my side of the counter and rewashes a pot I'd put on a dishcloth to dry. She dries it vigorously and puts it away, folds the towel into a perfect triangle that she tucks next to the faucet. She also whisks away the vodka bottle. Mac and I share an indulgent eye roll before he disappears down the long hall to their master suite.

"Black Dog?" She's still talking about the security firm. "They've solved a lot of problems for people we know," she says when he's gone.

"What kind of problems?"

Though she's cut Mac off, she pours herself another glass of wine. I've noticed that she starts at five and drinks continuously all evening, cutting the wine with splashes of club soda as it gets later. How much is she really drinking? It's hard to say. Not that I'm in any position to judge.

"You know," she says, with a kind of resigned sigh. "The kind of problems Mac's clients have. Do you remember the Kings? Their young son was kidnapped during a vacation in Mexico. A nightmare, but Tom's firm negotiated his safe release. Thank God."

I'd heard about that kind of thing before, of course. The industry of kidnapping and ransom. But Jack—he'd tromped all over the world, trekking through Rwanda's Bwindi Impenetrable Forest looking for mountain gorillas, partying in Rio, hurtling down the slim North Yungus Road, a fifteen-thousand-foot-high single lane in Bolivia, in a rickety pickup driven by a man Jack couldn't understand. He laughed when he recalled that white-knuckled trip between La Paz and Coroico.

The world is safe mostly, he always said. *Safer than you think if you keep a low profile.*

But he was so wrong. It was arrogance to think that the world was safe.

Still, though I haven't said as much, I have no intention of hiring that security firm. I'm also not sure I want to stay here for the rest of the week, hiding out in Layla's world. The truth is, I was starting to get my feet under me again somewhat before this happened. I want that feeling back.

And now Mac's questions are ringing in my ears. *Were* there things about Jack that I didn't know? Another side of him? I think of that wall of sealed boxes in my apartment, all the parts of Jack collected there, sitting fallow for a year. Meanwhile, there are slices of me missing, too. Days just blank; memories I've lost and haven't, if I'm honest, tried that hard to recover. What have I been afraid I'll find?

Layla dangles a set of keys from her finger, breaking me from my thoughts. Her gigantic diamond—the cost of which could feed the average family for a year—glints in the LED lighting. "I had your locks changed. And I did not leave a set with the doormen."

I take the keys from her. They're cold and sharp in my hand. Strange keys to a place that is not home.

"Tell me," I say. "About the day you found me."

She sits in the chair at the bar, leans onto the counter. She holds me in her gaze, assessing. "Are you sure?"

She'd tried to talk to me about it before, but I'd always shut her down. Once I accepted Dr. Nash's theory that the time wasn't coming back, or that it probably wouldn't, I decided to put those days behind me. It was part of my whole program of accepting unacceptable things. Or maybe I've just been running away, afraid of the truth.

"What happened—exactly?"

"Well," she says, releasing a breath that seems to deflate her.

It's a tone I've heard her take with Izzy and Slade when answering the difficult questions. *Why was Daddy sucking on your face last night? If Grandma is looking down on me from heaven, can she see when I'm using the bathroom? Why is that man sleeping in a cardboard box?*

I'm surprised to see her eyes well up; she wipes at them quickly. I reach for her but she waves me away. "I'm sorry," she says. "This is about you, not me."

"It's about *us*, okay? We both went through something."

She takes another sip of wine.

"You called me late," she says. "You didn't sound like yourself. There was something so bright, so gleeful about your tone. It was weird."

"What did I say?" How odd to have to ask that.

"You said that you had answers," she says. "That you knew what happened to Jack. That it was the end of everything."

"The end of everything?"

She takes a sip from her glass. "That's how I felt, too, when I thought I'd lost you."

After the funeral, that was the darkest moment. I remember that. That's when it was finally real. The terrible shock had been absorbed, leaving me rattled and wobbly. The funeral, the gathering, the slew of flowers, cards, the phone ringing and ringing, a hundred emails from friends, acquaintances, strangers. A million arrangements to be made, the police and all their questions, my mother sleeping on my couch, her lawyer escorting me to the police station. And then it all went silent. Jack was gone, all leads went cold, everyone else went back to the day-to-day of their lives. Even I intended to go back to work, thinking—what else? What else would I do? *Could* I do?

"It was late when you called, so I went right over, leaving Mac with the kids. But when I got there, you were gone. I tried your phone but it was dead, or off, went straight to voice mail. That was the worst moment, knowing your phone was dead, that my lifeline to you had been cut."

Layla puts her head in her hand, and I slide into the seat beside her, dropping an arm around her.

"I spent the next two days racing around the city—hitting the places I thought you might go. Just blindly. The park, the gym, restaurants you and Jack frequented, bars. Mac took time off work, we took turns looking or staying with the kids. I showed your photo around. Grayson did the same. I thought we'd *lost* you. There were no credit card charges, no way to track you."

She pours herself another glass of wine, and one for me, too. I don't even put up a fight. I take a deep swallow from the glittering glass, welcome the cool of it, the warmth that comes to my cheeks as more alcohol hits my bloodstream.

"Then when we were about to hire someone—Tom, in fact— you came walking into the lobby. I ran down to get you, but I barely recognized you. Poppy, in that dress, your makeup. You were someone else. When you saw me, you just passed out, collapsed right there in the foyer. Then for the next few days, you were just—out of it."

"Unconscious?" I remember nothing of those days in the hospital, either.

"No," she said. "Just rambling, wild-eyed, glazed. It was— surreal. I kept saying: *Come on, Poppy. Snap out of it.* But you weren't there. I don't know how else to describe it. And then, just like that, you were back."

I cringed at the thought of myself like that, what I'd put everyone through. I don't even have the slightest recollection. There's a black spot between the funeral and the day I woke up in the hospital with my mother reading a *People* magazine by the window.

Can I have a root beer? I asked her.

She looked at me, blinked a couple of times and issued a sigh of relief. *Welcome back, sweetie.* As if I'd been away on a long trip.

"Do you remember any of the things that I said?" I ask Layla, though part of me doesn't want to know. "*Exactly* what I said."

She shook her head. "It was just—nonsense."

"Like what?" I pushed.

"I don't know," she said. "It's hard to remember because it was all so disjointed. You didn't say anything meaningful, if that's what you're getting it. Clues to what happened to Jack, you mean? No, nothing like that."

Her mouth is pressed into a tight line, her gaze sliding off to the side. She's holding something back. We've known each other too long. I'm about to press when Slade calls from down the hall and Layla quickly slips off.

I drift into the living room, stare out the window into the dark of Central Park. The black of it, run through by the red veins of streets and paths, the glitter of streetlamps scattered like stars, is a void. If you look at an aerial photo of New York at night, its parks are these dark patches in a landscape of lights. One of those patches swallowed Jack. It swallowed me.

"You can bring it all to Dr. Nash, right? On Thursday?" says Layla when she comes back. "She'll help you sort it out."

I wonder. Dr. Nash hasn't been a big fan of pushing into that empty place in my life. Early on, I suggested hypnosis and she balked, said it wasn't part of her practice. She believed that my memories would come back when and if I was strong enough to handle them. She said she could refer me if I was adamant. I wasn't; to be honest, it scared me—scares me still. What will I find if I start to dig deeper into that dark void inside me? Where did I go? What did I do?

"Is there something you're not saying?" I press. "About that time."

She stands beside me at the window, laces her fingers through mine and looks out the window into the glittering dark. "I'd tell you if there was anything you needed to know. Anything about Jack. Of course I would."

★ ★ ★

Back in the guest room, my nerves are rattling. All I want is to tumble into a dark, dreamless well of sleep. I draw myself a bath, hot as I can stand, light the vanilla-scented candles that Layla has everywhere. I take three pills. I'm not sure what. Distantly, I'm aware that this is stupid. Beyond. In fact, it's self-harming. But it's just for tonight, just to get through this.

Then I step into the bath, the water so hot, so soothing. All my muscles relax, thoughts and fears receding swift and silent. I breathe deeply the way Dr. Nash taught me. In for three counts, hold, out for four counts. *The breath,* she said, *is always here for us. We can always soothe our nervous system with just some deep breathing.*

And pills. And liquor.

I focus on my breath, the hot water easing my tight muscles. The candlelight makes dancers on the wall and ceiling. I watch them dip and turn, swirl, and disappear, as the world slowly fades away.

You're a fucking liar!

I awake shivering in the water grown cold, the candles burned down to almost nothing, flames just tiny red dots on crinkled black wicks.

The sentence pried itself into my fitful, dream-riven sleep—where I endlessly trekked through the Fakahatchee Strand with Jack, that ghost orchid elusive. Where my phone rang and rang, Jack's name blinking on the screen. But I couldn't answer his call and couldn't make my finger dial him back. Where the sheets were stained with blood, like they were after my first miscarriage. The man from the bar, he looped his arm tight around the small of my back, pulled me in tight to his body, filling me with desire and anger.

You're a fucking liar!

I climb out of the tub, quaking with cold, quickly wrap myself in the robe that hangs on the back of the door. Was someone yelling in the house? Something from my own addled inner life?

Back in the bedroom, still shivering, I listen to the night. There's only quiet, just the faintest faraway hint of city noise through the double-paned windows and thick concrete walls of Layla's cocoon. My limbs icy and stiff, I dry and put on my pajamas.

I am not even going to acknowledge that I basically just passed out in the tub. How moronic, how dangerous. Candles burning. I could have started a fire in my best friends' home. Or I easily might have drowned. I cannot stop shaking with cold, anger at myself, fear at what might have been the consequences of my carelessness.

I leave the guest room and walk down the hall. Izzy and Slade are both sound asleep in the chaos of their respective rooms, night-lights glowing. Slade has his headphones on.

Layla and Mac's room is at the end of the long hallway, a suite separate from the rest of the enormous space. It's practically its own wing. The door is firmly closed and all I hear now is the measured, peaceful breathing of the kids.

9

I slip out with the dawn, leaving a note for Layla that I'll be back for dinner. I know she'll be worried, but I need to think. Rather than head to the office right away, I walk to the downtown train. The sky is a flat hard gray, clouds moving fast as a river, run through with fingers of the golden rising sun. Underground, the platform is oddly empty. The train when it comes, impossibly swift.

Why do the streets seem deserted, my heels clacking loudly on the concrete? I don't recognize the slim blond doorman sitting at the desk in the lobby: but he knows me.

"Good morning, Mrs. Lang." He waves at me and I do the same, breezing past him. My building lobby is cool, quiet in the pre–rush hour hush.

If there was any drama related to last night's episode, there's no evidence of it now.

The elevator is empty, and when I emerge on my floor, the long gray hallway stretches out silent and empty. A hair dryer hums. The sound of a television chatters. Wafting flute music is tinny and strange on the air. I've only seen one or two people since I've moved here. A thin bespectacled girl who the door-man told me was a famous writer. There's a couple—an archi-tect and his husband, lovely and smiley, always in a rush. They have two manic mini poodles who I occasionally, distantly, hear yapping. A building of strangers, myself included.

I pause at my door, fish the new keys from my bag, then move inside. I wait, listening, reminding myself that the locks have been changed. No one could have entered without the key I hold in my hand. Still, I walk from room to room, checking to make sure there's no one there. The orchid and the note are gone. The photo, too. Detective Grayson must have entered every-thing into evidence. He hasn't returned my call from last night. It's a niggle in the back of my brain. Why hasn't he checked in?

The box cutter is light in my hand as I head over to the pile of boxes stacked between the couch and the windows. They all have one word scrawled across their sides: *Jack*.

I've let them sit untouched for a year. It's been a topic of con-versation with Dr. Nash, when to unpack those boxes.

"Many people find it cathartic," she nudges. "To sort through the belongings of a deceased love one, to keep what's meaning-ful, and to discard the rest."

But I haven't wanted to let go of any piece of him. Jack's mom and I went through his things when I was packing up our old apartment. Sarah only took a watch that had belonged to Jack's father, and a picture of Jack as a child, fishing with his dad.

"It's only when you lose someone that you realize how little everything else matters," she said. "All the stuff. It's just gar-bage. Hold on to it, Poppy, until you're ready. Then let it go."

I put my head in her lap and cried that day—a thing I'd never done with my own mother. I carried everything I had left of him down to the new place in Chelsea. And here it sat, waiting.

I slice one open, and find a stack of his portfolios. Flip open the leather cover, and see an image of myself. She's almost a stranger, the girl there, her expression half amused, half annoyed. There are a hundred things she doesn't know. Behind her, palm trees bend in a strong wind; a fuchsia-tangerine sun sets over the ocean. Mexico, the night we met. He took a picture of me with my own camera.

And then I'm back there.

He was on assignment for National Geographic; I was on a press trip for a trade magazine, taking pictures of a new luxury beachfront hotel and spa. My assignment was a cushy one—all expenses paid, luxury accommodations, coaxing beautiful images from the lush landscaping, glittering pools, lavish meals. It was a shoot for a story designed to please a major advertiser for the magazine. Jack was following a team charged with releasing a pack of Mexican gray wolves raised in captivity back into the wild, part of a program to save the nearly extinct species. These two very different paths nevertheless led us to converge at an ocean-view bar at sunset.

He was with his team—journalists, naturalists, some local guides. They were dirty and scruffy and I'd barely noticed them as I breezed through the glittery space to the balcony to capture a few final shots of the sunset. It was a beauty—coral, violet, blazing orange lazing like a tiger against the black ocean.

"That's a serious piece of equipment for a tourist," he said, coming up from behind.

I spun around, startled, annoyed. "I'm not a tourist. I'm a photographer."

I wish I could say it was love at first sight. He claimed that it was for him, that he watched me from the moment I walked in and approached the minute he realized I was alone. But when I looked at him, I saw one of those guys—those sort of outdoorsy, adventure travel, adrenaline junkie guys. I'd known a few. Swaggering with ego, hard-bodied, they think because they risk their lives for nothing that they're special. They regale you with stories of their adventures, tell you how they want to suck the marrow out of life, expecting you to be riveted as they drone on and on. There's nothing more boring than a man who thinks only of himself.

"Canon 5D Mark III?" he asked, indicating my camera.

"That's right." Okay, so he's a photographer, I thought. I'll wait for the barb about how my press assignment is not as real, not as meaningful as his (obviously) journalistic one. I could tell by his scruffy arrogance that his was not a cushy gig like mine. Maybe some sexist comment about how mine is a good camera—for a woman because it fits nicely into a smaller hand.

"I heard the burst speed is slower than the EOS 5DS," he said.

"Slightly," I admitted. "But it's more ergonomic and the files are gorgeous."

"May I?"

I leaned against the balcony and handed it to him. It was his smile that did it, slow and mischievous. It brightened up his face as he lifted the camera and took a picture of me.

"You're right," he said, glancing at the screen. "Gorgeous."

And then I'm back in my apartment, staring at the picture in front of me. Time traveling.

When I look at that picture now, I see the irked amusement on my own face, the glitter of attraction. I'm glad that girl didn't know what lay ahead of her. Maybe she would have chosen to never love him, knowing how much it would hurt to lose him. That would have been a terrible loss for her, one she'd never even realize.

I am sifting through Jack's files when the phone rings. The ring sounds funny, distant, and I dig for it underneath the piles of debris I've unpacked. Detective Grayson.

"Mrs. Lang?" His voice sounds oddly measured.

"Mrs. Lang?" I say, with a laugh. "What happened to Poppy?"

There's a pause where I expect to hear him chuckle. But he doesn't. "Okay, then. Poppy. Where are you?"

"I'm home." But it doesn't sound right. This place has not become my home. "At my apartment."

"I thought you were staying with the Van Santens."

I don't love his tone—taut, officious. I find myself bristling.

"Is there a problem?" Last I checked I didn't answer to him or anyone for my whereabouts.

"Don't go anywhere, please. I'm on my way to you." He hangs up without another word.

Looking around at the mess I've made, there's a tingling sense of déjà vu. The portfolios of Jack's prints, the files of tax returns, business documents, medical records, contracts—there's nothing here I haven't seen, that I don't know about. What am I looking for? I'm not even sure—anything that helps me make sense of what happened yesterday, some piece of Jack that tells me why someone would want to hurt him, why someone is following me, breaking into my apartment, leaving me orchids and notes that bring back powerful memories of moments I shared with my husband.

I slice open another box. His clothes. Maybe it's my imagination, but the smell of him wafts up into the air and it's so fresh, so vivid that my whole body folds in with sadness. I reach for his New School sweatshirt and bring the ratty gray garment to my face, bury myself in its softness. His scent, the darkness, it wraps around me. I wish I could dive into it and disappear. But a soft click brings me back. Something has slipped from the front pocket of the sweatshirt.

I reach down and pick up a red foil matchbook. Embossed on the cover in silver: Morpheus.

I know it. Where? Where I have heard it before? The address on the back says Ludlow Street, Manhattan's Lower East Side, Jack's old stomping grounds. He went to the New School, lived in Alphabet City in the late '80s and '90s, when it was still gritty and tough and "real" according to Jack. Beautiful, he thought, in its tumbledown, graffiti-covered squalor. His photos from that time show his love for the streets, the buildings, the people in his neighborhood.

I open the matchbook; a pretty cursive, a woman's handwriting: Elena, it says, and a phone number with a New York City cell exchange. I stare at it, not sure what it means.

The pounding on the door startles me, and the matchbook drops back into the box. I stuff the sweatshirt on top and close the cardboard folds. I walk down the hallway, the knocking continues.

"Mrs. Lang?" His voice is stern and unfriendly. "It's Detective Grayson, please open the door."

As I reach for the door, it swings open and he steps inside. He looks different somehow, less rumpled, more alert, younger.

"What's going on?" I ask.

"I don't like having to track you down."

I shake my head, not understanding his attitude, what he's saying.

"What are you doing here?" he asks. His gaze is hard, suspicious.

I lift my palms. "I don't know," I say. "After yesterday, I just thought I'd look through some of his things. Maybe there's something I missed. Some piece of this."

"That's my job, Mrs. Lang."

"He's my husband," I say, my voice cracking. "It's my job, too, to understand what happened to him. Maybe—I found something."

But when I turn back toward the boxes—they're gone.

In fact, I'm not in the new apartment at all, but back in the Upper West Side place where Jack and I lived together. How? Confusion pulls the moment long. How did I get here? The furniture is all pushed around the way it was after the gathering of friends we had to mark Jack's passing. There are wineglasses, washed and lined up on the kitchen table, where Layla put them to dry. What's happening to me? Panic squeezes my chest.

"No," I say, my brain grappling. Outside the window, it's dark. Wasn't it just morning?

I startle to see Jack reclining in the chair by the window, his feet up on the ottoman.

"Let it go, Poppy," he says. His face is caked with blood. "Let me go."

A sob climbs up my throat. "Jack?"

The floor is soft, like it might buckle under my weight. The whole scene pulls long, and twisting.

"No," I tell him, moving toward him. "I can't. I won't."

I want to clean the blood from the side of his face.

"Get your coat," says Grayson. "You shouldn't be here."

I'm not here, I want to tell him. It's a year later, and I don't live here anymore. This isn't happening. Jack is gone.

"There was a matchbook," I stammer. "From a downtown club, with a woman's name written inside. Elena."

"Let's go."

"Wait," I say, panic ratcheting tight. I can't breathe. "Why won't you listen to me?"

"Because," he says, suddenly nasty, his face twisted with disgust and anger. "You're not making any sense."

He taps at his temple hard. "Because you're a fucking liar."

He grabs me hard by the arm and starts pulling me toward the door. His fingers digging in, hurting. I try to resist, but he is impossibly strong and I am powerless to pull away. Even my voice is gone. I try to yell at him, to rage, but there is only silence. The hallway stretches, yawning and dark.

10

Layla's guest room again. My heart is an engine, tears burning my eyes. I can't get a full breath as I push myself to sitting, try to orient myself in the space, hold on to what's real. I rub my arm, still feeling Grayson's steely grip.

But no. It never happened. The stretching hallway, his twisted face.

Not. Real.

Shit.

What's happening to me?

"Aunt Poppy?" Izzy is a long lean shadow in the doorway, wearing a nightshirt, her hair up in a knot. "Are you okay? I thought I heard you crying."

"I'm sorry," I tell her. "Everything's fine. Just a nightmare."

She's real. I know that much. As she drifts near, I smell the soap on her skin, that same organic coconut bar that Layla keeps in the guest shower.

"Do you want me to stay with you?"

Kids know. They know that no one wants to be alone after a nightmare as its tendrils still whorl about, reaching for you, threatening to bring you back. No one wants to dwell in that nether place between night and morning where every shadow is a monster, every noise the boogeyman outside your door. Izzy doesn't wait for me to answer, just slips into bed beside me.

"I thought I heard someone yelling before," I say.

"They were fighting," says Izzy, her voice heavy with sleep. "That's all they *ever* do. They hurt each other. They, like, hate each other I think."

I'm surprised to hear this from her. "Izzy, really?"

But she doesn't answer, sound asleep already. I teddy bear–hug her from behind and feel the rise and fall of her body, her deep breathing slow and soothing. Mac's dark tone, the obvious tension between him and Layla. Am I so caught up in my own mess that I can't see what's going on with my best friends?

I lie there with Izzy. Sleep doesn't come, just a parade of images, flashes. That matchbook, that name, the number I can't remember. Was *that* real? Something that I found and lost? Or forgot? *Who* is Elena?

Thoughts of Jack tumble; I time travel into memory.

"Can I buy you a drink?" he asked that first night.

I hesitated, then joined his group. We sat talking late into the evening. Alvaro was there that night, too. They were working as a team. Dark where Jack was fair, quiet where Jack was talkative, his stare brooding and watchful. He sat, drinking, not saying much. Eventually, though, he was gone, and one by one, so was everyone else until it was just Jack and me. We drank too much, and finally we were making out like prom dates, pressed against the wall in front of my hotel room.

"Are you going to invite me inside?"

"Definitely not," I breathed as he kissed my neck.

I'd known too many men like Jack. You meet them all over the world when you do this kind of work. For a night, or maybe even a weekend, it's a party, but then they're gone, on to the next assignment and whoever they meet there.

I ran my fingers through that sandy hair, kissed him long and deep, then I unraveled myself from his arms and pushed myself inside the hotel room, closing the door behind me.

"Seriously?" he said outside the door. "You're killing me."

"I doubt that." My whole body was tingling.

"Poppy Jackson," he said. "I'll see you in New York."

"Sure you will," I said to the door. It took a superhuman amount of self-control not to let him in.

"I have your card right here," he said. "I'm going to call you as soon as I get into town."

I smiled, figuring I wouldn't see him again. You *never* see this kind of guy again.

"Okay," I said. "I'll be waiting by the phone."

I didn't wait by the phone—not that anyone waits by the phone anymore. Now we just take it everywhere with us. And I didn't hear from him again right away. I thought of him a couple of times, but only to remember that heat, his smile, to be glad I hadn't slept with him or wanted more than a man like that could give.

A week later, he was waiting for me as I exited the SoHo Gallery where I was working between photo assignments. The address was on my card. He held a bouquet of poppies.

"Did you know that the poppy flower symbolizes sleep and death?" he said.

"I *did* know that," I said, drinking him in. He'd cleaned up some, but in khakis and a white cotton button-down, hair wild, he still looked as if he'd just emerged from the jungle—tousled, able, as if he'd seen *so many* interesting things. "But my mother just really likes the color red. That's why she chose that name."

"In classical mythology," he went on, "it represents resurrection."

"You've done your research."

"It also signifies remembrance." He moved in close and

handed me the flowers, their droopy scarlet faces fragrant and cheerful. "Do you remember me?"

"Vaguely," I said with a smile, looking down at the bouquet. It's not easy to get fresh-cut poppies; in some places they're illegal, or they must be special ordered from a florist.

He kissed me then, on the street, with people passing all around us, the afternoon humid and darkening. The world disappeared and it was only us from that day forward.

Lying in Layla's guest room, I wonder now: Was the note with the orchid meant to evoke that moment with Jack?

No, I decide. It's an innocuous question, uttered frequently throughout your life. It might be asked in hope or passion, in casual query: Do you remember me? Was there a connection? Have you been thinking about me?

I remember you. Don't you remember me?

If not that, then what did it mean? *Who* remembers me, when I can't remember him?

Mercifully, darkness recedes and the sun rises, light sneaking milky white through the blinds. With Izzy still sleeping soundly, I dress, gather my things and leave a note for Layla. I slip out the front door, shuttle down the elevator, pass the doorman, déjà vu shadowing me.

The cab carries me downtown, and the morning sun climbs, coloring windows golden. The city bustles by, even before 6:00 a.m.—the overachievers jogging, or dressed and moving with click-clack purpose up the sidewalk, headphones in, coffees or cell phones clutched in hand.

I wish—desperately—that I was one of them today, with nothing on my mind this Wednesday morning but maybe getting a workout before my early meeting. I'm addled, jumpy, back to feeling as I did after Jack died, after my breakdown: disconnected from the world, torn out, separated. Any schedule for my days or goals for my week scattered like debris after a bomb blast.

Back in my apartment for real this time, I stand before the boxes that line the far wall.

If there's something about Jack I didn't know, some secret self, maybe it's hiding in here. I read in one of those clutter clearing books that if you have sealed boxes in your life, then there are places within yourself you're afraid to confront. A warrior, I wield the box cutter and get to work. I tear them open one after another, rummaging through the contents, digging into the detritus of Jack's life.

Finally, I sink to the floor, my throat constricted with frustration. Piles of papers, files, portfolios, clothes form a chaotic circle around me. I don't find his New School sweatshirt; there's no red matchbook. Nothing there points to a different Jack, one I didn't know.

I pick up a small black box; Jack's wedding ring glints in the velvet cushion around it. I take it out and hold it in my palm. When I slipped it on his finger at our wedding, it almost didn't go on. We laughed as he forced it.

Layla thought I should wear it on a chain as a necklace. But no. He'd hate that. *Move on*, he'd surely say, just like the Jack in my dreams. *Let go.*

I look around at the mess I've made. It's all just *stuff*, void of his energy, drained of anything it might have meant once to him, to me. His mother already knew, that's why she wanted so little. Just that watch, a shadowy picture of Jack as a small boy and his lithe and handsome dad fishing on a dock. She'd lost her husband, Jack's dad, when they were still so young, in their thirties with a baby. She never married again.

There wasn't anyone else, not after him. No one ever compared.

I knew what she meant. I've never been one of those girls who mooned over boys—not like Layla. I never ached to marry, never saw myself with my hair done, wearing a white dress. Layla was already planning her wedding when we were in middle school. She'd steal bridal magazines from the drugstore, leaf through them on the floor of my room. She'd turn the pages slowly, gazing on all the perfect, airbrushed images of dewy brides and virile grooms—her hair would be like this, her dress like this, *oh, Poppy, look at that ring.*

Which one, Poppy? Which one do you want?

I don't know, I'd laugh. *Do I have to get married?*

To me then, marriage was angry conversations behind closed doors, cold looks, barbed comments, long silences. My parents weren't happy, always moving in wide orbits around me—him out in his shed, her in the bedroom with the shades drawn and the television tuned in to some old movie, him working late, her out at bunco, stumbling in after I was asleep. *At least there's no screaming*, Layla said. *At least the police don't come.* Yeah, okay. There was that. No black eyes, no arms in slings like at Layla's.

Of course you have to get married, Layla said emphatically.

But there was never some imaginary bridegroom for me; it was only ever Jack I wanted to marry. It was *his* baby I wanted to have when I eventually wanted that. Before him, I never did develop Layla's grand plans for marriage and children. I had no ache for that kind of life, the kind Layla wanted so badly—the happy home, beautiful children, the enviable love. I only wanted to travel, to hold the world in my lens. To take moments, those abstract slices of life and places and people, and make them say *something*. I wanted to make magic. That changed, of course.

Mac's words still knock around my brain. *Maybe we only knew a piece of him.*

When I photographed Jack, it was always slivers of him—the ledge of his stubbled jaw, his calloused hands, the smooth round of his shoulder. I sift through some of those photos now. Those moments, fragments, the shifting shadows that pass and can't be recovered. That's what's real, isn't it?

I put the ring back in the box and snap the lid closed, start piling things back where they were. Enough of this. Why can't I keep myself rooted in the present?

I am about to close the box when I see something silver glinting near the bottom. I rustle through the mess I've made and find a set of keys attached to a leather tab. The keys to his Jeep, which has sat untouched in a garage uptown since before his death.

He'd bought the Jeep on a whim after a big job, before we met.

"Oh," I said, on seeing it. "Wow."

"This." He swept his hand wide. "*This* was the car of my dreams when I was kid."

"Really?"

I rested a hand on its hood; my fingers came away brown with dirt.

"The ultimate freedom," he said. He gazed at it lovingly. "Your driver's license, right? A vehicle that could take you off-road. To places where there aren't any rules."

We were a month into our new relationship, sick with love, revealing ourselves to each other in moments like this one. There was a boyish light to his face, something I hadn't seen yet. It ignited something in me, a matching excitement that there was a whole new world out there waiting to be explored and held in my lens.

The Jeep was dusty blue, with fat, deeply treaded tires, mud-spattered. Inside, the leather seats were worn, all the gauges analog, glass foggy. There was a simple AM/FM radio.

"Remember what it was like to be in the car? No phone, no navigation computer, no screens. Just the radio, the sound of the tires on the road, the wind rushing."

"Uh." I didn't share his nostalgia. I remembered endless rides with my parents arguing over where they needed to be and when they needed to get there, a great flapping map, folded and unfolded, turned every which way by my mother before my father finally pulled over. I had my Walkman, the only saving grace, a giant device with a cassette tape I made. I let David Bowie, The Cure, The Smiths, Joy Division bury me deep in sound, staring at the landscape racing past the window, watching the sky, the clouds. That vaguely carsick feeling. That heavy boredom with no end in sight. Having to pee, not wanting to say so because I knew it would just aggravate my father, who was obsessed with "making good time."

Later, under my mother's hysterical, terrified tutelage, I became a nervous driver. I preferred to be a passenger in Layla's junker to driving my dad's old, well-maintained Ford.

"I remember."

"It was like this safe zone," he said. "No one could reach you. Maybe no one even knew where you were."

He held the door open for me and I climbed inside. Roll bars, a fabric roof.

"Is this *safe*?" I noticed a small rip where the "window" zippered on.

He bounced into the driver's seat, and the whole thing rocked. Shooting me a devilish grin, he coaxed the engine to life.

"I mean," he said. "What's safe *really*?"

"Uh." I fastened the seat belt, which looked a little frayed, gripped the armrest as he rambled onto the street.

"Where's your sense of adventure?" he teased.

We roared out of the city. Where did we go that day? It was spring, the air growing warm. We headed north up the Henry Hudson, spent the day hiking in the Catskills, dinner in Woodstock. He was right; our phones left behind, we were freed.

The Jeep—it has been on my list of things to deal with; I should sell it. But it's another piece of him I can't let go. I shove the keys in my bag.

After I've put things back in the boxes, I grab the black dream journal and write it all down, anything that I can remember. I even take some stabs at the phone number I saw in my dream on the matchbook. The name—Elena. When I have it all on the page, a black scrawl on bright white, manic, barely legible, I flip back again through the journal, this time looking under the filter of Mac's question. Was there something about Jack I didn't know? Are there secrets hiding in my dreams?

I'm surprised at how much I've written, almost the entire notebook filled. Written in that space between sleep and wakefulness, I barely remember writing most of it.

There are sketches, too, renderings of Jack, a sad self-portrait where I'm slumped over, eyes dark with circles, a maze, a room I don't recognize with a fireplace burning, and snow falling outside the window.

Before I picked up a camera, I used to draw. The lines are dark, heavy-handed, my talent middling at best. Flipping back and forth through the pages, there's an odd voyeuristic thrill, as if I'm looking at the diary of a stranger. Most of it is gibberish. I turn back to more recent entries, am about to close it altogether. That's when I see it, a single word embedded in a checkerboard of black and white squares: *Morpheus*.

The name of the nightclub embossed on the glass in my dream night before last. The same as the name on the matchbook: *Morpheus*. What does it mean, these spiderweb threads between two dreams? Is my subconscious playing tricks on me—or trying to tell me something? Using my phone, I search the word.

Morpheus, the Greek god of dreams, the king of night, he can take any form, bringing messages to mortals from the gods. Born of Nyx, the personification of night, he sends dreams to the sleeping through two doors, one made of ivory and the other of horn.

I click on an image where he's depicted as a winged angel, bending over the sleeping form of a young woman in a red dress. He holds her in his arms and whispers in her ear. I get lost in the image, its bold colors and delicate lines. Her peaceful sleeping face, the tenderness of his touch. *In the Arms of Morpheus* by Sir William Ernest Reynolds-Stephens, painted in 1894.

Morpheus: a character in *The Matrix*, or the origin of the word for the opiate morphine. Down a bit farther, I find a website for a nightclub on the Lower East Side, click on it. I scroll through the images there, mostly drunk people taking selfies in rowdy groups, grainy images of the dance floor. The home page is red with the name in elaborate script, an address on Ludlow Street, and hours of operation. It doesn't even open until 10:00 p.m. Have I been there before? Is it the place in my dreams? I can't be sure.

I write it all down, fatigue pulling at me, a buzz of anxiety persistent in my head.

What has Morpheus been whispering in my ear? What is he trying to tell me?

The bed beckons me. I could sink into its white fluffiness and disappear. But no. There's been enough sleep, enough of the maze of my dreams. Time to rejoin the living.

I put the book back by my bed and get in the shower. The water is hot, as hot as it will go, nearly scalding. I wash it all away, try to clear the cobwebs in my addled head. I have to get back to myself, to the waking world and figure out what's going on.

As I'm drying my hair, lost in thought, the buzzer rings.

"Detective Grayson here for you," says the doorman through the intercom.

It's only seven in the morning. Grayson was like this in the beginning, calling and showing up at strange hours as if time and propriety meant nothing to him. I can't imagine him sleeping in, taking a day off, living a life, though he must do those things. "Send him up."

I flash on my dream Grayson, his face wrenched in anger and disgust. I'm not sure how many or what pills I took last night, how much I drank. Right now, though I am tired, I'm oddly more alert than I remember feeling for a while. Maybe Dr. Nash is right. Maybe I am getting stronger. Maybe my brain is reorganizing itself, working through fear, anxiety, grief.

There was a time when Grayson and I weren't friends, when

I was his prime suspect as all spouses of the murdered must be. He battered me with questions for hours on the darkest day of my life until my mother's lawyer came and forced him to stand down. I hated him that day, feared him. Layla's words push through: *Maybe that wasn't a dream at all. Maybe it was a memory.* Or some facsimile of memory, some twisted depiction of how I saw him once.

Dr. Nash: *I really* do *want us to think of this as good news.* I doubt she'd say that if she knew that I was mixing pills, taking them with alcohol.

When I open the door for the detective, he's the man I know—steely-eyed, intense, but rumpled, dark valleys of fatigue under his eyes. He has that look he had at the beginning, as though he'd been up all night, slept in his clothes or not at all. There was a partner at first, an older man who smelled like hamburgers and cigarettes—who's since retired. Grayson hasn't been assigned a new partner that I know of. I haven't asked him about it.

"I thought you were staying at the Van Santens," he says.

He glances around, as he always does, eyes searching. Must be a cop thing, always looking, examining. Not unlike the photographer, always waiting for that moment, the perfect blend of light and shadow, the detail that tells the story. "I called over there. She said you left."

There it is, that niggle of defensiveness, as though I must explain myself. "I had to come back here for a few things before work."

He walks a loop around the room, his thick black boots heavy on the floor, casts a glance at the now open boxes.

"Finally unpacking?"

"Something like that."

I make us some coffee, and he comes to sit at the island that separates the kitchen from the living space, puts his cell phone down with a meaningful tap on the quartz countertop. Sometimes I feel like he's waiting for me to talk first, like it's a technique he uses to get people to fill silence.

"Did you talk to the building staff?" I ask, finally giving in.

"I did." He touches his phone and the screen comes to life. "Did you know that there are security cameras in the lobby?"

I guess I knew that. It might have been on the website or some of the glossy selling material the broker gave us when she was trying to convince Jack (I was already sold) that the exorbitant rent was worth it.

The aroma of Jack's favorite roast fills the room, deep rich coffee, with a hint of lemon, a note of something green and earthy. He'd wear the same jeans for a decade, but he'd spend nearly twenty bucks on nine ounces of Ethiopian Yirge Cheffe.

"Want to see what they caught?"

There's an unpleasant twist in my middle. Do I? My world is on such a tilt, I'm not sure I want to know what the camera caught in my lobby. I flash on that image of Morpheus, the prone woman in his arms. What's he whispering to her as she sleeps?

I stand beside Grayson as he opens an email with a movie file attached and presses Play. He's slow with it, thinking, not fluent with his device. His fingers are thick and calloused, cuticles ragged.

We watch the tiny screen as people move through the lobby—a bike messenger with a big bag slung around his tall wiry frame; two lithe women with high ponytails and yoga bags glide past, laughing, tossing careless waves at the doorman; a woman with a black German shepherd, holding tight to the leash as the dog pulls.

"You should get a dog," says Grayson absently, apropos of nothing.

"Just what I need." Surely, I don't need to remind him that I can barely take care of myself.

For a few moments, the lobby is empty.

"Wait for it," he says.

A boy, slim in jeans and a Yankees jersey, walks through the door carrying an orchid. He brings it to the front desk, says something to the doorman and leaves quickly. I see his face, dark-skinned, fine-featured, big doe eyes and a wide mouth. His hair is shorn close to his head, face slack and innocent like maybe it was his job to drop off the flower, that's it. There's nothing furtive about him, nothing nervous or edgy. Just a city kid.

"He just dropped it off, said it was for Poppy Lang, did not—according to the doorman—give an apartment number," says Grayson. "When they did the afternoon deliveries of packages, laundry, dry cleaning—which, again, cannot believe you let them do that."

He pauses here to again adequately express his disapproval of the arrangement, which never seemed like anything but a convenience to me. Or maybe it's more that I don't care about anything in this apartment. Which I guess is a whole other thing.

"They say that they brought it up to your apartment. Bruno, the guy who delivered it, said if he knocked the photo off the wall, he's sorry. He was wearing his headphones and maybe didn't even notice."

Grayson shrugs as I take the information in.

"I don't know," he goes on. "Seems like he would have noticed."

I want this to be true, that it was just Bruno the delivery guy in my apartment, that the orchid and card were left at the lobby desk. I've seen him in the hallways with his cart, headphones on, humming or singing. He's a big guy, plodding, not careful. I can imagine him, bull-in-a-china-shop-style, knocking the photograph to the ground with his shoulder. Could be he didn't notice. Or.

"Maybe he just didn't want to get in trouble," I offer.

I thought about how the photo was far from the wall. Thrown, I thought, not accidentally knocked off. The glass was shattered as if it landed with force. But really, how could you know such a thing? Chaos theory and all of that. Complex systems highly sensitive to changes in initial conditions. Who could say how he knocked it, how it fell, where it landed?

Grayson replays the video and we watch again.

"Recognize the kid?"

I shake my head. "Never seen him before."

"We pulled some security footage from other buildings," he says. We watch the slender boy—maybe fifteen or sixteen—walk easily up the avenue, camera angles shifting, then turn and disappear into the subway station on Twenty-Third Street. He has a city kid aura to him, watchful but fluent with the streets, how things work, when to jaywalk, when to wait, slithering quickly through slow-moving crowds of people.

"We lost him after that," said Grayson. "The flowers didn't come from an identifiable florist—no sticker on the pot, nothing on the card—so there's no lead there. Like you say, it's a common flower easily purchased at any corner bodega. He wasn't a delivery boy the doormen had seen before."

"No cameras in the subway?"

"Yeah," he said, rubbing at his temples. "There are more than four thousand cameras in the subways. But half of them don't work—electric problems, heat, water damage. So, we lost him."

Since 9/11 supposedly there are seeing eyes all over the city, but it's the second time those cameras have failed us. Jack's murder wasn't caught on camera, either, his killer not captured on film by one of the many security cameras owned by private businesses or the NYPD as he fled the scene. Eyes everywhere unless you want them to be, unless you need them to be, it seems.

"So. That's it?" I say. Anger, frustration edges my voice. "Another dead end."

He looks away from me, then back. There's an odd expression on his face.

"What?" I ask even though I don't want to.

"Let me ask you something," he says. He taps a finger on the counter.

"Okay."

"Have you been dating?"

My cheeks warm at the question. Do I have to answer that? I use the excuse of pouring and serving the coffee to turn away from him.

"Well?"

"I've been on a couple of dates," I answer, not bothering to conceal my annoyance. "I'm not seeing anyone seriously if that's what you mean."

"Dating site?"

I nod quickly. I stop short of telling him that it was Layla's idea, not mine. That, actually, I'm only interested in one thing at the moment.

"I saw you," he says. He looks a little embarrassed. "Online."

What am I hearing—judgment, disapproval? Whatever it is, I don't like it. How often do our conversations turn like this, where I suddenly feel on the defensive? Seems like whenever a lead goes dead, he comes back to the wife. I am reminded that even though our relationship sometimes feels like friendship, it's not that. It never was and can never be.

He rubs at his temples again, fatigued I guess—with work, with life, with me.

"What were *you* doing on there?" I counter.

"Same thing everyone's doing I guess." A lift of his eyebrows. "Looking. Hoping."

I recast him with this new information. His eyes on Layla yesterday, now the news that he's on a dating site, looking for love. What did I think? That he disappeared into nothing when he wasn't in my world? That he didn't have a life, needs, pain and loss?

"So, your point is?"

"Maybe one of the guys you've met," he says. "Maybe someone was just trying to be cute. Romantic."

I know he likes his coffee black, so I hand him a cup.

"That seems unlikely," I say.

I've been on three dates. Oliver the actuary, tall, cute in a geeky way—glasses, sweater-vest but with glittering dark eyes, and absolutely ripped from the intense daily workouts he did before heading to the office. He was soft-spoken, still reeling from an ugly divorce and fighting for more time with his kids. We had a nice dinner at Gotham, then went back to his place. I left in the hours before dawn. *Can I call you?* he asked, as he walked me to the door. *Of course*, I said. He texted later in the day. *I had a great night. Thank you.* Then he called the following day, but I didn't ring him back, or answer his texts. Finally, he stopped reaching out. Cold, I know.

There was Martin who worked in IT—metrosexual, into wine, travel, clothes, never married, pushing fifty. There was a twinkle of good humor to his gaze; he had a way of folding his hands when he was listening. There was something priestly about it. We didn't even bother eating. We went back to his place, a walk-up in SoHo. There was a copy of *The Life-Changing Magic of Tidying Up* on his shelf, and little else—everything spare and white. He was lovely in bed—gentle, considerate. He didn't wake up as I slipped out, never called.

Then there was Noah. Noah was tall, big through the shoulders, hazel eyes with thick lashes—a sculptor. There was a deep quiet to him, an astute listener. He had a ready laugh, talked about his parents, who lived all their lives in Long Island and died too young. His hair was a tangle of golden curls, darker but something like Jack's. And it wasn't long before I was back at his Tribeca loft, running my fingers through that hair. The space was dominated by his sculptures, towering abstract metal monsters—a dragon, a ghoul, a spider—that cast odd shadows on the wall.

Again, I tried to do a disappearing act.

"You were never here," he said easily as I pulled on my clothes. "Where were you?"

He lay on the bed, arms crossed behind his head. He watched with a smile as I shimmied into my skirt.

"Come back to bed for a while," he said, sitting up and putting out a hand. "You don't have to stay but you don't have to rush out, either."

I don't know why, but I sat back down on the edge of his bed and told him about Jack.

"I'm sorry," he said when I was done. "I'm so sorry."

He told me how his girlfriend died in college, killed by a drunk driver when she was home visiting her parents.

"Maybe I never got over it," he said. "Maybe she was the one, and that was it. That's why I can't make anything else work."

I lay beside him for a while, our fingers laced together, watching the shadows of his sculptures move across the wall with the headlights of each passing car. Finally, I told him I had to go, and he didn't stop me. Just pulled on his jeans and walked me to the door, kissed me softly on the lips and didn't say anything.

He called a couple of times, left a message:

"I don't want to seem weird. But I—feel a connection. Don't you?"

I thought about it, calling him back. I almost did. Finally, I just took the coward's way and sent a text: I'm just not ready for anything more than we already shared.

I understand, came his reply. You know how to find me.

"No one aggressive, calling and calling? Showing up places he shouldn't be?"

I think about mentioning the text I got from Noah yesterday, but don't.

"Nothing like that," I say. "Just professional people like me—like you—looking for someone."

"What about you?" he asks. "What were you looking for?"

I shrug, don't answer.

"It's not safe, you know. Meeting up with strange men, going back to their apartments."

"Nothing's safe," I say. "Not really."

He offers an assenting dip of his chin. "But in my line of work there are people who live high-risk lives and those who live low-risk lives. High-risk people drink too much maybe, then get in a car and drive, or get belligerent and start fights in bars. Low-risk people, if they drink too much, call a cab. They wear their seat belts, stand back from the tracks, wait for the light to turn before crossing, come in from the rain."

"And those people are safe?" I say. There's a bite to my tone that I didn't intend. "Nothing bad ever happens to them?"

"They're *safer*. Bad things can happen to anyone."

"And Jack? Was he a high-risk or a low-risk person?"

"You tell me."

I guess we both knew the answer to that—adventure traveler, someone who runs alone at five in the morning.

"Sounds like victim blaming to me," I say, this time less sharply than I intended.

He gives me that look he has, a thoughtful squint, nod thing.

"Are we not at least partially responsible for keeping ourselves safe, for lowering the risks in our lives?" he asks. "Locking doors, staying vigilant on the street? No one has a right to hurt us, even in a careless moment. But we have some—*some*—control over our level of risk."

"What are we talking about here?"

"We've known each other for a while. Maybe I'm out of line here. But humor me," he says.

I wait.

"Sometimes when we're grieving, depressed, we don't take care of ourselves," he says. "In fact, sometimes we *invite* darkness."

Invite darkness? It would almost be poetic if it weren't so insulting. I think about the dates, the pills, the alcohol, how last night I drank, took three sleeping pills and fell asleep—okay, passed out—in the tub. Insulting and maybe a little too close to the bone.

Grayson scratches at his head, then takes a sip of coffee. He doesn't look at me even though I'm staring at him.

"Is that what you think I'm doing?" I say. "By dating again. By trying to move on. I'm inviting darkness."

I wonder: Would we be having this conversation if I were a man?

"Yesterday you told me someone was following you." He drains his cup. "I found you banging on a door, yelling your head off on Fifth. You thought someone was in your place. Now we think maybe not. Some kid just delivered a flower from an unknown sender and the building delivery guy brought it in."

The way he says it makes the heat come up in my cheeks again. *Yelling your head off. Thought someone was in your place.* It reminds me of how everyone looked at me after my breakdown, as if I were a china cup tumbling, eternally in midflight from hand to floor. Something about to shatter.

My mother brought me home from the hospital after those strange days. I didn't want her there; she was not the person I called in a crisis. It was snowing, a light flurry, the first of the year. The sky was ash and the air bit at my cheeks as I sat in a wheelchair with the nurse behind me. My mother, slim and ever stylish in a long black wool coat, hailed a cab.

"We'll put this behind you," she said, coming back, offering me her hand. "This too shall pass."

This too shall pass. It's what she always said. Yes, this too shall pass. All of it. Every goddamn thing.

I took the hand she offered and let her tug me up, wrap her arm tight around me, usher me to the taxi. I was wearing thin gray sweatpants and a pair of Uggs, a thick black parka, a red stocking cap. A patient, unable even to get myself home. The reflection staring back at me from the cab window was not recognizable, someone hollowed out, haunted. I was still fighting for those lost days then, pressing hard into the black space of my memory until my head throbbed. How could there be nothing there? Meanwhile, my body ached with grief, every muscle clenched and painful.

"I was somewhere," I told my mother in the cab. "There was music playing."

"That's all right," my mother said. "Don't think about it, Poppy, any of it. Just forget it. That's what I did when your father died. You'll see. We'll get you well. You'll go back to work. You'll put one foot in front of the other, and one day soon, you'll be okay. You'll find someone else. You're still young and attractive."

Oh, Mom. Really?

Back at my apartment, everything was clean. The mess from the funeral gathering all cleared away. I didn't have to wonder. I could tell from the smell of lemons that Layla had sent her service over. There were fresh flowers, lilies on the table in the kitchen, poppies by my bed. Beside my pillow was, touchingly, Beans, Layla's stuffed tiger ragged and limp with his sewed-on mouth turned up into a smile. A note: *Beans will take care of you. Hold on to him as tight as you need to—and to me. Love you.*

Mom tucked me into my bed, turned the dimmer lights down low.

"I'm going to make some soup." She lay a hand on my forehead, her palm icy, her blue eyes searching my face. Then she left quietly.

I lay in the dim amber light, too destroyed even for tears, listening to my mother clang about the kitchen. Finally, I drifted off.

Later I heard her talking. *She was never strong. Such a fragile girl. After her father died, I thought she'd never recover.*

Layla's voice came terse over the speakerphone: *she's stronger than you think, Sybil.*

"Poppy." Detective Grayson has his eyes on me, that look again. "Where did you go?"

How often this happens, where I drift so deep into my thoughts, memory, that I lose the present.

"I've been thinking a lot about those lost days. My breakdown."

"What about them?"

I go out on a limb with the detective and tell him about my dreams—about the name, the phone number, the club. As I talk, his brow goes heavier with concern.

"I don't get it," he says after a moment. "Is this something you dreamed or something you *remember*?"

My head aches and now it's my turn to rub at the pain in my temples. "I guess I don't know the answer to that right now."

"Spell it."

I do and he taps it into his phone, looks up at me. He's probably scrolling through all the same listings I did earlier. "It's a real place. A nightclub on the Lower East Side. A hot ticket, on the *New York Magazine* top clubs list."

Just thinking about the throbbing music, the flashing lights, the cold filthy tile of that floor ratchets up the pain in my head. *Did* I go there? *Why* did I go there? When?

"Did I—?" I start, then stop.

"What?"

"Did we ever—talk about this before? Did you come here or to my other place? Did I tell you about the matchbook with the name and number on it?"

I don't say: *Did you ever call me a fucking liar, grab my arm and drag me down the hallway?*

He shakes his head slowly. "No," he says. "This is the first I'm hearing any of this."

But is there something off about the way he says it? There's a similar tension to everyone—to Layla, to my mother, when I ask about that time. Now I see it in the detective. A kind of breath held, a slight stiffening of the shoulders, an averting of the eyes. Was it *that* bad? I've wondered. A rush of shame keeps me from pressing him further.

Another thought crowds in but I push it away as paranoia. *Are they—all of them—keeping something from me?*

"What about the name—Elena?" I press. "Could it mean something?"

"Last name?"

I shake my head.

"I don't remember anyone with that name in his phone records or email. I'll take another look but—" He pauses a second, watches me with a stern frown. "We are talking about *dreams* here, right? This is not a real person, someone you remember."

Heat comes up to my cheeks again. Yes, we're talking about the dreams of a woman scattered by grief and pills. I think about my journal, filled with the scribbling and drawings of a crazy person, the jagged shards of my psyche in a manic black scrawl. Sleeping and waking, dream and memory; what's the difference? I used to know the answer. Now I'm not so sure.

"They're dreams," I say. "But—what if they're not? Some of them have felt—real."

"I don't dream."

"Everybody does."

"Yeah, that's what they say, but not me. Anyway, I can't work with that, Poppy, you know. The real, the concrete, that's what I need to find justice for Jack."

A pragmatist, like Jack. Solid, dealing in the now. I get it. He rises, rinses his cup in the sink, dries it with the cloth there and puts it away.

"Can I get those names?" he asks. "Of the men you've met?"

I hesitate, then give them to the detective. I scroll through my contacts, providing all the information I have on each of them. What choice do I have?

"I'll check this place out, okay?" he says, looking up from his notebook where he's been writing down the information. "And I'll keep looking for footage of that kid. If we find him, maybe he knows something. I'll look through Jack's phone and email records for anyone with the first name Elena."

I'll look here. I'll follow up this lead. I'll try to find this per-

son who may know something. All these winding roads to nowhere and nothing. The victim waits and waits and waits some
more for answers that never seem to come. My hands ache and
I realize that I'm clenching them into hard fists. What would
Jack do? Would he just wait around, hoping that someone figured out what happened to me? I know better.

"Can I go with you?" I ask. "When you go to Morpheus?"

"Uh," Grayson says, moving toward the door. "That's not a
good idea. Let me focus on this. You just keep yourself safe. Go
to work. Go back to the Van Santens. Be low risk for a couple
of days, okay? No dating. Just not right now."

I don't even bother to suppress my eye roll. "Here—I'll come
closer so that you can give me a little pat and tell me not to worry
my pretty head over dangerous things."

The corners of his mouth turn up in a patient nonsmile.

"Poppy." He releases a long, slow sigh, glances down at his
phone. "Just let me do my job, okay?"

When he's gone, I'm alone with the boxes of Jack's life, the
vague, disconnected images of my dreams and nothing but questions.

11

At the office, a tide of phone calls and email carry me away from the chaos of my dreams, my life, the impossible tangle they've become; even the dread of what might be happening in my waking world recedes. I swim in the blissful mundane, so underrated. The slog of the day-to-day can bury you—until the worst thing happens. Then you'd get down on your knees and pray for it if you thought it would do any good. The pill I took is helping, too. That sense of dread I've had since my chat with Grayson has receded all but completely.

My mother calls a couple of times, no doubt alerted to my recent troubles by Layla. Ben knows better than to put her through.

Mrs. Jackson, so sorry, she's in a meeting. Yes—still.

But when she starts texting—Poppy. I'm your mother. You can't avoid me forever—I have no choice but to call her back.

"Everything's fine, Mom," I say by way of greeting. As I get up and close my door, Ben casts me a knowing eye roll.

"That's what you always say," she says. "Just like your father always said. Everything's fine."

Her ancient cat mewls in the background, no doubt making furry figure eights around her legs. I can see the kitchen, sunlight streaming in the back window, the tall oak trees that dominate the yard. The house where I grew up, and where she still lives, is her personal art project, always some part of it under construction, being painted, wallpapered, renovated. It's a symptom of her chronic dissatisfaction; she can never just let anything be.

"Tell me."

I give her an abridged version since I have no choice.

"Anyway, it's fine," I conclude. "There was no one in the apartment after all. And I haven't been sleeping well. So."

"So."

"So. It's probably just that. Sleep deprivation."

It sounds like the lie that it is. There's a noise she makes, a kind of disbelieving grunt, followed by a pregnant silence. I have learned not to rush to fill this empty place, to clamor in with more words of explanation. So, I wait. Then:

"Do you want me to come—?"

"No," I interrupt, way too quickly, too adamantly.

"Okay, *okay*," she says, sounding injured.

I soften. "Mom. I'm okay. I'll tell you if I need you. I promise."

A sniff, then: "I suppose if Layla's hiring someone, there's not much point anyway."

Layla and my mother have a relationship of sorts, one forged during our childhood when Layla's own mother was absent in many ways—a broken and abused woman who never could rally herself, even for her children. Layla spent a significant amount of time with us. *She's there, you know. Sybil's a piece of work, but she's been there, even for me.* It was true—rides to the mall, concert chaperone, in the audience at all sporting events, plays and dance recitals. My mother—vain, passive-aggressive, almost Machiavellian in her manipulations—was always there.

"Layla's not hiring *anyone*," I say.

"Okay, well," she says, knowing she hit her mark. "What do I know? I'm just the mother."

"Mom."

"I just can't handle another one of those—" she pauses dramatically, searching for the right word "—episodes. It was so *frightening* for me, Poppy."

Guilt and shame duke it out in my chest. Luckily, I don't have to answer because it sends her off on a tangent about a friend of hers whose daughter *also* had a nervous breakdown. I pull the phone away from my ear and go back to the slew of unanswered email. Mom goes on, her voice falling and rising. I pick up on stray words—mental hospital, medication, suicide watch—make intermittent *I'm listening* noises.

I delete a bunch of junk mail, click, click, click. There's an email from my pharmacy, saying that the refill I've already picked up is ready. It reminds me that I wanted to do some research on sleeping medication side effects, and what to expect when lowering the dosage, which I've promised myself I'm going to do. Starting tonight. So, I enter the name of my meds into the search engine bar and start scrolling through listings.

Vivid nightmares. Sleepwalking. Sleep-driving. Sleep-*eating*—really? Withdrawal. Anxiety. Depression. There is a slew of Reddit confessionals. Blogs. Newspaper articles from around the world, extolling the dangers of sleeping pill use, and the difficulties people have getting off.

"That's terrible, Mom," I say.

It's a fair bet that whatever she's saying *is* terrible—some perceived wrong, or gossip about her neighbors, some maudlin memory of my father. From an article on my screen, an exhausted middle-aged woman looks back at me, her caption: "Better to never go on them at all than try to get off. It's been a nightmare."

The tired, haggard face floats. She looks so exhausted, so cored out—exactly how I feel. I type in: mixing prescription pills, and start scrolling through the articles there. Addiction. Confusion. Unusual behavior. Overdose. Coma. Brain damage. Death.

I wind up on a rehab site, clicking through pictures of a tree-shaded building, nature trails, smiling faces. *Are you ready to start your new sober life today? We can help.*

"You're not even listening to me," my mom says finally, grabbing my attention.

"I am," I lie. "Of course I am."

"You can come home, you know," she says. "Whenever you want."

I find myself smiling. I've always known that, that I can go home. That my mom will tuck me in and make some amazing chicken soup. I could curl up in my old bed and stay there for as long as I needed to. I'll never hear the end of it, but I can go home. That's not what I want.

"Thanks, Mom."

"You should listen to Layla," my mother says. "She's a sensible girl." *Unlike you*, she doesn't say and doesn't have to—*flighty, head-in-the-clouds.* What was the word I heard her use that night? *Fragile.* Layla and I need to have a conversation about running her mouth off—especially to my mother.

"I have to go," I say. "Sorry. Love you. Bye."

"Poppy," she says. Something in her tone stops me from ending the call. "Honey, you don't sound like yourself."

I'm not myself, I want to say. I've never been further from the person I used to be.

"I'm fine," I say instead. "Really."

There's that pregnant silence, so full of meaning between mothers and daughters.

Then: "Remember, sweetie, no one knows you better than your mother does. Like it or not."

After we end the call, the phone rings again mere seconds later; I answer without looking at the screen.

"What *is it*, Mom?"

There's a pause, then a throat clearing.

"Poppy?" A male voice—deep, familiar.

"Oh," I say. "I'm sorry."

"I didn't think you'd answer." A quick glance at the caller ID reveals a number I don't recognize.

"It's Noah," he says in the awkward pause that follows.

A rush of recognition, embarrassment. "Noah," I repeat, biting back the urge to apologize again. I remember my conversation with Grayson, how I turned over the names and phone numbers of the people I've dated. Has Grayson been in touch? Is that why Noah's calling? How embarrassing for both of us.

Ben's at the closed glass door, pointing at his wrist, which doesn't have a watch on it. But I get his point. My next appointment.

"This is not the way it works, right?" Noah says when I stay silent. He laughs a little. I like the sound of it, easy, throaty. "When someone doesn't return your calls these days, you're supposed to just drift away. Ghosting—that's what they call it now, right?"

"Um," I say stupidly.

"You're not ready for anything real—you said so in your text. Which I also get. And you didn't answer my last text. So, I should just disappear. I just…can't stop thinking about you."

I don't say anything, feel frozen. Grayson and I were just talking about this, about him. *No one aggressive?* he'd asked. *Calling and calling? Showing up?* Does this qualify?

"Too stalker?" he says into my silence.

"No," I say. My heart's fluttering a little. "Unless you *are*. Stalking me?"

"Uh—"

"Are you?"

"What? Stalking you? *No*." He sounds mortified.

The man on the subway, the cracked picture of me and Jack, that drooping orchid blossom. The images flash rapid-fire.

"Did you recently send me flowers?"

Another pause where I think he may have hung up.

"Did someone send you flowers?" he asks.

I think about Noah, what he looked like. He *was* a big guy, muscles lean and developed from his work as a sculptor. I remember how he looked, lying there with his arms folded behind his head. But, no, he wasn't hulking like the man I'd seen—or thought I saw. Noah and I had lain in bed and talked about people we'd lost. When he left his last message, he said he felt a connection. If I'm honest, I felt it, too. But I wasn't looking for a connection, that wasn't the point of my newfound "dating" life. I was looking for an escape, a doorway *out* of feeling.

"My life is a little complicated right now." It sounds short, dismissive.

He lets out a breath. "Life's always complicated, isn't it?"

Not *this* complicated, I want to tell him. "I guess you're right," I say instead. "But—"

"How about just one more drink? Tonight?"

Grayson's warning bangs around my head: *Be low risk for a couple of days, okay?* Somehow in my memory it takes on the tone of a dare. You're not my daddy, Detective Grayson.

"Have you heard of place called Morpheus?" I ask.

Another pause.

"A club, right?" he answers finally. "On the Lower East Side."

"Yeah," I say. "Are you up for it?"

It's quiet again. A nightclub probably wasn't what he had in mind.

"Have you been there before?" he asks. His voice is masculine without being deep; there's something soothing about it.

"No," I say, then add: "I don't think so."

He's going to make some excuse, beg off.

Then, "Sure," he says. "Why not?"

12

My dad had this shed in the backyard, big enough for his desk, his chair, shelves of engineering texts, stacks of magazines, boxes of I don't even know what. My mother called it "The Junkyard" because it was a maze of broken things scattered and stacked throughout the space—old computers, ancient phones and appliances, boxes of wires, coaxial cables, parts of power tools.

Tucked into the far corner, completely hidden from view, was a cot. My mother ruled the house—a spotless showroom of chintz and floral patterns, breezy draperies, plush carpets—but the dank and musty space, located at the end of a path through the trees belonged to my father and me. I used to lie on the cot and read, the bare rafters water-stained above me, my dad click-clacking on his keyboard, or leafing through the pages of some text. He was an aeronautical engineer who dreamed of building a robot.

That dusty, dangerously cluttered old hut was hot in summer, freezing in winter. But there with my dad—reading, doing homework, talking about his robot, our conversation ebbing and flowing, rain sometimes leaking through the roof into a metal pot kept there for just that purpose—it was the favorite space of my childhood. Though my princess bedroom with its pink walls, four-poster bed, window seat, walls of books, toys, stuffed animals and dolls was the envy of all my friends, I never felt quite as if I could *be* there.

That shed, my dad. They were my first subjects as a photographer. Him with his head bent over his notebooks, the way the light shone in through the milky window, him dozing with a robotics text on his lap, a tilting pile of broken parts. He let me take pictures of him in any state, ignoring me completely, like all the best subjects. My mother wouldn't let me near her with my camera.

Layla was my other favorite subject. She preened and vamped before my lens, loving every minute. But she was the most beautiful—as are we all—when she forgot about the camera. When she caught the photo bug, too, we learned together, my dad picking up the tab for classes at the local community college, renting darkroom time for us and shuttling us back and forth. Then I was *her* favorite subject.

The girl I saw in the mirror was awkward—her nose too long, too many freckles, eyes too close together—something just off enough to never be quite pretty. Too tall. Shoulders too hunched. *Stop slouching, Poppy!* Flat-chested, breakout on my chin.

I never recognized the person Layla saw through her lens, the one who turned up in the darkroom, dreamily appearing in a chemical bath. Someone lithe and dark, with sparkling blue eyes—lying in the grass, dreamy, or staring directly at the lens—serious or teasing, laughing or thoughtful.

Maybe you can tell how someone feels about you by the image they capture, the moment they choose to snap the shutter. Layla loved me and thought I was beautiful, and so in her images, I was. Likewise, Jack's photos.

The photos I thumbed through this morning—the night we

met, pictures he took of me in Riverside Park that afternoon he met me outside the gallery, a picture he snapped while I was reading, lounging on his bed after making love—that was a woman I'm sure only existed for him, with him. Our faces, our body language, the changing light of a room, every second is different than the one before or after. The photographer chooses one among the infinite. It's both a lie, a trick of light, and an irrefutable truth.

These thoughts tumble, mingling with Mac's words about how maybe all we ever know of each other is a sliver, a fraction of the real person.

"I need my space," I say to Layla, who finally caught me on the phone. "I can't stay with you forever, Layla. You have a life, a family."

"Not *forever*," she says. "Just until we get this all figured out. And you *are* my family."

It's true; Layla couldn't be more my sister if we were biologically related.

"I'll think about it." But I'm not going back there tonight. "And, hey, can you not call my mother and tell her everything about my life?"

"I didn't!" Her voice comes up an octave in a mockery of innocence. Then, "Well—*she* called me. Said she couldn't reach you."

"Okay, regardless of who called who, she doesn't need to know everything. And—PS—I am not hiring that security firm."

There's a pause on the line where I think I've lost her. I am still in front of my computer, so on a whim I enter the name *Elena* into the search bar. A character from a television show, an animated heroine, a listing on a baby name sight. A Spanish variation of Helen, the name means bright, shining light.

"Poppy." Layla's voice snaps me back. I hate that tone, the "be reasonable" tone.

"Layla." I try to mimic it back for her, but she's the undisputed master of the mom voice. "This is not a discussion."

Another pause, then an annoyed "Fine. So, what *are* you going to do?"

Ben, who has been hovering outside the door, finally pushes it open. "Your one o'clock is *here*. Like, in the lobby."

"Gotta go," I say. "Call you later."

"Setting a place for you at the dinner table," she says, her voice growing tinny as I move the phone away from my ear. "Carmelo's picking you up at the office."

I end the call without commenting. Sink my head into my hands. What is the line between caring and controlling? What is the line between being foolish and stubborn, and being independent, take-charge? I try to tell Izzy when she longs for her imagined adulthood full of limitless freedoms that it's not all it's cracked up to be. Hang on to being the beloved, pampered kid that you are. In your grown-up life, there will be more questions than answers.

Poor Ben looks like he's about to lose it.

"I need five minutes," I tell him, stepping out of my office finally. "Then bring her into the conference room."

Fatigue tugs as I head down the hall. I am already thinking about that vial of pills. Is it too soon to take something else? Am I ready to start my new sober life? Uh, no. Clearly not.

At the head of the long table, I open the file and read through the résumé there—a student at Parsons School of Design, a young woman looking for an internship. We've had a lot of students cycle through the agency, aspiring photographers, graphic artists, some business majors, looking for college credit and experience. It was a program Jack instituted and loved, believing that all aspiring artists needed to understand the business side of being a creative, and all people looking to be in the arts business needed to understand the creative personality. Ben was one of Jack's picks; Maura was, too. Both started working for us when they were still in school and were offered jobs when they graduated.

I scan through the information in front of me, skim predictably glowing letters of reference. After a few minutes, the door opens and a slim girl walks through, closes it behind her with a click. I take a deep breath, put on a smile.

When I stand to offer my hand, she takes it shyly.

"I'm Poppy Lang," I say. "Welcome."

Her hand is cold, limp, which immediately puts me off. Her stare is strangely intense. Eyes dark pools in a fine landscape of caramel skin, set off by a mane of black hair wild around her face, cascading over her shoulders.

She looks familiar. Where have I seen her before? She doesn't say anything; maybe she's nervous.

I motion for her to take a seat, which she does, keeping those eyes on me. Okay. Weird. My prediction: this is going to be a short interview that doesn't result in a callback. Silent and sullen are not good qualities in an agent. I glance through her class schedule, looking for some common ground.

"Ah, I see you have Photography and Cinema with George Pitts," I say. "He was one of my favorite professors."

Silence.

When I look up, there's a kind of stutter to the room, a hard wobble. The lights above issue an unpleasant buzz. The girl before me is covered in blood. Her face is bruised and swollen, a thick, viscous line of blood dripping from her mouth.

"I knew your husband," she says, her Latino accent thick.

When she smiles, three of her teeth are missing.

Lashed to the chair, a scream swollen and lodged in my throat, I roll back in fear and hit the wall hard behind me. Time, the room around me, pulls long, twists.

"*This* is what he did to me," she says, leaning closer to me. I'm pinned to my seat.

I shake my head. "No." Just a croak, barely a word at all.

"Oh, yes," she says. She rises. "You know it's true."

Then she's crawling across the table like a panther, her eyes filled with malice, her face twisted and hideous with rage. I am paralyzed, breathless. Please.

There's a hard knock on the door then. Another, louder. I want to scream but no sound comes. Then that hard stutter, like someone flipping the lights on and off. The knock comes again, the door swings open and Ben steps through. He stops in his tracks, his polite smile dropping.

"Poppy," he says. His brow creases into a worried frown. "Are you ready? For Ellen Rausch?"

There's no beaten, bloodied girl on the conference table. I am alone, a file open in front of me, the surface gleaming, empty.

I swallow hard, try to orient myself. The room tilts, but I hold on. A young woman stands behind Ben. She's pretty and bouncy, looking past him toward me with a wide smile. *Get a grip, Poppy. For fuck's sake, pull yourself together.*

"You okay?" Ben asks, moving in a little and shutting the door a bit behind him. Poor Ben, what must he think of me?

"Yes," I say, straightening up, slowing my breathing. "Of course. Send her in."

I plaster on a smile, rise unsteadily.

"Mrs. Lang," says the impossibly young girl as she strides over to shake my hand. She's slim, dark-skinned with hazel eyes and an exuberant puff of inky curls. The fresh, high energy of youthful ambition comes off her like fairy dust. "I'm so excited to be here."

"Welcome, Ellen," I say, sheer, white-knuckled willpower keeping that smile in place. There's a siren in the back of my head. *What's wrong with me?*

The world is spinning as we talk about her classes, her passion for photography, her high GPA and her desire to learn about the business side of the industry. On another day, I would have taken pleasure in chatting with someone so young and bright. Jack would have loved her, too, her sincerity, her obvious enthusiasm.

But I keep flashing on the bleeding girl, hearing her words: *I knew your husband.*

I hope Ellen Rausch doesn't notice my hands are shaking, that I don't even want to look at her.

13

Dr. Nash squeezes me in that afternoon. I hate to leave the office again; it looks bad for me to be gone so often.

"I'm sorry," I tell Ben, packing up my laptop. Pictures of Layla and Mac, Jack, the kids, smile up at me from my desk, faces from another time in my life when things were normal and I was happy. Those times—weekends at Mac and Layla's Adirondack house, afternoons in Central Park with the kids, days at Rockaway Beach—it's another planet, a home world destroyed, no way back.

"Don't worry." Ben moves in close, lowers his voice and puts a hand on my shoulder. "Everyone gets it, Poppy. I promise. You've been through hell and we have it covered."

He pulls me into a hug, and I hold on, grateful for him. Then I hustle out before I lose my grip completely.

The truth is, no one really understands grief, or mental illness (that's what this is, right?)—not unless they've grappled with these things personally. A year ago, I'm not sure I would have understood, either. I wouldn't have understood how grief takes the floor out from under you. Or how the world can alter itself until it's unrecognizable. *I'm sorry, Jack. I wish I was stronger than this.*

As for our agency—his agency—I know that when no one is at the helm, the ship veers off course. I should be doing a better job for him, take better care of this thing we built together. But really, what choice is there? I am obviously losing my mind.

On the street, every man looks like an assailant. Even the cabbie's apathetic silence seems ominous as we snake uptown, traffic heavy, horns bleating. It's hot again, tricky October edging toward winter but still clinging to summer. Rolling down the window lets in more hot air, and the city stench.

Finally, in the embrace of Dr. Nash's office, I feel myself start to calm. I am soothed by the cool, bright space, the nature photographs—a vista of the Sangre de Cristo Mountains in New Mexico, a great blue heron balancing on one slim leg in the Florida shoals, a house nestled in woods by a lake. My breathing comes easier; shoulders drop their tension. I tell her about the man on street, the orchid, my wild dreams, and finally about the bizarre event in the conference room. I can hardly look at her when I'm done. It all sounds so crazy. She's definitely going to have me committed, right?

"Well, first thing," she says gently. I look up at her. She's concerned but not shocked. "We'll return to the original dosage on your sleeping pills to make sure you get the rest you need. Poppy, you look exhausted. That's not helping, of course."

Her blue eyes are amplified by the green frames of her glasses. I still don't tell her that I have been taking some creative mixture of Layla's pills and mine, sleeping pills, antianxiety meds. That I'm not sure how many I've been taking. Not to mention the alcohol last night. Wine. Vodka. I don't tell her that I passed out in the tub. Sins of omission.

"What's happening to me? Am I—hallucinating?"

"I don't think so," she says thoughtfully. "When the brain is sleep-deprived, it takes what we call *microsleeps*. In your case, you're working through a lot. We've lowered the dosage on your sleeping pills, maybe causing you to remember more of your dreams. So your brain is getting less rest. I think your stress is manifesting itself in the form of these nightmares."

I take in and release a deep breath.

"These events might seem like hallucinations, but they're more like dreams. You know the types of dreams you have when you're just drifting off—when you're falling, or something leaps at you from the dark. The state is called hypnagogia, the transitional phase between sleep and wakefulness, or between wakefulness and sleep. The sensations there—be they visual, olfactory, auditory—are often quite vivid. I suspect that's what you're experiencing."

I don't argue. But she was *there*, that woman. The way the blood pooled on the table in front of her, the purple-black bruises on her swollen skin, that throaty voice. It was so real. My heart starts to race again at the thought of her.

"So, I think if we can get you a couple nights of solid sleep, we'll be in a better place."

Again, I almost come clean about what I'm doing. But instead I promise myself that I'll toss all the other pills and only take exactly what she's prescribing now. I'm not lying exactly. I'm just not telling Dr. Nash the whole truth. Like I'm an addict trying to hide how bad my habit has become. Maybe that's what I am. But I can get a grip on this. I know I can.

"The fact that you couldn't move this afternoon tells me the REM atonia had set in, the paralysis that one experiences in a dream state, accomplished through inhibition of the motor neurons."

"English."

"The body is almost completely immobilized during sleep, to prevent you from acting out your dreams. That's why I believe you were dreaming, not hallucinating."

I flash on the image again. *In the Arms of Morpheus*—the whispering angel, the prone woman in red.

I wasn't sleeping, I want to say. But maybe I was. The truth is that I'm not sure.

Outside the window, clouds drift, misty slivers of white in the bright blue. A plane, distant and tiny, zips across the sky, leaving a trail of white. As a kid, the sight of an aircraft filled me with wistful longing. Who were those people jetting off to exotic locales, I used to wonder, living different lives, and *when* would I be one of them? I have that feeling now, wishing that there was a plane that could take me away from whatever is happening to me.

"On the train the other day, when you felt like you were back in your bedroom. I am guessing that was a hypnagogic state. And today, as well, with the woman in your conference room."

The hard stutter, the startle; the experience *was* like those twilight dreams. But when did my dreams go rogue, invading my reality?

"So how do I know what's a dream and what's real?"

"How do any of us know?" Dr. Nash peers at me over her glasses, gives me a smile.

I laugh a little, though it's mirthless. She's being philosophical.

"I *used* to know," I say. "Before Jack died, before my breakdown. There was never anything like this."

She tucks a strand of her silver-blond bob behind her ear, leans forward.

"We know why you keep going back to that morning before Jack died—on the train, frequently in your dreams, in our conversations here. You've identified that as the moment where you could have effected change. You revisit it subconsciously to reconcile, to accept that the past cannot be altered. But this woman. What did she mean to you?"

"Nothing," I say. "I've never seen her before."

Dr. Nash watches me. "Nothing."

I dig into my memory, but there's nothing.

"The woman's name on the matchbook in your dream from last night. Elena, was it?" presses Dr. Nash.

Last night, this morning, asleep, awake—it's all running together.

"That's right."

"Elena is a Spanish name," says Dr. Nash. "The young intern whose résumé you were reading, her name was Ellen."

I try to remember what I was thinking about, feeling, while reviewing the documents in the conference room. Was the dream in my mind, that name knocking around my head? But, no, I was present, awake, just reviewing the documents in front of me. Trying, in fact, to forget everything else. But—

"Just before my meeting, I searched the name on the internet."

"Okay."

"You think the intern's name—Ellen—triggered that dream, or whatever it was?" I ask.

"Not necessarily," says the doctor, pushing up her glasses. "I think you may have dozed off—or *microslept*—and the detail of that name wove itself in, the way things do in our dreams. Your husband's murder is unsolved—he was beaten as you say this woman was—there are days missing from your memory. Those are dark mysteries at the center of your life. It makes a kind of sense, that this beaten, bloody woman says she knows your husband."

"So, scenes from my nightmares are weaving into these hypnagogic states?"

She leans back in her chair and regards me.

"'All that we see or seem is but a dream within a dream.'"

"Edgar Allan Poe," I say. "Very literary."

Dr. Nash smiles, kindness and empathy radiating. "I'm not being flip, Poppy. I am just saying that the mind, our dreams can be labyrinthine. If we follow those paths, no matter how twisty and dark, sometimes we find answers about ourselves."

It's the exact opposite of Detective Grayson's position. *They never make sense. They're not real.*

I have a headache, a bad one. We fill the hour with more talk about my dreams that frankly leads nowhere. Jack thought psychotherapy was a pseudoscience. *There's nothing wrong with most people that can't be cured by a few hours in nature, in silence.* Maybe he was right.

"What about the hooded man?" she asks. "Have you seen him again?"

"He's real." I feel the need to assert this. I break office rules and take the phone from my bag, pull up the picture and hand it to her. She squints at it.

"I don't doubt that you saw *someone*," she says handing it back. "But—"

She pauses a second, measuring her words. "I just think it's notable that both times you've seen him, *you* pursued *him*. Most women, when confronted in that way, would run in the other direction, or call the police. But both times you chased after him."

I don't know what to say. She's right.

"Both events, in the telling, seem very dreamlike. He's there, you chase, he slips away. No one else sees him. Even in the picture, yes, there's a man, but he's one in a crowd of other people. Just standing there."

"You don't think there's a hooded man." There's a swelling of shame, uncertainty.

"I didn't say that," she says easily. "I'm just asking you to think about it—when it happened, how you were feeling at the time. What did you feel when you were chasing him?"

"Just this—" I search for the right word "—this *urgency* to see his face."

"And when he got away?"

"Angry," I say. "So angry, so frustrated. And after that, just exhausted."

She's quiet a moment, letting the words settle.

"It's hard work chasing someone you can't catch," she says finally. "Someone who is always just out of reach."

I know what she's implying, but why bother asserting again that he was real? The more you must assert your reality, the more unstable you seem.

"Am I going to remember those lost days? Are they going to come back?"

"As your psyche grows stronger, as you recover from the post-traumatic stress symptoms and grief, those days may come back. You might get fragments, images, bits and pieces in your dreams. Or it could all come back in a rush."

A bird alights on the windowsill, feathers shiny black, then flaps away.

"I have a suggestion," she says. "Why don't you take some time off, Poppy? Rest up, stay with your friends or go visit your mother. Some time away can make a world of difference when we're healing."

It's solid advice, coming from all directions. Layla wants me to move in with her. Grayson wants me to be "low risk." Ben tells me he can handle the office, that I should just take a few days off. I could do that, go back to that CPW womb, let Grayson do his job. I could let Layla and Mac hire that firm. It's tempting, so tempting. But it also scares the hell out of me. If I stop moving, the weight of everything will crush me. I might never get up again. And Jack will just keep getting further and further away.

I make a promise to myself. I'll go back to the prescribed sleeping pill dosage and stay on it. Normalize. Then I'll work on getting off it altogether. And no alcohol. No other pills.

"That's a good idea," I say with a smile. "I'll think about it."

Leaving Dr. Nash's office, the thought of going back to my dark and quiet apartment, all those open boxes with Jack's name scrawled on them staring at me, presses down on me, a terrible weight. I can't do it. I can't go to Layla's. There are so many questions, such an ache at the base of my skull, too many things I can't remember. Something my mom said has stayed with me. *No one knows you better than your mother.*

I get on the 1 train and take it uptown.

14

I have been riding this train all my life, watching. All those lives crowded together—mothers and students, businessmen and panhandlers, club kids, thugs. The rich, the poor, the hustling, the ground down, the old, the fresh, all swaying to a rhythm of a train taking them in the same direction to different destinations. On the way uptown, I do something I haven't done in a while—I take out my phone and start snapping pictures. The reflection in the window of a man reading his newspaper, a young mother with a child sleeping on her chest, a girl with a quivering little dog in her bag.

The details, the moments, leap out at me. A girl wearing red mittens, an older woman clutching a rosary, her eyes closed, a middle-aged man reading a novel, wearing a peaceful smile. Just moments for them, one they'll likely forget before they go to sleep tonight. But that moment, captured on film, will last an eternity. The photographer is a thief, stealing time.

At 116th Street, Columbia University, there's a big shift, lots of people getting off, others crushing on. I sit in the farthest seat, pushed against the metal wall by a large man, a redhead in a suit. I don't mind. I'm ensconced, like a wildlife photographer hiding in a blind, undetected.

When the train hits an elevated stop at 125th Street, I send a text.

Mind if I come by? I've been thinking about you.

The response comes right away: Of course. You're on my mind every day. When do you want to come?

Now?

I'll be here.

The train rumbles and I feel its rocking lull as people come and go, a river, life flowing around me. I get to my feet quickly, accidentally jostling the guy next to me, who has started to snore.

"Sorry," he grumbles, drifting off again. His head tilts, mouth gapes. I watch him a moment, envying whatever sense of security he possesses that allows him to just fall asleep on a city train.

I can't afford to have Morpheus start whispering in my ear again.

The train is a stop-and-go crawl. The farther uptown it gets, the more it empties out.

My sleepy seatmate gets off at Dyckman and I'm alone in the car, still standing, holding on to the pole as the train bucks and moves. Then it starts to slow between stations, the windows only looking out onto black tunnel walls. When it comes to a full stop, the car lights flicker. Darkness, then light, then dark again.

When the lights come back up, I see him through the glass.

He stands legs spread and arms akimbo on the far end of the other car. The hooded man. My heart squeezes, adrenaline surging. My body, every muscle, nerve and instinct demand that I move away.

Then something else washes up: anger, white-hot and irratio-
nal. Who is he? Instead of moving in the other direction as good
sense dictates, I break into a run toward him, burst through the
doors between the two cars.

"Hey," I call out as the door clangs shut behind me.

He stands a moment, then simply turns and walks away, ef-
fortlessly fast, long legs striding. He's through the doors before
I am halfway across the car. I keep my eyes locked on him; he's
not going to get away this time.

I pass an old woman who eyes me with the suspicion of a lifelong city dweller; a young man, headphones on, has dark eyes
on me, too, wears a kind of smirk.

"Did you see that guy?" I ask as I pass quickly.

He just shrugs, looks away with a sullen *tsk* of his tongue.
I keep going, my breath ragged, slam through another set of
doors, leaving the unhelpful strangers behind.

What am I doing?

The dark figure glides, a wraith, heading toward the front of
the train. With a hard jostle the train starts moving again; I'm
knocked against the seats, almost losing my balance. But I re-
gain my footing, keep moving through the cars.

He's always just ahead of me, doors crashing closed behind
him. The train seems to stretch and bend, as though there's no
end to it, like it would just keep going, the hooded man always
just ahead of me.

The train pulls into the station as I reach the final car, the
doors to the platform sliding open. And he's gone. If he has exited, I don't see where. I step out onto the platform. Other than
a few tired commuters—the woman I saw dozing, the young
man with his headphones and backpack—there's no one in sight.
The kid looks back at me, shrugs again, lifting his palms.

I go after him, catch his denim-clad arm. He turns, annoyed,
pulls roughly away.

"Did you see him?" I ask. "The man in the hood."

"What's your problem? Are you high?" he says, nasty, disdainful. "I didn't see anyone. Just you, running."

The chime. Stand clear of the closing doors.

"This your stop?" he asks. "Get back on the train."

His blank coldness, the face of an uncaring stranger—it pushes me back. This city, this world—it can be so hard, so unforgiving. I swallow a rush of sadness, of shame, slip through the doors before they close, my hands shaking. I walk back through the train as it moves out, scanning the platform. He's nowhere. I walk the whole length of the train before the next stop.

If he was ever here, he's gone. I can't stop it, the flood of tears. I lean against the cool metal and let myself weep, alone in the rattling car.

By the time the train reaches 242nd Street in Riverdale, I'm still quaking inside like a prey animal—even though I was the one doing the chasing. My blouse beneath my jacket is sticky with sweat.

I exit the train onto the elevated platform and descend to the street, walking quickly, looking over my shoulder. The sky is ash and the air grown frigid, the streets and low buildings a line drawing of black and gray. Van Cortlandt Park, in wild contrast, is an autumnal watercolor behind me as I jog up a flight of concrete stairs, pass a coffee shop, a dry cleaner, a café—finally coming to the wooded street where Jack grew up. When the house comes into view, his mother, Sarah, is standing at the door, looking out for me.

She descends the steps as I open the gate. She takes one look at me, tilts her head in empathy and opens her arms. I practically run to her, let myself be enfolded in her soft embrace.

"Come inside," she says gently, leading me into the warmth of her living room.

It's a shrine to him, to them, the men she's lost. Everywhere my eyes rest, there's a picture of one or both, or photographs taken by Jack. There are many of me, as well—our wedding day, shots from our honeymoon, Christmases we spent together, a selfie Sarah and I took during a weekend we spent at the beach. She's the rare mother-in-law who also becomes a friend, a friend who, in my grief, I've sorely neglected.

Jack and I spent so much time in this house together—cooking with Sarah, decorating her Christmas tree, taking care of her after minor surgery a few years back. But today I feel like a stranger, my life unrecognizable from what it was when Jack was alive, this place crowded with memories of another self.

The room is orderly—magazines fanned out on the low cocktail table, soft navy couches accented with gray pillows and soft throws, Staffordshire dogs on the fireplace, an oil of an Amsterdam canal by the shelves where books are arranged tidily by size. I, in contrast, am shattered, carrying around the broken pieces of myself, my reality.

"I've been out of touch," I begin weakly.

But she lifts a palm. "It's okay," she says. "You don't have to explain. I know where you are right now, Poppy. I get it."

A copy of the photo that was smashed on my hallway floor sits intact on her mantel in a simple white frame. Her kindness soothes me. She locked the door behind us, and I feel safe here with her. Whoever it is out there; he can't get in here.

"It's just good to see you today," she says. "I'm glad you came."

The ice water she brought me goes down quickly. I'm surprised at how dehydrated I feel, how fast I drain the glass. She gets up to fetch me another, her eyes on me in concern.

"How are you doing with it?" I ask when she comes back.

Something does battle on her face, a sad arch of the eyebrows, a hard press in her mouth. She wears a soft pink wrap around her narrow shoulders, pulls it tight across her middle. Finally, she offers a crooked, mirthless smile.

"Let's just say I'm doing the work. Moving away from anger and toward acceptance."

I know the journey we the grieving must take. I've just lost my way.

"I'm volunteering back at the hospital in the pediatric ward," she continues. She was a nurse in a small local doctor's office all her career, working while Jack was in school, home with him in the afternoons. "The night shift."

An identical snow globe to the one that sits on my desk is on her end table, a little house beneath trees. I pick it up, make the snow twirl, then put it back down.

"Because that's the hardest time."

"For everyone," she says. "Let's just say the work helps me keep it all in perspective. Reminds me that there's plenty of pain to go around. It keeps me from sinking too deeply into the quicksand of mine."

We sit a moment. Outside the trees sway and a bird chirps manically on a feeder close to the window. The city, that train, the hooded man feel a million miles away.

"I'm remembering things—I think," I say. "Maybe. From those lost days."

Sarah leans back in her chair, takes off her glasses. There's so much of Jack in her face, in the shape of her eyes, her high cheekbones. The same sandy curls. I look away, giving her the abridged version of my dreams, tell her what Detective Grayson told me in the park, about the hired killer. There's no reason to tell her about the hooded man; it will only scare her.

She seems to shrink before my eyes, rests her head on her hand.

"I'm so sorry, Sarah," I say, stopping. This is the reason I don't come here much. Her grief is possibly more profound than my own; it hurts to see that darker mirror of my pain.

"It's okay," she says quickly, opening herself back up. "The detective told me about the lead. It's hard to believe that people like that even exist."

We both sit for a moment, lost in our imaginings.

"He never seems to get anywhere with any of it, though, you know," she continues. Her voice tightens. "It's a year this month. We're still no closer to understanding."

A year—for most people it's a heartbeat, days rushing into weeks into months that pass in a blur. For the grieving, it's an eternity, life aborted, days dark and slogging.

"Jack talked to you, Sarah. You were as close a mother and son as I've known. Was there something wrong, anything bothering him that he couldn't share with me? Would anyone have wanted to—hurt him?"

I didn't even realize that this was my reason for coming. Now that some of my memories might be returning, I want more. Jack and I—we talked and talked about everything—our pasts, our careers, our friends, family, thoughts, dreams, philosophies. We were friends, best friends. But maybe Mac was right. Don't we only ever know facets of each other, like those strangers on the train, moments in time, slivers of self? I wouldn't have thought he'd keep things from me—never even considered it— but maybe.

"Poppy," she says, looking away. She picks up her glasses, cleans them on the bottom of her crisp pink-and-white-pinstriped shirt and puts them back on.

"It's not a betrayal to tell me," I press. "Not now."

She twists at a blond curl with long elegant fingers. She still wears her wedding ring. I wonder if she's noticed that I've removed mine. What would she think about my assignations, my newfound dating life?

"Please, Sarah."

"There was nothing," she says. "The detective came. He wanted to know the same thing. Maybe he seemed more distracted, more worried than usual. But when I asked him about it—"

She looks down at her hands.

"What did he say?"

"Honey," she says softly. "He was worried about *you*."

I draw in a sharp breath of surprise. "Me?"

"He was concerned that—"

My heart is hammering again.

"What? *Tell* me."

"He thought that you were drifting away from him. The miscarriages. He thought you blamed him, that on some level you believed he didn't really want children."

The miscarriages. There were two. I flash on the image of the sheet beneath me covered in blood. The second time, in the shower, I looked down to see the dark red water running down the drain. It was devastating, both times. She's right. It did put a strain on us, a big one.

"I didn't blame him," I say. But was that true? The sadness, the dark blanket that settled over me—it didn't seem to affect him in the same way. He seemed to blithely move on—*Honey, this happens. We'll keep trying*—while it dragged me down into despair.

"He said you two were spending more time apart," she says. "He wasn't sure how to reach you."

We were both working long hours at the agency. He was out more with Mac and Alvaro. I had been begging off some client dinners. Nothing dramatic, nothing so unusual. But maybe that's how it starts; maybe the fissures are tiny at first, then start to widen, deepen under the pressure of life. Before you know it there's a valley between you.

"He wondered if you might be—" she pauses, her cheeks flushing a little "—having an affair."

The words land hard, a sucker punch. I let the information sink in. Outside the sun dips, afternoon shifting to a purple gloaming.

"An affair. No," I breathe. "I wasn't."

She shakes her head, looks at me imploringly. "I *told* him that.

I know how much you loved him, Poppy. I could always see that in you. I see it in you still."

She rises from her chair and comes to sit beside me on the couch.

"He wasn't certain, just *worried*," she goes on. "He said there were times he couldn't reach you. That you said you were one place, and then it turned out you weren't there."

"What?" I say, confused. "No, that's not true."

I search my memory for what she might mean. When was that? When had he looked for me and not found me? How could he think I was having an affair? The distant echo of that dream voice: *Who is she, Jack? Who is she?*

"I believe you," says Sarah, her voice comforting. "He felt like maybe you didn't love working for the agency the way you thought you would. That you missed being behind the camera. He said that the two of you were fighting. A lot."

My throat is dry, constricting. "No," I say. "*He* was the one drifting. *He* missed the camera. Not me. I was the one holding on—to all of it."

The passion that comes up surprises me. "I might have said all the same things about him."

"*Every* couple has these moments in their life together," Sarah says, knowing and kind. "You two—you should have had the time to work through it all. But that was taken from you."

For the first time in a long time, I let myself think about our last year together. In the shock and grief of his death, everything that came before—the miscarriages, the frequent bickering, all of our problems—faded, cast in a gauzy patina. The truth is that it wasn't the best year of our marriage. If I thought he was drifting, and he thought I was, maybe we were drifting away from each other. What would have happened? Would we have found our way back to each other?

"When?" I ask. "When did he tell you this?"

"Just a few months—" she stops again, takes a breath and releases it "—before."

The grandfather clock in the corner chimes the quarter hour. The room is growing dark but neither of us gets up to turn on the lights. We just sit.

"If you thought I might be having an affair," I say, "why didn't you tell that to the police?"

She shifts away from me just slightly, bows her head. "I did," she nearly whispers. "I had to, of course, in case—it had something to do with what happened."

It cuts deep, just when I thought I couldn't hurt anymore. I hate that while she was grieving her son, she had to think this of me, that something *I* did might have led to his murder. That she had to tell that to the police. I remember how Grayson asked me repeatedly about affairs—Jack's, mine, how the police checked my email, my phone records. That Jack questioned my fidelity in the time before he died—it crushes me. How could he?

I reach for her hands. "I would *never.*"

For a second I'm back there, in the club, the stranger kissing me, feeling that heat. I push it away. If it happened, it happened after Jack was gone.

Sarah takes both my hands in hers. "The detective says that there was no evidence to support that, nothing to suggest that you were anything but happily married. Which of course I knew."

"What must you have thought of me, Sarah," I say.

She just smiles, puts a hand to the side of my face. "My husband and I—we had ups and downs, good times and bad. We were both guilty of mistakes, bad judgment."

She sighs, glances over at our wedding picture on the end table. "That's marriage—people make mistakes. We are all so flawed. If we want to stay together, we forgive and move on. I told Jack to figure it out and work it out. He loved you, sweetie, so much, and he wanted the things you wanted. He might have been afraid of fatherhood—his dad maybe wasn't the best role model, not around like fathers are today. But his father loved him. And Jack would have been a great dad."

"I'm sorry," I say, not even sure for what. She wraps me up in her arms.

"Don't be sorry, Poppy," she says. "Be well. Be strong. There's life on the other side of this for you. I'm sure of it."

I wish I could be as sure that was true.

My eyes fall on a photograph sitting on the end table beside me, one I haven't seen before. It's Jack, standing between Mac and Alvaro, an arm on each of them. He wears a wide grin, behind him, lights, a crowd. Mac stares straight at the camera, a typically reserved smile on his face. Alvaro is laughing, arms crossed in front of his chest. It's a good photo, lots of energy, movement, personality.

"I haven't seen this." The frame is heavy in my hand.

"Oh," she says, looking at it. "Alvaro came by, brought that as a gift."

I can't take my eyes off it, this piece of Jack, this moment captured. He looks light, happy.

"When was it taken?"

"Hmm," she says, her mouth pressed into a sad line. "He didn't say exactly when. One of their last nights out together."

There's something funny on Mac's face, is it tension, or just the normal discomfort some people have in front of the lens? It could just be the light or the angle.

"Who took the picture?"

"Oh, huh—don't know," she says. "Maybe they asked someone to take the shot?"

I look for clues in the frame. The shirt Jack wears, a black button-down with a faint pinstripe, was one I bought for him. When? A while back, too long ago to remember where or when. Just that he loved it. A drink in one hand, nearly empty. Judging by the color, it might have been bourbon.

Behind them—where are they? A club? A bar?—there's a mirrored wall, smoky and obscured. There it is—the shadow of the photographer, slim, small, camera raised. Just a ghost, though, a figure without a form or face, unidentifiable. Possibly female just judging by size, the dip at the waist.

"When did Alvaro come to see you?"

"A couple of weeks ago."

"You see him often?"

"Not at all," she says. "Not since the funeral. He said he was sorry, that he's been struggling with Jack's death. That he'd been losing himself in his work, trying to move past it."

"He stopped by my office the other day. I wasn't there. He wanted me to call but I haven't yet."

"People tend to reach out around the anniversary," says Sarah. She drifts off into thought a second. Then, "He said something strange that day. I didn't think anything about it at the time, but it rang back to me later."

"What was that?"

"Something like—Jack was one of the good guys. And he wished that he'd been a little less good."

"What does that mean?"

"I didn't ask," she says. "You know how sometimes it's only later that things seem odd."

Sarah looks so tired suddenly, like the conversation has drained her. How could it not?

"Maybe he meant that he was too trusting," she says, her voice growing softer. "I told him not to run so early in the park. Both of you, in the dark, alone."

She's gone to that dark place I visit so often myself, the spiral of what-ifs and if-onlys. It's a sad, dizzying spin into nothing. Now it's my turn to wrap her up. When I do, she holds on tight. I don't know how long we stay that way.

Outside Sarah's house, I'm surprised and not surprised to see Carmelo leaning on the hood of the Lincoln. I'd be mad about it if it wasn't such a huge relief, dreading as I was the walk through dark streets, the train back downtown. All the shadows around me have form, menace. My talk with Sarah hurts, her words like blows that have left bruises. I was looking for pieces of Jack, and now I have one. He thought we were drifting, that I might be having an affair. Our last year together and he wasn't happy; maybe I wasn't, either.

"How did she find me?" I ask Carmelo.

He shrugs, gives me a smirk. "I don't ask questions. Just do what I'm told, ya know?"

He swings the door wide and I slip into the warm leather embrace of the car, too exhausted even to feign resistance. My phone buzzes with a mind-reading text from Layla: Find My Friends, remember. I've been tracking you for a year. In case you're wondering how Carmelo found you.

You know that's weird, right? Like, really creepy and strange.

I don't think so. I track Izzy and Slade.

Not your KID, Layla.

We're having turkey burgers for dinner.

I stow the phone in my bag. "Carmelo, I'm going to need you to take me to my place, okay?"

He pauses a second. "Mrs. Van Santen's not going to be happy."

"If you take me back to Layla's, I'm just going to get a cab home from there."

I can see his worried eyes in the rearview mirror. "I'm not in the business of kidnapping," he says with a shrug.

"Good to know."

The world outside is velvety dark, run through with the twinkling lights of windows and cars and streetlamps. I'm still reeling from my visit with Sarah, the encounter on the train. But deep inside, there's something else, too.

There's a girl not hopped up on pills, not rattled by grief, not being stalked or disappearing into dreams. It's me—the person I used to be—strong and capable of managing her life. She's still in there. Despite the things my mother-in-law said, seeing Sarah reconnected me to the old me. She had a piece of Jack, but she had a piece of the old Poppy, too. Maybe healing is not just about finding him, but about finding myself.

Back in my apartment, instead of popping my one prescribed pill and crawling into bed—which I very obviously should do—I shower again, and make myself a big pot of coffee.

It's not time to sleep, Poppy. Jack's voice, loud and clear. *It's time to wake up.*

Fatigue tugs and pulls at me, but there's no way I'm going down that rabbit hole. I fight it back. I find my old prescription and Layla's mystery vial, then dump it all down the toilet. They float in the water like confetti—red, yellow, blue, white. With a tumble of elation and dread, I flush and watch the rainbow swirl disappear.

15

Noah's picking me up in a couple of hours and I am going to use that time to press into my lost days, keep searching through those boxes, get quiet and start digging into my memories. That nightclub on the Lower East Side—Morpheus. If I've been there before, I need to know that. If there are any more answers in the boxes—about Jack, about myself—I am going to find them tonight before I sleep.

Two cups of coffee and a few boxes later, fatigue gnawing and frustration growing, I am about to give up. Then, at the bottom of the last box, I see a flowery printed surface embossed with gold print. A tattered deck of tarot cards, a gift from our next-door neighbor Merlinda. She's another person I've let drift, holding on to her friendship too painful as the line to my old life was wrenched away from me.

My visit with Sarah has convinced me that I need to go back to go forward. If anyone had a front row seat to my life with Jack, it's the woman who lived next door to us for five years. I find my phone, ignoring Layla's angry texts and voice mails, and call Merlinda.

"Ah, my friend," she says by way of greeting. "It's been too long."

"I'm sorry," I say. It feels like all I do is apologize.

"I'll tell you what. This *building*?" she says. "Never the same since you left, lovely Poppy."

The sky outside my window has grown dark. Curled up on the couch, I cradle the phone, remembering the Hudson River views from our old apartment.

"That's sweet, Merlinda," I say.

Our old building seemed to mourn Jack; the neighbors were devastated by his murder, in their own backyard. I couldn't get out of there fast enough. Away from the memories of our happy, quirky life, away from his ghost at the mailbox, in the elevator, on the street. After the hospital, once I had my feet under me again, I left. I regret it now some days; maybe I should have stayed longer. Maybe I wouldn't have lost myself as I have.

"No, I mean it," she goes on, her voice deep and smoky. "And then when that other family moved out—what were their names? Who can remember? Still. It's just all the old crazy people now, the ones they can't get rid of. Like me!"

Her raspy laugh makes me smile until it devolves into coughing. I wait, listen with mild alarm, as she walks away from the phone, then returns.

"Merlinda? You okay?"

"Fine," she says finally. "Never mind about me. How *are you*, sweetie?"

There's that tone. From anyone else, it makes me cringe. It's the posttragedy prying. The deep, meaningful looks, the heavy sad voices. The stare that tries to get underneath the facade you're working very hard to present. But from Merlinda, I can handle it—because she's so well-meaning, so purely good.

"You know. Good days and bad." I usually put a better face

on, but with Merlinda I don't bother. She sees all, the great Merlinda. We were more than neighbors; we were—are—friends.

She draws a deep breath and releases it.

"Yes," she says. "I understand. Poppy, my dear, I dreamed about you last night."

More dreams. Just what I need. This one from the resident psychic-slash-fortune-teller-slash-hypnotist-slash-tarot-card-reader.

"You were in a maze," she says. "Walking and walking, trying to find a way out."

Sounds about right.

Merlinda came to our New Year's Eve party, the last one we had before Jack died. By popular request, she'd given tarot card readings. We turned the dining room lights down low, lit some candles. Holding court in a wild green-and-orange muumuu, her dyed red hair wrapped in a sequined scarf, Merlinda played her role to perfection—predicting love and success, peace and joyful surprises for everyone who sat with her at our dining room table. Even Alvaro, silent cynic, spent some time with her, deep in conversation.

"What did she tell you?" Jack asked Alvaro when he finally broke away from her.

"You know—" Alvaro said, after taking a deep swallow of the beer Jack handed him. "Fame, fortune, women falling at my feet. The woman's got a gift."

He was talking to Jack but he had his eyes on me. Always. That guy was *always* looking at me in a way I didn't quite understand, like I was a problem he just couldn't solve.

"What about you, Poppy?" Alvaro asked. "What's your future?"

His gaze, his question made me uncomfortable, but I smiled anyway.

"I'll let you know," I said. "I'm up next."

Merlinda was waving for me to join her, and I did, slipping into the chair beside her at the table.

"What do you want from the year ahead, pretty Poppy?" she asked. She put both her warm hands over mine. I looked at the ropy veins, her thin fingers heavy with gaudy rings, nails painted red. I longed for a camera to take that shot.

"I have everything I want," I told her. But it sounded false, insincere.

"No one has *everything* they want," she answered. Her energy, the sudden intensity of her jewel-green gaze, it wrapped around us until there was no one else in the room.

"I want a baby." The words were out of my mouth before I could stop them, and I was surprised and embarrassed to find myself tearing up. I gazed over at Jack, who was making drinks at the bar we'd set up. That had been the year of my two miscarriages. I'd tried to take them in stride the way everyone seemed to think I should. But those losses, they pulled at me, kept me up at night.

Merlinda smiled kindly and squeezed my hands. She handed me a tissue and I wiped quickly at my eyes.

"And I want Jack to be happy."

Again, I had no intention of saying that. I looked over at my husband again, who had his head tipped back laughing at something Alvaro was saying. Probably something dirty, or mean—which seemed to be most of what came out of Alvaro's mouth. Jack never said so, but I wondered if, on some level, he envied his friend—his ever-growing success, his globe-trotting lifestyle, an endless string of beautiful women. Jack had settled down, by his own choice. Did he regret it? *He's a dick*, Jack had said when I asked. *Clueless. If I envied anyone, which I don't, he'd be the last person.*

Merlinda kept her head bent for a few moments. Then she

held the deck out for me, and I made three choices. She spread them out between us, then flipped the first well-worn card.

The Lovers. An angel held blessing hands over two nude figures as glorious rays of sun shone down from above.

"You and your husband are in love," said Merlinda. "Well suited, complementing each other and with a deep respect for each other's passions, dreams and desires. Don't lose faith, there are children in your future."

I smiled at her, grateful. I knew Merlinda was a fraud, that she had no special psychic powers. But it was still nice to hear those words. Maybe just saying them, putting them out in the universe had a kind of power. Behind me, Layla's voice broke, bright and exuberant, through the party noise, as Jack greeted her and Mac. They were late as usual, juggling myriad social obligations that night. It was almost midnight.

Merlinda flipped the next card, but then Jack was tugging me away. And then Layla was pulling me into a hug. *Happy New Year, girl.* The countdown began—*ten, nine, eight*—

"I love you, Poppy," Jack whispered, as everyone shouted around us.

He took me into the melting embrace that always made my knees weak, and when the clock struck midnight, I lost myself in his kiss. How could he have thought I'd be unfaithful to him? I loved him. *So much.* When I looked back at Merlinda, her gaze had gone grim and she had shuffled away the cards into the deck. Whatever my future was, I figured it was better off as a mystery.

"I have some questions, Merlinda," I say now. "About the days after Jack died."

"Of course you do," she says. "And I have answers."

Her apartment buzzer rings, tinny and distant. "But I can't talk now. Come tomorrow, as early as you can."

"Wait," I say. What does she mean by that? That she has answers? It's not at all what I expected her to say.

"I'll wait for you tomorrow."

And then she's gone, the line dead. I stare at the phone in my hand, feeling the cold finger of dread press into my belly. I try her back, but my call goes straight to voice mail.

It's a moment before I realize that my own buzzer is ringing.

"Noah Avidon here for you," says the doorman when I finally answer.

16

I try to shake off the conversation with Merlinda, peer at myself in the bathroom mirror. Though I've made every effort to cover the circles under my eyes, I'm still looking pretty bad—gaunt, pale. Haunted, even. I've tied back my long black hair, am wearing the simple black sheath dress that is my go-to, a pair of black heels. It's the best I can do. The phone is buzzing, vibrating on the sink below the mirror. Layla. She's relentless.

This is a bad idea. Please don't do this.

I made the mistake of telling her about my plans for the evening. I can never keep things from her. And she's been texting me every quarter hour since. I ignore her.

I've thought about my night with Noah—more than once. A wash of guilt; it's disloyal, isn't it? Even though Jack is gone, I'm still his wife, still in love with him. Jack's mother never remarried. And even though my parents weren't exactly happy, my mother never remarried after my dad died. *There's only one real love in your life,* Mom said mysteriously. I had a feeling she wasn't talking about my dad. Was that true? Was there only one? Had I already loved enough?

The phone vibrates again with another text from Layla:

Which one was Noah? Is he hot? I think you said he was hot. Do NOT sleep with him. You're not in a good place right now.

I finally text her back: Stop.
I can practically feel her fuming.

Fine. Do me a favor and don't stagger into my lobby not remembering your own name.

Seriously? That's what she's going to write?

Wow. That's a low blow.

Sorry. ☹ I'm just worried about you.

I stow the phone in my evening bag and give myself a final once-over.

A knock on the door. I take a deep breath before opening it. Layla's right; this is a bad idea. But there he is, hands dug into his pockets. He's bigger than I remember, broad and tall. There's a scent—fire and linseed oil. Moments from our date come back, how he held the door, how he listened intently when I talked.

"Hey," he says, leans in for a quick peck on the cheek. "You look—amazing."

I know he's just being kind, as I've recently just come from the mirror, where a washed out, frazzled woman stared back at me.

Still, my cheeks warm. "Thanks," I say. "You, too."

Triple black—shirt, jeans, boots. He runs a hand through those silky curls and his hazel eyes rest on me. There's something, a magnetic draw, between us. But instead of moving closer, we stand awkwardly in the doorway a moment until I step aside to let him in.

"Nice place," he says.

He follows me to the kitchen island, his gaze lingering on the boxes. It's one of those details I guess, that wall of boxes with my husband's name written over and over. If he's intuitive, it probably screams: *Hasn't let go. Can't let go. Head for the hills, dude.*

"I didn't have you pegged for a girl who wanted to go to clubs." He takes a seat across the quartz countertop from me.

"I'm not—usually."

"I feel like maybe there's something else going on," he says. "Want to talk about it?"

I open the fridge and offer him a beer, which he accepts. He twists off the cap with his hand and I see how it's burned and scarred from all the metalwork he does. Those sculptures, black and twisted, dragons, and ghouls, a phoenix, a man with a knife. He's successful, his work displayed in galleries around the world. I know not because he told me but because I Googled him after our date.

I am sticking with Perrier. No more mystery pills, no more booze. Time to get clean, get right.

Noah gets the abridged version, a kind of hybrid truth that makes me sound slightly less crazy than I might be. He already knows about Jack and my breakdown from our first night together. I share with him some of my dreams, the suspicion that maybe they're memories of my lost days. When I'm done, he's quiet.

Part of me expects him to get up and leave, because—really— who wants this kind of baggage? When he called, he was probably just looking for a repeat of our last evening—good sex, easy, no strings. But he stays, takes a swig of that beer.

"This club," he says, looking down at the bottle in his hand. "You've been there? Or you think you've been there? Or maybe you just dreamed about it."

I prepare myself to say goodbye. He rubs at the stubble on the hard ridge of his jaw.

"And what do you hope to accomplish by going there?"

"I thought maybe it would jog my memory," I say. It sounds weak, every bit as unsound and illogical as it is.

"Can I ask you something?" he says. He's squinting, tentative.

"Sure."

"Have you considered just letting him go?"

It doesn't sound condescending or judgmental the way it could. It's more like the musing of someone who's been there. Dr. Nash, Layla, my mother, they've all expressed a similar sentiment. The idea of it, that I can just release the life Jack and I shared and move into some new, unexpected phase, that I might just accept this new path, and once grief has passed, move on— it's always just within reach. And yet.

"I can't," I say. "Not until I understand what happened to him."

So, there it is. Maybe I do want closure, after all. Maybe it does matter who killed Jack, even if it doesn't bring him back.

He puts the bottle down on the bar and slowly nods, considering.

"Fair enough."

Again, I expect him to get up, make excuses. But he stays rooted.

"That night we were together," he says. "I told you about my college girlfriend?"

I nod. "She was killed by a drunk driver. I'm sorry."

"I became obsessed with the man who killed her. Who was he? What had he been doing that night? What kind of monster gets behind the wheel of a car drunk and kills a girl? Takes her from her family, from the kid who loved her and wanted to marry her? He didn't just kill her—he killed my future, the future her parents imagined. The injustice of it shredded me."

He's loose, though, not tense and angry with his words. I

can see that he's on the other side of it, a place so far away from where I am.

"But you know what? He was just a man. A middle-aged guy who had a few too many at happy hour with some coworkers. His company was going under. He had two kids and was going through an ugly divorce. He was a struggling, unhappy guy who made a mistake one evening and ruined lives—his own included."

"I'm—sorry." Because what else can you say?

He lifts a hand, but looks away. The shadow of it darkens his face.

"Because I was young, arrogant, couldn't believe someone *I* loved, something *I* wanted had been snatched from me, that made it worse. The randomness of it was impossible to accept."

He leans toward me a little.

"I held on for years, going to the trial, writing letters to the guy. I put Bella on this pedestal in my mind. She was the one, the only one. There would never be another love like the one we shared. But the truth was that we were just kids. We loved each other, sure. But would we have shared a life? I don't know. I wasn't the best boyfriend. I'd cheated on her, blew her off sometimes."

He looks down at his hands.

"She wanted to be a doctor, had a long road ahead of her education- and career-wise. I was less directed, an art major prone to slacking off, not sure how or if I'd make a living with my art. We weren't that well matched."

The words hung between us. Outside and far below a siren wails up the street low and distant. I try to envision her, a studious young girl in love with an artist, dreams of being a doctor, life ended tragically, suddenly, as she drove home to see her parents. It hurts, though I never knew her, the waste of it.

"What you're going through," Noah says. He reaches across for my hand. His fingers are cold from the bottle, soothing on the heat of mine. "It's not the same. I'm not trying to diminish it. Your husband was murdered. You were happily married, in love, probably getting ready to start a family. I'm just saying that even when you have all the answers, you still have to make the choice to let go."

"When did you let go?"

He shakes his head. "I kind of hit rock bottom with it. Failed out of school, moved home with my parents. My dad came down on me, told me to get my act together. I wound up taking an apprenticeship with a local artist, got into the metalwork. It was that work, that discovery that saved me. I worked through my grief in the studio, forged a new path."

"But you never met anyone else. Never married."

"No, nothing serious. Nothing that lasted."

Then, "Metal. It's solid. Nearly indestructible. Hot, you can bend it, mold it, hammer it. But cold, it takes its shape and you can't change it. You can melt it down, but it will just take another shape. Everything else leaves, changes, disappears."

Jack's already fading. That's the hard part. The sound of Jack's voice, the feel of his hands. What it was like to lie in his arms, to fight with him, to laugh with him. How annoying it was that he took forever in the shower, and could never decide what to order at restaurants. He was prone to mansplaining. It used to drive me nuts that he assumed a total air of authority about everything. He hogged the blankets. He made the best omelets, brought me coffee in bed, could always find a solution to any problem large or small. The whole world disappeared when he kissed me. It's all fading, rising like steam from the lake of my memories. If I am trying to hold on to him, to us, if that's what I'm doing, I can't.

Noah comes around the bar and reaches for my face, wipes away a tear I didn't even know was there. I try to turn away from him. I don't like for people to see me cry, though everyone has now. But he holds on to me gently, a hand on my arm.

"I am going to give you the thing I needed and didn't have then," he says.

He touches my cheek to turn my gaze back to his. I rest my hand on his waist. When our eyes meet, there's a jolt of electricity through me. He's so close, I can feel his heat.

"What's that?" I ask.

"A friend."

I smile at the word that can be so loaded between men and women, especially when they're standing as close as we are, when the attraction is so strong. It would be easy to lose myself in him tonight, to take some pills and forget. The phone in my pocket buzzes and vibrates, manic.

"What does that mean?" I ask.

"It means I'm going to help you find out what you can about your husband, about those lost days. If you want to go to this club, if you think it will help, I'm in."

He steps back, offers his hand, and I take it in mine. His gaze is warm, giving, and heat spreads through me.

Then, when I look away, there he is. Jack. Sitting on the couch he would have hated. That hard, gray uncomfortable slab, so sleek and modern. A jolt of alarm sets my heart to pounding.

I try not to stare; he's bloodied and beaten. Face swollen and purple like the girl in the conference room. I didn't identify Jack's body. Mac took on the horror for me. I'll never forget Mac's face when he returned to me from the morgue, ashen and drawn, eyes glittering with pain.

"Oh my god, Poppy," he said, voice breaking. "I'm so sorry."

He tipped into Layla, who let out a strangled wail of grief as she held him, then pulled me in. We all three stood there, holding on to each other. Mac sobbed like a little boy, helpless against his sorrow. My own voice, a whisper, a prayer: *nononononono*.

"He's a good-looking guy," says Jack. "He kind of looks like me a little, don't you think? What would your shrink say about that?"

The sound of his voice sends a jolt through me. But I don't answer him. After all, he's not there. Instead, I take Noah's empty beer bottle and put it in the recycling, busy myself as if I'm getting ready for us to leave. But he's so real. I could walk over and take him in my arms, wipe the blood from his face. What's happening to me? I'm not dreaming. But I am. I must be.

"Poppy," Jack says. He stands, wearing his running clothes that are smeared with mud and blood. The side of his head is mashed, unnatural. "Don't do this. Keep looking for answers and you're going to find things you won't like. Take the advice everyone keeps giving you and let me go. I'm gone. Long gone."

"You okay?" asks Noah.

There's that stutter, that world wobble, and then Jack is, thankfully, no longer in the room with me.

"I'm just—sleep-deprived," I say, trying to slow my hammering heart. What had the doctor called it—hypnagogia? I think about trying to explain it but it sounds way too crazy. He was so real. He was *right there*. "Prone to blanking."

He moves back around the bar.

"So, let's go do this and then get you to bed," he says. He must catch something on my face; his cheeks color slightly. "You know, to sleep—alone. I mean, if that's what you want."

His discomfort—it's charming. "Thank you."

I'm grateful for him, this stranger who didn't know Jack and who doesn't truly know me. Everyone else in my life lost something when Jack died; they all just want me to be better, to be well and each of them has ideas about how that's going to happen fastest. But Noah only sees who I am right now, a fractured girl trying to put herself back together, to understand who killed her husband. And he has offered that person his friendship, maybe simply because he knows the way down this dark and twisting, bending path better than most.

He doesn't ask what I mean. He knows.

A quick glance at my phone reveals a screen full of texts from

Layla—lots of angry emoji faces and those big red exclamation points, a missed call from Izzy's phone (Layla calling from Izzy's phone to try to get me to answer, an old trick that's worked more than once). There's a missed call from Detective Grayson. If I call him back, I'll need to lie to him. I don't even consider it. If it was anything important he'd have come here. I hear his warning again, though: *Be low risk for a couple of days, okay?*

"Ready?"

Noah's watching me. He hasn't glanced at a phone once; not on our last date, not tonight. It's rare that someone doesn't have a device clutched in his hand, isn't staring at a screen all the time, relationships scrolling out in bubbles, text disembodied from voice and body, language pared down to barest meaning and, so, far less meaningful than actual conversation.

How did we let them do it, separate us from each other while making us seem more connected than ever? How did we let them strip voice and touch and tone from our interactions? I like this about Noah, that he's more present than most people. More present than I am. He pulls the door open for me as I stow the phone in my evening bag, vowing not to look at it again.

A quick glance behind me reveals that the apartment is mercifully empty.

17

Jack and I fought the night before. In fact, Sarah was right, we'd been fighting a lot in the months and weeks before he died. *Couples fight,* Layla said when I confided this in her during one of our long talks after his death, after my breakdown. *You go through phases, good times, bad times. Everyone wants you to think their relationship is perfect. But nothing's perfect, no matter what they post on Facebook.* She's right, of course, but I hated that our last few weeks were characterized by bickering, silences, hard words.

Mac and Layla were frequently stiff and snappish with each other. Over the years, I'd seen the frayed edges of their relationship—Mac's immersion in his work, parenthood, Layla giving up her art to raise a family—how stresses and little resentments bubbled up into blowouts. Still, I knew the way he looked at her, and she at him. The way he held her, the way they kissed, long and sweet when he got home from work (usually). The way she laughed at his stupid jokes that were not funny to anyone else. The way he held her coat. A marriage is a mosaic, comprised of pieces—some broken and jagged, some shiny, some dull, some golden. The pieces don't matter as much as the whole picture of your life together.

The truth was, it seemed different with me and Jack. What we had, was it somehow less solid? Were we less bound to each other than Mac and Layla? I suspected it was the lack of children, the miscarriages. They unstitched me in a way I wouldn't have imagined. But Jack didn't grieve in the same way. My desire for a child began to consume me.

"I think we should take a break," he said over dinner that last night. I'd been staring at the pasta on the plate, moving it around. I didn't remember the last time either of us had spoken since sitting at the table. He had his laptop open. I looked up from my plate.

"A break?"

"From *trying* so hard, I mean."

That was it, the strained silence. I was ovulating; we both knew that.

He reached for my hand, but I pulled it back. Part of me heard what he was saying, and even agreed. Sex had become about making a baby, not just about connecting, about pleasure, about love, about lust. I didn't love that about our life, either. But I sensed something else, another layer.

"I'm starting to think I want this more than you do," I said. Sadness, anger, seemed to always simmer beneath the surface now, a fight always ready to boil over.

"I want it, too," he said, looking away. He closed his laptop. "You know I do. It's just—the business is growing. We talked about my taking assignments again."

It wasn't just the words, but his tone. Soothing, reasonable—but distancing somehow.

"You said you didn't want that. That you're *all in*." My voice bounced back peevish, mocking in a way I didn't intend. But Jack was easy, slow to ignite to anger. He lifted his shoulders, took the napkin from his lap and laid it on the table.

"When the business is solid, I *might* want that again."

I put my fork down, leaned back.

"I'm just saying," he went on, leaning forward to bridge the distance I created. "Let's take the pressure off. If it happens, it happens, you know? Let's stop tracking your cycle, get back to good old-fashioned *fucking* because we're *hot* for each other. You're still hot for me, right?"

I felt the energy of a smile.

"I'm not just a baby machine to you, right?"

He came around to where I was sitting, knelt beside me and took my hands. He had that smile on, the one that melted anger and any kind of resolve.

"What if it doesn't *just happen*?" I asked.

He shrugged. "There's more to life than kids, Poppy. Right?"

I flashed on the sheets covered with blood, the wail that came from a place of sorrow inside me I didn't even know was there. I thought of Izzy and Slade, the magical products of Mac and Layla's love. The world before they came was somehow *less* than it was after their arrival. Who would Jack and I bring into the world? I desperately wanted to know.

"Like what?" I asked.

He blew out a laugh. "Like art and travel, late nights with friends, freedom. Like *us*, Poppy—*you and me*—doing whatever we want for the rest of our lives."

It cut deep, the way his face lit up with excitement.

"You're saying that it doesn't matter to you whether or not we have kids."

There was something about it that was so crushing; I couldn't have even said why. Before Jack, I never really thought about kids, either.

"I'm saying *you* matter, *we* matter. Whatever else happens, I'm good with that."

"I heard you," I said. He frowned at my tone.

"What do you mean?"

"Talking to Alvaro last night."

He shook his head, looked down.

"You told him about the miscarriage and what did he say?"

You dodged a bullet, man. Kids are the end of everything else in your life.

I only heard because Jack had him on speakerphone while he was typing. He quickly picked up the phone.

"That's fucked-up, man," said Jack in a low voice. "Poppy's hurting."

Not *we're* hurting. I didn't hear more after that, just walked away.

"Alvaro only cares about himself," he said with an eye roll. "You know that."

"I knew that about him, yes," I said, rising. I picked up my plate and moved away from him. "But I didn't know that about you."

"Come on," he said, staying on the floor. "That's not fair."

He called after me, but I went into the kitchen, cleaned up, then went into the bedroom. The cold I'd been fighting had me too exhausted to even be angry. I brushed my teeth, changed and climbed underneath the covers. A few hours later, he crawled into bed beside me, wrapped me up.

I love you, he whispered, his breath hot in my ear. *I love you so much. I'm sorry.*

I pretended not to hear him, to be sound asleep, and finally he moved away.

Noah and I don't wait in the line that stretches up the block. He slips his arm through mine when we exit the cab and strides us up to the doorman, who glances at us briefly, lifts the velvet rope without question. They exchange a nod, and for a second it seems like they know each other. Has he been here before?

Before I can ask, we are in a maze of bodies, music thumping. Almost immediately I am sorry we've come. The club is a breathless crush, the usual blend of chic, and grunge, and after-work, and punk and whoever, whatever else. The space, too small for so many people, throbs with deafening house music.

Still I push my way in, am immediately assaulted by moments, images. I wish I had my camera. Behind it, I can hide and observe, separate myself from the chaos; behind it, I am lifted from the moment, above it. Instead, I'm buffeted by bodies, Noah pulling me through the crowd. In the throng, I wait for the sense that I've been here before.

But the club in my dream was not like this. Glancing about, there is nothing familiar, no one and nothing I recognize. I take the phone from my bag, breaking the vow I made less than an hour ago. The phone camera, though not my preferred piece of equipment, will do.

Once I have it, the world captured on a screen, the chaos around me makes more sense. The world segmented into moments: a couple presses into each other, makes out against the exposed brick wall; a girl blows bubbles from the rickety loft up high, dancing bodies all around her; a DJ onstage, intent, head bent, disappears into bulbous red headphones. Blue lights glitter from the ceiling like neon stars, a young man bows his head into his hand. Girls spin on poles, stage lit. A disco ball sheds rainbow shards on a woman in a glittering purple dress. I capture Noah staring at a golden mannequin, the naked torso of a woman. I recognize that look, an artist studying form, asking questions about shape or light. He turns and stares at me through the screen, smiles. I put the phone away, and he slips his fingers through mine, pulls me toward the stairs.

On the flight down, it grows quieter, darker. Drunk people clamor around a freezer-temperature room dedicated to serving vodka shots. Their laughter and shouts, whoops and cackles follow us down a long dark hallway. I was never one of those people, drunk and laughing in a group. I was always the one outside, looking in, wondering what the hell was so funny. Maybe that's the natural condition of the photographer, to stand in the margins, to observe, to document. Or maybe some of us are just hardwired to be the outsider, and that's why we paint or write or hide behind a camera lens.

"There's another bar," he says. "It's quieter."

"You've been here before," I say. But he doesn't hear me above the din, keeps walking.

We make our way down a long hall, the shoes I'm wearing already hurting, squeezing my toes and biting at my heels. The music throbs, vibrates through the floor. A red light casts a strange glow and the wall is a patchwork of stickers, writing in marker and pen, Polaroid pictures, a thousand faces, messages, images. Déjà vu dogs me. We press through the crowd. This place, maybe it *is* vaguely familiar; but there's nothing solid to cling to, no real reference point.

The relative quiet of the other bar is a relief. But if I've been here before, it's buried so deep that I can't reach it, and I'm no detective. I realize that I don't even know what questions to ask, or of whom to ask them. Detective Grayson wanted me to stay out of it and now it's clear why. You can't investigate yourself.

"What are you drinking?" asks Noah. Though it's quieter, we still need to shout a little.

"Club soda."

Noah yells something to a male bartender with a large ring through the middle of his nose like a bull.

"So," he says, leaning in close. "Anything?"

I look around at the room, people crushed into semicircle booths, lights too low to see much. I just shake my head. It's embarrassing to say I don't remember, that I can't be sure.

He's watching me with that same intensity I noticed earlier, the artist looking for the truth. There's something, the whisper of a memory then, but it's gone as fast as it came.

"I'm sorry," he says. There's a gravity to it that I find moving, though I'm not sure why he's apologizing. Maybe it's just because, for some reason, he cares about this errand, maybe about me. He wanted to help, and is disappointed for me. I am, too. Or maybe he just feels sorry for *me*. The stupidity of this endeavor is humiliating.

"Will you be okay for a moment? If I hit the bathroom?" he says.

"Of course."

I watch a young woman twist, arms up, on the dance floor. She's in her own head, not with anyone, just one of a few people dancing in the space, much smaller than upstairs, the music coming over speakers mounted on the ceiling. I snap a few pictures of her; no one notices. In fact, that space is riven with those rectangles of light, the bright stutter of flashes. Everyone's photographing themselves or someone else, texting, or scrolling through feeds. When did we stop seeing with our eyes?

When I turn back to the bar, recognition is a rocket—her violet contact lenses, her arms sleeves of tattoos. The bartender from my dream. For a moment, I'm breathless, reality stretching. I think of Dr. Nash, her answer to my question about how I know when I'm dreaming and when I'm awake. *Do any of us really know?*

She puts our drinks down and I reach for her arm before she can shuttle away. Looking up, her violet eyes flash annoyance. Whatever she sees in my face softens her.

"Do you know me?"

She shakes her head, her smile curious. "*Should* I know you?"

"I may have been here once." My voice sounds weak, and I feel strange and out of place here. "Maybe a year ago?"

"I meet a lot of people." She glances down the bar, looking I guess for other customers who might need her attention. The music seems louder now that we're talking. We're almost yelling to hear each other.

"I was wearing a red dress," I say. "I wasn't feeling well. I was with someone, a man."

Listening to myself, I'm aware that my descriptions sounds

like a hundred women who must have been here over the last year, messed up, with a strange man, even wearing a red dress. I'm suddenly so tired, I can hardly stand. I sit on the barstool, leaning closer to her. On her arms, brightly colored fairies frolic in a flowering landscape. A rainbow twines through; there's a unicorn in a pen. From the speakers above us, a remix of an old Grace Jones song weaves through a modern dance beat.

"Maybe." A squint, a tilt of her head, pink hair spiky and unmoving. "Maybe you look familiar."

"But you don't remember that night." How could she? One of a hundred booze-soaked evenings.

That's when she realizes that I'm not hitting on her. She seems to consider me a moment longer, then shakes her head again, and starts to move away. "I'm sorry."

A dead end. What did I think would happen here? I watch her go, wondering *what next?* What would Grayson ask her? Or that firm that Layla wants to hire. Surely there's some technique that professionals have. Some way of teasing information from people, finding clues. This was a mistake.

But then she turns back and stares a moment, returning. The girl takes out her phone, taps at it with her thumbs and starts scrolling.

She looks up, gets someone a glass of water, still staring at her phone, then comes back again.

"I take pictures sometimes—you know, for my blog. I never delete anything from my phone," she says. "Maybe—when did you say this was?"

"A year ago," I say, leaning toward her.

She glances up at me, then back to her phone. Finally, she turns the screen so that I can see it.

"Could this be you?" she asks.

A woman, long and lean, slender pale hands on the wide dark shoulders of a man, almost pushing him away. She leans back, but he has her solidly, arm wrapped around the low of her back, bent over her like a sickle, kissing her. Blue lights glow above and behind. There's a mascara trail of tears down her face.

Her face. My face. It's me. My heart thrums.

"And him?" I ask, still staring.

She lifts her shoulders, turns back toward her waiting customers. "Some girls I remember. Guys, not so much. I'll send this to you, if you want."

The music gets louder, the vibration of it moving through me, making my head ache again.

"You haven't seen him since that night?"

"No."

"Would you recognize him?"

"I don't know. Maybe."

He's a wraith, the man in the image, wrapped in darkness, a shadow. I can't see his face. He's swallowing me, a ghoul enveloping me, black devouring red. I think of the masked man in the shadows of my life. A shudder of fear moves through me. Is it the same man? Did I meet him that night and has he been following me all this time?

"I remember now, I think. You danced with him—but you seemed *so* out of it. Then you disappeared into the bathroom. You were in there for a while. I figured you were trying to blow him off, but he waited. Finally—I think you left with him.

"It's weird, I know," she continues. "But I took your picture. In case."

"In case?"

"I don't know," she says, looking sheepish. "It didn't seem right. You were a wreck. He was watchful in this weird way, not like just some normal guy looking to get laid."

Unsettling to hear a story about yourself, one you can't recall. *You were a wreck.*

"So you took my picture in case—something *happened* to me?"

"Yeah." She shrugged. "And you guys were making out, there

was something kind of beautiful about it—the colors, the shape of your bodies, the blue light."

I give the bartender my number and she texts the photo.

"If you remember anything else, or if you see him again, will you call me? I'm Poppy."

"Sure, Poppy," she says. She has a sweet smile, somehow confident and shy at the same time. She winks at me, then she hurries down the bar again.

I drift toward the bathroom, take a deep breath before pushing inside. Red stalls, black-and-white-tile floors, walls covered in graffiti, scrawled notes, phone numbers, bumper stickers. Over the sinks, smoky mirrors reach the ceilings. When a girl stumbles out of the first stall, I move inside, door banging metal on metal. It's filthy like I remember it—or dreamed it, the odor strong. The wall is a mess of scrawl, a bulletin board broadcasting phone numbers and email addresses, dirty comments, cryptic messages:

You were the girl with the purple butterfly tattoo. We met on the dance floor and you said I was hot. Call me. The number was long since rubbed away, just a smudge now.

Maria is a slut.

Bobbi and June TLA.

I hate you. I hate myself more.

This place sucks.

I sit on the toilet and keep reading all the messages of the party crowd, the music getting louder, then quieter again, as the door opens and closes, opens and closes. I use my phone to snap pictures; I don't even know why except that it occurs to me suddenly that this is the way to hold on to reality.

If I can capture the image, save it on my phone, then it's real.

I press the reverse button and my own face appears on the screen. I stare at myself a moment, a tired-looking woman with big blue eyes, and blush-pink lips, someone who looks both older and younger than she is. Who is she? Who am I? Before I sink into a full-blown existential crisis, I take the picture. Then I quickly leave the bathroom to find Noah waiting by the bar looking content, patient. He sips at his drink, watching the dance floor. When I join him, he hands me my club soda.

"I thought you ditched me," he yells over the music. His smile is warm, pleasantly devilish. I take a sip, then more. I'm hot suddenly and the icy liquid fizzes pleasantly in my mouth.

"I wouldn't do that," I say.

"Happens all the time."

"I kind of doubt that. You don't look like the kind of guy girls ditch."

He lifts his glass, then drinks it down.

"Anything? Dreams, memories, something you recognize?"

I want to tell him about the bartender, but it seems too hard with the music so loud. I look over in her direction, but she's not there. A young man has taken her place, tall with a mop of inky hair, dark eyeliner.

I start to panic—another microsleep? Another hypnagogic dream? But then I scroll through my texts, see the strange picture she sent, her number. Okay. It works. Reality captured and cataloged. I lift the phone, and Noah appears on the screen.

"Smile," I tell him.

He does, a little self-consciously. He runs a hand over the crown of his head, and I take his picture. There. Now he's real, too.

"Any chance we can get out of here?" asks Noah.

I think I said yes. I'm sure I did.

18

The lights are out, but I hear him moving around in the bathroom. A cough. The water running. Though my head feels like it's full of gauze, and my throat is raw, I force myself out of bed, stand and stretch. The room is cold and full of shadows, amber light leaking between the blinds from outside.

"You coming?" Jack stands in the doorway, a shadow in a dim rectangle of blue light.

"Yeah," I answer. "It'll be good for me."

He moves over close, lays a hand on my forehead. "You sure? You were coughing a lot."

"I have to shake this thing."

"I'm sorry." He runs a hand through my hair, holds my gaze. "About last night."

I rest my head on his shoulder, take in the scent of him. We went to bed angry; he feels a million miles away. Or maybe I'm a million miles away.

"It's okay," I say. I mean it. "You were right."

He was right; that's why it hurt so much.

"I want the things you want, Poppy." It's just a whisper, hot in my ear. "I swear I do."

I believe he wants this to be true, though I'm not sure it is. It's okay, though. We don't have to want the same things, do we? To love each other?

I lean up to kiss him, and he bends to meet me. Desire comes up hot and fast. His arms tighten around my back, his mouth finds my neck, my lips. I'm ravenous for him in a way I haven't been for a while. The heat—it's just for him. Outside the wind howls, a cold morning, still dark. In the glow of the streetlight, raindrops glitter like glass.

Then we're tumbling back into bed. I strip him out of his running clothes, his sneakers bouncing softly to the wood floor as he kicks them off. His skin is so hot, so soft. He tears off and tosses my thin sleep shirt; it flutters away like a ghost.

I feel his need for me, but I make him wait, kissing him—his eyes, his neck, his chest, the silky insides of his arms. I take him in my mouth until he's groaning, helpless, and then I climb on top of him. Slow, wide waves of pleasure, milky light making dancing shadows on the wall. A dog barks outside, faint, far away.

With an easy flip, he has me beneath him, staring up into the pools of his eyes, arms tight around him. It's desperate—as though we haven't been together in months and maybe we haven't, not like this, not just because we want each other, because we love each other.

Later, we lie wrapped up in each other as the dark morning grows light, and outside the world starts to turn. I hear the coffeepot come on; it's set for six.

"That's better than a run," he says with a grin.

"There's always tomorrow."

Maybe, I think before I drift off again, we are enough, just us, if it comes to that.

I'm wearing the clothes I wore to Morpheus with Noah, but now I'm lying on my bed, covered by a blanket that was on the couch. It's 3:00 a.m. Another wake-up from a revisionist dream where I live another reality with Jack—then lose him again. So vivid this time, it didn't seem like a dream at all. No wonder I had a nervous breakdown. How many times can you lose someone? There are an infinite number of scenarios I could concoct where he doesn't leave me that morning. Will I live them all? I think of those pills in the toilet, wish I hadn't flushed them. Right now, I'd take just about anything to dull the pain in the middle of my chest where my grief has lived. God, he's still here. He's still with me.

I push myself up and walk down the hall to the living room, where I find Noah asleep on the couch. He's sprawled on his back, one leg on the floor, one arm over his head. He stirs as I walk into the room.

"What happened?" I ask.

He pushes up, rubs his eyes. "You fell asleep in the cab. I walked you in but you were dead on your feet. It didn't seem right to leave—or to stay. So."

He looks at the couch, where he's piled up some pillows. "I thought I'd just crash on the couch awhile. In case you woke up, needed something."

I wrap myself up, arms tight around my middle, and stay by the door. It feels like a betrayal to have him here; Jack is everywhere. His essence, our love, it's still on my skin, under my skin. I still belong to him, maybe I always will.

"By the way," he goes on. "This is *literally* the most uncomfortable couch in the world. It actually seems to be *pushing* me away."

He has a nice smile, kind and warm, in on the joke of it all.

"Thank you," I say. I sit across from him, still wrapped up.

"For what?"

"For coming with me tonight, for seeing me home. For not..." The sentence trails.

Noah hangs his head, seems to sense the distance that's opened between us. After a moment, he rises.

"I should go, I think. Right?"

I want him to *stay*. I want to lose myself in him, if even for a while. I want him to leave; I need to be alone. Alone with my memories of Jack, my unwanted dreams. That's the tug-of-war inside me. Move on? Stay rooted? What hurts less? Either way, it's not fair to Noah. A friend, maybe in another version of my life, something much more.

"Maybe," I say. "I'm sorry."

Noah is a shadow among shadows—of boxes, the hard couch, his silhouette cast against the ambient light from outside, the city a field of stars behind him. Another pang. I should have stayed in our old place with the mice and the outdated kitchen, the place where our love lived. Nothing lives here. Nothing can; it's too cold, barren. Like a museum, Jack said.

"A couple of years after Bella died, I went to see a psychic," he says into the quiet. "One of those people who talks to the dead?"

I find this surprising, that he was the type of person to see a psychic. I don't know him well. But it's hard to reconcile this information with the man who stands before me, the one who hammers metal, bends and twists it into enormous, menacing shapes. He seems so grounded, so solid in the world. It's hard to imagine him reaching beyond what he can see, what he can touch.

"That doesn't seem like something you'd do."

He draws in a breath, offers a shrug.

"Desperation can separate us from ourselves. I couldn't stand how *random* it seemed. How there was no justice or logic to her death, no meaning that I could see or intuit. It defied what I thought I knew about the world. Of course, then, maybe even now, I knew nothing about the world. Who does know anything?"

"So, what happened?"

He sinks back down onto the couch. The light from the hall

shines on his face and I can see the fatigue under his eyes, his sleep-tousled hair. He rubs at his temples.

"I was on this waiting list for months. Finally, I get a call, drive out to a town called The Hollows and I meet with a woman named Agatha Cross. She has this big white house in the middle of nowhere."

The name of the town rings a bell, a place that Merlinda has mentioned. A vortex, she called it. A girl went missing there a couple of years ago and it was in the news. There's some kind of dark history, haunted tours, woods, abandoned iron mines.

"She had this remarkably soothing energy. Just sitting with her, I felt some of my anger, some of my grief drain away. There must have been a hundred chimes on her porch, and the wind blew in this weird way, like it was *whispering*. We talked for a long time—about Bella. About how I wanted her to know that I was sorry we fought, sorry about everything."

He is quiet in that abrupt way men have when emotion overtakes them. I sit quiet, waiting.

"She knew things she couldn't have known," he continues. "That Bella got pregnant, an accident. That I asked her to marry me, then she miscarried. That we'd fought, were angry at each other when she went to see her parents."

"I'm sorry."

"At the end of our session, she told me something that stayed with me."

He's staring at me, his eyes dark pools. There's a draw, a pull. Something that doesn't have anything to do with Jack, something that's just me and him.

"She said that everyone thinks the dead haunt the living and sometimes they do. But the living can also haunt the dead. Bella needed me to let her go, so that we both could move on. She told me: you had your time together in life. And it's over now. That's it."

He stands up again, picks up his jacket that's draped over the chair. He moves over toward me, leans down and kisses me gently on the forehead.

"Good night, Poppy."

I let him leave, just sit there in the dark listening to his footfalls down the hall.

When I hear the door close, I get up and rummage through my bag for the one prescribed bottle of sleeping pills I kept. I hold the rattling bottle in my hand. Sleep in an amber vial. Rest. Darkness. I hesitate, then stuff them back in my bag.

In bed, I sit and write everything that happened that night, my dream, the things that Noah said. The photos, these journal entries, that's how I'll know tomorrow what's real. Ink on paper, moments captured in digital memory. Everything else fades. Those things remain.

19

"Did you sleep with him?" Layla asks immediately when I call her in the morning. I'm already in a cab heading uptown.

"No," I say, trying and failing not to sound defensive.

The conversation Noah and I had still rattles around my head, but I don't tell her any of that. I tell Layla about the club, what the bartender said, the picture she showed me. I can feel her vibrating on the line. I get it. If situations were reversed, I'd be after her, too, for her recklessness, for shutting me out. I've dragged her out of bars when she wanted to go home with the wrong guy, taken cabs in the middle of the night to outer boroughs to rescue her when she did. She threw a drink at a guy who groped me in a club, stayed with me for a week when my father died. I've sat up all night with her when Slade was colicky and Mac needed to sleep for work, taken Izzy to school in the morning. We've been there. As long as I can remember, no matter what. I'd be railing, chasing, bitching a blue streak if she were doing the things I was doing.

There's an annoyed pause when I've finished recounting the

evening: "So what's your endgame here, Poppy? What are you looking for?"

"I need that missing piece of myself back."

And if I find it, I might be closer to understanding what happened to Jack. I don't say that, though, because it sounds a little wobbly, doesn't it? Like I'm on a mission to find out who killed my husband. This isn't something stable people do, is it? And it's not the whole truth.

"Okay, I get it," she says, even though I know she doesn't. "If you don't think the police are doing their job, we have people who can help. People who can look out for you, and find the answers you want. Tom at Black Dog, he already has a plan. Let him handle it and you come back here. That way you stay safe."

"No one's safe."

"*Safer* than you are now. Look—it's selfish. I'll admit it. I *need* you. The kids need you."

The guilt card; it's a powerful one. I feel myself weakening.

"You're not safe right now, how you're acting," she goes on. "It's like—you're purposely putting yourself at risk. I mean—is that what you're doing, Poppy?"

Grayson's warning comes back to me. *Sometimes we invite darkness. Is* that what I'm doing?

Anger bubbles up from nowhere. Why does everyone think they know how to live my life better than I do?

"Layla, I have to go."

I hear her saying my name as I end the call.

Returning to my old neighborhood is a journey through space and time. Versions of Jack, of myself, vivid close memories dwell on every corner—in line at the coffee shop, reading the paper at our diner, jogging down the street toward the park. Even the fall of autumn leaves littering the ground, their earthy smell, reminds me of him, of us.

There is a tightness in my chest as I climb the stoop to our old building and push through the door.

I expect to see Richie, stooped and smiling. But the uniformed young man at the desk is a stranger. The smell—wood, floor polish, decades—is so familiar, so evocative of our life together, that it nearly buckles me over.

"Can I help you?" he asks.

He has a crooked nose, as if it was broken once and never healed quite right. But there's a sweetness, an innocence to the sea-glass green of his eyes.

"Where's Richie?" I ask. I look to the doorway behind the reception desk.

"Oh," he says, turning to follow my gaze. "He retired, moved to Florida with his wife. He's been gone a few months now."

He always said he would; we never believed him. He was a fixture, an old New Yorker in an old New York–style job. I'm happy for him, but it's just another reminder of how you can't stop things from changing. Why does it never stop being a surprise?

"I'm here to see Merlinda, 7B." I want to tell him I used to live here. But I don't.

Instead I take it in, the towering ceilings, the marble floor, the dark wood wainscoting. New York, prewar, with the kind of character Jack loved, things that stood the test of time, that weathered and grew more beautiful. What I saw then was the water stains on the ceiling, the creaking old elevator that didn't work as often as it did, the rust on the mailboxes, the cracks in the floor. I wanted crisp and new, clean, modern.

"Ma'am?" He's looking at me as if he's been trying to get my attention.

"Sorry."

"She says to come up." His name tag reads Sam. I thank him and head down the hall, summon the elevator, wait to see if it's working. The door opens and I climb in; it rumbles slowly up.

On the seventh floor, Merlinda swings her door open, strides quickly toward me and pulls me into a pillowy, fragrant embrace. She draws away, puts papery ringed hands to my cheeks and stares deep into my eyes as if she's searching my very soul. I can feel my phone vibrating—does it ever stop—but I wouldn't dare look at it. Merlinda calls them soul stealers, thieves of life.

"You've met someone," she says. I look down the hallway toward our old door. Who lives there now? I won't ask, because I don't want to know. How can someone else be walking the same floors, cooking on the same stove, showering in the same old claw-foot tub?

"No." I shake my head. "Not really."

Lines crease her brow in a worried frown. "I'm making tea."

She breaks away from me, glances in the direction of our old apartment, then ushers me inside hers. Cluttered, dusty—every surface covered with crystals and statues, lamps with ornate shades—her place hasn't changed a bit.

She motions toward the low couch and I sink into it as she glides off, long skirt swishing, bangles on her wrists jingling. From the window, I can just make out leaves from the park up at the end of the street. She's been in this apartment for decades, rent control the only reason she can still stay in this neighborhood. Out on her fire escape, a hundred different wind chimes clatter—wood, shells, bits of metal and glass. It reminds me of my conversation with Noah, about the living haunting the dead. Is Jack trapped somewhere, trying to move on? But I'm holding on too tight.

When Merlinda returns from the kitchen, she's carrying a bag I recognize, something I've carried all over the world because, lightweight and quick-drying, it makes a great day pack and folds into nothing when it's empty. It was hot pink when I bought it. Now it's faded and frayed from hundreds of hours out of doors.

"Where did you get that?"

She cocks her head.

"You brought it here to me," she says. "It was late. After—Jack. You asked me to keep it until you came back for it, to tell no one. I thought that's why you came. You don't remember?"

She hands it to me. That I have no memory of this encounter is deeply unsettling. Life, awareness, memory have always been firmly in my grasp.

"And you kept it?" I ask. "Jack was murdered, and for a time I was a suspect. You weren't worried that I was hiding something from the police?"

She waves me away, sits across from me.

"You? Lovely, sweet Poppy? You're one of the good ones. And trust me, there aren't many. If you want me to keep something for you, I don't ask. I just do."

I want to open the pack; it's heavy in my lap. But I *don't* want to open it, either. It's Pandora's box, once I crack the lid I won't be able to close it again, or control what I find inside.

"Afterward, when I learned you were in the hospital, I tried to see you," she says. "But they wouldn't let me."

This is news to me.

"Who? Who wouldn't let you see me?"

"Your friend, the rich one," she says with a sniff. "And your mother."

"What do you mean?"

"She told me—your friend—that you had enough problems without memories from your life with Jack, especially me with all my messages from the beyond."

It sounds like Layla—fiercely protective, sharp-tongued. She'd have viewed Merlinda as a threat to my moving forward and treated her as such, though she never mentioned it.

"I'm sorry." Then: "Did you? Have a message from the beyond?"

"No," she says. She presses her lips together regretfully, shakes her head. "That's not my gift. Me, I just read the cards. And

I see the heart. I cut through all the layers and people are laid bare before me."

Her thing about seeing to the heart—I believe it. I am relaxed here, with her, in a way I haven't been. She knows me and I don't have to pretend; I don't have to don the layers I put on at work, even for family and friends. In this strange room, with this funny fortune-teller, I can just be.

I look down at the bag again. It sits in my lap like a pet; I rest my hands on it as though it might try to get away.

"What's inside?" I ask.

She shakes her head vigorously. "I wouldn't look. That's your business."

"What did I say when I brought it to you? Exactly."

She closes her eyes, as though trying to remember. Then she looks at me carefully, her eyes full of empathy.

"You said that you knew what happened to Jack. That they were all liars. You were very upset. I tried to keep you with me, but you said you had to go."

I toy with the tied knot. What's inside? What message did that lost Poppy have for the woman I've become? What did she know that I've forgotten? And what was so horrible that it drove her to a nervous breakdown? Or was she already so far gone with grief that when she came to Merlinda, she had already departed from herself? The answer is in the bag, but I can't bring myself to look.

"Can I take your picture?" I ask Merlinda.

She leans back, folds her arms and stares at me with eyes, heavily lashed, shadowed in ice-blue. I lift my phone and take the shot. The resulting image is a chaos of color—her eyes, her bright orange blouse, dyed red hair, the rich fabrics all around her, the way her gnarled ringed hand rests on her folded arm.

"The world is a patchwork quilt," she says. "We are all bits of scrap stitched together. It doesn't always make sense to us—

things don't always match. But that's because we can't see the big picture. No one can—only God."

Her wind chimes sing in the breeze and the curtains billow. She's prone to this, waxing philosophical. Around her apartment, there are statues on every surface—the Virgin Mary, Jesus on the cross, a laughing Buddha, a golden Ganesha, the goddess of overcoming obstacles. There are altars of candles and dried flowers, clusters of prayer beads, black rosaries. Merlinda thinks that there's only one God and the various religious practices are just different ways of speaking to Him—or Her. She'll call on any saint, god or goddess from any religion for help and guidance. She doesn't discriminate.

I see it then, her deck of tarot cards. It sits on the old dining room table, which is too big for the small space. It's a beautiful old thing with legs ornately carved, heavy wood. Varnish fading, covered in nicks and scars, cold candle wax dripping from its edges.

"On New Year's you were reading my cards," I say. "We got interrupted. You never finished."

She looks away from me for the first time, down at the ground beneath our feet, then out the window, seems at a rare loss for words. "The cards are flawed, just like the reader. Just like life."

"What did I draw?" I press.

"I don't remember."

"Merlinda. Please."

She takes and releases a long breath, threads her fingers together.

"You drew the Seven of Swords," she says finally. "In the three-card reading, it was for the present."

I know a little about the tarot—that every card has dual meaning depending on which way it is laid upon the table, that no message is dark or negative really, that every negative has a positive, that every end is a beginning.

When I don't say anything, she goes on.

"It's the card of deception and betrayal. When I draw that card, it means that either the person before me is hiding something and it's about to catch up. Or it might mean that she is the victim of deceit, trusting people who should not be trusted."

Layla's voice bounces around my head. *You're a fucking liar!*

"What else?" I ask. "There was another card."

Again, she hesitates, shifts in her seat. Then, "In the future position, you drew the Devil."

I know the card, the image featuring a satyr and a couple chained to him. It's only after looking closely that you see the chains could easily be removed. "It can represent hidden forces of negativity in your life—addiction, attachment to unhealthy ideas or relationships. Or it could mean that there's someone in your life who doesn't wish you well."

A memory comes back to me, sharp and vivid. I am standing in the dark, in the hallway outside the living room. Jack's talking, his voice low but vibrating with fear, anger.

"Look." He stands by the window, huddled over the phone, clearly trying to keep from waking me. "I can't just walk away from this. It's not—right. I won't do it."

I want to enter the living room, to confront him.

Who are you talking to? What are you talking about? Tell me.

Something stops me. Instead, I return to bed.

"What's going on?" I ask when he returns to the bedroom. He's quiet, the way he is when he doesn't want to answer my question. "Who were you talking to?"

"Alvaro," he says. It's a lie. I don't believe him. "He's having some issues."

"What kind of issues?"

"Nothing important. Can we talk about it in the morning?" He kisses me on the cheek, then turns over.

I want to press him. But I don't want to be that kind of wife—

needy, prying. I wish I had been. I wish I had turned on the light and made him tell me the truth.

"Poppy," asks Merlinda, shuttling me back to the now. "What is it?"

I shove the pack into my tote and rise.

"Nothing," I assure her. "I'm just—tired."

That word has taken on a whole new meaning. She rises with me, a bustle of fabric, a jingle of bracelets, and takes my hands.

"Be careful, Poppy," she says. Her eyes have turned dark with worry. I promise her I will be, and leave clutching the tote to my body.

The day outside has turned frigid and gray; I can't get a cab so I start walking downtown.

I call Ben to tell him I'm running late.

"Nothing on the calendar today anyway," he says lightly. Then: "Are you going to tell me what's going on? Can I help?"

"I wish you could," I say. "There are just some things I need to figure out. Holding down the fort there is the best thing you can do for me right now. Okay?"

He lets go of a sigh and I can envision him massaging his beard, looking thoughtful and millennial. "You got it. Don't forget—I've got mad skills. I can help with all kinds of things."

"How could I forget?" I say. "I'll check in later. Promise."

Still no cab to be found and my head is swimming. After writing in my journal last night, I did take the single prescribed pill—but nothing else since I flushed it down the toilet. Now I have a sleeping pill hangover, and my thoughts are wild, bouncing between dreams and memories, memories and dreams.

When my phone vibrates again, I fish it out of my bag. The detective.

"So now you're not returning calls?" I never called him back last night. A glance at my phone reveals that there's another message from him, too.

"I've been—busy."

"I know that," he says. "You're not good at taking good advice, are you?"

I think about Noah, the nightclub, the mystery bag I can't bring myself to open.

"I don't know what you mean."

"Let's get together," he says. His voice has a coldness to it that puts me on edge. "We need to talk."

20

I am shivering in my too-light jacket as I push into the diner. Overnight it seems that winter has come. The cold has seeped into my bones, where it will stay until spring.

Detective Grayson is in the far booth, nursing a cup of coffee. I've noticed this about him before, that he chooses the seat from which he has the greatest vantage point of the room. Detectives and photographers, maybe not so different. Always watching.

A cup of coffee, still warm, waits for me, too, as I slide in across from him. The air is heavy with the smell of frying grease and burnt coffee, loud with people shouting orders and customers chatting on cell phones, waiting for to-go egg sandwiches.

"What about being low risk did you not understand?"

I bristle. "Are you following me?"

He pins me with his gaze. "I told you to stay home. Not to go to a nightclub with your new boyfriend and start asking questions."

"Sorry, Detective." I hold the cup in both hands, hoping to leech off some of its warmth. "You don't get to tell me what to do."

He rubs at the bridge of his nose, pressing hard with his thumb and forefinger, a gesture that seems to express his state of perpetual fatigue with the world.

"Okay," he says. "Look. I'm *not* telling you what to do. I'm *trying* to look out for you. Someone's following you, right? We still don't know what happened to Jack. The way I see it you're either going to fuck up my investigation or get yourself hurt."

I hang my head, thinking of the backpack, which is tucked inside my tote, still unopened. I am afraid of what's inside. I should give it to him, open it right here in front of him and face what's in there together. But I don't. I can't. Something powerful stops me.

"So those names you gave me?" he says. "I did some looking. Two of them seem okay. No records, nothing weird online."

He takes out his notebook, flips it open, old-school. Squinting, he slides on a pair of black reading glasses. "But this guy—Noah Avidon. Some kind of artist, right? He's got quite the history with women."

Noah—his words are still ringing in my head about the living haunting the dead. And more. The feel of his hand in mine, his kindness, his willingness to take me where I wanted to go, to make sure I got home safe.

"What kind of history?"

I sip the coffee. It's typical diner swill. No excuse for a brew this bad in a city where there's a barista every few blocks.

"His girlfriend in college was killed."

"A car accident," I say. "He told me."

"Well, maybe not," he says holding my gaze. I want to take that notebook out of his hand and read what he has there for myself, rather than wait for him to dole out the information he's gathered. "The police report indicated that she'd broken it off with him, and he'd been stalking her. That he was following her in another car at the time, that he tried to force her off the road, causing the accident that killed her."

My stomach does an unpleasant flip, and I feel a kind of shaking, uncertain anger. Did he lie to me? Did he misrepresent what really happened in his past? The man standing in my living room last night was good, respectful of my space, offering a piece of his hard-won wisdom. I try to reconcile this with Grayson's news. It doesn't quite fit.

"He told me it was a drunk driver," I say.

"He was following her," he says. "It's in the report."

"Was he convicted? For causing her death?"

"According to the arresting officer, there wasn't enough evidence to support the charge. Mr. Avidon is a person of means. His family hired a powerful lawyer," says Grayson with a cop frown, skeptical, knowing. "And the other driver involved in the accident was, in fact, drunk."

I let the detective's information sink in while he taps a finger on the table, knocking out an impatient beat. What had Noah told me about it? That Bella had been killed by a drunk driver while visiting her parents. Did he ever mention that he'd been there, following her?

"There was *another* woman," he continues into my silence, "who also claimed, according to the restraining order she filed, that he was stalking her. They met online, dated once. She ghosted him, stopped texting, returning calls, tried to disappear. He showed up at her work, at her apartment. Get this. He sent her orchids."

I remember you. Do you remember me?

A little roar starts in my ear. The sound around us seems to ramp up—the chatter, the clanking of silverware on dishes, the drone of a jackhammer outside.

"He got loud one day in her lobby. That's when she called the cops and got the restraining order. He backed off after that."

"Well," I say, not wanting this to be true. "That could be like a *he said, she said* thing. Right?"

"There's a video," he says. "Of the guy losing it in the lobby. It isn't pretty. He's got a nasty temper."

I try to imagine the soft-spoken, easy person I know raging in someone's lobby. I can't picture it. Am I so out of it that I can't see what's right in front of me, that I'd think he was a good guy when actually he was a stalker? The thought turns my stomach to acid. Layla was right. I'm not in a good place; my judgment is off.

"How long ago was that?" I ask, taking a breath.

"Three years or so."

"Nothing since?"

"No," he says with a shrug. "Nothing on the books."

"People change?"

"No." He shakes his head. "Guy like that—in my experience— he gets worse. Older, angrier, accruing more bitterness against women."

"I don't see it."

He shrugs. "You wouldn't," he said. "Not yet. If you saw it, you'd be miles away already. That's how predators work. They give vulnerable people what they want or need, at first. They see a need, a desire, then they exploit, manipulate. When you're hooked, that's when the abuse starts."

Is that what I am, a vulnerable person, someone broken and attractive to predators? Now it's my turn to be exhausted by the world. It doesn't fit, not with the guy I know. But then I guess I don't really know Noah Avidon. Lately, I don't even know myself.

"So, this guy," says Grayson. "He's someone new in your life?"

"Yes, of course," I answer. "I told you that."

"Are you certain?"

He's twisting at that indentation on his ring finger, playing with a ring that's no longer there.

"I met him online." *Keep your voice neutral, don't get defensive, answer simply and honestly but offer nothing more than you must.* That's the advice my mother's lawyer gave me when I was a "person of interest." Why do I feel like I'm back under suspicion? The angry Grayson from my dreams, that face twisted with disdain and judgment. It floats between us. "That was the first time we met."

His cup is empty. He turns it by its rim.

"The bartender at that club? Morpheus? She said that she'd seen you before. She told you as much, right?"

"So—you are *following* me."

He ignores the accusation with a dismissive frown.

"But she said when you two were talking last night, she didn't see *him*."

I'm confused. "Who?"

"The man you were with last night, Noah Avidon. She'd seen him before, too. With you."

My throat catches with fear. I remember the intensity of his stare when I couldn't say if I'd been there before, how the man at the door seemed to know him.

"She said she called after you when she saw him, but you didn't hear. She tried to text, but you didn't answer."

It's not true. It can't be.

"I'll ask you again," he says. His voice is low and he leans in close. "Is he new in your life? Or did you know him before? Maybe even before your husband died."

"What are you asking me?" My voice comes up an octave, is too loud. The couple in the booth next to us stops their conversation to stare.

"Just answer the question."

"No," I say, leaning across the table, lowering my voice. "I've already told you how and where I met him."

"How do you explain what the bartender said?"

"I can't. I don't know. She must be mistaken." My certainty fades, replaced by a cold dawning. "Or—"

"Or," he says. "Or you met him during those days you don't

recall. That blank space in your memory. And he's been watching you ever since."

I close my eyes and press into the dream memory for the face
of the man who was with me. But there's just nothing there.

"*Or* you knew him before."

"Before?"

"Before your husband was killed."

Sarah's words come back, that Jack thought I might be having an affair, that she'd told Detective Grayson that. That's why
we keep coming back to me, my habits, my relationships. My
cheeks grow hot with shame, with anger.

"There was never anyone but Jack," I say.

He lifts his palms. "I'm not saying an affair," he says. "Maybe
you met him, he developed an obsession with you. Maybe without your even knowing. And—"

A woman laughs too loudly, her voice a grating cackle.

"What?" My voice sizzles with fear, with anger. "And then
he hired someone to kill my husband? No. No. That's impossible. That's *crazy*."

Grayson backs away a bit—a kind of surrender. "Is it?"

"Yes." My voice is an angry, frightened hiss.

"Well, we're bringing him in." Voice flat, assured. Grayson
never doubts himself, does he? He never wonders if the world
around him is real or a dream, if he's right or wrong. He doesn't
care. "Just for questioning."

What can I say? He'll do what he wants. Part of me wants to
call Noah, to warn him. But unlike the detective I'm certain of
literally nothing. What if I *did* know him before? What if Noah
is the hooded man in the periphery? Was he devious enough
to then play the role of concerned friend, edging his way into
my life? That bitter coffee turns to acid in my stomach, the cup
has gone cold.

"On another, darker note," he says. Great. A darker note.

"The guy, the one who claimed he could identify that killer for hire?"

"Yeah?"

"He's dead."

The words land hard, knocking the wind out of me. *"How?"*

"Beaten to death," says Grayson. He must see me wince. "Sorry."

"What does it mean?" I ask when I catch my breath.

I hate how my voice shakes, how afraid I sound. I used to be stronger than this. It's as if Jack's death was a blow that broke every bone in my body. Now I'm just a rattling mess, waiting to fall apart.

"Not sure," he says. He flips his notebook shut. "But it does lend a certain credibility to his story."

I've seen this before in Detective Grayson, the practicality that borders on apathy. He's not wearing a suit today, instead a John Jay College sweatshirt and jeans, a worn denim jacket. A black cap and gloves rest beside him on the table.

"But you haven't found the man, the one in the sketch."

Grayson shakes his head, presses his mouth into a frustrated line.

"Is it another dead end?"

The detective looks down at his hands. His knuckles are swollen and red; he trains at a boxing gym on the Lower East Side, he has for years. He shared this once. He works out all his stress there, which must be considerable.

"Maybe," he admits with a dip of his head. "I'm sorry. But I haven't given up."

The room is spinning—Merlinda, Noah, the unopened backpack. My dreams, the hooded man. My life is a Tilt-A-Whirl.

"You okay?" he says. "You look pale."

"I have to go," I tell him.

"Poppy," he says, face grim. "Be easy for me to find."

There's the look I remember, a deep, probing stare, cold and searching.

Who are you? it asks. *What have you done?*

I feel it on my back as I slide away from him and walk quickly through the loud, crowded space.

Outside, the cold air hits me like a wave. A light drizzle falls; cabs speed past me as if I'm invisible. I walk past my office, my phone buzzing in my pocket. I should go in, go to work, call Layla, let her bring in her team of investigators and bodyguards. I should call my mother's lawyer, tell him about my conversation with Grayson, bring the pack and whatever is inside to him. I could retreat behind the curtain of powerful people in my life. And there, I'd be safe—from whatever is happening in my mind, from what happened to my husband, from the man in the shadows.

But I've been sleeping for a year. I broke apart when Jack died, and I've been hiding beneath a blanket of grief and pills, numbing my pain, pushing away the truth, pretending it doesn't matter. It does matter. Who we were, what happened to him, what's happening now. No one can fix this but me.

I pull out my phone to see a text from Noah: Can we talk? The police came to see me. I know what they're going to say to you. There's more to me than that.

My screen is filled with texts and phone calls from Layla and my mother, too. I see the text from the bartender. She's sent me another picture, one of Noah as he stood at the bar waiting for me. He's staring at his drink, his face contemplative. It's him, her text reads. The guy you were with tonight is the same man from last year. Did you already know that?

I stare at him. There's nothing on his face that gives him away as a liar, as a stalker, as a man who rages at women. All I see there is wisdom, kindness. I remember how his lips feel, his touch. But hey, I'm crazy, remember? Completely losing my grip. So what the hell do I know?

Layla: Where are you?

Mac: Hey, Poppy. Layla's driving me crazy. Can you please just go back to our place before she blows a gasket?

Mom: Call me.

Noah: I just want a chance to make you understand.

Layla: Poppy, please, just come home.

21

\

The space is spare, white walls, high ceilings, innards exposed—the venting, wires, an artful tangle above my head. It's constructed like a maze, each surface showcasing a large format image—a bear covered in snow, a congregation of monkeys high in the trees, the soulful face of a gray wolf, eyes a sad, searing yellow. Some of Jack's images hang here, too—a lone man atop a boat, pushing himself with a pole down the muddy waters of the Amazon River, a little girl with startling blue eyes kneeling in a field, hands and face marred with dirt but her gap-toothed smile wide and pure.

Soft flute music plays as I wind through the images. I have the sense of traveling to exotic, distant places, though Alvaro's East Village gallery space can't be more than seven hundred square feet. He has a small darkroom in back, also a room where he lives when he's in the city—a bed, a desk, his computer and a wall of equipment. I've been here a few times—for Jack's shows, for Alvaro's.

What am I doing here? It's like a safari into my past—Sarah, Merlinda, now Alvaro. I'm tracking the big game of my memory, my life with Jack. But the truth, now that I'm really look-ing, seems elusive, always slipping into the shadows, just ahead or just behind.

As I near the back, Alvaro emerges from a door built into the drywall, one that when closed disappeared almost completely. A chime announced my entrance, and there are cameras in two of the four corners of the room, red eyes blinking. He must have been watching me make my way through the gallery space.

"Poppy," he says, shutting the door behind him.

We stand a moment, regarding each other. He has his black hair pulled back, his dark eyes trained on me. His face is all hard angles, his mouth a thin line. I should feel closer to him, I think. He should connect me to Jack, shouldn't he? But there's that familiar distance between us.

He tries to bridge it, moves closer, and takes me into an awk-ward embrace. His body is hard, stiff, as if he's pushing me away even as he's pulling me in.

"How are you?" he asks, releasing me. "It's—good to see you."

He looks older, fuller in the face. There's something changed about him, maybe something softer, sadder through the eyes. Grief, I suppose. It ages us, introduces us to new ways of look-ing at the world. Alvaro, however I feel about him, lost his best friend.

"It's good to see you, too." I say it just because it seems rude not to.

And maybe it is good to see him in a way. I never felt quite relaxed around him, sensed that he was silently judging me and finding me not good enough for Jack. *He's just like that*, Jack used to defend. *He's a watcher.* But today what he thinks of me—or what he thought once—doesn't matter much. He's another per-son with a piece of Jack that I need to collect.

"Ben said you stopped by, that you needed to talk?" I say.

Alvaro and Jack share the same fashion sense, faded jeans and threadbare T-shirts, hoodies, boots. The I'm-too-cool-to-care look. His faded, ripped T-shirt reads *Art should hurt*.

"I just wanted to see how you were doing," he says with a shrug. "I've been thinking about you, about Jack. A lot lately. How *are* you, Poppy? Really."

I almost tell my favorite lie: *I'm okay. Everything's fine. Don't worry about me.* But I don't bother.

"Can you stay a bit?" he asks when I don't say anything.

I nod, not trusting my voice.

He walks over to the street door and locks it, and I follow him into the back.

The space is nicer than it used to be. He's created a cozy sitting area; there's a large screen television on the wall. The galley kitchen still only consists of an espresso machine and a microwave, a small sink. He motions for me to sit on the couch and he brews us some coffee, walks over with two tiny cups, handing me one. He sits across from me, and for a while we don't say anything.

There's a mirror on a stand in the corner and in it I see a wreck of a girl, my gray sweater washing me out, my jeans too big, my hair tied back messily. I try to smooth my hair out, but what's the point?

"You went to see Sarah," I say after an awkward moment of silence.

He nods. "A while back, before I left for the Congo."

That was the kind of assignment Jack would have loved, travel to somewhere exotic, weeks in nature, searching for something elusive like newly released okapi, beauty leaping out at him everywhere—an adventure.

"Jack—he's on my mind a lot," says Alvaro. "Out there I was thinking—man, he would have loved this one."

Is there going to be some jab about how Jack gave up the work he loved to settle down with me? How even if he'd been alive, he'd have turned down that job. But no. He's watching me with that new stare; but it's not judgment I see. It's sadness.

Honestly, maybe the distance between us wasn't just about thinking he didn't like me. Maybe it was more that I never liked him. Alvaro was bad for Jack, luring him into behaviors that he wanted to leave behind—drinking too much, smoking, staying out too late, being wrecked for work and cranky at home the next day. He was *that* friend, the guy who doesn't grow up, who connects your husband to the single, wild man he used to be. Maybe that's why we could never be friends. I wanted Jack in one world; Alvaro wanted him in another, places utterly incompatible with each other.

"Jack would have wanted me to be there for you," he says when I stay silent. "I haven't been."

This surprises me; that sadness I see has etched itself into the lines around his eyes, aged him. There's a hard stab of guilt at my selfishness. Grief can be so myopic. You forget about what other people have lost.

"When things get rough, I tend to disappear," he continues. "Jack knew that. You probably know that, too."

This admission softens me.

"I disappeared, too," I offer. "I fell down a rabbit hole."

He watches me, as if he's looking through all my layers.

"Your breakdown?"

Yes, my breakdown. Fragile Poppy couldn't hold on to reality after she lost her husband. I search for the usual judgment on his face but it's not there now.

"Tell me what happened? I heard some from Ben, from Maura, just the company line."

I recount how two days after the funeral I disappeared, turned up in Layla's lobby, spent a few days in a private hospital, and returned to reality with no memory of those lost days, and spotty recall of the days immediately preceding Jack's murder. It sounds exactly as crazy as it is.

"And those memories—they won't come back?"

"Actually, they might be coming back," I say. "I guess that's why I'm here."

I tell him what's been happening to me, the hooded man, my dreams that might be memories, the new leads Grayson is following up.

I could tell him the details about my visits to Sarah and Merlinda. But I don't. I'm still not ready to look into that bag, and I don't want him to know that Jack suspected I was unfaithful. I guess I just want the sliver of Jack that he had. In the same way that Layla knows a version of me that no one else does, maybe that's true for Alvaro, too. Maybe if I can collect enough of those fragments, the picture of our life together—and his death—will be clearer.

"Was he happy?" That's not the question I meant to ask. But maybe it's what I really want to know. "With his choices? With our life?"

Alvaro blinks. "Don't you know?"

"Was he hiding anything from me?"

Alvaro leans back in his seat, keeping his eyes on me.

"He *loved* you," he says. "I have to admit, I didn't *get it*. I thought he was giving things up—for the agency, for you. It seemed to me like he was settling down, when there was still— I don't know—so *much* out there."

He lifts his shoulders, looks at some point past me.

"I didn't understand. A wife. Trying for a baby. All the responsibility of an agency, a business. The Jack I knew—he was a wild man, an adventure junkie. It all seemed like an anchor to me. Maybe what *you* wanted, but not him."

There's a squeeze on my heart, a kind of tremble inside. "Is that how he felt—ultimately?"

"No," said Alvaro. "He never felt that way. He loved you— more than anything. He was happy. Truly happy."

We sit in silence a moment. It's a different picture than the one Sarah painted, one where Jack was worried about me, our marriage, whether I was faithful or not. But maybe both these versions are equally true. Different moments in the same life.

"I understand now," he says finally.

This new softness—it suits him. Maybe he's in love, I think. Nothing else changes people as much, as quickly.

"He knew that—there's nothing out there." He points toward the front of the gallery. "The more you chase, and roam, sleep around, wake up hungover and empty, the further it gets—whatever it is."

I watch him. I always thought he was just another jerk, another blowhard, a threat in some ways to my happiness with Jack, a lure back to the life of the roaming photographer. Maybe beneath the dark exterior, there's more to him.

"It—whatever it is—it's in here." He taps at his chest.

I remember Maura talking about him in the conference room, my suspicions that she had feelings for him. Ben mentioned that Alvaro came by to pick her up from the office. I put the pieces together.

"Maura, right?" I say. "You've been seeing her?"

He smiles. "Yes," he says. "And the big news is that she's pregnant."

There's a hard and sharp twinge in my heart. I think about what Noah said, about how when you lose someone you don't just lose that person, you lose the hope of everything you thought you'd be together. I thought we'd be parents, Jack pushing our baby in a stroller. I saw the birthday parties, the graduations, one day maybe taking her to college. Maybe we'd be travel photographers again, maybe. Retirees, eventually. One day, grandparents. All of those versions of us died with him.

Alvaro shifts toward me. "I wish I could tell him that I finally understand. He was always the smart one."

I swallow back my sorrow.

"I'm happy for you, and for Maura." It's the truth, despite the pain. "Jack would have been, too."

That seems to please him, something lightening in his gaze. But this is not why I came to see him.

"Was there ever anything that happened—on assignment, or when you were out without me?" I ask after a beat. "Can you think of any reason that someone would want to hurt Jack?"

He looks away, then bows his head and looks down at his folded hands. When he looks up again, that softness is gone.

"Everybody loved Jack. Who would ever want to hurt him?"

It feels like a dodge, a nonanswer.

"*Someone* did. Someone did want to hurt him and now he's gone."

He runs a hand over the crown of his head.

"The detective was here, asking more questions—questions like yours, about people we knew and things we might have done even long ago," he says. "But I told him and I'll tell you, there was nothing like that. Jack—you know—he was always a straight-up guy."

The phone in his pocket rings, he takes it out but declines the call, keeps his attention on me.

"When you went to see Sarah," I say. "You brought her a photograph I've never seen."

He nods, a shadow crossing his face. "Yes, just a picture of the three of us, one of the last nights we were all together."

"Where was it taken?"

He shrugs, wrings his hands. "Some club downtown."

"Morpheus?"

"Yeah, maybe something like that."

"Who took the photo?" I ask. "Who was with you that night?"

He rises, issues an uncomfortable little laugh. "The waitress, I suppose. Those nights were pretty debauched, Poppy. I hate to say it. They're all kind of blurred, run together a bit."

There is a gallery wall of black-and-white pictures behind
him—all of him in various shoot locations around the world,
with other photographers, accepting an award, one of Jack and
him in a blind photographing a wall of parrots in Guatemala.

"That club—it was in my dream. It means something."

He looks at me oddly, an expression I can't read. "Maybe he
mentioned it to you? It was a while ago that we went there."

It makes a kind of sense. Maybe long ago, he did mention
that place and my subconscious just held on to it. That's how
dreams work, details from your life, even things you've forgotten get woven into their fabric.

"You said something odd to Sarah. That you wish Jack hadn't
been such a good guy. What does that mean?"

He's still standing, carrying some tension now in his shoulders.
"Did I say that? Maybe I just meant that he was too good, you
know? Doesn't it seem like the best people get taken from us?"

It does seem like that—my father, Jack. The rest of us are just
left to muddle through without them, to try to make sense of
the world in their terrible absence.

"What are you doing, Poppy?" he asks softly. "What are you
looking for?"

I'm looking for Jack, for myself.

"Answers," I say. "I want to know what happened to my husband. It's been a year and we're still no closer."

"I wish I had those answers for you," he says. He bows his
head. "But I don't."

Another dead end.

Alvaro disappears into the darkroom.

"I have something for you, too," he calls through the door.

He returns with a print of Jack and me on a dance floor. Jack's
wearing a tuxedo, and I'm in a gauzy dress that drapes nearly
to the ground. My hand is in his, his arm firmly at the small of
my back. He's whispering something in my ear, a look of mis-
chief on his face. My smile is bright and wide, head tipped back.

Where were we? The upstate wedding of our friends Bill and Claire Simpson, hence Jack's rare formal attire. He complained miserably about the black-tie dress code, but he was devastatingly handsome that night. *I'm literally swooning*, I told him. We drank too much champagne and danced like idiots, had a blast with Alvaro and his then girlfriend—can't even remember her name, some shy blonde. This was maybe six months before Jack died. Before the second miscarriage, and all the fighting and tears that followed.

"This photo says everything about the two of you—how you loved each other, how you laughed. Look how relaxed, how intimate you are. His eyes shining. Your smile. The way he holds you."

We both regard it. A sliver of our time together, so long ago—or so it seems. I ache for it, for him. I haven't thought about that wedding in ages. How happy Bill and Claire were, how beautiful was the weather, the venue. It was a wonderful evening, not boring or stilted like weddings can be. It was easy and light; we truly had fun. Was it the last time I felt so free and easy, before all the heartbreak that would follow?

"It was just a moment." I feel oddly guilty that he thought that one joyous moment typified our life together. Other moments that followed between us were not so lovely. Not something you'd post on Facebook, or put in a frame.

Alvaro puts a heavy hand on my shoulder.

"But our lives, they're just a series of these moments. Some people never have one like that with *anyone*."

God. I miss Jack. So damn much. I want to reach through that picture, go back and tell myself: *Hold on to him, don't let him go. Don't fight over things that can't be changed. Don't waste time.*

"I was *jealous*," Alvaro says when I stay silent. "Not sure I even realized it. But I was. I wanted what he had. His talent, the love you two shared."

More surprises. His dark, disapproving stare; his eyes always on me. It felt like judgment, dislike, but it was envy.

"After my miscarriage, you told him that he dodged a bullet," I say.

He has the decency to hang his head. "I regret that," he says softly. "I'm an asshole. I talk too much, say things I don't mean."

I regret things, too. So many things.

"I've made a lot of mistakes," he says, voice heavy. "There are things I wish I could—undo."

Staring at the photo, my gaze moves to the other couples dancing, lights glittering overhead, a band playing. The image has a ghostly aura, cast in the shadow of everything that came after it. Mac and Layla dance beside us, both stiff, unsmiling. Layla's eyes glance off into the distance. I find myself following the line of her gaze, scanning the other faces. Ben's there, dancing with a willowy brunette. And someone else.

Standing on the edge of the dance floor, clearly watching the dance floor, a slender woman with dark hair, piercing black eyes. Her expression is blank, unreadable. She's still and grim, alone among the gleeful crowd, people chatting, laughing, dancing all around her.

"Who is that?" I ask Alvaro, showing him the image.

Alvaro looks at it, gives a slow shake of his head; there's something strange on his face, the shade of a smile.

"Not sure," he says. "I don't know her."

But I do. The woman on the computer screen in my dream. The bloody woman in my conference room. Elena. My breath is suddenly thick in my throat. Her face. I reach for it; it's right there.

Who is she?

When I look back at Alvaro, he's watching me. Is there a dark glee in his eyes? But then whatever I saw—it's gone.

"What is it?" he asks. "You recognize her?"

There are footfalls slow and heavy behind me. The front door.

Alvaro locked it when we came back here. The room feels small and hot. Is there another exit? Another way out. There must be.

"Who else is here?" I ask him.

"No one," he answers with a frown.

But the footfalls grow louder, heavier, until finally he comes around the corner. Jack. The front of his sweatshirt is soaked with blood. His glasses are cracked.

"Stop asking questions, Poppy," warns my husband. "I promise you. You don't want the answers."

He's not there. A dream. A microsleep. Hypnagogia. I wipe the sweat from my brow, try to calm my jangling nerves and look away. Just breathe, Dr. Nash would surely say.

"You don't know this woman?" I ask Alvaro again. I don't believe him, though I'm not sure why.

"Do *you* know her?"

I do. I should. This woman from my sleeping and waking dreams. Who was she to my husband? Why is she standing on the edge of our life, watching us?

"She looks—familiar."

I push in deep like I used to when I was first trying to recover my memories. I sink back into the leather of the couch and dip my head into my hands. But everything shifts and swirls. She's a ghost, there and gone. Just like Jack. Just like me.

Someone I used to know.

When I look back up, Jack is gone again.

"Poppy, what can I do?" Alvaro's face is a mask of concern. "Can I call someone?"

You can tell the truth, I think. *You can stop pretending to care about me. You can leave me alone.* But I don't say any of those things, because they make no sense. I don't know if he's my friend or my enemy. I never have known.

"Can I keep this photo?"

"Of course," he says. He takes it from me, slips it into an envelope. "It's yours."

I get up and start to move toward the door.

"Stay awhile," he says. "Let me call a car."

But I'm already weaving through the photographs, heading for the door. An image I recognize as Jack's, a young woman in a burka, her dark sad eyes visible through the black netting, She's hidden, deeply veiled, but she's there looking out into the world. It's the last thing I remember seeing.

22

The sun is dipping low when I find myself back in front of my apartment building. My reflection in the glass doors stares back at me, and I must confront the fact that I have no memory of the last couple of hours. I left Alvaro's gallery and just kept moving. I remember my head spinning, trying to process what Grayson told me about Noah, the photograph Alvaro gave me. How the information twisted and tangled up with my grief, with the shadow on the edges of my life, with my conversation with Merlinda, the pack in my tote. There was a twister inside me, turning, shredding, filling my head with its roar. And then there was nothing.

Dr. Nash: *Our psyches are only designed to take so much. We all have a breaking point.*

The clock in the lobby says it's almost five, that's almost a full workday since I walked out of the gallery. Where have the hours gone?

Before Jack, I would just head out in the morning with my camera and wander. I'd walk until I got tired, then get on the train. I've explored the city this way, been places most young female Manhattanites don't go alone—the ruin of the South Bronx with its wide streets, crumbling towers and fields of rubble; the riot of Spanish Harlem, the avenues always crowded, legs dangling from fire escapes, music pouring from windows; the Meatpacking District with its daytime aura of desertion, where transsexual prostitutes used to rule after midnight, stalking in heels beneath yellow lamplight, and if you wanted to visit a bondage club, that was the place. You can go anywhere with a camera in your hand; you're invisible.

The city will hide you. You can lose yourself inside its grid, walk its streets endlessly. Thirteen miles from tip to tip, you can travel through time, through the world. You will pass thousands of people—the wealthiest and the poorest, the most successful and the most broken, the most beautiful, and the wretched—and still be completely alone. With a camera in your hand, you are recognizable for what you are—an outsider, an observer, not part of anything and so you fade into the scenery.

I was always happiest there, in the space of the observer, before Jack. It's so much easier to stand apart from the chaos and document it, attached to nothing. As a child, if I just stayed quiet, I could move around unnoticed. My father always bent over those robotics texts, my mother zoned out in front of the television—soap operas and old movies. This was before the days of the helicopter parent, where every movement is monitored, every second cataloged. If I didn't make noise, if I didn't want anything, they let me be. I could watch them, their expressions, their unconscious gestures, body language; people are more knowable when they think they're unobserved.

Poppy the spy, my mother used to call me. It's true. Stay quiet, stay hidden, so that you can see.

I have a sense now—a memory of street noise, voices, the squeal and rumble of the train, the ache in my feet—that I've been doing that today, wandering like I used to. I reach for my phone, to see what pictures I've taken, but it's gone dead, the screen blank. I feel a little jolt of alarm. Grayson told me to be easy to find; Layla is going to be worried.

You forgot your tether, Jack used to tease about my smartphone. *How will Big Brother know where you are? How will he communicate with you?* He carried an old flip phone—no email, limited texts, grainy pictures. He'd leave it when he went out, or let it go dead. *When did we give up our freedom?* he'd ask when I complained.

I push through the glass doors into the blissful warmth of the lobby, realizing for the first time that I'm chilled to the bone. As I near the elevators, I hear the doorman call after me, his footfalls heavy and quick behind me on the marble floor. But I let the doors close without waiting to see what he wants. I don't want to talk to anyone; I can't.

In the hallway, there's music, a faint strain of something classical; there's the smell of something savory cooking. When I push through the front door, I realize that all of it is coming from my apartment. Oh, no.

"Poppy? Is that you?"

Mom.

My mother sits primly in the living room, rises when I enter; Layla stands by the counter, arms folded across her middle. Mac stands behind her, an arm on her shoulder. There's also a man dressed all in black; he digs his hands into his pockets and offers me a polite nod of greeting. He's a stranger, but I have a pretty good idea who he is. Anger bubbles up from my middle.

God, this is the last thing I want.

"What is this?"

"Poppy." Layla moves over to me from her place by the tall windows. She puts her hands on my arms. "Where have you been? We've been—so worried."

I can see it etched in her face, the lines at her eyes, the flat of her mouth. I look over to Mac, who offers me a kind, worried smile. If he's left the office to be here, Layla must have been a wreck.

"Why?" I ask. "Did something *happen?*"

She draws back a bit at my tone. "We—we couldn't reach you."

"When did I give up my freedom?" I ask. My voice is sharper, angrier than I intended. But my anger is hot, to the boiling point. "Do I *answer* to you?"

Layla steps back, hurt and anger coloring her cheeks.

"Poppy," says Mac softly. He moves toward me. "We were worried. Really worried."

"There's a history, dear. Don't act like we don't have reason." My mother, in her most annoying "be reasonable" voice. She looks slim and well turned out, as ever. She's wearing her ash-blond bob a bit longer and it becomes her, highlighting the cream of her skin, her high cheekbones, how well she's aging.

"And you have a stalker," says Layla, coming to stand beside her. Damn, they look so alike, it's weird. Hands on hips, same expression of concern, worry. They could be mother and daughter.

"Who's *this*?" I gesture toward the stranger by the couch, who is watching the encounter, head cocked, taking in all the details.

My voice bounces back to me, too sharp. Where is all this anger coming from?

"This," says Layla softly, "is Tom. The man we told you about. He runs Black Dog Security and Crisis Management. He's going to help us figure this thing out."

"What?" I move a bit closer to her. "I told you no, Layla. I don't want this."

"We're going to take care of you, Poppy," says Mac. His voice is soft and pleading. "We owe that to you, to Jack."

"Mac and I are handling this," says Layla. "All you have to do is come home, be safe."

Layla's doing that thing she does, drawing back her shoulders and sticking out her chin. *Mac and I.* It drips with the condescension that comes, apparently, with great wealth. I have the means, it says, to bend the world, bend *you* to my will. She wears it well, as if she's always worn it. And maybe, in a way, she has. Even though she comes from poverty and abuse, Layla has always been powerful. She wouldn't have survived otherwise. Now, she's put herself up high, where no one can hurt her.

"I don't want you to *handle* it."

"Poppy," she says, her voice going cool. "We're trying to help you. Where have you been?"

I don't want to tell her that I don't know. I can't tell these people that. My mom is watching me, her expression gentle, worried. She looks a little confused, too, like she's not sure that what they're doing is right. I move away from them, rage tickling at the back of my throat. I plug my dead phone in; it's the only way I'll be able to piece together my recent past. I decided last night to take pictures, to document. I imagine I stayed with that program during the last couple of hours. I hope I did.

It stays dead, though, in the way it does when the battery is really and truly run down. It will be a few minutes before it comes back, even plugged in. I take a few deep breaths, and everyone is quiet, staring.

"If I may?" It's Tom, the man in black.

"Please," says Mac, as if it's his permission he's asked. Maybe it is. After all, he's paying the bills. Layla goes back to the floor-to-ceiling window, leans against the glass and stares out. She's always been good at looking long-suffering.

"You seem angry," says Tom. "You know, I think I would be, too. You've been ambushed. Or so I'm sure it seems."

There's something soothing about his voice. Some of the tension in my shoulders drains as he continues.

"It really doesn't matter where you've been, Poppy. You're right. You're a grown woman and what you do is your business. You're safe now and I think that's all anyone cares about."

Both my mom and Layla watch him, nodding, as if he is casting a spell. I catch myself nodding in agreement, too, calmed by the sound of his voice. I can see him managing all sorts of crisis, handling every kind of problem.

"Layla had a call from Detective Grayson. He was looking for you. He told her that you left your conversation with him very upset and that he'd tried to reach you since."

Was that true? Had I been *very upset*? There's that feeling again, when someone tells you something about yourself that you think is inaccurate—but you're not *really* sure.

"So, naturally, when she couldn't reach you, Layla became concerned, called your mother, and Mac contacted me. Did they overreact?"

I glance over at Layla, who shrugs. *Maybe.*

"Given what's happened to your husband, what's happening to you now, and—yes, I'm sorry—your recent history, I don't think they did. To be honest, I wish someone cared about me as much as your friends and family care about you."

Layla doesn't look vindicated, as I expect her to. She casts me an apologetic look, then looks down at the ground. My mother moves in, slips an arm around me, and I surprise myself by sinking into her. My mother is not much of a hugger; she's all bones and hard angles, stiff with physical affection. But she's soft now and so am I. I let her lead me over to the couch.

Layla comes to sit on the other side of me. She drops a hand on my thigh. I let them surround me. Mac stands by the kitchen island nodding his head, relieved. He casts a glance down the hall toward the door. *Problem solved*, I can see him thinking. *Can I go back to work?*

"Detective Grayson told you about your friend Noah, his past," said Tom. "My team thinks he's a suspect when it comes to who might be following you."

In the light, I can see a scar on Tom's face. It trails down the center of his right cheek, almost a straight line from his eye like the path of a tear. There's a flatness to his gaze that I have seen before in soldiers, eyes that have seen things that make them want to stop seeing. A shade, a veil comes down. His trim waist, broad shoulders, the way he moves with the measured ease of someone in superior physical condition—it's all part of him. But it's that scar, that's the telling detail. Pain.

"We have a team on him," he says. He lifts his palms at something he must see on my face. "Just watching. We're not in the business of harassing innocent people. He'll never even know we're there. If."

"If?"

"If he doesn't bother you again," says Mac.

Bother me again. He didn't bother me, I want to say. *He was kind to me and I felt something for him. He's my friend. More than that maybe.*

I can see why Layla likes Tom, though; he's one of those guys. The guy who handles things other people can't handle. A fixer. I want to say that I don't believe Noah has anything to do with this. I get it. I know what Grayson said; it just doesn't mesh with the man I am getting to know. *Was* getting to know. I'm a better judge of character than that, aren't I? If he were some stalker, if there was something that wrong with him, I'd know it. Wouldn't I? But I just stay silent.

"Meanwhile, we have a team going over the police investigation of your husband's murder. NYPD did a passable job—we're not pointing fingers. Grayson seems like a good cop. But we bring a fresh perspective, as well as unlimited resources to an investigation. If this was something more than a random mugging, we'll have a bead on that pretty quickly."

"There's something else," Layla says quietly. She looks up at Tom, who begins a slow pace by the window.

"What?"

"You asked me the other night if there was anything I remembered about when I found you. Anything you said."

"You told me no."

She looks down at her fingernails, a gesture I recognize well, something she does when she's nervous, uncomfortable.

"You told me that you suspected Jack was having an affair," she says. Her words take the air from the room.

She lifts her palms. "Which you'd *never* said before your break. But you kept saying her name over and over."

"What was it?"

She hesitates a moment. "Elena."

That's when the room seems to fade out and back in again, and she's standing in the corner—silent, radiating rage. Elena— her eyes purple, teeth missing, a swath of blood down her shirt, watching me. *I knew your husband.*

Jack's there, too, lounging on the couch.

Don't look at her, Poppy, he says. *She's not there.*

I ignore them both. Hypnagogia. Am I awake or asleep?

"You thought it had something to do with this affair, why he might have been killed," says Mac moving closer to us.

The matchbook, that scrawled name and number. He thought I was having an affair, according to Sarah; I thought he was, according to Layla. But Jack's not alive to say what he was thinking then. And I, shamefully, don't know. How very far apart we were when he died. I wonder not for the first time: Would we have found our way back to each other?

"Why didn't you tell me?" I ask.

Layla shakes her head, looks past me.

"I told Detective Grayson at the time. But there was no evidence that either of you were having an affair, nothing in Jack's effects that suggested it. No one in his contacts, no evidence in his phone records. You forgot about it after you came back to yourself. I thought—why cause you any more pain than you were in already? Especially if it wasn't true."

"A confabulation maybe," says Tom. "Something the mind does to explain things that can't be explained, to make things more manageable."

My head. It's a siren of pain; nausea twists at my insides. I'm shaking, wipe at my forehead, which is damp with sweat. I know enough to know I'm detoxing. Those pills that I've been taking to numb pain, to take the edge off my anxiety, the pills I flushed down the toilet. What I wouldn't give for one of them now.

"Honey," says my mother. She shifts forward on the couch. "Why don't you sit down?"

I realize that I've risen from the couch and I'm moving toward the door. Mac seems poised to make a grab for me, edging closer.

Elena's gone but Jack's still there, lounging across from Layla and my mother.

Were you? Were you having an affair? Was it all too much—the miscarriages, my desire for a child, your avoidance of it, the day-to-day slog of it all? Did you meet someone beautiful and exotic, a model at a shoot maybe, another photographer? I want to ask him.

I hear that shrieking voice again, a vibration from a dream.

You're a fucking liar.

My phone buzzes then, coming back to life. I walk over to it, feeling all their eyes on me as I do. The screen is filled with texts—from Noah, Layla, my mother, Ben. There are voice-mail messages. I ignore them all, go straight to the photos, start scrolling. The last picture on there is Noah from last night—there's nothing from today, no pictures of Merlinda, no city scenes. Wherever I went, whatever I did, it's gone. Confusion and fear are a roar in my head. What's happening to me?

"Poppy." It's Mac, cool, reasonable and in charge.

Almost. I could almost go to him. Our eyes lock; there's always been a connection. A shared love of Layla, yes, but something that's just us, too. If he and I had met first, we'd have been friends.

I move over to the tote on the chair. Inside, there's no pink pack—just my wallet, some makeup, a brush, receipts—the usual jumbled mess. I remember holding that pack in my hand, the heft of it. I remember the scratch of the fabric, how the seam was coming unstitched.

I had it.

I know I did.

Merlinda's apartment, snapping that image, the colors, her ringed hand, the wind chimes, the aroma of incense—I was there; I know I was. My throat is tight and dry, my heart stuttering.

"What *is* it?" says Layla.

The photo, the one Alvaro gave me. It's still there in the envelope he slipped it inside. I take it out, show it to Layla.

"Who is she?" I point to the woman in the picture. There's a flash, a quicksilver microexpression of fear, then her features fall into a practiced mask of ease and patience. Mac just stares at it, silently confused.

"Who?" she says.

"This woman," I say, tapping my finger on the image. It's real, as I remembered it. She's still there. "Do you know her?"

"Where did you get this?" she asks, eyes drifting from the photo to me, then over to Tom, who leans in, as well.

"From Alvaro," I say.

"You saw him? When?" asks Mac.

"That doesn't matter," I say, exasperated. "Do you know *who she is?*"

"When was this?"

"The wedding upstate—Claire and Bill Simpson. Remember?"

She makes a show of staring at the image, showing it to Mac and smiling a little. "I don't know who that is, Poppy. Do you?"

Mac offers a helpless shrug.

I want to say that it's Elena—the woman in my dream, in my conference room, the scrawled name on the back of the matchbook. But I don't know if that's true. And it just sounds so crazy. I'm sweating, sick to my stomach.

"Look, Poppy," says Tom, so calm, so soothing. "If you think this is a lead, we can help you follow it. We'll find this woman. We'll ask the right questions. If it has something to do with Jack, we'll figure that out."

You can't, I want to say. *She's dead. Just like Jack.*

But I don't know if *that's* true, either, or why I even think that. I only have my disjointed hypnagogic dreams to guide me.

I can't take this.

What I need is to get out of here. Right now. I grab the phone and the charger, shove them into my bag and shoulder it. "I have to go."

"That's not a good idea," says Tom. "Poppy, let's talk. Let us help you. But more importantly, let us keep you safe in the meantime."

He sounds so reasonable as I move toward my front door. They all follow slowly, Mac with his hand outstretched. "Come on, kiddo, don't do this."

"Poppy, honey," says my mom. "Stay with us. Everything's okay."

But it isn't okay. It hasn't been okay in so long that I don't even remember what it feels like. They're all standing there, all of them wanting to help me. But I can't stay here, with them. Because that means I just crawl into bed and let them "take care of it," let them do everything they can to "help me."

But that's not going to work. Because it's time to take care of myself. It's time to wake up and remember what happened to Jack. What happened to us.

I turn and run for the door, lock it behind me from the outside. As they struggle inside to undo the inside lock, I open the doors to the stairs and let it swing wide, then slam shut. I run around the corner and wait. Tom, Mac and Layla race out, head down the stairs through the still-open door. Their footfalls clattering on the concrete, their voices urgent.

"Poppy!" Layla calls. "Poppy, *please* come back."

"I'm calling Detective Grayson," my mother says, the door closing.

When the hallway is empty again, I press the call button for the elevator.

"Poppy."

"Mac," I breathe, startled. "I have to go."

"You don't," he says. He has both his palms up in a gesture of surrender. "Look—you're sweating. You're pale and shaking. You're not going to help yourself, or find out what happened to Jack—not like this. But Tom can help us. He has the resources."

I back away from him, though he makes good sense. Any reasonable person would listen. But I can't. I can't. I can't go back to sleep. And something else—my heart is racing. I am afraid. I don't know of what, of whom.

I hear the ding of the elevator arriving and Mac takes a step closer.

"What are you going to do? Physically restrain me?"

Something strange crosses his face—sadness, something else.

"Come on," he says. A final plea.

"Let me go, Mac."

He lets his arms drop to his sides, shakes his head.

"Don't do this to her," he says. "She can't lose you again. You're the only family she has."

Guilt, it's a stab in the gut. But when the elevator door opens, I step inside and watch Mac, sad and defeated, disappear. I go all the way to the basement and exit through the service door in the back of the building.

On the street, I hail a taxi, climb quickly inside.

"Where to?"

"Uptown," I say. "Just drive."

And then we're racing up Broadway, the city a blur of light and color. I scroll through my texts, looking for anything to orient me.

Noah: I can explain things. It's not what it looks like. Please give me a chance to tell my side of this.

Ben: Hey that guy, Rick? Rick in finance. He's persistent. Wants to keep the date, says he'll hang there for a while in case you change your mind. It's just a drink, he says.

"Where to?" says the driver.

Where to?

"Hey, lady," he says, impatient, dark eyes staring in the rearview mirror. "Where do you want to go?"

I wish I knew that answer to that. Do I want to go back? Do I want to go forward? I give him an address and he keeps driving. I lean my head back, fighting sleep.

Jack is breathing in that deep and even rhythm that I know means he'll be difficult to rouse. I can slip away before he even knows I'm gone. He is always most soundly asleep in the hours between three and five.

I lie there for a moment, feeling the distance between us. We are inches apart, but a gulf, a deep divide separates us. When did it start? After the last miscarriage? No, before that. When I confided in him how desperately I wanted a baby, how the desire came on me powerfully and would not be denied. It wasn't an intellectual decision. Do we have the time? The money? What about the business? What about the work? None of those questions or their answers were a part of this. It was something that welled from inside me. He didn't understand, though he pretended to. He complied because that's who he is; he wants me to have the things I want.

Maybe that's it. Maybe it's causing him to drift away, the fact that I want something he doesn't want as much. It casts into stark relief our differences. When we met, he said, you told me children weren't a priority. That you hadn't ruled it out, but that it wasn't a driver for you, not something in the plan.

That was true then. Something changed. People change.

I slip from the covers, that unrelenting cold still with me, clogging my sinuses and making my head heavy. My throat is raw from coughing. But I need to get out there, into that hour before dawn, and run. I need to think about all of this—our fight, my miscarriages, that desire, how I feel now. About a baby. About Jack. Things were easier when I was alone. Lonelier. But easier.

His breathing goes deeper, and I reset the alarm. Then I quickly dress in the living room, pulling on the clothes I left out there, my sneakers, my down vest. I take Jack's wool cap and even a scarf. I'll have to strip them off as I heat up, stick them in my pockets. But the wind whips up our street, a frigid corridor.

Outside, the air is even colder than I anticipated. I start moving right away, a light jog past the row of awnings, doorways golden with the light inside, doormen cozy and warm at their desks. I wait at the light, then enter the park. My heart rate is up, and I'm already getting warmer, the wool at my throat growing scratchy.

I stay on the main path, which is already populated with other runners, many of whom I recognize from keeping this routine for so long. You run into the same people morning after morning, maybe you wave, notice when a few days go by without seeing the guy who runs in the same red shirt and shorts every day, even in winter. Or the woman who sprints then jogs, sprints then jogs. The lean, muscular girl who walks, arms pumping, and is faster than a lot of the joggers out there, her face a mask of dogged determination.

Then, I don't know why, but I veer off onto the path that takes me deeper into the park, into the dark, away from the other runners. The city looms tall and glittering around me as I take the incline, pass under the first bridge. I am not afraid. I know this city. And more than that, I am fast. I pick up speed, feeling my temperature rise, my heart working. It all drops away, my fight with Jack, the pain I've been carrying around, even the heaviness of my head cold. My sinuses clear, and the endorphins start to pump. I pick up my pace.

The sky turns the milky blue-white of dawn. By the time I return to the apartment, it will be light. As tension, anger and sadness leave me, pushed aside by the brain chemicals of exertion, I realize that Jack's right. I've let my desire for a baby, and my sadness over my miscarriages drain some of the love and passion from my marriage. I've turned sex into something scheduled, something burdened with expectation. Maybe I need to recast my thinking. Maybe we are enough, I realize. Even if there's no one and nothing else, we're enough.

It comes from nowhere, the blow to my side, and I am flying, land-

ing hard on the ground. *Struggling for orientation, the world in a hard tumble—what happened? I tripped. It must be. Then another blow, hard to the ribs. The air leaves me, pain flooding my senses. No. No. A weight on top of me, then a hard knock to the jaw, a bottle rocket through the crown of my head, down my spine. My arms are butterfly wings, flapping powerless. Hands on my body. Grabbing. Feeling. I writhe, try to slink away. A prey animal, terrified, helpless.*

Money. I. Have. Money.

My mother drilled it into my head, never leave the house without cash in your pocket. You never know. Hand it over. If you get mugged, give them everything. It doesn't matter. Only your life matters.

My rings. Take them.

But the blows keep coming, my stomach, my face again. I taste blood, metallic and strange. I feel myself lift, go elsewhere.

I can't see him. He's wearing a hood or a mask. His face is just a shadow, as the blows keep coming. A rain of pain.

And then I'm floating, outside myself. I look down as he rises, a hooded figure. He stands over the broken version of myself. Not me. Someone else. She is very still, arms out, palms up, legs askew. A deep black pool spreads out from beneath her. He's panting, shoulders heaving with his effort. The stranger, the golem, the monster who waits in the shadows to destroy, to change everything you think you know about the world and your place in it. I watch as the scene gets more and more distant, until it is gone, until I am gone.

I wish. I wish it had been me.

23

"Can I see you home?" Rick. Rick in finance.

We're on the street. Our awkward date, if you can even call it that, about to draw to a merciful close. The world tilts on its axis, sidewalk askance beneath my feet. I shouldn't have come here. What was I thinking?

"You okay?" he asks.

His concern seems exaggerated, almost as if he's mocking me. There are other people on the street, a couple laughing, intimate, close, a kid with his headphones on, a homeless guy sitting on the stoop.

"I'm fine," I say again, feeling defensive. I didn't have *that* much to drink.

But then he has his arm looped through mine, too tight, and I find myself tipping into him. I try to pull away from him. But he doesn't allow it. He's strong and I can't free my arm.

"Hey," I say.

"Hey," he says, a nasty little mimic. "You're okay."

Of course I'm okay, I want to snap. But the words won't come. There's just this bone-crushing fatigue, this wobbly, foggy, vague feeling. Something's not right. The world starts to brown around the edges. Oh, no. Not now.

"She's okay," he says, laughing. His voice sounds distant and strange. "Just one too many I guess."

Who's he talking to?

"Let go of me," I manage.

He laughs; it's echoing and strange. "Take it easy, sweetie."

He's moving me too fast up the street, his grip too tight. I stumble and he roughly keeps me from falling.

"What the hell are you doing?" I ask.

Fear claws at the back of my throat. I can't wait get away from this guy. He pulls me onto a side street; there's no one around.

"Hey." A voice behind us. He spins, taking me with him. There's someone standing there. He looks distantly familiar as the world tips. Somewhere inside me there's a jangle of alarm. He has a dark hood on, his face not visible.

It's him.

He's big, bigger than—what's his name? Reg, or something. Rex? The big man blocks our path up the sidewalk.

"Hey, seriously, dude," says Rick. Yes, Rick, that was it. "Step aside. I've got this."

But things are fading fast, going soft and blurry. There's a flash, quick-fire movement. Then a girlish scream of pain, one that touches all my nerve endings, a river of blood. Black red on lavender. The sidewalk rises hard and unforgiving.

Arms on me. Very strong.

He lifts me and begins to carry me down the street. I can still hear Rick from finance keening, a swell of other voices, but the hooded man moves swiftly and the noise fades. He's impossibly powerful.

"Hey, hey!" a voice calls after us. But it fades away. We are moving so fast, and then it's dark. Disoriented; nothing makes sense.

"What did you do to him?" I ask. But my voice is weak, too soft. "Where are you taking me?"

I try to writhe away from him, but I'm a rag doll. Am I dreaming again?

Then all I hear are his footfalls on concrete, things pass by in an unpleasant blur—parked cars, concrete pillars, the metal of elevator doors. We're inside, gray walls all around. Silence. The opening of a car door. He lays me into a deep leather seat, leans in close to fasten my seat belt.

"Where are we going?" I can't seem to focus, on him, on anything.

The interior of the car is warm, the leather buttery. The soft glow of the dash, the red and blue of the controls, the dark outside, the quiet hum of the engine. We are flying into space.

I don't know how much time has passed, or where we are. I sit up and look outside, but there is only darkness.

"What did you do to him?" I ask.

No moon in the sky, stars obscured by trees like sentries on the side of the road. I am not bound, just strapped in to the seat. I turn, look at him. It's him. Did I know it all along? Maybe.

"I kept him from taking advantage of you," he says.

"And what are *you* doing?"

"I'm taking you someplace safe," he says. "You've been there before. Do you remember?"

"No," I say. "I don't remember."

He slows the car, pulls onto the shoulder and comes to a stop.

He turns to watch me. His hands reach for mine. My fingers find his face instead. I look at all the lines, the shine and intensity of his eyes, touch the shadowy places where the darkness pools. His face is open and honest. Desire, I see it. But I see kindness too, the face of hard lessons learned, pain and loss.

I remember him. I met him on the dance floor of Morpheus— I was alone and he joined me. What drove me to a nightclub on the Lower East Side, I have no idea. The throb of the music, how it moved through me, how I lost myself—it all comes back. We danced. He looked so much like Jack, I just closed my eyes and let him be Jack.

I remember his kiss, how he led me out into the street, asked me if I wanted to go home with him to his house in the country. I was weak with grief, brain addled. I said yes. It all comes back, a rush of memory—just like Dr. Nash said it might.

"Let me see your purse," he says.

I hand it to him. He digs through and pulls out that last bottle of pills.

"What is this?" he asks. "Have you been taking these?"

I tell him that I have, and more than that, and mixing pills with alcohol. Anything to numb the pain, to sleep, to forget. I knew it was dangerous, the risks. Maybe the truth is that I didn't care.

"Are you ready to be done with this?" he asks. The vial sits in the wide palm of his hand. "Are you ready to wake up, Poppy, and face whatever it is you're running from? It has to be you. It has to be your decision."

"Yes," I say. "I'm ready."

He rolls down the window and throws the bottle out onto the road. The cold air, the wind rushes into the car, and then he slides the window up. For a second I'm terrified; I want to run out onto the road and gather them all up.

"Come with me? Or go back?" he says. "The choice is yours. Right now, I'll take you anywhere you want to go."

I still have my hands on him, now resting on his forearm, his hand on my leg, leaning in. Staring into the deep of his gaze, there's only us, this moment. My life, outside the confines of this car, is a chaotic swirl.

"Do you want to wake up or go back to sleep?"

"I want to wake up."

He lifts my chin and forces me to meet his eyes.

"Call someone and tell them you're okay, so that they're not worried."

I make the strange decision to call my mother.

"Poppy," she whispers, her voice heavy with relief. "Where are you?"

"Mom," I say. "I'm okay. I just need some time to understand what's happening to me. Tell them—Layla, Mac, Tom—that I'm fine. That I just need some space."

I can hear Layla in the background. *Let me talk to her.*

"Sweetie, please," Mom says. Her voice cracks with emotion. "Just come back and let us help you."

Let us help you.

"Mom," I say. "This is something I have to do alone."

"Where are you going, honey? Tell me that at least."

"I'll call you," I say. "I promise."

I end the call and turn off the phone. He puts the car in gear and starts to drive.

I leave everything, everyone behind.

Then I am nothing but pain. I am grief. I am rage. The days pass in a rushing river of physical illness; I am as sick as if I have been poisoned, head throbbing, body rejecting food and water. Detox at its ugliest.

The nights are impossibly long, endless twisting tunnels of misery, where I piece together all the missing fragments of my memory. The nights are filled with ghosts. In my journal, I write and write—my last year with Jack, the miscarriages, the terrible fights, my unhappiness without my art. The truth, all of it, not just the story I told myself and others about my life.

You're a fucking liar.

The voice I heard was my own.

And then the grief of losing him, losing us, in a violent and totally random way. How angry I was at the injustice of it. That all the things between us would never be resolved; that the story of us had no ending. We didn't come through our challenges stronger than we were before. We didn't choose to end our marriage, both of us finding another, better path. He just died. Wrong place. Wrong time. All issues unresolved. No time to say goodbye. A story with an end we didn't choose.

Slowly, the pills, the chemicals flooding my system begin to recede like a tide. And my mind clears. He's there.

Listening, holding on, offering the things he's learned. Lying beside my bed on the floor while I writhe, or standing outside of the bathroom.

"Think of it as a purge, a releasing," he says helpfully through the door.

"Shut up," I wail. "Stop talking."

"Yep," he says. "Gotcha."

And then, one night, I sleep. A deep dreamless slumber from which I wake into a bright, clear morning, my head light with freedom from pain. The ghosts are gone, and I can think again. I feel myself solid in the world. He sleeps in a chair by the fireplace, looking bent and uncomfortable. I rise from the bed and walk over to him.

"I am awake," I tell him when he opens his eyes. I take his hand and he rises. He runs his fingers through my hair, rests his hands on my shoulders. His gaze is warm, those faceted hazel eyes glittering.

"Nice to meet you, Poppy," he says.

"Nice to meet you, Noah," I answer.

In his arms, I think of Jack, when he found me outside the gallery where I was working then.

"Did you know that the poppy flower symbolizes sleep and death?"

"I did know that," I said. "But my mother just really likes the color red. That's why she chose that name."

"In classical mythology, it represents resurrection."

"You've done your research."

"It also signifies remembrance." He moved in close and handed me

the flowers, their droopy scarlet faces fragrant and cheerful. "Do you remember me?"

I do. I remember him. I remember myself. I remember everything.

Those lost days after Jack's funeral, it all comes back in a rush.

PART TWO
Awake

You are not wrong, who deem
That my days have been a dream.
—Edgar Allan Poe, "Dream Within a Dream"

24

The days after Jack's funeral...

Tap, tap, tap.

The sound leaks unpleasantly into my consciousness. *Tap, tap, tap.*

I bury my head beneath my pillow, sleep holding on tight. Then, the sense that everything around me—the scent on the air, the sounds, the feel of the sheets beneath me—is wrong, off somehow.

Tap, tap, tap.

Black winter branches scrape against a windowpane in a pale dove gray and white room. Flecks of snow hit the glass, drift down leaving trails of tears. Milky light washes in and I am alone in a place I've never seen. A plush chaise languishes in front of a fireplace where embers still burn. Shelves of books, an abstract oil in blues and silvers hangs on the wall. A red dress drapes over the chair, matching heels askew on the floor.

My head aches, limbs filled with sand. Beneath there's a hard pulse of fear—where am I? This is not right. But the fog in my mind is thick and so heavy. It's an effort to shift to sitting, the world wobbling. Adrenaline starts to pump, a surge of energy gets me from the bed, even as the world tilts. I pull at the drawer in the bedside table, looking for my phone, my wallet. It's empty, smelling like new wood.

I'm wearing a big T-shirt, black, worn to softness. It drapes almost to my midthigh. Another door leads to a bathroom. In the mirror, I catch my haggard reflection—hair wild, circles deep and black under my eyes, skin white, void of any color. I lean on the sink, run the water and splash it cold on my face.

Wake up. Christ. Pull yourself together.

I stumble back out into the bedroom, lurch for the door and try the knob. Locked. Panic wells, a tide that washes through making everything feel disjointed and strange. I twist and pull at the door, which sticks fast, then I move to the window. It's just a solid pane of glass in a frame, thick, no mechanism for opening. Outside, just snow and snow and the black twisting branches of dead winter trees reaching into that gray the sky turns when snow falls.

My panic is silent; I don't call out. Who would I be calling? Where the hell am I?

I hear a sound outside the door, footfalls. I watch, nearly paralyzed with fear. It's quiet for a moment, then the door softly pushes open.

"Hey," he says. "You're up. How are you feeling?"

Sandy curls, a few days of stubble. Big, broad. I touch my lips. Do I still feel him there? He frowns, concerned. "You okay?"

"Where?" I manage. "What is this place?"

He moves closer, which causes me to move back, knocking into the bed and sitting heavily onto the mattress. He lifts his hands—surrender, supplication. He waits, keeping his distance.

"My place upstate," he says. "We came last night."

I shake my head. There are remnants of myself knocking

around, none of them coming together in a whole I can understand.

"Where's my phone?"

"In your purse," he says. "I put it in the drawer."

He opens a drawer and takes out a clutch and hands it to me. Money. My platinum card, my driver's license. My phone is dead. There's no charger.

"I have to go," I say. "I have to get back to the city."

"It's snowing pretty hard," he says, pointing to the window where the view outside is quickly whiting out. He sits on the chaise, watching me.

"Why was the door locked?" I ask.

He looks back at the way he entered, as though confused by the question.

"It wasn't," he says. "It just sticks sometimes. I restored this house, but it's old. The wood swells and shrinks, lots of strange noises."

The bed is soft and the room is warm. I know him. I have known him. I find that the panic, the fear—it's subsiding.

I have a place upstate. We can get away for a couple of days. You'll regroup, decide what to do next, decide who you think I am. Those words bounce around the walls of my memory. When did he say them? In the car, when I asked him where we were going.

"Why don't you just rest awhile longer?"

"I need to call someone," I say. "They'll be worried. Layla, my mother, Detective Grayson."

"There's no landline," he says. "I'll get my cell phone, okay? Just stay here and I'll be right back with it. And some tea. Are you hungry?"

I am ravenously hungry suddenly, cored out and empty with it.

"I'll leave the door wide open," he says. There's an easiness about him, something gentle. "You're safe, okay?"

I believe him even though there's something I know I should

remember but don't. After a while, he brings the phone and puts it beside me. The bedside table is a carved, solid piece of wood, like a piece of a gigantic trunk. I run my fingers along its finished surface where the knots and grains are visible. The phone, slim and modern, looks out of place, almost an insult to the organic lines of the surface beneath it.

"I made that," he said.

"It's beautiful."

He has a tray and rests it on the bed. He hands me a cup of tea, warm in a misshapen ceramic mug.

"And this mug," he says, with a smile. "Let's just say I haven't mastered the potter's wheel."

His hands are covered with scars, the discoloration of burns, white lines, knuckles swollen, calloused. He sees me looking. "From the metalwork," he says, regarding his hands as if they're new to him. "Burns and cuts are part of the territory."

That's right, a sculptor. This place is where he comes to work; he's told me this. There's a barn—an isolated property. Sometimes he spends months here alone. It's in a town called The Hollows. I've read about it—an energy vortex some people call it. Bad things happened here—missing children, fires, hauntings.

"The signal is pretty good." He takes a seat on the hearth, nods toward the phone. "Better than it used to be. I was happier when I was cut off against my will. Now I have to apply the same discipline here as I do in the city."

He stokes the fire and the dying embers come back to life. I stare at the phone. I should call. But.

"Driving conditions are pretty bad," he says. "But we can brave it if you need to get back."

I find that I don't want to leave and return to the life I've left in the distance.

"Jack and I fought the night before he died." I don't know why I say it.

He closes the screen in front of the fire and sits in the chair beside it. I don't remember telling him about Jack, but I know I did.

"We were fighting a lot. Daily."

He rubs the stubble on his chin, watching. There's something about him that reminds me of Jack. The artist's eye, the one that sees and absorbs, doesn't judge.

"Conflict," he says. "It's normal, right? I mean, they don't sell it that way. It's all flowers and moonlit walks. But the real thing—it's not that."

I think of my parents, Layla and Mac, all the fights, the slicing words honed sharp to hurt, the bleak silences where there's just nothing left to say. I always wanted to do better. Maybe you can't. Maybe when two people occupy the same space, the same life, there is necessary struggle. My parents, they never seemed to fit, but they stayed together.

"He loved you," he says. "You loved him. If he'd lived you'd have made up, gone on."

I flash on something. New Year's Eve. Merlinda's veined, ringed hands, The Seven of Swords. The card of deception.

"Maybe," I say.

He waits, draws a breath and releases it. Outside the wind sighs, scatters icy bits, branch fingers scratch the glass.

"I miscarried. Twice."

"I'm sorry."

"That grief—the grief you're not really supposed to feel— maybe it changed me. Changed us."

He blows out a breath.

"Life is brutal. Naturally, it changes us. Why does that always come as a surprise? The galaxy is in a constant state of change, an explosion, ever moving outward. The planet—shifting, erupting, continents drifting, tsunamis, fires raging. Why do we try to stay the same? We can't."

There's a small black sculpture on the hearth, the stick figure of a man, fallen to his knees, arms outstretched, thin fingers splayed, reaching toward heaven, head bent back. The agony of loss.

"You lost someone."

"I did."

He tells me about Bella, his college girlfriend, how she died in a car accident, how a week earlier she miscarried the baby they hadn't planned. The world; it's unimaginably cruel.

"We were fighting," he says. "The pregnancy—it was an accident. We probably would have already split months earlier if not for that. We were young and so, so dumb. We thought we could stay together for the baby, make a go of it. And suddenly that reason was gone."

"But you loved her."

"I did. I still do. The idea of who we might have been. Who our child might have been. But it's just a dream. A fantasy. Who knows how things would have been, really? We might have grown to hate each other."

The wind picks up and starts to howl; the house perceptibly groans.

He watches me, legs crossed, the fire behind him. He's a shadow against the flames, a stranger. And yet, I am relaxed, feel that I've known him a long, long time.

"Should I give you some privacy to make those calls," he asks.

I pick up the phone he's laid beside me. The signal is strong. I should call Layla, my mother. How frightened they'll be. Something stops me, a tangle of voices, something I can't remember, a deep, bright core of anger, something as hard as a stone inside me.

"The loss of hope—a miscarriage, a death," I say. "You lose the person and everything you thought your life would be. You lose yourself, too."

He dips his head into his hand a moment, then he rises to come stand in front of me.

"Poppy," he says.

I rise and he stands before me a moment, then I slip into his embrace. I let him hold me in powerful, muscular arms, pulling me into the tight, flat warmth of his body. I allow my head to drop to his shoulder. And we stand there, swaying slightly, for I don't know how long—the fire sighing, the snow tapping.

Finally, he pulls back the covers, and I climb inside. He tucks me in like a child, kisses me on the forehead and leaves. The phone still lies beside me, but I don't touch it.

The next day when the snow has stopped falling, the world outside is a brilliant diamond white, pressed crisply against a gunmetal sky. The dead winter trees an ink drawing. I bundle into ill-fitting clothes, his jeans, a thermal undershirt, parka, and he straps boots and snowshoes onto my feet. We crunch through the winter hush, the world starkly silent except for us. Heat comes up from my core, and I sweat even though the air is frigid. Above us a lone hawk circles, gliding wide and effortless, dipping, climbing.

In the quiet, in the effort, I am clean. Something releases. This is what Jack wanted, a place away from the city, away from the crush, the hustle, the constant hum and nag of it. Noah walks ahead, slim and dark, black against white.

In the emptiness of snow and sky, all the horror—the police, the lawyers, the funeral, the well-meaning friends and family— it slips away. I can hear myself, feel myself. I allow the raw grief to tear through me, the loss of Jack, the children we never had, the life we won't live. No one rushes at me with words, using their bodies and their voices to comfort me. There is no comfort for this. It must rage through me, this pain like a typhoon. It must be allowed to destroy, take me down to the ground. I let the beast ravage me. No tears. This is beyond tears.

Suddenly, it rushes through—a wrenching wail of grief and pain and sorrow. The sound carries—a flock of winter birds call in alarmed answer, flap away into the sky. Then it is silent again. I am silent again.

He stops and waits. As I approach, his eyes search my face. Something like a sad recognition pulls down the lines of his mouth. He keeps walking. I follow. How long? How far? I don't know. It's dusk when we return, the sky black-and-blue like a bruise.

Inside, I strip off my cold clothes; he stokes the fire to raging in the great room, where there are high, vaulted ceilings, windows and windows and more windows staring out into winter.

I don't remember the last time we exchanged words.

"Do you do this a lot?" I ask. "Rescue women who have lost their minds?"

"Almost never."

His smile is easy, doesn't ask for anything, as he hands me a cup of tea. I sit holding it, letting it warm me.

"I can hear myself. I can feel what I want to feel here."

He dips his head in understanding. "That's why I come. I don't work as well in the city."

Out in the space between the house and the barn, there's an enormous structure—a great swirl of hammered black metal. Two figures locked in a dance, or a battle, arms thrown, legs in wide stance, the impression of hair flying. Gaping Os for mouths, black eyes. Anger, fear, love, joy—I can see all the raw elements of existence.

"Agony," he says.

He's watching me look at the sculpture; it's nearly glowing in the setting winter sun.

"That's where I was when I forged that."

"I see it. The one upstairs, too."

I can't stop staring at it, the way the lines seem fluid, in motion, almost like liquid. How the shape of it communicates pain.

"I have regrets," I say, though I didn't even know I was thinking that.

"So do I," he says. "Maybe everyone does."

"What do you regret?"

He draws in a deep breath, releases it, looking off into the middle distance.

"I've held on too tightly to things that weren't mine. I've let anger get the better of me, let it isolate me, alienate me. Coming from that place of anger, I've mistreated people."

His aura is calming; he seems so grounded and real. I can't imagine him acting out in anger. There are so many facets to us, so many different shades of truth. For some reason, his words make me think of that last New Year's Eve with Jack. Merlinda, the cards on the table, the countdown—Layla, Jack, Alvaro and Mac. There was something there, a moment from which I was excluded. Seven of Swords—the card of deception.

"There are so many layers to everything, everyone," I say. "How do you ever know what's real?"

"Maybe you don't need to know," he says. "Maybe it's all real in the moment, even if the next moment it's something else."

The wind outside howls.

"Do you think the world is a beautiful place or an ugly one?" he asks.

The question hurts, somehow makes me think of my father and his robotics obsession, how he wanted to make the world better, less lonely, from the shed in his suburban backyard. How he died there instead, alone. I think about the bloodstained sheets. My husband murdered. Of Izzy and Slade, of the elusive ghost orchid, how it shimmered, hovering, a white specter in a dark place.

"Both," I say. "You can't have one side without the other. That's the joke of it."

25

And then I'm running, wearing that red dress, those heels, wobbling up an icy drive. The air is frigid and the cold hurts—my face, my legs. But still I run, the windows of the house glowing behind me like eyes staring.

He calls after me.

"Poppy, wait!" His voice bounces off the trees. "Don't do this."

But I keep moving, making it finally to the street, which is deserted, lined with black, impenetrable trees. I am shivering to my core. I've never been so cold.

"Poppy!"

I hear his footfalls behind me, and I pick up my pace, heart hammering. I turn to see his shadow behind me, moving fast. I take off those shoes and clutch them in my hand. The ground feels like shards of glass on my bare feet, slicing, the cold burning. But I dig deep, find my strength and start to run on the muddy shoulder of this deserted road.

Twin headlights appear ahead of me, golden suns of hope. I veer into the road, put myself in the path of the car and start to wave my arms. I turn to see him drop back into the shadows. The vehicle slows and comes to a stop, a big man in a barn jacket and a thinning head of sandy hair climbs out.

"Hey," he says. "Are you okay?"

"Please," I say. "I need to get out of here."

He looks behind me. I turn, too, but the shadow is gone. He nods toward the passenger seat.

"Get inside," he says. "I'll just get you a blanket from the trunk."

Wrapping myself up in my arms, I climb into the leather interior. The SUV is older, but well maintained, surfaces clean and polished. In a strap on the driver's visor, a picture of a pretty woman with copper curls, and a boy who is a younger, slimmer version of the driver.

I shiver, an uncontrollable quake from deep within. I thought it was a myth, that your teeth chatter in extreme cold. It isn't; they knock against each other comically. He comes to the passenger door with the blanket and hands it to me. I wrap it around myself. When he climbs in the driver's seat, he cranks the heat.

"Do we need the police?" he asks.

He looks like a cop himself, something in the trim way he keeps himself, the directness of his stare. I wonder what he must see when he looks at me.

"No," I say. I'm confused, scattered. "I just need to get back to the city. I lost my wallet, my phone."

"New York City. How'd you get all the way out here?"

"I'm not sure." I shake my head, sink into the blanket, keeping my eyes on the road outside.

"Where did you come from?" He gazes back toward the direction from which I ran. "Is there someone I can call?"

"No," I say. "There's no one."

"I can take you to the train," he said. "Give you some money for a ticket."

I smile at him gratefully. "If you give me your information, when I get back, I'll get you your money. I promise."

"That's all right," he says easily. "Just let me know you got back safely?"

How rare. The solid, upright person who does a kind thing for a stranger. Who puts his life on hold, goes out of his way.

He calls his wife. "I'll be a little late," he says. "Yeah. I'll explain when I get home."

He waits with me in the car at the train station.

"So, what happened?"

It's late; the last train into the city arrives in twenty minutes. He's bought a ticket, given me some money, grabbed a candy bar and a cup of coffee from the concession machines. I can't stop thanking him. The blood has started to circulate through my body again, my limbs, fingers, toes tingling unpleasantly. How long would I have lasted out there? How long until he caught up with me?

"Fight with my boyfriend," I say. It's a lie. I don't want to say that I'm not sure where I was, or why I ran out into the street, no coat. I grasp for it, but it slips away, reality a wraith.

He regards me, then shakes his head. "No."

"Why not?"

"It just doesn't seem like that," he says. "Something else. Something more."

When I don't answer, he gives me his card. Jones Cooper Private Investigations.

"You'll get everything back," I say. "I promise."

He looks toward the lights of the oncoming train. They're far in the distance, two yellow eyes in the night. "I believe you," he says.

I shake his hand and climb out of his car, reluctantly leaving the blanket behind. He tries to give me his jacket, but I refuse. "You've done enough," I say. "Thank you."

Embarrassment and gratitude mingle as I make my awkward

departure. The train is nearly empty, just a smattering of people, a couple nestled in the back talking in urgent soft voices. A
man in a suit, already dozing off. I find a place as far away from
the others as I can, sit near the window. Jones Cooper sits in his
car, watching as the train pulls away. I lift my hand in a wave
and he does the same.

Then I see him, sitting in a sleek, new BMW. Noah. Or just
the shadow of him. Or maybe it isn't him, just a hooded man
sitting behind the wheel of a car, watching as I head away.

Back in the city, I make my way through the streets to Layla's
building. In the lobby, the doormen all get up to greet me, faces
stern as if I'm a homeless person who's wandered into their plush
universe, a stain on the white cleanliness of their environment. I
manage to croak out Layla's name. One of them recognizes me,
rushes for the phone. A minute later, I see her, her face tense
with fear, no recognition, then bright, washed soft with relief.
She runs to me, and I collapse into her arms.

Oh, Poppy. Oh, sweetie. Where have you been? What happened?

I want to tell her about Noah. About the snow. About Jack.
About everything. But the words just jam up in my throat and
I start to sob.

*It's okay. You're home now. We'll take care of everything. We'll
take care of you.*

Dr. Nash thinks I'm ready to go home. Though my days
here—and what came before—are a blank space in my memory,
I have returned to the present. I am aware that I had a nervous
breakdown after my husband's funeral, that I disappeared, returned to Layla and was brought here to this psychiatric reha-
bilitation center somewhere in Manhattan. Everyone's thrilled
that I have grasped this completely, even though there's a gaping
black hole in my memory that may never be recovered.

We sit in the office Dr. Nash uses when she comes here to see me, and for the first time in a couple of days I am wearing my own clothes. My mom has brought my soft gray sweatpants, and a cashmere sweater that Layla gave to me ages ago and has become my favorite. The fabric drapes on my body the way only fine things do, soft and warm like an embrace.

Layla casts things off, impossibly expensive things, to me—gorgeous bags, clothes I wouldn't even bother to glance at in stores, shoes she's worn once, if ever. I joyfully accept, knowing at some point Izzy is going to get in my way. Layla and I have always traded clothes, possessions, even boys without resentment or possessiveness. Like sisters, without any of the sibling baggage, without that undercurrent of competition, that primal struggle for resources.

"How are you feeling today, Poppy?"

"Other than the fact that I can't remember the last week of my life?"

"Yes," Dr. Nash says evenly. "Other than that."

"Pretty good, then, I suppose. A little numb. A little foggy."

"Are you ready to go back to your life?"

"My life without Jack." It's a black tunnel. No light at the other end.

"It will get better. I promise," she says. The doctor manages to strike a tone of empathy that contains no trace of pity. "You will get through this pain and find a new normal."

I offer an assenting shrug because it's an acknowledged fact that time heals and grief fades. I have emerged from dark days before. In the year after my father died I just went through the motions—getting up, going to class, collapsing at the end of the day, exhausted just from being alive with him gone. I don't tell the doctor that I saw my father everywhere then, had long talks with him in dreams that seemed to stretch on and on, seemed real when I woke up. There was comfort there when there was comfort nowhere else. Likewise, Jack is everywhere, alive inside my dreams, lingering in corners, beside me in my bed.

"Your mother says she's going to stay with you awhile," Dr. Nash says. "Until you find your footing."

"Great."

"I know the relationship has its challenges," says Dr. Nash. "But I think it's wise. Can you handle a week?"

"Maybe."

She gives me an approving smile.

Detective Grayson comes to see me later that day. I should decline to talk to him without my lawyer present. Instead I allow myself to be escorted to the sunroom, more out of boredom than anything else. The place they've put me, Dr. Nash, it all has the mark of Layla and Mac. It's more like a spa; my room is as well-appointed as a suite at the Ritz. I have not seen another patient since my arrival.

Grayson is standing by the window when the nurse opens the door for me. She slips away quietly and I stay by the door. Why did I agree to see him? I don't even know.

"I've never seen a hospital like this one," he says, still standing.

I just watch him, stay silent.

"There's no smell," he goes on. "You know that institutional undercurrent—bedpans and medication, fear—"

"Who killed Jack?" I ask, interrupting him. "What happened to my husband?"

He draws in and releases a breath. "I don't have the answers yet. I wish I did. I'm sorry."

I had wanted to stay standing, but my legs won't hold me against the weight of my fatigue, which is the only thing I feel. It's settled into my bones and joints, my eyelids. Must be the meds. I honestly don't even know what they're giving me.

"I wanted you to know that you're no longer a suspect."

I guess I should be relieved. Instead, I'm just annoyed.

"Also," he says. He moves closer, takes a seat in a huge wing-back chair. Against the rich, plumb fabric, beside the lavishly framed oil landscape painting, Grayson looks like a down-at-the-heels encyclopedia salesman. He has a mustard stain on his jacket; his slacks are wrinkled. "I was hard on you, on the worst day of your life. It's my job, but—"

I lift a hand, not interested in apologies. "Detective. Just find the person who took him from me."

He leans forward and bows his head for a moment.

"I have to be honest, Mrs. Lang." I doubt anyone has ever accused him of not being honest. "I've got nothing. No leads. No witnesses. He had no debts. There were no affairs, secret addictions. You had a thriving business. By all accounts, a happy marriage."

A happy marriage. Did we have that?

"Is there anything you're not telling me, Mrs. Lang?"

"Poppy."

"Poppy, do you have any thoughts on who might have wished your husband harm?"

I shake my head. "No."

"Otherwise, I'm going to have to treat this like a random street crime. And, unless I catch a break, that's going to be a lot harder to solve."

"What are you doing here, Detective?"

Layla stands inside the door. She has a bouquet of tulips; they droop prettily in her arms.

The detective stands and walks toward her.

"I'm doing my job, Mrs. Van Santen."

He glances back and forth between us, maybe waiting for me to say something. But I just look away from him.

"Get out of here," Layla says. "You talk to her through her lawyer."

"She's no longer a suspect."

"Good," she says. "Then get out."

I marvel at what a fierce bitch she is, always has been.

"I won't stop, Poppy," he says. "I promise."

Layla moves away from him, dismissive and cold. She comes to sit beside me and doesn't even look at him as he exits.

"Why did you see him?" she asks, resting a hand on my arm.

I shrug. "I wanted to know if he found anything."

Something shadows her features. "Has he?"

"No."

She lays the tulips on the table, puts a strong hand on my shoulder. "You look better," she says. "Rested."

"What is this place?" I ask. "It's not a hospital."

I stand and walk over to the drapes, finger the heavy silken fabric. It was my mother who taught me how to feel fabric, the difference between polyester and silk, between wool and cashmere. Silk is like water through your fingers, so soft it might drip away. Polyester scratches, even when it's soft. Wool is always stiff; cashmere flows.

Layla looks around, runs a hand over a chenille throw, an oversize pillow.

"No," she says. "It's more like a retreat, a private place where wealthy people come to rehab from whatever—drugs, alcohol, breakdowns. Strictly confidential."

"And Dr. Nash?"

"She's my therapist," says Layla. "She's helped me work through all my shit. Well, some of it, anyway. She can help you through this."

"Should we have the same shrink?"

She shrugged. "Why not? We've shared everything else."

"I can't afford this place," I say.

She pats the couch beside her, and I sink into the spot. I feel small, a wreck next to Layla. Her skin glows, and her hair, golden in this light, is clearly blown out. Everything—her nails, the cut of her simple clinging maroon dress, exudes style, wealth, ease. I, on the other hand, wouldn't be out of place on a street corner, holding a cup and begging for quarters. Not that I care.

"Do you remember the night that you and your dad rescued me from my father?"

"Of course."

How old were we? Sixteen. The phone rang late, a single note. My dad and I were in the kitchen, bent over the table while he tried to help me with my trigonometry homework—which, PS, addled my brain and has yet in life to reveal its practical application. My dad got up to answer, but the line was dead. He peered at the caller ID screen.

"Layla," he said.

My heart did a little stutter, even though I couldn't say why. In gym that morning, I'd seen wide black-and-blue marks on her arm, fingerprint bruises where her dad had grabbed her.

"I'm going to drive by her house."

My dad wore a worried frown, rubbed a hand over his thinning dark hair.

"I'll ride with you."

Easy. It was always easy with him.

I picked up the phone and dialed, hanging up after one ring.

This was not a thing we had planned or discussed. But I knew what that single ring meant: *I'm in trouble.* In her house, she knew the meaning of mine: *I'm coming.*

My dad and I pulled in front of Layla's house, her neighborhood a lot like mine—low ranches mostly, built in the sixties, some newer, bigger homes. Working class, middle class, some nice cars but mainly old-model Chevys and Fords. Towering oaks that shed mountains of leaves, bikes tilted in driveways, uninspired landscaping featuring weedy flower beds and anemic shrubs. Trash cans at the curb, sprinklers ticking on summer nights. My first photo of Layla, she sat frowning on the top step of her brick stoop, chin in hand—a teen, suburban Thinker.

God, I hate this fucking place.

You'll leave. We both will.

You bet your ass.

My dad and I sat, waiting. Voices carried—her father's anger a blue streak, a flame. Her mother's: shrill, hysterical. Something smashed, the sound reverberating. Then—quiet.

"We need to call the police," said my dad, growing anxious.

"No." I spun to him, grabbed his arm. "They'll take her away."

"Poppy," he said slowly. "She's not safe."

"She can live with us."

He blew out a breath. A sixteen-year-old thinks she understands the world. There's only black and white, right and wrong. Life hasn't taught the important lesson of gray. Shades and shadows elude.

I flashed the lights, just once. And then I held my breath, body tense, waiting and waiting. Finally, she slipped from the side of the house, duffel over her shoulder, climbed into the back seat as casually as if I were picking her up to go to the mall.

"Hi, Mr. Jackson," she said. Her eyes were rimmed red, her face still and set.

"Layla," he said. "Everything okay?"

I moved into the back seat with her and let my dad take the wheel. Layla rested her head against my shoulder; I stroked her hair.

"What do we need to do here?" my dad asked.

"Take her home," I answered. "We'll call the police there."

"She won't press charges, though," said Layla. "She never does."

"She doesn't need to," my father answered. "The police will do that."

"They won't," she said softly. "They don't. And it will just be worse for her."

None of us said anything. It was all true, no point in arguing.

"Some people don't want their problems solved," Layla went on into the silence of the car.

"That's true sometimes." His voice was solemn in the dim

light. "But sometimes they just don't have the right tools in their toolbox to fix things."

Layla didn't live with us after that—not officially. But mostly. She had clothes in my closet, a toothbrush in my bathroom, a place at our dinner table.

"You saved me that night," she says now, *so* many years later. "You and your parents have saved me a hundred times."

She laces her fingers through mine. "Right now, let me be here for you. Let me do what I can for you."

We're sisters, more than that. We're soul mates. I let her help me, let her wrap me up, take care of everything. I have no choice. I am flotsam, tumbled in the tsunami of grief. Without her, I might go out to sea.

Those days come back in fragments. There are still pieces missing. But part of that black space recedes, revealing my memories; I know who I was, what I did—mostly. There's a deep sense of relief, like a thorn has been removed from my heart. I am grasping my way to wholeness.

26

Now…

The sun streams in through the narrow window as I come to sit with a jolt, startling Noah, who is in the chair by the fireplace. I am soaked through with sweat, the sheets damp, my heart still racing. But my entry into this day is crisp and bright, no fog in my mind, no heaviness around my eyes. I remember it all: the apartment ambush, how I fled Layla and Tom, my date with Rick, the altercation on the street. I remember the choice Noah offered me, that bottle of pills in his hand, the choice I made.

Images from my dreams cling: I hold a baby in my arms, then I'm running up a dark street, pursued, then I'm lying in Jack's arms whispering I'm sorry, I'm so sorry. But on this morning, I am clear on where I am, where I've been. What's real and what isn't.

The misery of the last few days is close and present in my mind—the raging and sickness of detox—but now I am light, as though after a period of long illness I can breathe again. Noah is watching me.

"How long has it been?" I ask.

"Two and a half days," he answers.

There are dark gullies of fatigue under his eyes; I think he's been wearing that same shirt since I got here.

"I had a dream," I say.

"Another one?"

"Yes," I say, though it's fading fast. "I had a baby. He was so beautiful. I can still feel him."

I can. I can feel his weight in my arms, smell the shampoo in his hair, hear his sweet voice, feel his fingers wrapped around mine. My heart aches with it, wanting to hold him again. But he was just a dream.

Noah comes to sit beside me, folds me into his embrace, though I am not fit for embracing. I realize that I'm weeping; it's a cleansing, a letting go.

I take a shower so hot it's almost scalding. I drink a gallon of water. Noah cooks for me, and at the table he's made with his own hands, we eat as though we're starving. Which maybe we are; I can't remember the last time I had a meal, a real meal at a table.

After we eat, we sit by the fire. Outside a light snow falls. I am tucked beneath his arm and I can feel the rise and fall of his breath. He is solid, a grounding force. We are the only two people in the world.

"Why did you do this for me?" I ask him. "Why would you put yourself through this?"

He doesn't answer right away and I think he's fallen asleep. I look up at him and his eyes are closed, but he's wearing a slight smile.

"Don't you know?" he asks.

He met me at a nightclub—Morpheus—when I was another version of myself. Still, a year later, I haven't quite stitched myself back together. I've run away from him, forgotten him completely, blown him off, asked him to help me find answers to the dark question at the center of my life, led the cops to his door.

"I guess I don't."

He draws in and releases a breath, looks down at me.

"Life, you know, it can feel like a war. Like you're fighting battles inside and outside. Once or twice, you meet someone and you see through all the layers, recognize an ally. Do you know what I mean?"

I think of Layla, my lifelong ally and friend, my sister. I think of Jack, my love, my partner, the only one who knew my desire to hold the world in my lens, to find the beauty and truth in a moment and share it. I look up at Noah, into the jewel facets of his eyes. I know exactly what he means.

"Some people are worth fighting for," he says.

He laces his fingers through mine, and we stay like that a long time, watching the fire cast dancers on the wall.

"I have questions," I say. "There are things I need to understand."

"Of course."

"When I last talked to Detective Grayson, he told me things about you. He said that you were following your girlfriend the day she was killed, that you were stalking her. He also told me that you followed another woman, raged at her, sent her orchids. He had a theory that you were the one who sent the flowers. He suspected already, even though I didn't remember, that we met during those lost days—or maybe earlier—and that you've been following me ever since."

He bows his head, and is quiet. I move away from him so that I can see his face.

When he looks up at me again his expression is stoic but there's sadness there—and shame.

"He's right," he says. "It's true. I've made terrible mistakes in my life."

I blow out a breath I didn't know I was holding.

"The day Bella died, I *was* following her. We'd had a terrible fight and she'd left. I couldn't let her go, so I went after her. I certainly never tried to force her off the road, or to hurt her. I just—didn't want her to leave so angry, so sad. Or maybe, I didn't want her to leave *me* so angry and sad."

He pauses, his eyes searching my face.

"She was furious with me, crying, yelling at me on her cell phone. *Leave me alone, Noah*, she was screaming. *I don't love you anymore.* A few minutes later, she collided with that drunk driver."

The air in the room is thick with sorrow, with tension. We're both silent for a moment.

"Was her death my fault?" he says finally. "Yes, I think in a way it was. I *didn't* kill her. But maybe if she hadn't been driving so upset, if she wasn't so mad at me for following her. So yeah, I blame myself and I always have, maybe I always will."

Maybe I always will. I've heard him say this before. He's told me this.

"Have we talked about this before?"

"We have. Should I go on?"

I nod to indicate that he should.

"The other woman Grayson told you about. Her name was Amy. She and I dated a couple of times, then she blew me off. I liked her, sent her flowers. She kind of played around with me a little. She'd ask me to meet her, then not show up. She called me once in the middle of the night, asked me to come to her place—you know, that kind of call."

He gets up, walks over to the fireplace and leans against the hearth.

"I went—I mean, of course I did. What guy isn't going to answer a midnight call from a hot girl he likes, even if she had blown him off a couple of times. But when I got there, she wouldn't let me up. I lost it in her lobby, my outburst caught on film. She took out a restraining order against me. But no, I didn't stalk her. After that night, I never tried to see her again. It starts to look bad, though. More than one suspicious incident with women."

Maybe I shouldn't, but I believe him. He has the aura of a man who's learned hard lessons and grown stronger for it.

"And what about us?"

"You and I met, yes, the first time during your breakdown."

The man in the bar, his arms on me, his lips on me. The image on the bartender's phone, that dark form enveloping me, the mascara trails down my face. Noah. I realize of course that I knew it all along, that scent of fire and linseed oil, the heat of him.

"I realized quickly that something wasn't right with you, that you were in some kind of trouble. I asked you if you needed help. And you said you did. Right or wrong, I brought you back here."

I remember—the walk through the snowy woods, all the things we talked about, the burning fireplace.

"I let you rest here, get well. I fed you, took you for long walks, let this place heal you like it healed me. I never touched you, though, I promise you that. I never took advantage of you."

It's all coming back, a river, a deluge—just like Dr. Nash said it might. But it's not unsettling, it's freeing, like I can breathe again after being submerged in dark water, swimming, swimming toward the light, not sure if I'll ever surface.

"But when you came back to yourself, you didn't know me, or where you were. You ran and I let you go. I've done my work, you know—therapy, anger management, all of that. I'm older. When someone wants to leave you, you don't hold on."

I want to reach for him, but I don't. Instead I wrap my arms around my middle.

"The next year kind of passed in a rush, so much work, so many commissions. But you were there, always on my mind," he continues. "When I saw you on that online dating service. I reached out. Then there you were that night, all those feel-

ings I tried to forget, they came back in a rush. You didn't remember me. I would have told you, but I wanted you to get to
know me again, when you were well and whole. I planned to
tell you everything, but then you ghosted me."

He smiles wryly, rubs at his temples.

"I called a couple of times, just hoping. I felt something
powerful—I hoped you would, too. Yes, I sent the flowers,
not knowing everything else that was going on in your life. I
didn't cop to it on the phone, because you already thought I
was a stalker. It's kind of a shame trigger for me. I'm sorry. I
guess I should have told you everything right there, right then."

I want to move to him, to comfort him, but I can't.

"So, the other night when you left your apartment, after the
ambush, I was there, waiting outside. I knew you weren't going
to return my calls and I wanted a chance to tell you my side of
things. But you raced out of there, never even saw me."

He pauses and sighs. "I'm not proud of it, but I followed you."

"You hit him," I say. "I remember the blood, him screaming."

"We had words, yeah," he says. "There was an altercation.
You were out of it and he was taking advantage of you, Poppy."

"You're the hooded man."

He shakes his head emphatically.

"No," he says. "That last night is the only time I ever followed you. Whoever that is, *whatever* it is, it's not me. I swear."

I believe him and tell him so. He stays over by the fireplace,
though, keeping his distance.

"I've made mistakes, a lot of them," he says. "But I'm a better man than I used to be."

The fire crackles and casts dancing shadows on the wall. I
rise and move to him, and he takes me in his arms. I touch his
face and his mouth finds mine, then my throat. The soft of his
skin, the silk of his hair, the steel of his arms; I could lose myself. The heat, the hunger between us, it could devour me. But.

"I can't," I whisper.

He groans. "I know."

"I'm not whole," I say. There are still so many questions, so much I don't know about Jack, about myself, about what's happened to me. "It's not right."

He kisses my head, holds me tight. His words are just a breath. "I'll wait."

27

"You always hated the country." She's a little breathless.

"That was you," I say. "*You* hated the country."

"I still do," Layla says, though the flush on her cheeks suits her. We're walking on one of the trails on Noah's land; he keeps some of them shoveled so that he can get to his studio. The snow that's fallen is piled high all around us.

"Remember when it used to fall like this in the city?" I say. "There were walls along the sidewalk after the plows came through, cars buried till spring. It doesn't snow like that anymore, does it?"

She comes to a stop. The trail we're on is steep. "I have a cramp. Too much yoga, not enough cardio."

"It's always a challenge to do something different."

She puts her hands on her hips and looks up at the sky.

"What are you doing out here?" She drops her gaze to me. I can see her anger, her worry. "With this *guy* you barely know. You've walked out on your life."

I've been out here nearly three weeks, thinking, healing. I couldn't keep her from coming, though I tried. Once I had my phone on again, she tracked me with Find My Friends—again—and showed up. Carmelo waited in the car, stoically lifting a hand to me when I opened the front door for her. She started to cry when I stepped out onto the porch; so did I.

"No," I say now. "I haven't. I'm finding it for the first time since Jack died."

"What about the agency?" she asks. Her breath plumes in the cold air.

"I don't know," I say. "Ben and Maura are running the show right now. We'll see."

I keep walking and after a moment, she follows.

"I'm not sure we really knew what we were giving up," I say when she reaches me.

I've been thinking about this a lot. "The agency was something Jack thought he wanted, and I just went along. But being away from his art, the travel, all of that—I think it contributed to the problems we were having. He grounded himself to be with me, so that we could have the things I wanted."

"That's what people *do* in a marriage," she says sharply. "You become a 'we,' not just an 'I.' You make decisions for the couple, for the family you want to become. Maybe you sacrifice some things."

"But when you give up too much of yourself, maybe resentment sets in."

She doesn't say anything for a while; I listen to her labored breathing.

"What about us?" she says finally, her voice small. "What about Izzy and Slade?"

I come to a stop so that she can rest, smile at her, take her hand. "I'm right here, silly. I didn't fill out an application to go to Mars."

"Might as well be on Mars," she says sulkily.

She looks up again, this time suspiciously at the towering pines around us. We walk a little while longer, then come to a spot I like, a fallen log cleared of snow. I sit, feel the cold through my jacket. She sits beside me, leaning against me.

"If he turns out to be a killer, no one will hear you screaming."

"He could have killed me already—a few times."

Above us a hawk circles. A lonely hunter, searching for his prey, a warm body beneath the shelf of snow. I watch, breathe.

"It's my fault, isn't it?" she says.

When I look at her, she's sixteen again, that same sad, angry, lost little girl, hiding the bruises on her arms, huddled in the back seat of my dad's car, sleeping in the bed beside mine.

"What's your fault?"

"The pills," she says. "I should never have given you the stuff I was taking. When Dr. Nash wanted you to stop, I told you to keep taking them. I knew you were drinking with them."

I shake my head. "It's no one's fault but mine."

"I wanted to protect you, to take care of you, like you've always done for me," she says. "I thought that meant helping you avoid the pain you were in."

This surprises me. In the story of our friendship, it was always Layla taking care of me. She was the strong one, the one who knew what was right, so sure of herself.

"I'm doing it, too," she continues. "Zoloft, Ativan. I have a couple of bottles of Xanax floating around. The sleeping pills. And, of course, the wine every night."

The fog lifted, I see my friend for the first time in a while. She looks so tired, so sad, and angry.

"Layla. Tell me what's going on."

She breathes out, looks at her fingers pink with the cold. "Mac and me. It's been bad for a while. I've made mistakes—he has, too. We're so angry with each other. So far apart. I don't think we know the way back from here, or forward."

I hear Izzy's whispered words: *They were fighting. That's all they ever do. They hurt each other.*

"So instead of working on our issues, we just withdraw from each other. For me, it's the pills—that's my escape," she says. "For him, it's work."

She pauses a moment. The hawk above us lets out his high-pitched cry. "Whatever we do to avoid the truth of our life, to avoid pain, that's our addiction."

I should have seen it. I did see it; I just turned away from them, caught up in my own mess.

"You never told me," I say. "That you two were in trouble."

She's wrapped her arms around herself.

"You and Jack—it always seemed so right. Your art, your business together, your freedom. Mac and I, it's like we're rotten at our foundation. I couldn't face it."

Rotten at the foundation? Surely not. "It's just a rough patch. Everybody has those."

She presses into me shivering and I wrap my arms around her. We should go back; it's getting colder, the sun dipping lower. But we stay awhile longer.

"And then, after everything you've been through. How could I burden you with the problems in my marriage?"

I pull her tighter. "I'm here for you, always. I *want* to be, no matter what else goes on in my world."

She lets out a little sob.

"I gave up too much of myself, Poppy," she says between breaths. "For Mac, the kids—I thought you had to give all of yourself over to it, make everything perfect. I'm not even sure who I am anymore."

I know the feeling, hold on to her tight. "We'll talk it all through. Figure it out. Like we always do."

She sits up and wipes her eyes. There's the shade of a smile, that steely glint in her eye. That's the real girl, the one beneath all the masks she wears, tough as nails, a fighter.

"You were always the strong one," she says. "The one with all the answers."

"That's scary," I say. "I thought it was you."

We both laugh then, and it carries through the gloaming, scaring a murder of crows from the trees. There's more she wants to say, I can feel it. But she stays quiet, and I don't press. After a while, we head back to the house, where inside the fire we left is still burning in the hearth.

"How long are you going to stay out here?" she asks, shifting off her jacket.

Noah's been in to the city, getting things from my apartment. I gave him the keys and he brought Jack's Jeep to me, so that I have my own car.

"Not sure," I say. "I'm seeing a new therapist, someone who doesn't prescribe. There are good AA meetings here. Noah wants me to stay. And it's comfortable for me here, peaceful. There's distance, mental space."

She looks around with disapproval, though I can't imagine what she sees that she doesn't like. Maybe it's just that she's not in control of this space, can't take over here.

"Are you sleeping with him?" she asks. She takes off her boots and lines them neatly next to mine beneath the coats.

"No."

She scoffs. "Bullshit."

"Seriously," I say. "We're—friends. Well—I don't know what we are, really. Or what we'll be."

Most of my lost days have come back, not the full linear picture, but images, moments, enough pieces that I see a clearer picture of where I was and what I did.

Except.

I don't know who killed Jack. I still don't know where that bag is. Or if there was a bag. Or what was in it. I don't understand who the hooded man is—or if he was there at all. There's no real clarity on what caused me to lose my grip that first night when I wound up in Morpheus and met Noah for the first time. How can I enter a relationship when I'm not whole?

The new therapist I'm seeing has some thoughts. "Your memory loss, the recent episodes could be attributed to some combination of the pills, the trauma of your husband's murder, your grief. But we don't really know what contributes to a psychotic break in someone with no history of mental illness. And there's so much about the nature of memory that we don't understand. You may get everything back. But maybe not."

We sit and I tell Layla everything I remember, everything I know. She listens, and for once in her life, doesn't interrupt. She lifts a sculpture that sits on the coffee table. It's a smaller version of the one behind the house. Two figures in a dance, this one looks more like a battle with the larger figure besting the smaller, an arm lifted as if to deliver a killing blow.

"How do we trust this guy?" asks Layla when I'm done. She turns the piece around, staring at it from every angle. "He's practically a stalker."

"He's not a stalker."

"No?" she says. "You met him during your psychotic break. He brought you out here. You ran away from him. He found you online nearly a year later. You slept with him then, right? He kept calling. He's the one who sent the flowers, right?"

I admit that he was.

She raises her eyebrows, that look that says she knows everything and she just hopes I'll catch up at some point.

"Didn't he stalk someone else?" she goes on. "Wasn't he a suspect in his girlfriend's death? That's what Tom said."

I try to explain it to her, but she's not listening. She's made her decision about Noah and it's going to take time or an act of nature to get her to change her mind.

"He's got an anger problem, at the very least," she concludes sagely.

"You should talk."

"I've grown out of that," she says, hiking up her shoulders. "I had a lot to be angry about as a kid."

"So, people change."

She puts the sculpture down, but keeps her eye on it like she thinks she might have to fight it if it comes to life.

"It's not a good idea to be in a relationship when you're in recovery," she says. "That's, like, AA 101."

I smile at her. "Thank you, doctor. I'll keep that in mind. Anyway, like I said, we're friends."

"Friends who live together. Who *have* slept together in the past."

She moves over to the hearth, lifting her hands to warm them against the heat. She stares into the flames.

"Do you think you dreamed—or hallucinated—that bag?" she asks.

"I honestly don't know."

"No idea *at all* what was in it?" I've already told her this. Why is she asking me again?

"What about Merlinda?" she asks.

"Her number has been disconnected," I say, feeling the familiar bite of frustration. There's another dead end at every turn in this maze. "The doorman said she moved out six months ago."

She lifts the fire poker, moves the logs around, and the fire burns brighter. "So, you were never there at all? You never saw her."

"It seems that way," I admit, though it doesn't seem possible; my memory of our meeting was so vivid, so real—the wind chimes, the smell of incense, Merlinda's warm embrace.

"You did a web search?"

"There's nothing," I say. "Just a cobweb site with an email that bounced, and her old number."

"I'll have Tom dig around." Tension settles into my shoulders. The thought of him makes me uncomfortable, anxious. I don't want him digging around in my life.

"Thanks, but Grayson's investigating. I called him and told him everything I remember, all the details of my dreams. I'll

just stick with the police. At least Grayson's agenda is clear—
he's not a mercenary."

Layla regards me for a moment. There's something odd in
the air between us.

"There's no clearer agenda than a mercenary's," she says easily. "Money. Plain and simple."

She says that like it's a good thing.

"And I'm just supposed to leave you out here with this guy?"
she says, putting the poker down and turning around. "Grayson
had his suspicions about Noah, told you to stay away. What's
changed there?"

I release a sigh.

"Noah is not a suspect in Jack's death," I answer. "He's been
questioned and investigated. There's nothing linking him to
Jack, or to me before the night we met at Morpheus."

The missing piece at the center of my life and who I am now:
Who killed Jack?

"I'm okay here," I assure her. "I'm safe. Safer than I've been
in a while."

She shakes her head, disapproval, skepticism pulling the features of her face taut.

"How do you know you're not dreaming now—or hallucinating?"

"Or in a hypnagogic state."

"Whatever."

I smile again but the question rubs against the raw places inside me. "How do any of us know?"

She dips her head in acknowledgment, but a cloud of worry
darkens her face.

"What about the hooded man?"

"He's gone," I say. I still find myself looking for him in the
shadows, but he's not there.

"Coincidentally," she says with a smirk. "Now that Noah has
you to himself."

"It wasn't him."

"So you say he says."

"Layla."

She sweeps her arm around the room. "This isn't right, Poppy. You out here. It's not you."

How can she be so sure of who I am and where I belong when I'm no longer sure myself?

"What are you going to do?" I ask, flipping the conversation back to her. "What are you going to do about Mac? Counseling?"

"He won't do it," she says. She rubs her hands together as if she's trying to warm herself, looks away. "He says he won't air our problems in front of a stranger."

I blow out a sigh. How stubborn we all are, how we cling to our ways, our ideas.

"I don't think there's anything left to fix," Layla says. "Maybe we're just together for the kids."

"Don't say that," I say, leaning toward her. "You loved each other once."

She doesn't say anything for a moment. "That was a long time ago."

There's that strange flatness to her tone again—resignation. Then, "You said it yourself. People change. Except sometimes it's not for the better. Or maybe it was always wrong."

"You loved him once," I say again. I saw it. It was real.

"Did I?" she asks, musing, not really wanting an answer.

She stays awhile longer, then has to get back for the kids. I walk her out to the car, where Carmelo leaps out to open the door. Poor guy. I'd forgotten all about him. I didn't even make him a cup of tea.

"Carmelo will come for you, day or night," says Layla.

"I will, Miss Poppy. Call me and I'll be here."

I nod toward the Jeep, which sits powder blue and waiting for adventures it might not get.

"Thanks but I have my own wheels," I say.

She seems about to make some quip, but finally she just nods and climbs into the car. As Carmelo pulls away, she opens the window and sticks her hand out in a wave. I watch the car disappear, wrapping my arms around the hole that's opened my middle. I feel as if there's something I should do for her that I haven't done, something she needs that I haven't been able to give. I think about calling her, telling her to come back. But in the end, I let her go.

28

The next day I head back into the city to purge my apartment. It's time to finally, fully unpack those boxes, to sort through Jack's belongings, and to release the things I want to let go. And maybe, maybe in my new, sober state, find parts of us I couldn't see before. Or not.

Maybe it's time to accept that Jack was the victim of a random street crime, one that will, like so many crimes, remain unsolved. He was in the wrong place, the wrong time. Even though our story ends in an ugly, brutal way, it's an ending I'll have no choice but to accept.

"I'll come with you," Noah offers.

"I'll meet you there," Layla suggests over the phone. "You know I'm the purge and organize queen. The life-changing magic of getting rid of your shit and all of that."

But I don't want to be the problem that one or the other of them needs to fix. I have a grip on my life for the first time in a while. I am detoxed, free from the chemical fog I've been in. That raw scrape of grief has eased; and I am reclaiming authority over my reality. This is a trip I want to make alone.

It's winter now, gray and cold. There's snow on the ground, bowing the branches of the trees. In the driveway, Noah thumps his hand lovingly on the hood of Jack's old Jeep. "This thing is a classic."

I love that he loves it, saw what Jack saw in it.

Last week I told him that if I was to stay here, I wanted my own car. He took the train into the city and brought it back for me. I want to be behind the wheel from now on; I want to say where I go and how I get there.

Noah stands, looking down at the ground, his hands buried deep in his pockets. I know he's wrestling with his own demons, trying not to hold on to me too tightly.

The energy between us is electric, but we keep our distance, dancing around each other. Layla's right that I'm fragile and vulnerable now, in recovery from the things that have happened to me, the things I have done to myself. I haven't completely let go of Jack, and big parts of me still belong to him. There are so many unanswered questions. It's not fair to either of us to go too far.

His touch sends energy up my arm. The sun is just over the tree line, the morning golden. He tugs me close, loops a strong arm around the small of my back. It would be easy to just stay, to sink into him.

"Having you here—" His voice is a rasp as he lets the sentence trail.

The air is frigid but all I feel is the heat between us. I never forgot that, the night we shared in his loft. How his skin felt on mine, his hunger, his restraint, his tenderness.

Whatever he was, whatever mistakes he's made in his life, he's been a true friend to me. More.

He whispers, his lips touching the skin on my neck. "Don't forget me again, Poppy."

"I won't," I promise.

I am at the wheel of my life now. I won't lose my grip again.

★ ★ ★

Traffic into the city is heavy. The old Jeep rumbles, the heat cranking loud and rattling. People in their suits and shiny luxury cars look and smile. There's something about a Jeep that makes people think of adventure, surf and sand, off-roading—a life like Jack's before we met. Free from the restraints that our choices put on him—a business, a wife who wanted children, his camera packed away. I didn't see it then. I believed we made choices together, but perhaps he made choices to please me and then regretted them. And I made choices to please him. Maybe that happens to all of us. We think we want one thing, and then we get it. We find ourselves on one path and wish we'd chosen the other.

If Jack *was* having an affair, maybe that was why. Maybe it was an escape hatch for him, like my assignations have been for me after his death. It hurts to think he might have loved, or been with someone else. And it doesn't track with what I thought I knew about my husband. Mac's words ring back, though, over and over again. *Maybe we only ever know pieces of each other.* During my episode, I told Layla that he was having an affair, that it was the reason why he was killed. What led me to think that? What did that Poppy know, that I've forgotten? *Who* is Elena?

Parking the Jeep in a lot and walking the few blocks to my building, I realize it's my first time on these streets sober. I've been taking pills since the day Jack was killed. In this new, clearheaded space, not dogged by the hooded man, the streets seem different, less manic, less full of shadow and menace. How much of what we know and see is colored by our mental state? All of it maybe.

Inside, the apartment is quiet, that long hallway stretching out before me. I stand inside the door, but not for long. I'm here to do one thing, not leaving until it's finished.

I make a pot of coffee, put our music on shuffle and mercilessly dig in to those boxes. I don't stop until everything is out on the floor, a giant mass of paper and clothes, books, leather portfolios, files, photos. Time to sort. His clothes to Goodwill; he'd have wanted that, to know that his things were helping someone else. His old files, bills, contracts in the shredder; our lawyer has all the important documents. Jack hated paperwork, considered it the worst thing about life—other than flossing.

Ruthlessly, I bag everything else—old notebooks, prints of photos I know we have stored digitally. When I'm done there's a small pile of things I want—his ring, our wedding album, the portfolio of some of his early prints, letters he wrote to me, a poem. It's tiny, that stack of items. But it's precious. The sight of his words on a page, his boyish script, fills me with love.

I've put this off for so long, imagining that it would be un-bearably painful. But even through the heaviness and sadness of the task, there's a freeing sense of relief, the knowledge that I can keep what I loved about us, and let everything else go.

After a couple of hours, everything repacked and sorted, I open my laptop for the first time in days. My email box is filled with hundreds of messages. Though I know Ben's been staying on top of it in my absence, the mail still pops down from the server in a river of notes from clients, queries from photogra-phers, potential assignments from editors, junk mail. My mail-box fills with a manic series of chimes, in a sluice of wants and needs, demands, requests. I skim through, reading and deleting, until I see one from Ben, sent just a couple of hours ago. The subject line reads RE: Who is this?

Hey, Poppy,

It took me a while but I used those 'mad skills' of mine to find this woman. I dropped Bill Simpson a line, forwarded him the image from his wedding that you sent me. They've been out of the country on assignment, and he finally got back to me.

He says she's a longtime friend and colleague of Claire's: Elena Montoya. The unsettling news is that Elena Montoya has died since the wedding. Bill was vague, but I got the sense that her death was unexpected, that there was something mysterious about it.

I haven't had a chance to dig in to this yet. Do you want me to look further into the circumstances of her death? Alvaro and Jack must have known her. Bill says they all went to Parsons at the same time.

Ben
Xoxo

My hands are shaking as I scroll down to see what image he means. For a moment, I have absolutely no idea what this email is about. I see it then—the picture that Alvaro shared with me in his gallery, the one where Jack and I danced, happy and laughing, the strange woman staring on the edge of the frame.

I don't remember sending an email to Ben. However, I follow the chain and see the message that is obviously from me. The image attached to the email is a picture I must have taken with my phone. I can see my thumb holding the photograph, the back of the cabdriver's head obscured by the thick plastic divider. I've marked it up, drawn a red circle around the girl. I wrote: Ben, can you find out who this is?

I quickly type the name into my browser, scroll through listings—her website, some articles crediting her photographs, until I find a news article. I've seen it before, in my dream—or was it a memory?

It comes back like a slap, that night, Jack on the couch, reading in the wee hours of the morning.

"Who is she?" I asked.

"Someone I used to know."

"Someone you used to know? What does that mean?"

"A friend from college. I've mentioned her, haven't I? We had classes together. I see her from time to time on assignment. I've thrown work her way and vice versa."

"Yeah, maybe," I said. We both have a long list of friends and contacts, aren't in the habit of keeping tabs on each other. Maybe her name sounded familiar.

"What happened to her?"

I read the article now:

Elena Montoya, a photojournalist living in Manhattan, was murdered in her East Village apartment. In an apparent home invasion robbery, Montoya was beaten to death by her assailant, tens of thousands of dollars of photo equipment was stolen and never recovered. Her killer is still at large.

Elena Montoya, the girl on Jack's computer screen, late at night. The girl, beaten and bloodied, in the conference room. The name on the matchbook. A girl standing on the edge of the dance floor, watching us.

Another memory comes then, whisking me into the past.

The matchbook, the one that wove its way into my dream hallucinations. Jack had tossed it carelessly with his wallet and keys on the kitchen counter one night.

"What a cliché!" I said, picking up the red Morpheus matchbook the next morning, reading the scrawl inside. "Picking up women in bars, now?"

"Huh?"

He'd had a late night out with Alvaro and Mac, was groggy at the kitchen table over coffee, cranky about an upcoming meeting with a client who he couldn't stand but who brought a lot of money into the firm. He had a contract open in front of him, glasses on.

He looked up at me, glanced at the matchbook in my hand.

"Honey," he said, raising his eyebrows, faux smarmy. "I can't help it if all the ladies want me. You know. I just got that special kind of magic."

"True," I concede, tossing the matchbook down on the table. He picks it up, peers at it through his glasses. A slight frown wrinkles his brow, eyes to me, then back to the computer.

"That's not mine."

"Really."

"That's—uh—Alvaro's pickup," he says. "Seriously."

"Then what are you doing with the matches?" The funny thing was, that name on the matchbook—whatever it was—wasn't what worried me at all. Despite what I said to Layla, I don't recall ever once questioning Jack's fidelity in all our years together.

He offered me a sheepish grin. I smelled the smoke on him when he came to bed. Cigarettes.

"Seriously?" I said, disappointed. "You haven't smoked in a year."

The late nights, the drinking, the smoking—all of it only happened when Alvaro was in town. Even Layla complained about their nights out, what a bear Mac was the next day. Our husbands were straight arrows—until Alvaro was around. Then they were teenagers again, out too late, drinking too much for men their age. It was pathetic really. Meanwhile, Jack and I had just started trying for a baby. We needed to be healthy. But I didn't say anything else. He was a grown man after all. And I wasn't his mother.

It was only after he left that I noticed that the matchbook had disappeared with his wallet, keys and phone.

I briefly wondered, just for a second: An affair? All the usual signs were there. Late-night phone calls. Excuses to run out for a while in the evenings. A diminished interest in lovemaking, though we still had a pretty robust sex life. I thought it was just the scheduled nature of our "dates." He was never an on-demand kind of guy. We didn't keep tabs on each other, always allowed each other freedom of movement. No. I knew something wasn't right, but I didn't doubt his love for me. He was a wild man, but I always believed he was faithful and good.

Who is she really, Jack? I wonder now. A young woman, a photojournalist, beaten to death. She knew us. She stood on the periphery of our life and watched us dance. Was she something more to him than he said that night?

I pick up the phone and call Detective Grayson.

"Funny you called," he answers. "I was just about to ring you."

"I need to talk," I say. "Can we get together?"

"Where are you? Some strange nightclub? An alley? At the isolated home of your stalker?"

I find myself smiling a little. I still wish I never had occasion to have met Detective Grayson. But I like him just the same. We have a history now. Not a pretty one. But a history nonetheless.

"Home," I say. It doesn't sound right. "In my apartment in Chelsea."

There's silence on the other end and I think he's hung up, heading my way. Then, "You sound different."

"Do I?"

"Stronger," he says. "I don't know—clearer."

"Working on that."

"Good for you," he says. "Stay put. I'm on my way."

When we end the call, I survey the apartment and find that it is free from ghosts—Jack and Elena, both dead, both murdered, are nowhere to be seen. There's no disconnect from reality, no fog or wobble. Without the pills, there's no confusion between my dreams and my reality. I just have to wonder—how bad is my reality about to get?

29

While I wait for Detective Grayson, my phone pings as a text comes in from Noah.

How's it going?

I might be getting somewhere.

There's no reason to tell him about the article yet, the memories that have returned. I am just staying quiet with it, letting the information move through me. Her name, those memories, the story of her murder, what else will it trigger? What else will I remember?

Did you find the bag?

Even though we didn't discuss it before I left on this errand, we both know I was at least partially looking for that pink backpack. It's been something we've wondered about. I can't let go of the idea that there's something in there that I need. That it's real, not a figment of my previously addled imagination. My hope was that maybe it was buried in those boxes, or hidden somewhere in the apartment. But I've been through everything now and it's not here. Does it even exist?

No. I didn't. It's not here.

There's a pause. I almost put the phone down. Then:

Come home.

My body floods with warmth. That house, that land, Noah. It already feels like home.

Soon.

When he arrives, Detective Grayson and I regard each other for a moment. Even he seems different somehow—solid, soothing. We're on the same side. I suppose we always have been.

"The last time we got together here you told me to be low risk."

"I also told you to stay away from Noah Avidon," he says. He glances at the row of boxes and bags. "But I guess we're on a program where I ask you to do one thing, and you do the opposite."

I offer him coffee but he waves me off. "I'm overcaffeinated as it is. Thanks."

We move into the kitchen, and he takes his usual seat on the barstool.

"You're lucky your *other* boyfriend isn't pressing charges," he says.

Noah punched Rick from finance in the face the night he brought me back to his house. I remember the blood, the way Rick wailed in pain. Serves him right; no wonder he's not pressing charges. What was he planning to do to me?

"Neither of them is my *boyfriend*." What a stupid word, anyway, so infantilizing. "Meanwhile, Noah saved me that night. What was that you said about predators? That they look for the vulnerable and give them what they want."

"I was talking about Avidon."

"Who knows what would have happened if he hadn't been there?"

"Like I said." He does that exhausted temple rubbing thing he does so often in my company. "High-risk behavior. Avoid it."

I pour us each a glass of water. I've had a little too much coffee myself.

He glances around the room. "Moving out?"

I shrug. "Just getting rid of things I don't need anymore. Letting Jack go a little."

I tell him everything I've learned about Elena Montoya, what I remember from my dream memory, the morning I found the matchbook. I turn my laptop over to him so that he can see my email, the articles I bookmarked. Part of me expects him to be dismissive, to say he already knows all of this and it doesn't mean anything. But he's quiet, scrolling through the items on my computer.

"When was this?"

"The day I found the matchbook must have been nearly a year before he died. We had *just* started trying to have a baby. It was before the miscarriages."

He glances at the screen. "And she was murdered just a few months before Jack."

I show him the photograph of the wedding that Alvaro gave me, the image I took with my phone. I don't know what happened to the original picture. The last time I saw it was when I handed it to Layla.

"She *knew* us," I say. "She was at this wedding."

"And where does this wedding fall on the timeline?"

I think about this. "Somewhere between the matchbook and

Jack's murder. I can get the exact date, sometime in June I think."

He holds me in that dark gaze. "This is a lead, Poppy," he says. "I'll follow it up. I promise."

I want more urgency than that. Not just another *I'll follow up*. "How? How are you going to follow up? When?"

"I've got a few things I need to discuss with you first," he says. "Related to some of the other information you gave me. You might want to sit down."

We walk into the living space and he sits on the couch across from me.

"So, since you called me from Avidon's and talked to me about your friend Merlinda, I've been doing some digging."

I draw in and hold a breath, bracing myself for I don't know what.

"I'm sorry." He holds my eyes, practiced at delivering bad news. "She's gone. She passed away."

The news lands hard, bringing tears to my eyes. "How?"

"After a battle with cancer, she died in hospice."

How did I not know she was sick? It hasn't been that long since she lived next door to me, was my friend. Another person I neglected in the myopic nature of my grief. I close my eyes and say a little prayer for her. *I'm sorry, Merlinda. I hope there was light on the other side for you.*

"I have to admit, I was skeptical about what you told me. You know I don't have much faith in dreams. Real memory is tricky enough. But I promised you I'd do my best." Grayson is quiet a moment. Then, "So as part of this investigation, I went to see the attorney handling your friend's estate, and they have, in fact, been trying to reach you. They've left messages at your office, sent a letter to your old address."

He hands me the letter. It looks vaguely familiar, a letterhead I've seen. In the fog of the last year, did this fall through the cracks? Did I weave the information into my dreams?

"There *is* a safe-deposit box containing something Merlinda left for you."

"Did you get it?"

"I can't do that without a warrant," he says. "I thought I'd see if you want to go together to the lawyer's office."

I know I should refuse him, that I should go alone and bring whatever it is to my own attorney. Let him handle it if whatever is there needs to be turned over to the police. But I'm tired of games, tired of waiting.

By the way Grayson's shoulders are hiked, and how he's leaning so far forward on the couch it looks like he could topple off, I know there's more.

"What else?"

"Do you remember that killer for hire, the one my murdered CI told me about?"

I flash back to the sketch he showed me in the park. It seems so long ago now, but I won't forget that face, the heavy brow and deep-set eyes. I nod to indicate that I remember.

"A body matching that description washed up by Chelsea Piers," he says. "Same tats my CI mentioned helped us identify him. A career criminal by the name of Joe Knight—foster care, in the system from age 15, armed robbery, aggravated assault, manslaughter. He fits the profile, matches the description of witnesses at the scene of Jack's murder."

My first thought is a selfish and cold one: great. Another dead end.

If someone hired him to kill Jack, now we'll never know who. I've taken so many strange and winding roads away from Jack and back again, walked so many dark alleys deep into my own dreams, twisted memories that weren't even real. There have been so made dead ends in this maze. I'm afraid I've lost him forever.

"First thing I always ask myself about a guy like that," says

Grayson. There's a smile beneath his grim expression. He obviously loves his job, however dark. "How is he getting paid?"

I think about this a moment. "I'd guess it's a cash business."

"You'd think, right?" There's a little glitter of excitement in his eyes.

He takes some folded paper out of the inside pocket of his jacket and hands it over. It's a copy of a bank statement. I scan the charges and withdrawals. Hit men use their debit cards at Starbucks just like everyone else, apparently. They watch Netflix and shop on Amazon. Some of the charges are highlighted: an army-navy store, a pawnshop, a shooting range.

There are regular cash deposits, some small, some large. There's a larger, recurring deposit that seems to come consistently every two weeks like a paycheck. At first I don't recognize the company name. It knocks around for a moment. When it clicks, I take in a sharp breath, can't get any air. The room starts to spin and the bottom falls out of my world. Again.

But this time, I'm still here.

30

The small bank is quiet as we enter, an older branch with worn carpets and uninspired Formica surfaces, unflattering fluorescent lighting. The place has an air of desertion. A woman in a dark coat argues quietly with a young male teller, but otherwise it's empty. Do people even go to banks anymore in this online world? Money has become just numbers on a screen, debits and credits, red and green. Even our cash comes from machines.

"I'll wait for you here," says Grayson, taking a stance by the door like a security guard. "Give you some space with it."

Part of me wants him to come with me, to be there when I see what's waiting. He's right that I'm stronger. The world seems solid, the ground beneath my feet firmer now. But what kind of wormhole will open in my world when that safe-deposit box lid comes off. What's in there? Hesitating a moment, I finally leave him to approach the teller. She's a young woman who looks old, wearing a retro lime green shift, her red hair pulled into a tight twist, a quizzical frown on her face.

"I have a key for a safe-deposit box that was left to me by a friend who's passed," I tell her. She squints at the paperwork through bug-eyed specs, enters a few strokes on the keypad in front of her, then without a word retrieves a ring of keys.

"This way, please."

What did Merlinda leave for me? I think I know. But my only memory is a dream, something I'm not sure ever happened.

My throat is dry with fear as I follow the tiny woman, her kitten heels clicking purposefully on tile floors. We travel down a long hallway and finally at the end she pushes us through a heavy door, into a bright room that's as cold as the interior of a refrigerator.

I imagined something different, a wood-paneled space, maybe with an oak table and rows of copper doors. Instead, it's more like a gym locker room, the same lavender and gray of the branch lobby.

She puts a key in number 329, and leaves me alone, closing the door with a click that seems final. I breathe against my hammering heart.

Whatever it is, it's been sitting for a long time. How can it hurt me now? How much more pain is there left in my universe?

"What is it?" I ask Jack, who is sitting on one of the molded plastic chairs that tuck inside the cubby where you're meant to bring your box.

But he doesn't talk much these days. When I do see him, he's usually walking ahead of me on one of the trails I wander. Sometimes he lounges by the fire. These are all the things he would have loved about a house in the woods.

I still dream of him, too. The other night I dreamed we had a child together, a little boy who looked just like him with sandy hair and wide, soulful eyes. They walked ahead of me on a wooded path, hand in hand. I followed but they drew farther and farther away. The faster I chased, the more distant they became until they turned a corner and were gone.

He was ambivalent about fatherhood, but he would have been a good dad—a great one. Loving, patient, fun—exactly the kind

of husband he was. I never knew his father, beyond what he and
Sarah told me. A hard worker, honest, maybe too strict, a stick
figure in Jack's life, someone consumed by his job, plugging
in now and again for awkward games of catch, or fishing trips
steeped in silence. Maybe that's what Jack remembered about
fatherhood. Maybe that's all we know, what our parents model
for us, until we try to do better.

"It wasn't just that," ghost Jack says. "The world. I always
thought it was a beautiful place—magical and full of awe-
inspiring surprises. But it's dark, Poppy. You see that now, too,
don't you? Whatever light there is gets swallowed."

"I'm sorry," I tell him. "But you're wrong. It's both. Shadow
and light."

I turn the key in the lock. Then I pull the drawer from its
sleeve and open it slowly.

I let out a long breath when I see my pink backpack stuffed
inside. I lay my hand on it, feel the shapes of things beneath the
thin fabric. I wore this pack when I trekked the Fakahatchee
Strand with Jack, searching for the ghost orchid. It was on my
back as I rode a boat down the Amazon River, hiked a lush and
twisting trail to a stunning waterfall on Kauai. Once, it caused
me to get stuck in a tight spot spelunking a lava tube in Iceland.
Jack had to shimmy it off my back so that I could get free. It has
an energy I can feel in my palm.

I heft it out and lay it on the table, pull the zipper slowly and
start to remove the contents. There's a slim black notebook, filled
with Jack's scrawling handwriting. A burner cell phone, its battery long dead. And there's a large envelope, which I open to
retrieve a manila file. Inside there's a stack of photos.

Then, I'm time traveling again.

Everyone was gone. Jack's funeral was over. Layla had sent
my mother packing under some weak protesting. But I think

Mom was relieved to leave my grief behind her. Real emotion made my mother uncomfortable.

I could cry to my father, throw myself at him in adoration, follow him around with my camera. But Mother bristled at too much of me. *That's enough, Poppy.* A quick pat, a kiss on the head, and then a little push away. I was glad to see her go, too. On the other hand, I didn't want her to go, either, and part of me resented her for leaving. The complicated twists of the mother-daughter dance.

"Just try to keep moving, sweetie," she said as she left. "Try to not *wallow.*"

We left the dishes in the sink.

"Someone will come in to clean tomorrow," Layla said. Her face was as drawn and exhausted as mine. Mac stood by the window looking out. His phone convulsed on the countertop; for once, he ignored it.

"I'll do it," I said listlessly, lying prone on the couch. The pills Layla gave me, who even knew what, had me numb to my core, empty of feeling.

"You will not," she said. I think she'd taken something, too— and she'd been drinking. As had I. I relished the nothingness, the distance of my pain. "You'll rest. Or do whatever you need to do. No one ever needed to do dishes to feel better."

"No," I agreed. "No one ever did."

Mac seemed cored out, his shoulders sagging, eyes dark with fatigue. "We're going to do whatever it takes to get you through this," he said, taking me into his arms. "I promise that."

Thank God for them, I thought distantly. Where would I be without them? Friends are the family you choose.

"Come with us," Layla begged.

"It's okay," I lied. "I'll come over first thing in the morning."

All I wanted was dark and quiet, my nerve endings raw, my body aching. Just quiet.

"Then I'll sleep on your couch," she said. "You won't even know I'm here."

Mac drew her gently away. "Stop smothering her, Layla," he said. "She needs some space."

"I'm not smothering her," she said, high-pitched and defensive. "Am I, Poppy? Okay. Okay. I am. I'm sorry."

And then they were gone. The silence expanded. The apartment rambled. I floated on a medicated cloud, lying awake in a haze, blissfully blank. There's no tomorrow, I thought, no yesterday. Just this empty, disembodied moment. On the bedside table, there was a bottle of pills that Layla had left. Ativan, did she say? Or Bennies. What was that even? It sat like a sentry, ready to rush in and save me from the waves of pain, grief, rage that were beating distantly at the inside of my brain.

What if I took them all? Jack disappeared through a dark doorway in the world. Couldn't I just follow him? The bottle rattled in my hand, the water glass right there. How long would it take? How quickly would the darkness swallow me?

That's when I heard the beeping, somewhere muffled, so faint. Then it stopped. Long enough that I could think maybe I hadn't heard it at all, or that it was in another apartment, or something outside, down the hall.

Then it started again. It went on and on, until finally it drew me to my feet. I walked from room to room, finally coming to stand inside our closet. The beeping stopped but I stayed, waiting. The shelves lined up to the ceiling, the tallest of them only Jack could reach without a step stool. And that's where he kept all his old junk. When the beeping started again, that's where it was coming from.

I grabbed a chair from the dining room, hauled it awkwardly down the hall, banging into walls. After digging through piles of sweaters, shoving aside boxes that had sat unopened since college, stacks and stacks of photographs and term papers, I found it, far back in the deepest corner. My pink pack, a single red flashing light shining through the thin fabric. It was heavier than I expected as I took it down to the floor and tore it open.

A phone, beeping with the alert that it was about to die. The matchbook with Elena's scrawled name. Photographs. A slew of articles. *Oh, god. Oh, no.*

Back in the ugly white light of the bank vault, I let all the feelings from that night wash over me. The wrenching betrayal, the terror, doubles me over once more, and tears come with a strangled sob. That drawing in my journal, where the tiny figure falls and falls into the widening spiral. That's me.

I remember thinking that I had to get as far away from everything, everyone, as I could. I dressed and took that pack, brought it to Merlinda. Why did I bring it to her? I'm not sure what my logic was. Maybe it was because she was a friend who wasn't connected to the mess of my life. Because I trusted her, her goodness, her wisdom. Maybe because she was right down the hall, and someone no one would—if anyone was looking—suspect as my confidant. Scenes come back in a slide show of foggy memories: Merlinda answering the door in a robe, worried and kind.

Please, Poppy, stay with me. Let's call your friends.

No one can know about this.

The hallway, the elevator, Richie the doorman calling after me. Then I ran, as far away from my life, from myself as I could.

Everything, I remember thinking. *Now I've lost everything.*

What's real and what isn't real? It's a question I never thought I'd ask myself. We're asleep for half our lives, our bodies at rest and our minds journeying to another space and time, a twisted world woven from our experiences, our imaginations, our desires and fears. And something more maybe.

Jung thought that dreams were a doorway into the collective unconscious, into the mystical. Freud thought they were a canvas for the id. Before Jack died, before the pills altered my brain chemistry, I didn't have an especially active dream life. The idea that there might be any confusion between those two worlds never occurred.

The camera lens is the unwavering, seeing eye. And photographs are moments irrevocably captured. That trick of light and shadow, of here and gone, that is the passage of time foiled by the captured image. That moment, whatever it was, however brief, was real, the photograph says. It is the prisoner of this frame and it cannot deny itself. The eye is unreliable, memory even less so. The photograph in its pure form is the unimpeachable witness to what was.

"Don't do anything stupid, Poppy."

This was Detective Grayson's warning as we parted ways in front of the bank. My head is spinning with what I learned from him, from the contents of that pack. Finally, everything makes sense, and I desperately wish it didn't. I remember the advice from ghost Jack: *Stop asking questions, Poppy. You're not going to like the answers.*

"Get yourself someplace safe," Detective Grayson went on. "And stay there for a while. This is up to me now. Wait for my call."

"Be low risk for a while?" I say.

"Can you handle that?" he asks, skeptical.

I don't go back to Noah's, or to Layla's, or to my Chelsea highrise. Instead, I wander around the old neighborhood—past the café where Jack and I used to sit and have coffee and read the paper. Past the corner deli where he used to stop for flowers—not orchids. Past the entrance to the park where we most often entered on our morning run, and where he entered alone on the last morning of his life. I sit on the bench there and listen—to the traffic, to the birdsong, to the kids shouting and laughing on the playground.

Jack's ghost is everywhere, and so is mine. The girl I was then,

Jack's wife, Poppy Lang. But Jack is gone. Mac, Layla and I released his ashes off the Brooklyn Bridge, as was his wish. And I am gone, too. The woman who walks these streets today is not the same. I died that morning in the park with him, have died a hundred times since then, in dreams, in my imagination. I am someone new.

I need to call Layla, can't keep this from her—even though it's the end of everything, for both of us.

She answers on the first ring.

"Where are you?" she asks, her voice wavering. I can tell she's been crying. Does she know everything already? Have the police already called her?

"Nearby," I say. "What's wrong?"

"The kids—I've arranged for them to be picked up from school for sleepovers with friends." She takes a shuddering breath. "I'm leaving him, Poppy. It's worse between us than I've told you. *So much* worse."

I don't know how to tell her that it's even worse than that, however bad it might be.

"I'm on my way," I say instead.

"Don't, Poppy." There's something strange in her voice: fear. "I think he's coming here. He's so angry. I have no idea what he'll do. I need to be gone before he gets here."

"What are you *saying*, Layla?"

A picture starts to coalesce, like an image emerging in the chemical bath of a darkroom lab.

"He's dangerous," she whispers. "There are *so many things* I've never told you. I've been so ashamed. God, I'm just like her. I'm just like my mother. How could I have let it get this bad?"

Her voice, she's that teenager afraid and angry in the back of my dad's car. And my whole body vibrates with the urge to rescue her. How could I not have known? How could I have missed Mac and who he really is?

"Go to my place." I get up and start to move. "I'll get the Jeep and pick you up."

"Okay," she says. "Okay."

Then I hang up the phone and start to run.

My apartment is empty when I arrive. I wait and wait, but she doesn't come. I pace the rooms, calling her over and over. Desperate, I phone Mac. The sound of his voice on the message makes my stomach churn but I keep my voice steady and light.

"Please call me, Mac. Let's talk."

Finally, I ring Carmelo, but only get his voice mail. I resist the urge to hurl the phone in anger and frustration. Where is everyone?

"Carmelo," I say, trying to sound calm. "I'm looking for Layla and Mac. Do you know where they are? It's—an emergency."

Grayson's phone goes straight to voice mail, as well.

"I think Layla's in trouble," I tell him. "I think he has her. He's dangerous. Please do something."

Panic wells, the walls are closing in. I'm so damn helpless. I can't just stand here, waiting for Grayson. Should I call 911?

I almost call Noah, but then I don't. How can I ask more of him? How can I pull him deeper into this mess?

Then I remember Layla's favorite trick, how she tracks me and her children all over the city: Find My Friends. I quickly open the app and there she is, her little blue dot, pulsing. She's on the Henry Hudson, heading north. Relief makes me weak; that blue dot—it feels like proof of life.

But where are they going?

And, then, before my eyes, the dot stops pulsing, seems to freeze.

I refresh the screen and a message pops up. Final and cold: Layla Van Santen is unavailable.

No matter how many times I refresh, the message stays the

same. I remember how Layla described her despair when she couldn't find me. *It was like my lifeline to you had been cut.*

Think, think.

Where would they be heading up north?

Mac's fishing cabin. The place he goes to unplug, no internet, no phone. Jack spent some time up there with him. Mac's had it for ages, even before they had money. It's a little shack of a place, sitting on acres in the woods—just a single room with a couch that turns into a bed, a galley kitchen, a sleep loft for the kids.

It reminds us how little you really need—just love, your family and friends, a place to be warm, good food. What else is there really, at the end of the day?

Yeah, I quipped. *Because only rich people need to be reminded of how little they really need.*

"I'm coming," I say out loud. "I'm coming."

There's only one problem. I'm not totally sure where that cabin is, don't have an address to punch into my GPS. It wasn't Layla's favorite place and it has been years since I was up there.

Still, I run to the parking garage where I left the Jeep and plan to head in the right direction, hoping to find my way. I burn out of the lot, only to get caught in a crush of traffic headed toward the highway. I snake through cross streets, practically crawling out of my skin and finally, finally get on the Henry Hudson, head north.

When my phone rings, it's Carmelo.

"Miss Poppy," he says, sounding concerned. "Something up?"

"Carmelo, where are they? Mac and Layla?"

There's a pause. "I don't know," he says. "Mr. Van Santen, he gave me the day off. He, uh, I guess he didn't seem like himself. I took him to the garage where he keeps his other car. And he told me he wouldn't need me for a couple of days probably. Which is, you know, kind of out of the ordinary."

"Where's the cabin?" I ask. "The old fishing cabin."

There's a pause where I think I've lost him. Then:

"It's not my place to tell people where Mr. Van Santen is, Miss Poppy. I'm sorry. Part of my job for him is discretion."

"I'm not looking for *Mr. Van Santen*," I snap. "I'm looking for *Layla*. She's in trouble, Carmelo, and I *need* you to help me."

He clears his throat. "What kind of trouble?"

"Please—" I'm desperate enough to beg. "Tell me where the cabin is."

I'm leaning on that feeling of friendship between us, hoping it's not just me, that I'm not just the friend of his employer— someone he tolerates politely.

The speedometer pushes past seventy as I weave between lanes, the phone on speaker—no Bluetooth. I can barely hear him over the sound of rushing wind through the poorly insu- lated Jeep.

"I wouldn't ask this of you if it wasn't important. Please."

"Okay," he says with a reluctant sigh. "I'll text you the ad- dress."

Then he hangs up. A moment later, my phone pings with the address. I tap on it and bring up the map and directions.

The isolated cabin buried deep in the woods is more than an hour away. *I'm coming*, I silently tell my friend, press my foot to the gas.

31

Mac was right.

How well do we ever really know each other? As children, we lay ourselves bare—we run around naked, blurt out anything that pops into our minds. We can't keep secrets. We can't hide without laughing. But as we grow older, something changes. Somewhere along the line we step behind a veil, create one facade for the world and live another life inside. The modern world lets us construct avatars of ourselves, post a curated version of our lives for everyone to see. Supposedly, this keeps us connected. But maybe, just maybe, it keeps us apart, keeps the world at arm's length, only allowing people to see what we want them to see.

Jack. Layla. Mac. Alvaro. They all had secret selves. Some of those secrets got my husband killed. The Seven of Swords; all along I was holding the card of deception. And I had no idea.

The cabin sits small, surrounded by a stand of trees. The night is dark and moonless, the air icy cold. I bring the Jeep to a skidding stop and kill the lights. I don't have a plan, my whole body vibrating with fear. I just jump out of the car and race to the front door. Reckless. Thoughtless. Acting out of fear for Layla. And something else—that dark rage that comes after betrayal.

But the door is locked tight, and inside the cabin is dark. It's bigger than I remember it, much bigger, as if rooms have been added on. Layla never mentioned a renovation, but then, this was always Mac's place.

I peer in the window and only see the shadows of covered furniture. Then I move around back.

The sky is pitch-black, moonless, stars obscured by clouds and the trees all around me. It's so quiet that my footfalls are loud on the soft ground, fallen leaves rustling. I come to a glass-paned back door that seems to lead into a kitchen. It's locked tight, too. I stand listening but there's only the hush of things gone quiet around me.

All my anger wells and I start pounding on the door.

"Layla!" I yell, my voice ringing out in the silence. "Layla!"

I realize that I didn't see Mac's car—or any vehicle—when I arrived. My stomach bottoms out. Oh my god. I've come all the way out here and they're not here. Maybe I've driven hours *away* from the place I need to be to help her.

I reach into my pocket for the phone to try Grayson again and find that I've left it in the car.

I hear something then, something muffled and far away. A voice. A cry. Every nerve ending in my body is tingling.

That's when I do something crazy. Okay, crazier. I grab a large rock from the ground, walk over to the back door and use it to smash the pane, shattering the glass. I reach inside the hole I've made, my jacket protecting me from the sharp edges, and unlock the door. Then I push inside, the glass crunching beneath my feet.

But there's only silence and I begin to feel the weight and foolishness of my actions.

"Layla!" I call.

Then, he stands there in the doorway leading to the rest of

the house, his dark shadow blocking my path. For a second, my heart pumps. The hooded man? But no, it's Mac. As I draw closer, his face comes clear—a deep scowl darkening his features.

"What are you doing here, Poppy?" he says. His eyes move past me to the door. "Did you break the fucking glass? What the hell is wrong with you?"

"Where's Layla?" My eyes fall on a gleaming row of Wüsthof blades; I keep the long marble counter between us.

"She's *my* wife, not yours," he says, his tone dark.

"Where is she?" I say again, louder. "Layla!"

The silence that follows expands and fills me with dread.

"You don't need to know where she is every single fucking second, do you? What's with you two, anyway? It's not normal, you get that, right? Your friendship."

I stare at him, the dark expression on his face, the cool edge of his tone. He seems like a different man, not my friend—a person I have loved and trusted for so many years. He's a stranger.

"I know what you did," I say. "I know about Elena. I know about *Jack*."

The words burn my throat.

"You shouldn't have come here."

The electricity of bad possibilities thickens the air between us. I'm frozen, not sure what to do. Then he laughs. It's a strangled, unpleasant sound.

"You know—you're just like him." He shakes his head slowly. "Relentless. You guys—you were well suited."

The words knock me back like a hard slap to the face. But I edge closer. He stands firm, a guard at the door.

"How could you do this to us, to him?" I wonder briefly if this is what Detective Grayson meant by not doing anything stupid. Anger flashes across Mac's face, widening his nostrils, pressing his mouth into a grimace.

"You have no idea what you're talking about." His voice is a growl. "You're a wreck, Poppy. You always have been. You're out of your mind and everyone knows that."

His voice is cold, his words so cruel.

"There are pictures. I think you know that." My voice is calm and steady, though I'm anything but. "I saw them."

There's a flicker of uncertainty, then he blows out another disdainful laugh. "Another dream. Another hooded man in the shadows. You don't even know what's real anymore, do you?"

Layla was always the wild one, the one to stand up to bullies, the one most likely to throw the first punch when necessary. But the disdain in his voice, what I know about him now, the fact that I can't hear Layla, something hot and red takes over. All that rage that has been brewing since I lost Jack, its release is volcanic.

I rush for him, with a kind of warrior's yell that blasts from some place deep inside. But I just hit him like a wall. His flesh is as unyielding as brick. I reel back, stunned. He grabs me hard by the shoulders, shakes me like a doll.

"You shouldn't have come here," he says again, teeth gritted. "*Why* did you come here?"

He's so fast, so strong. The blow, when it comes, is a backhand to the jaw—shocking, disorienting. It knocks me on the ground where I lie, my mouth filled with blood that spills out down my chin, onto the ground. A hard kick to the ribs bends me over with white-hot pain, radiating, taking my breath away. I look up at him, this man, my friend, and his face is so twisted with rage, I don't even know him.

"Mac," I breathe. The pain, it's not just in my body. My heart is broken, too—again. "Please."

He bends down, his face a mask—or maybe the mask is gone. He raises his fist one more time, and then there's nothing.

The ground beneath me is cold and hard as I come ragged and disoriented back to myself.

There is nothing but pain—my back, my shoulder, my jaw.

Blood and saliva mingle, a metallic taste in my mouth. A hard-wood floor, bunk beds. I recognize it immediately. I'm in the sleep loft. Layla lies still, just feet from me, her face swollen and purple, her arm twisted. I try to move to her but the pain, it's a lightning strike through my body, and my arms are bound behind me. What the fuck? Is this another dream, another hypnagogic nightmare? No. It's brutally, miserably real.

"Layla," I whisper. "Layla, *wake up.*"

She moves at the sound of my voice, issues the faintest groan. Relief is a river, giving me a rush of adrenaline. She's alive, we're alive. There's still hope, isn't there?

My phone? Where is it? The fucking car. What *an idiot.* Who would do this? Come bursting in here without a cell phone, without a plan to take on a monster, without letting anyone know where she was going. That electronic tether that Jack so disdained would really help us now.

The only person who knows I've come here is Carmelo. How much does he know? Whose side will he be on? I didn't tell Detective Grayson because I thought he'd try to stop me, or Noah—because—I don't know why, maybe because this is not his battle to fight. And I've asked too much of him already.

Or maybe the truth is that I'm inviting darkness with my high-risk behavior. Maybe on some level I am purposely bringing this kind of mayhem into my life. Isn't this what I wanted all along, why I kept chasing after the hooded man? I wanted a showdown. A confrontation. Well, I got one and lost.

Voices. Male voices, low and deep, rumble downstairs. Or maybe not. Now there's just silence, the wind outside, the scratching of a branch at the small octagonal window.

"Poppy."

Layla, voice weak and scratchy, eyes swollen nearly shut and trained on me. Her lids are an unsettling purple, there's a gash from her forehead to her eyebrow. I want to rush over to her, clean it, hold her and tell her we're okay. But I can't because we're both bound. And we're not okay at all.

"You're not the whole rescue party, are you?"

"In fact," I say, "I am."

"Seriously?" She tries to move but issues a groan of pain. "You didn't call *anyone*? Did you at least dial 911?"

There's no good explanation for my reckless stupidity or lack of foresight, so I just stay quiet, trying despite the pain to wiggle free from the bonds at my wrist. What is it? Duct tape?

"What happened?" I ask. "What's *happening*? Did he do this to you?"

She makes a noise that's somewhere between a laugh and a sob. "This is what happens to you when you try to leave Mac. He always told me that he'd kill me if I tried to leave him. In my heart, I didn't believe him."

I can hardly believe that he'd hurt her so badly. But then I remember his face as he stood over me, an ugly twist of rage, the face of someone unhinged, detached from consequence. Had I ever seen it in him before? In all these years—where we ate together and drank together, where he helped Jack and me with the business, when his children were born, when we all traveled together. No, I am ashamed to say. Never. Maybe only in the way he couldn't really be photographed, how he always looked hulkish and strange, his features poorly defined, a shadow over Layla.

"Why didn't you tell me he was hurting you?" I whisper. "How could you keep this from me?"

"You want to do this now?" Even beaten and bound on the floor, she still manages to have an attitude.

"Layla—I could have helped."

She groans, starts shifting toward me. "The twist of it—the violence, the kids, the shame. It's so fucking complicated."

"I know," I say. "But I could have been there for you."

"It starts small, you know. Comes out of nowhere. In fact, the first time he ever touched me in anger was here in this cabin. I can't even remember what we were fighting about—something stupid, like I'd forgotten to get something at the store. It just escalated, got hotter. This was before the kids. He pushed me against the refrigerator and I hit my head. He cried and cried—he was so sorry. It was years before it happened again."

She blows out a breath. There are bruises all up and down her bare arms, just like the ones she had as a kid. She hid them under her sleeves.

"I was so hard on my mom, so angry at her for her weakness. I get it now, how it starts small, how every single time it happens you just get weaker and weaker. That sometimes I'd goad him into it, just because it sort of becomes the only way you connect—which is sick. But I used to hit him, just to make him mad so he'd seem *human*. We'd throw things, break things. Afterward, the tearful, passionate making up. It's a drug. Then the kids come, and it's a secret you think you're keeping from them. All the apologies, the promises, you just keep hoping it will go back to the way it was."

She looks at me through her swollen lids. "What a cliché I am, right? And here you are saving me from another abuser."

I fight back angry tears. There's more to tell Layla about her husband—so much more—but I'm not sure this is the time. But there may not be another time.

"Layla—" I begin.

"Shh" she says through her broken lips, her eyes darting past me. "There's a gun locker out in the shed. It's where he keeps the hunting rifles. There's a shotgun, too. The ammunition is on the shelf above."

"Layla." I am still struggling with my bindings. They're looser, but not loose enough for me to slip a hand out. "Turn around so that we're back-to-back."

She lies still, exhausted. "I can't," she says, her voice going sleepy. She's fading out. That head injury; it can't be good. There's *so much* blood. On her face, her neck, on the floor. Too much.

"Layla!" My voice is a sharp hiss. "Stay with me. I need you. You don't get to bail right now."

Her eyes flicker. Underneath the blood and bruises, her skin is an unsettling white. "Okay. Okay."

I shimmy myself closer to her, and with effort we both turn.

"I'll work on yours," she says. "You're stronger right now. If you get free, run. You know the code to the locker. Same as everything."

Izzy's birthday.

"Do you know what it feels like to truly hate someone?" she asks. "To wish him dead."

I draw in and release a breath, flash on those entries in my dream journal, that terrible rage that surfaced when I faced Mac.

"I do now."

We fall silent at the sound of footfalls approaching. The ladder leading to the loft starts to creak. We freeze, my bindings still tight, both of us beaten and weak. We're no match for whatever comes next and we both know that.

"When you start to fade out," I whisper. "Think of Izzy and Slade. We're not leaving them behind. Not with him."

I hear her draw in a sharp sob. Then the dark form of head and shoulders looms.

"Girls," says Tom, his face full of compassion, his voice gentle and reasonable. "Let's talk."

"I think that we can all agree things have gotten out of hand here," says Tom easily.

He's helped us both down the ladder, and now Layla and I sit on the couch side by side, Layla so out of it that she's leaning heavily against me. That cut on her head is still bleeding. The pain in my side is so excruciating, it's hard to concentrate.

We're going to die here.

Mac stands in the corner of the room, arms folded across his middle, staring balefully at Layla.

"I'm sorry," he says. "I'm so sorry."

Sorry: the favorite word of the abuser. How many times did Layla hear it from her father?

I find myself thinking about her wedding day. Of all the dashing and handsome men she'd dated in her life, why Mac, I'd wondered. Sweet enough, sure, but a dyed-in-the-wool geek. She'd been with photographers and models, adventure guides, all of them strapping and charming, head over heels in love with Layla. Mac was, as I understood it then, a banker. A number jockey. He sat behind a desk. I asked her: *What is it about him, Layla? Why Mac? Because*, she said, as pale and beautiful as a ghost bride. *Because he'll take care of me. He'll never hurt me.*

How could she have been so wrong? Or, on some level, did she know? When you come from abuse, do you forever confuse it with love? Do we invite darkness as the poet detective once suggested?

Mac starts to weep softly, he leans against the wall and sinks to the floor. Hatred tastes like bile in my throat. I wish I was strong enough to kill him with my bare hands. That rage, I allow its power to pulse through me; it's keeping me conscious.

"So who killed Elena Montoya?" I ask Tom. No point in beating around the bush. "Was it Mac himself? Or did you hire Joe Knight?"

Mac looks up at me and Tom goes very, very still.

It was all there in Jack's notebook, the notes he started keeping after Elena was killed. Pieced together with what I learned from Detective Grayson, the ugly picture is starting to come clear. Silence now would be the better choice, but I just can't keep the words from coming.

"You met her through Alvaro and Jack, right, Mac? Did Alvaro invite her that night to Morpheus? Or maybe even Jack? He had a talent for keeping up connections. Elena was their old friend and colleague, their fellow alum from college. That's how you met Elena?"

He says nothing. It's so quiet that I can hear my own breathing. Out the window there is only blackness. This cabin; it's miles from any other structure, sitting on a private lake. There's a rickety dock, a boathouse where they keep a small dingy. Cell service here is spotty at best, which is what Mac liked about it best. His place to disconnect.

"So, what happened?" My words sound too loud, too strident. "Was it a single night? Or did you have an affair?"

"Stop," whispers Layla. "Don't do this."

I look over at her. Does she already know?

But now that I know the truth, what's real, what pushed me over the edge, it won't stay in. It was a poison, a toxin, it almost killed me. It needs to be *purged*.

"Jack thought that Elena wanted more than you could give, Mac. You thought it was a one-night stand, but Elena wanted a life with you, threatened to tell Layla. When she couldn't have that, she started blackmailing you. Hell hath no fury? It happens, right? Wealthy guy has a fling with the wrong girl, things get ugly. Rich people problems. Did you handle it yourself? Or did you call in your *fixer*?"

"Miss," says Tom. That scar, that fixed stare, it's unsettling. "I think you need to be careful with your accusations. We're all in a place where we can work things out. Let's not cross the point of no return."

I should listen to reason, knowing what happened to Jack, Elena Montoya, what's already happened to Layla, to me. But I'm too far gone. Maybe Mac's right, maybe I am crazy. Too crazy to save us.

"I saw the pictures she was using to blackmail you," I say. "Very graphic. Did she set you up? Lure you to her place for that purpose, or was it just her kink, how she got off? I don't believe you were aware she was taking that footage. It doesn't seem like your style, Mac. I had no idea you were such an animal, so—*unhinged*."

The weeping has stopped; now he's glaring at me again.

"You're going to get us killed," Layla hisses. "Shut up, Poppy."

That's what she doesn't get. We're already dead.

"Jack must have put it together when she was murdered," I go on. "Someone made it look like a burglary gone wrong. But he didn't buy it. How did he get all those pictures? Did she send them to him, too? It looks like he was *investigating*, trying to figure out what happened to her. It was *haunting* him."

"I didn't kill her," said Mac. "It wasn't me. I tried to tell Jack that, to make him understand."

"But Jack couldn't let it go, could he?"

"Mac." Tom's voice has taken on a tone of dark warning. "Don't say a word."

There's a breath where I think Mac's going to deny everything.

"No," he says finally, his voice a growl. "He couldn't. He *wouldn't* let it go."

Layla draws in a breath, starts to sob.

"She was *nothing, no one*." Mac's voice is high and indignant. He stands now, starts pacing. Layla shrinks against me, afraid. My brave, tough friend shrinks *from him*. That rage, it's rumbling.

"It was *nothing. Nothing*, Layla. One stupid, drunken night, one stupid drunken mistake. She set me up, had those cameras planted and waiting."

Arms waving, face red.

"That's enough, Mac," says Tom with a sigh. "Quiet now."

"No, Tom, no. It was a *setup*. For all I know Jack was even *in on it*, from the beginning. And he would have ruined all our lives—mine, Layla's, the kids'—even yours, Poppy."

"Jack? In on it? He was your *friend*," I say, incredulous. "He *loved* you."

"Then maybe it was Alvaro," Mac says. "*He* was in on it with her. I'm sure of it. She wasn't working alone."

Something about that strikes a note. That picture. Why would Alvaro give that photograph to me and pretend not to know who Elena was? He *knew* her. Did he hope it would jog my memory? And his words to Sarah: *I wish Jack had been a little less good.*

Was Alvaro capable of something like that? Setting Mac up to blackmail him? Did he figure Mac would just pay any amount to keep his affair from Layla, never imagining the dark turn things would take?

"Just tell me everything, Mac," I say. "Make me understand what happened. The truth. God, for all of our sakes."

"I advise you again to say nothing." Tom again, looking a little red in the face.

Mac waves him off. "What does it matter now?" he says.

"Mac," says Tom. "It *matters.*"

"I always really liked those guys, you know—Jack and Alvaro," Mac says.

He rubs at his bald head. The Mac who met me at the door is gone. Now he's more like the man I thought I knew. But that's the trick of the abuser, soft one moment, a monster the next. Unpredictability is his best trick.

"When Alvaro was in town and we hung out, it was *cool.* I felt like one of the guys. Alvaro was kind of a dick, but—you know—he was funny. The girls *loved* him. We partied. I never had friends like that before. For me it was all school, work, work, work, then family."

He starts pacing the room again. Tom stands still by the door, fists clenched.

"Alvaro introduced me to Elena. We danced. She was *so hot,* you know. Not beautiful like Layla—but eager, willing. With Layla, it had been so bad for so long. I can't even remember the last time we—you know. All we do is fight now, right, Layla?"

"God, I hate you," she moans. I glance down at her; the look on her broken face is pure revulsion. She sits up higher, seems energized by her hatred for him. I can feel her working on her bindings, too. Who *are* these people?

"See what I mean?" He looks at me with palms up, a caricature of the innocent man, eyes pleading. "You know what a bitch she can be, Poppy. *Come on*, you know."

"Mac, please," says Tom, an exasperated parent with a difficult child.

"I ditched Jack and Alvaro, and I went back to her place that night—Elena's." He stops, blows out a breath. "And it was totally off the hook, crazy."

"Okay," says Tom. But Mac's not listening; he's caught up in the telling of this.

"I told her that I was married. That it was just for that night. She seemed cool with that. But I saw her a couple more times. I mean, she was so—easy. Just light and fun. Then, I tried to end it. I mean, I have kids. I love Layla—despite it all—I do."

He puts his hands in prayer at his chest, closes his eyes. It's disgusting, how well he plays the role, the guy who made a mistake, one who is sorry for it.

Tom stands, shaking his head, totally focused on Mac. Slowly, carefully, I work at the bindings. Layla's quiet but I can still feel her moving. My mind is focused on that gun locker. If I can get loose, I will run. I'm fast when I need to be.

"First, she sent the video to my phone," he says. The darkness settles into his voice now. The anger. "I was at the dinner table *with my kids*. Then the pictures came to my office by messenger."

I see it start to creep into the features of his face. The hardness, the indignation.

"And she wouldn't *stop*. Money. That's what she wanted. She didn't want me. She didn't want *a life, a relationship*. She just wanted money, more and more of it. That was all she ever wanted. I didn't know what to do. For a while, I just paid up.

But she wouldn't stop, started showing up places. I think she was getting off on it, watching me dance like a puppet on a string."

He stands in front of me, his expression dark, but still pleading. He wants me to understand. I nod carefully, giving him what he wants.

"So, you couldn't take it anymore. You called your security firm. There was a problem that they needed to handle," I say, trying to keep my voice soft, understanding. "What else could you do?"

"That's right, Poppy," he says. "What else *could* I do?"

I'm free. While Mac was weaving his tale, and Tom focused on how much of the story Mac was going to tell, I managed to shift out of the duct tape at my wrists.

But I leave my hands behind my back for now, stay very still.

"Tom is the fixer. And if Jack had just stayed out of it, everything would have been fine. It would have—" he makes a burst with his fingers "—gone away. The police, they bought the burglary thing."

He sinks into the chair across from me and we regard each other. He seems drained of anger again. Tom's angry flush is gone; his expression frighteningly grim. Layla hasn't issued a sound, made a move. Now she lies heavily against me. *Oh, please, Layla. Please hold on. Don't black out now.*

"He just didn't get it," says Mac. "That was Jack's problem."

I feel a shaking begin in my center. "What didn't he *get*, Mac?"

"That the world isn't big." He swings his arm wide. "It's small. It's *tiny*."

I shake my head; what is he saying?

"Jack was a bleeding heart." He lets out an angry laugh, waves a finger at me. "He thought that it was the big picture that mattered—justice for this woman, what's right and wrong. He thought *that's* what mattered."

A cold poke of fear presses into my belly.

"Jack—you know I loved him—but he was selfish. When

you miscarried, Poppy, lost *his* child, he didn't shed a tear. You know what he told me. That he was *relieved.*"

He practically spits the word; and it hurts, it slices, because I know it's true. The power of rage is leaving me, crushed by sadness.

"That he wasn't sure *he* was ready. His child *died* and it was about him, some ideal he had about parenthood and whether he could be ready for it. How disgustingly selfish is that?"

The air is leaving my lungs, my head spinning.

"So, if he didn't care about his own child, why would he care about mine? Why would he care about *Layla*? What finding out about that woman would do *to them*? I had to fix that problem and he just didn't get it."

He's gone weirdly blank. The man before me is once more a total stranger. The Mac who was married to my best friend, who I thought of as family, who held me when Jack died—he's gone. Another friend lost.

"You're right, Poppy. He couldn't let it go. He didn't understand that for most of us it isn't about *justice for the world*, or *capturing beauty*. Life is not about art and travel and high ideals. What matters is our children, the life we've built, whether the people we love are safe. The world is not big. It's small. *You* know that, Poppy. He didn't."

The irony that he's just beaten his wife and her best friend seems lost on him. He's the crazy one. He's the one who's lost his grip.

"Mac," I whisper.

"*He made* me call in Tom," says Mac miserably. "He forced my hand. I had no choice."

"Jack became a problem." Tom, cool and level. "He was a threat to the Van Santen family. I was empowered to deal with the issue as I saw fit. It might have gone differently if Jack had cooperated."

Mac looks to Tom, then back to me, his face earnest.

"I didn't know *how* he would fix it, just that he would," says Mac. He seems pale and weak suddenly. "I swear it, Poppy. I didn't know what was happening until it was—too late."

I remember his grief, how he wept that day. It was real. Just like his weeping after beating Layla was real. Remorse changes nothing.

Mac sinks his head in his hand. His body sags, and I feel that wild thing come up from inside me again, that terrible rush of rage and grief. And I'm glad for it. Adrenaline. It's all I have now. It's a kind of electricity in my body.

Now Layla and I know everything. Which means they're going to kill us both. Fear twists at my insides, and I try to nudge at Layla, but she's heavy on me, not moving. Is she just pretending to be out of it? Has she gotten her bindings free? Or has she passed out completely?

Layla, please wake up.

How will they fix this? I wonder. When Layla and I disappear—how will it be explained? It can't be. Grayson will know what happened. They won't get away with it. But it will be too late for Layla and me. What will happen to Izzy and Slade?

"The police know everything, Mac. I've turned everything over to Detective Grayson. I found the safe-deposit box, the pack with all of the evidence Jack collected."

"Then where are they?" he asks, with a smirk. "Why are you here *alone*?"

"I'm not," I lie. "They know where I am. They're on their way."

Tom pulls on a pair of gloves. "You've been here two hours. Your rescue party is late."

"I didn't know how much Jack told you, Poppy," Mac said. "I was relieved when you lost your mind. You should have stuck with that play. It would have been better for you. I don't want this, you know. *You* did this."

It comes up from deep inside me, a wail of rage so pure. I

lunge for him using all my speed and weight, and take him down hard to the floor, tipping the chair over, his head cracking against the wood, releasing a groaning breath as I land on him. I sit up and punch him hard in the face, again, again. Blood sprays, my hands throbbing with each blow.

All the grief, all the rage, all the pain—it flows out of me just like it did in my dream. The blows land one after another, Mac prone beneath me, my breath ragged, my knuckles splitting, fists screaming with pain.

There are hands on me; then a sharp pain in my arm. I turn to see Tom standing behind me with a needle in his hand. The world starts to shake and wobble, nausea creeping up, everything dimming around the edges.

"No," I say, grappling to hold on to consciousness. "No."

I fall to the floor, gripping at the pain in my arm, fighting to hold on to the dimming room. When I look back toward the couch, Layla is gone.

32

A vise grip on my wrists, I'm being dragged across the floor.

"Let's get her outside and into the trunk. We're going to have to burn this place as it is. What a mess you've made here, Mac."

"I'm sorry," he says, a teenager whining with regret.

"Then we need to find your wife," says Tom, like he's checking an item off a list.

"She won't get far—there's nothing but woods for acres."

They're both breathing hard, suddenly stop dragging me. I try to struggle, but whatever they've given me, I am weak to the point of near paralysis, my limbs heavy, useless. This is it. I've failed Jack. Layla. Myself. Oh my god, Izzy and Slade. That spiral of fear and despair, it's spinning wide beneath me, pulling me into its depths.

"What is that?" Mac's voice, distant and tinny. I strain to hear, but there's only that awful, endless silence. I am lying on the floor in the hallway. Jack leans against the ladder to the loft, looking somber, bleeding from that horrible gash on his head. *I told you to let it go, Poppy.*

"What?" says Tom. "What do you hear?"

"Listen."

I hear it; it sounds like the whine of a mosquito, a wail off in the distance. Then, the outside door swings open with a crash. Layla. She stands, bloodied, ragged, with a shotgun in her arms.

"Put her down, Tom. Step away from her."

Tom complies, lifting his hands. "Be reasonable, Layla."

"Where did you get that?" asks Mac. He seems frozen; his hands coming up in the air as he backs away from me.

"From the gun locker, you idiot," she says.

"Don't do this, Layla," says Tom. "We can all still come to an understanding. We can still fix this."

"Fuck you, Tom."

The room explodes with a blast so loud that my ears start to ring. Mac lets out a scream, hits the wall. Then a strange widening silence. There's something else. That wail is drawing closer.

Tom stands very still. His hands go to his middle and blood leaks through his fingers; he looks at me in shock and pain. Then he falls in a heap to the floor, revealing a black-red burst behind him on the wall. A river of blood flows from his mouth. Layla turns the gun to Mac.

"Layla," I whisper. I know what she's going to do next. "Don't."

"All her life she was afraid," says Layla. "She walked on eggshells in that house. We never knew what was going to set him off. It could be anything—someone used the last of the peanut butter. He couldn't find the remote. He didn't like what she made for dinner."

"Layla," says Mac, his voice a whisper. "I'm sorry."

"Shut up," she says. Her voice is so cold. "Don't say another fucking word."

She squares her stance, but I can see she's wobbly, her hands shaking.

The world, the room spins and tilts. That wail grows louder. Please.

"I hated her," says Layla. "Because she was weak. Don't get me wrong. I hated him, too. But I think I hated her a little more, because you know what? She forgave him. Every. Single. Time. Every time he brought her flowers, or cried, or was in a good mood, she opened to him like a flower. She loved him. I could see it. She loved him more than she loved us."

"Forgive me," whispers Mac. "I can do better. It hasn't always been like this."

She moves in closer, the barrel of the shotgun pointed at him. Tom's body sits horribly, like a dropped toy.

"Honey," I say, struggling to sit. "You don't have to do this."

"Once he hit her so hard she lost three teeth," she says, voice breaking. "The next night I walked in on them dancing in the kitchen, swaying to some slow song."

She laughs, a sad, mirthless sound.

"We're all flawed, Layla," Mac says. "We're all broken."

She shakes her head. She's swaying now, pitching from side to side. "Not all of us," she says. "Not like you."

Now he's weeping, a blustering, disgusting sobbing.

"Put it down, Layla."

The voice surprises us both. She jumps, startled, but she doesn't turn, keeps the gun trained on her husband. I see her face grow harder, her mouth pulled into a grim line. I know that look of determined anger. She can't be stopped.

Detective Grayson walks into the room from behind her, his gun drawn. "This is not what you want."

"How do you know what I want?" she asks, looking between him and Mac, back to me.

"Maybe he doesn't," I say. "But I do. You want to be safe. You want to love your kids. You can have all that, Layla. Just put the gun down. Walk away."

In a breath, I see our life together—riding bikes, and driving in her beater car, the sleepovers, the proms, our weddings, all the dried tears, and belly laughs. Her strength, her flaws, her toughness. Through joy and grief, laughter and pain, she's been there. Our friendship has been the most solid thing in my life.

"Whatever comes next," I say. "We face it together."

Slowly, she drops the gun, sinks to her knees and lays it on the floor. She bends over in a sob. And I struggle through my pain and weakness to move toward her. As I do, out of the corner of my eye, I see Mac scramble to his feet and dive for her. His wail of rage fills the room, but I use the last of my strength to throw myself between them, and take the full brunt of his weight as he knocks me to the ground, my head hitting hard against the solid wood floor. I have nothing left, no strength, no will to fight. I can barely lift my arm to fend off the blow I see coming.

Then a deafening shot rings out and Mac seems to freeze midstrike, his arm raised, a flower of blood blossoming on the white of his shirt. The moment pulls strange and twisting. His face goes slack and he falls off, hitting the floor beside me. Layla's wail fills my head as she crawls to me.

Detective Grayson, my enemy, my friend, the poet detective comes to kneel beside me. And his is the last face I see before the world fades to nothing.

33

Jack stirs beside me and I lie still, listening. It's dark, amber streetlight sneaking in through the blinds, the room a familiar field of shadows—his clothes in their eternal slouch over the chair, the little-used fireplace dark, a stack of files on the narrow desk by the window. He's awake, lying there, wondering if I'm awake. I am, barely. The cold medicine I took has me foggy, my limbs heavy. I don't move. The fight we had last night still aches at the back of my throat. Angry tears burn behind my eyes. After a moment, he slips from bed. Still, I don't move.

Water running in the bathroom; he'll be splashing cold water on his face, running his wet fingers through his sandy mane of hair, then brushing his teeth. I can see him as if I'm standing beside him, so familiar is he, this routine. Normally, I'd be squeezing next to him in our postage stamp of a bathroom, jockeying for position at the sink—reaching for the brush, a tie for my hair. *This bathroom*, I might complain. *This apartment.*

The water goes off and there is quiet except for the street noise. I haven't moved a muscle. The bathroom door opens and a rectangle of light slides across the floor.

"Poppy?" Just a whisper. There's apology in his voice, a plea.

But I'm heavy. Heavy with this cold, with the medicine I took to stop coughing. With the fight we had last night, with the fear that things between us are too far gone. How did we get so far apart? When did it happen? It's not just one thing, not even what we fought about last night—though that's a big chasm between us. I could turn around and look at him. It's still there, whatever it is that brought us together. If I reach for him, he'll still come to me. But I don't move.

I listen as he pulls on his running clothes, laces his shoes sitting on the bench at the foot of the bed. He pauses at the door; I can hear him draw and release a breath. It's not too late. I could still hop up and hustle into my clothes, too, head out into the morning with him, take our daily run in Riverside Park before the sun comes up. The sky will start to glow over the horizon as we make our two-mile loop, our breath in clouds. He might take off, leaving me behind for a bit, but I'll catch up by the underpass. What I lack in speed, I make up for in endurance. On the bench at Ninety-Sixth Street, we might stretch. That's when we'd talk, probably make up, or achieve some peace that will get us through a few more days.

So many mistakes, wrong choices. His. Mine.

I let him go, listen as footfalls creak on the hardwood floor, as he opens the door, closes and locks it behind him. The ding of the elevator, faint and distant. Still. I could still get up and go after him. Maybe I'll catch him by the playground; maybe he'll be moving slowly hoping that I'll come out after him. But I don't. This cold, a kind of fatigue that's settled in over our life together, a crushing inertia keeps me lashed to the bed. I sink in deep, sleep wrapping itself around me, pulling me down, down, down. We'll talk when he gets back. We'll work it out. We always do.

No. Something gets me up. I hustle into my running clothes,

find my shoes by the door. I don't wait for our ancient elevator, I take the stairs, burst through the lobby.

"You can still catch him," Richie calls after me. "He wasn't moving too fast this morning."

"I'll catch him," I call back with a laugh.

The air is so, so cold. But I don't waste time warming up. I break into a sprint. I see him crossing the street.

"Jack," I call. But he doesn't hear me. He jogs across the street just as the light turns, disappears into the park.

I wait for the flow of traffic to pass. When the street clears, I cross and follow, moving faster, faster. He seems always just ahead of me, his speed effortless, his hoodie pulled up against the cold, drawstring tight. He probably has his headphones in. He can't hear me; he doesn't know I'm right behind him. He picks up speed.

I dig down deep, move along the path faster than I'm used to running, a stitch sharp in my side. He turns the corner; I think I'll lose him. But true to form, he slows by the underpass.

"Jack," I call, my voice loud, resounding off the concrete.

Finally, he hears me, stops and turns.

He's just a shadow standing there, a hooded man in the dark edge of my life. But I don't slow down, run right into his arms. He wraps me up and holds me tight, pulls me into a kiss. That kiss, our kiss, the one that always melted me and made wrong things right again.

"I'm so sorry." Pulling back his hood, I put my hands to his beloved face. "I love you."

I swim up through the layers of sleep, resurface in dim light. Breathe in wakefulness like air. Dreams and memory twist and mingle, a confused tumble. Don't bother trying to sort them; it doesn't matter. What's real? What isn't? Who can really say?

"Poppy?"

My throat is dry, head heavy.

"I'm ready," I tell Jack. "I'm coming."

There's a moment, a beautiful suspended moment where I float in that final dream space with Jack, where I catch him at the underpass, feel his lips on mine. And it's all okay again; we live to fight another day. And maybe in another universe, somewhere on another plane of existence, we leave the park and go back to whatever life we'll live together. It's right there. I can almost touch it.

"You're probably not going anywhere for a while."

Not Jack's voice.

Instead, a rumpled Detective Grayson sits grim as a gargoyle in the corner of what looks like a hospital room.

"Where are we?"

Then it comes back in an ugly Technicolor rush—purging the apartment, Grayson's visit, the pack with all Jack's evidence about Elena's murder, my race upstate, Mac, Tom.

"Layla," I say, sitting up painfully.

"She's okay." He comes to stand beside me. "She'll be okay. Just—lie back. You don't make things easy, you know that. Do you know how crazy that was? You almost got yourself killed."

"Is Mac—*dead*?" I ask.

He pauses a second, then offers a solemn nod. I wait for waves of grief or sorrow, some feeling. But there is only a deep and total numbness. Pain will come. Of course it will. We're old friends now.

"They killed Jack," I tell him. "I understand what happened now."

He holds up his palm. "We don't have all the pieces yet, but it looks like Van Santen and Elena Montoya shared a night that she caught on film for the purposes of blackmailing him. She was aggressive, apparently, demanding more and more money, showing up places to unsettle him, like that wedding for example. He empowered his security firm to handle the problem. And they did."

"Jack found out."

"From what was in that pack, it looks like he suspected that Mac had something to do with Elena's death, investigated and confronted him."

"Where did he get those pictures," I ask.

"I don't have the answer to that," says Grayson.

"He never told me anything," I say. "I didn't know."

It kept him up nights. It explains why he was so distant, so tense in those final months.

"*Why* didn't he tell me?"

"Obviously, he wanted to protect you," says Grayson.

"I wish he had protected himself."

He presses his mouth in a grim line, squeezes my hand. "I do, too."

"Why didn't he just go to the police?"

"From the texts on that disposable phone it looks like he was trying to convince Mac to get a lawyer and turn himself in, turn in Tom's firm Black Dog Security and Crisis Management. Mac and your husband were friends, it seems. Jack didn't just want to go to the police. My guess is that he was trying to make things easier on you, Layla and the kids."

That sounds like Jack.

"Mac was hurting Layla. There was abuse in their marriage and I never saw it."

"Sometimes we only see what people want us to see, you know."

It reminds me of Mac's words. The thought of him—what he's done to all of us. The betrayal is so deep, it's a gully through my middle. I wish I could go back to that night when Jack was staring at Elena's picture on a screen and force him to burn it all down right there—go to the police, report Mac, save us all. But we can't go back, no matter how hard we try, or how badly we want to. I fight helpless tears, but they come anyway.

Grayson takes my hand and says nothing. There's nothing to say.

"What did he give me?" I ask. My arm still throbs, my awareness still thick and slow. "He put something in my arm."

"Some kind of sedative, I think," he says. "Just rest now."

There's a doctor then, and a nurse. Questions, light in my eyes. Grayson gets pushed out of the room; he lifts a hand and disappears. I drift away again.

When I open my eyes, it's dark outside the window. Noah dozes in a chair beside me, his hand over mine. I watch him until he opens his eyes and looks back. He startles a little, smiles, sits up. I lace my fingers through his and he holds tight.

SIX MONTHS LATER

34

Above us, a hawk makes wide, lonely circles. It dips and turns, wings motionless, lofting on the air. Silver white and black around me. My breath. Snow crunches beneath my feet, as the cleats on my snowshoes find purchase.

Once you awaken, you cannot go back to sleep.

This is the last of winter. Soon the snow will be gone. I can already see the green buds on the black branches. In places, blades of grass push up through what's left of the snow.

"It's not that bad out here," says Layla. "I am starting to like the quiet."

"How much longer?" complains Izzy.

"This sucks," adds Slade, huffing and puffing down the trail. "I can't, like, *breathe*. Can we go home now?"

"I guess we'd better head back," Layla concedes, dropping a comforting hand on Slade's head.

Back inside the kids collapse on the couch, immediately returning to their devices—Izzy on the phone, Slade with his iPad. Despite all that's happened, despite the fact their worlds have imploded, they seem—okay. Less light and exuberant, more prone to meltdown and tears. Izzy's lost weight; Slade has gained some, a constellation of acne on his chin. Grief and sorrow have taken up residence in their eyes.

But they'll be okay; we'll make sure of it. They have Layla; they have me. We have each other. Friends are the family you choose; and family pulls you through your darkest days.

Layla and I make hot chocolate for the kids.

"Stay the night?" I offer.

"No," she says. "We should go home. I'm trying to keep their routine."

I get it. Trying to find that new normal after tragedy. It's a slog; one foot in front of the other. She's taken them out of school and they are attending classes online now until she figures out what to do, where to go, what's next.

We don't talk much about what happened, about the years of abuse she suffered with Mac, the fights turned violent, the affairs, or why she hid it all from me, or why I didn't see it. We don't talk about that final night in the cabin when I saved her, then she saved me, and then Grayson saved us both. We've been saving each other all our lives. It's what we do.

"I don't know if you heard," she says. "But the magazine hit the shelves this week. The television news feature runs on Wednesday."

"Yes," I answer. "I know."

She walks over to her bag and slips out an envelope, leaves it on the counter.

The story of what happened to us—the blackmail of an ultra-wealthy hedge fund manager leading to the murder of a young woman, followed by the murder of the photographer who tried to find justice for her—has been headline fodder. Now it's a crime feature in a major magazine.

I've seen it online already. It's a searing account, sparing no detail, including my breakdown, memory loss and my flight to save Layla from her abuser and the man responsible for the murder of my husband. On the page, it's one thing—a sensational story with all the right elements of mayhem to be eagerly consumed.

On my soul, on our lives, it's a wound that is just now starting to, maybe, heal. Layla and I refused to be interviewed for the article, but the reporter got his information anyway.

Layla still moves with a hitch in her step, has a scar under her eye from Mac's last beating. She is no less beautiful. She's amped up her kickboxing, hired a trainer to teach her self-defense. She, Slade and Izzy are all in twice-weekly therapy.

"The cycle of abuse stops here," Layla told me. "I brought it forward into my adult life. But Izzy and Slade aren't taking it forward into their lives."

Mac, Tom Jager and Joe Knight are all dead. As for me, I try not to think about any of them. I work through my feelings of rage, betrayal, inconsolable sadness in therapy, in meditation and try to leave it there. There's no evidence to tie Alvaro to Elena's blackmail of Mac, the place where all this darkness started to leak into our lives. But I keep going back to our last meeting. He knew something—or maybe he just suspected. I don't know how much. He won't return my calls. And, right now, I don't have any energy to chase.

Occasionally, I dream about Mac, that same dream where I beat him with my fists and enjoy every minute of it. I usually wake up weeping. I don't tell Layla that sometimes I miss him, the man I thought he was. He was funny and smart and could hold his liquor.

Once upon a time, he was my friend, someone who laughed and cried with me. That he was someone else underneath the skin, somehow doesn't mitigate the loss of who he was to me.

After hot chocolate, we all walk out to Layla's car. The air is growing warmer, has that fresh, clean scent of new beginnings. We say our goodbyes, embrace, exchange kisses. We are all broken, limping, but we are whole and healing. We'll be okay. This time, it's no lie.

When Noah comes back from his studio, I have let the room go dark except for the fire. There's a chili simmering on the stove. I am deep in thought as I often am here, far away from the cacophony of the city, of all the powerful voices in my life. He leaves the lights off and comes to sit on the hearth, warming his hands after the cold walk home.

"More snow tomorrow," he says. "Spring's not ready to come just yet."

I don't answer, just point toward the magazine on the table. He picks it up and looks at it in the firelight, then back at me.

"I'm sorry," Noah says, leafing through the pages. "I am sorry for what happened to him, to you. I'm sorry for *this*."

He tosses the magazine on the table in disgust. It lands beside the snow globe I used to keep on my desk, the one Jack gave me with the little house and winter trees, snow falling all around. I lift it from its place and stare inside. I'm here, without him.

I rise and Noah meets me in the middle of the room. His arms enfold me; his lips find mine. I lace my fingers through his hair, run them down his back to lift off his shirt and let it fall to the floor. Heat comes up between us fast and bright.

His mouth on my neck, his breath in my ear, as he strips away my shirt. The firelight makes shadows on the wall. Darkness settles into the valleys of his face, pools in the dips of his body. After a few moments, there is only skin, only desire. All the dark players in my life recede from the stage, and it is only us.

He lifts me and carries me to the couch, where he lays me down, running his hands along my arms, my legs. And then we are a tangle of flesh, wrapped around each other. Pain melting into pleasure, grief over the past releasing its grip on my heart, allowing space for more.

"I don't remember who I was before you," Noah whispers. "I am someone new with you in my life."

I let the moment expand—the fire dying to embers, the room growing colder. Outside the wind howls and the branches scrape at the windows. There is no time but now, no one but us.

What path were Jack and I on? That last night together, the one I have visited and revisited in my dreams, what would the next day have brought if he had not risen before me and gone for his run? What if I had not miscarried? What if I had stayed at the table and listened to him, rather than walk away? All these decisions and events, large and small, twists and turns in the path of our lives. Once a way is chosen, there is no way to know what might have happened on the other path.

In the firelight, Noah rests his head on my bare belly, listening. I have just barely started to show, just the tiniest bump. I feel his joy, his anticipation. He has bought a stack of books, wants to get started on the nursery, is tracking my pregnancy with an app on his phone.

"Today, he's the size of a grape. Or she," he announced that morning.

"Who's in there, do you think?" he asks now. "Who will it be?"

"We have to wait to find out," I say, running my hand along his shoulder.

I know the miracle of children, vividly remember both of Layla's pregnancies, attending the birthing classes with her when Mac couldn't. The surprise of meeting Izzy, then Slade, who each arrived, clearly of Mac and Layla, but wholly their own selves, too. I can't imagine who will arrive when our child is born.

There are difficult times ahead; I know this. Days so dark, it will be a struggle to remember joyful ones. And there are joyful days ahead, as well, times so full of life and happiness that the possibility of dark days will be distant. But, for right now, there is only the warmth of our bodies, the depth of our new love, the child inside me.

★ ★ ★

Later Noah sleeps, his breath deep and even. It's one of those nights when sleep won't come and I accept that. Instead of railing against it, the night has become my time to write, to think. There are so few silent spaces in this modern world; I have learned to relish the gift of insomnia. Out the window I stare at the wide full moon that glows blue white over the trees, casting the world in silver.

When I look down, I see him. The hooded man. He's waiting.

Quietly, I dress at the door, slip into the frigid night. On the porch, I strap on my snowshoes and crunch out into the moonlight. He turns and disappears into the darkness of the trees.

The canopy above blocks the glow of the moon, but my eyes adjust quickly to the dim ambient light. The dark hulking form moves away, silent, nearly drifting and I follow.

Distantly, behind me, I hear Noah's voice, my name on the night air. I chase the hooded man into the dark, deeper into the woods, farther from the house.

Then we're in a clearing and the moonlight creates a blue-white day. I stand and wait.

He drops his hood.

Jack.

How flawed we all are, how imperfect and yet how fiercely we can love each other. We can build lives, and care for each other. We can fail each other, break each other's fragile hearts. We hold on so tightly to the stories we tell ourselves, to the dreams we have of our futures. And when the worst thing happens, we rage. We rail, and cling. We try to hold on, though it's the one thing we can't do.

"I wish we had more time."

My voice is just a whisper in the wind and he is only light and shadow, the rays of a distant, long-dead star. He's fading into the snow and trees, the sparkle of moonlight on ice.

"Poppy."

Noah is behind me, full of breath and heat. I glance at him, and when I turn back, Jack's gone. Noah comes closer, puts his hands on me, gentle.

"Where are you going, Poppy?" he asks. He looks past me to the clearing, then back. "Are you all right?"

"I am," I say, and mean it.

"Were you sleepwalking?"

He's flushed with the effort of following me through the snowy night, his breath coming out in white clouds, mingling with mine.

"No," I tell him. "I wasn't."

I am present. I am awake. I am alive.

★ ★ ★ ★ ★

ACKNOWLEDGMENTS

Everything begins and ends with my husband, Jeffrey, and our daughter, Ocean Rae. They are the foundation of my life, keeping me grounded, loved and loving, laughing, and fully in the moment. I've said many times that I'm most at home at the keyboard, lost in story. But that's not true. I'm most at home with my beautiful, loving family in the happy sun-drenched world we create together.

Thanks to my agent, Amy Berkower, for her calm, her wisdom and her steely navigation of the white water of the publishing world. Thanks also to Alice Martin and Abigail Barce for their intelligence, good humor and uncanny knack for taking care of business. Writers House is a stellar agency and I'm honored to be represented there.

What a gift is a smart, insightful, funny and wise editor! Erika Imranyi is all those things and more. Many thanks to her for stellar editorial work, helping me find my way through a Tilt-A-Whirl story, and bringing me on board at the super exciting and high-energy Park Row Books. I'm thrilled to be among such a fantastic group of writers, supported by such an enthusiastic team. It takes a lot of people to bring a book into the world—many thanks to the talented and dedicated folks in the art, marketing, publicity and sales departments.

Thanks to Jay Nolan, photojournalist extraordinaire, for taking some pretty amazing photos of—me! He made me look A LOT better than I do, all the while answering my million questions, offering his insights into his profession and giving me a little window into his world.

I continue to be inspired by Carl Jung and his writings, most especially for this novel *The Undiscovered Self: The Dilemma of the Individual in Modern Society*. Further, I found tremendous inspiration in *On Photography* by Susan Sontag. Her insights into photography and its place in the modern world are profoundly relevant, and in many ways prescient, to our current experience where we photo-narrate, curate and document all the minutiae of our lives. *Camera Lucida: Reflections on Photography* by Roland Barthes is the essential study on subject, the role of the image and how the photograph affects us. Some other books that informed and inspired me during the writing of this novel: *The Interpretation of Dreams: The Complete and Definitive Text* by Sigmund Freud and *Zen and the Brain: Toward an Understanding of Meditation and Consciousness* by James H. Austin.

I am blessed with a truly heroic network of family and friends. My parents, Joseph and Virginia Miscione, and brother, Joe, are tireless supporters, promoters and pals. My mom is one of my earliest and most important readers, along with forever friend Heather Mikesell. Erin Mitchell is reader, proofreader, promoter and buddy. Special thanks to the endless support, love and advice of my mentor and dear, dear friend Shaye Areheart.